CRITICAL TIMES

EK Jonathan
Cover design by EK Jonathan
©2016. All rights reserved.
www.criticaltimesnovel.blogspot.com
Edition 1.0

This is a work of fiction and is a product of the author's imagination. Although the events portrayed in this novel are based on things foretold in the Bible, they should not be viewed as predictions. This book is in no way sponsored by the Watchtower Bible and Tract Society.

Dedicated to my love.

TUESDAY, OCTOBER 13

2:27 AM
LUKE

It's foggy and unusually cold for October and I'm nodding off to the beginnings of a post-carb-binge nap. The heady odor of a greasy cheeseburger and fries hangs in the air. I submit to the food coma and feel my consciousness ebb away. It's a quiet night, and the worst I can expect for a little shut eye on the clock would be a mild tongue lashing from Captain Pryce, and even the best officers do it from time to time. It's called the graveyard shift, for crying out loud.

The dispatcher's call cuts through the air like the hiss of a welder's torch, threatening to ignite the space in my stuffy Dodge. I jolt to attention and crank the dial.

"This is a code three, repeat, a code three," barks the voice. "We've got a fire reported on Castle and Paso. Unit twenty-three, do you copy?" I clear my throat to force the sleepiness into retreat.

"Unit twenty-three here, copy that. En route to Castle and Paso. Has the fire department already been notified?" I crank the key in the ignition, lighting up the dash and bringing the engine to a throaty rumble.

"Affirmative, unit twenty-three. HFD on its way."

I flip a switch on my console, splashing blue and red light across the sleepy Shell station. A baggy-eyed teenage girl with faded pink extensions leans over the counter in the glass box convenience store at the far end of the pumps and stares. A break in the drudgery of her night shift, no doubt. My sirens split the night as I peel from the station.

I blink away dry eyes as my adrenaline surges. The sluggishness is gone; in its place is the usual flood of concerns that come with any call. What will be waiting for me there? What kind of decisions will I need to make? Will everyone walk away unharmed? A code three can be anything from an overturned grill charring someone's front lawn to a full-blown industrial blaze, though at half-past two in the morning, neither seems likely. I do my best to picture the intersection where

Castle Lane and Paso Avenue meet and wonder what might've started the incident.

The Pylons. That's what people call that part of town, the name itself a dismal reminder of all it's come to represent. Long ago, the city promised big things for the area. They put up billboards all around town with ads for Coming Soon strip malls and Big Box stores. They pumped millions into developing a monorail linking the area to the city hub. Contractors even showed up for awhile and began forming the concrete pillars that would eventually support the track. But when the new mayor took office four years back, he reallocated the funds to counteract the rising crime rate and the monorail project was abandoned. The pillars were never torn down, however, and now jut from the landscape like the skeletal remains of some long-dead beast.

What sparse development eventually came this way turned the Pylons into a semi-commercial, semi-residential, semi-industrial mishmash, as if the urban planners threw their hands up and left everything to chance. There's a Goodwill nestled between stucco condos and an overgrown park, a library set against the rear parking lot of a Taco Bell and a recycling plant. It's ugly.

In the Pylons, packs of youths prowl around like hungry wolves, showing off the chrome bulges of handguns from beneath their waistbands. I think about these kids now, the ones I see from time to time throwing cinderblocks through the windows of abandoned cars or getting high behind one of the dilapidated strip malls, and wonder if it's one of them who has something to do with the code three.

With one hand balancing the wheel, I reach over the console and swipe a finger across my Toshiba. The tablet's screen glows to life in a webwork of colorful lines set against a black gradient. My Dodge is a blinking red triangle, 023, at the center of the map. I tap the corner of the screen to zoom out, and two more triangles appear. They're the two other officers on duty, but I see from a glance that they're well outside the response radius. I'll be the sole responder.

I slip off the freeway leading into the Pylons and immediately note the orange smear of a fire reflected overhead in a clot of low lying clouds. I thumb off the sirens and roll down my window. The air is sharp with the acrid scent of burn. A couple of hooded teenagers sit on the curb a few doors down from the fire, snapping at the destruction on their smartphones and snickering. I consider chasing them off but think better of it. They could be packing, and I don't have backup. I park my

Charger across the street and aim its hood in the direction of the blaze. Whatever happens, my dash cam will catch it all.

I emerge from my squad car and feel myself pushed back by a stifling wave of heat. Something explodes, sending a cascade of sparks onto the concrete driveway that leads to the rear of the property. I check my watch. 2:45.

Curious neighbors are beginning to creep out of their front doors with faces like frightened animals emerging from the woodwork. Lights on porches flicker on. I hear yells as neighbors assess the danger.

"You just gonna stand there?" shouts a woman in my direction. I ignore her. A baby in someone else's house is shrieking.

"Hey, I'm talkin' to you!" The woman repeats, louder this time, her voice competing with the hiss and crackle of fire. I give her a curt nod and hold up a hand to let her know she's been heard.

"Ma'am, I'm gonna need you to go on inside now," I say in an even voice.

"Or what?" she sneers, taking a step off the porch. The light from the fire sends strange shimmering patterns across her silk nightgown. Pastel curlers bob like buoys in the turbulent sea of her white streaked hair.

"Ma'am, the fire department is on its way, so it's best you go inside. You'll be safe there."

"Safe? I got Dante's inferno down the road and the cops sitting around doin' nothin' and you tellin' me it's safe?"

"Ma'am…" I begin, feeling the exasperation creep into my voice. But before I can finish the thought, a second, more violent explosion rips from the flames. Glass splinters shower onto the sidewalk and something metallic lurches from the roof and crashes to the ground. People are shouting. The baby's screams go up a notch. I stagger backwards and glance again at my wristwatch. Where are the firefighters?

More commotion in the neighbors' houses now, lights turning on, people stumbling onto the sidewalk with flashlights. An old man hobbles down the sidewalk with a bucket, who knows what for. Flames leap higher and higher into the atmosphere. The air glows with specs of red, like a swarm of fireflies caught in a black glass bottle.

I approach the burning building and circle it cautiously. At least it's a safe distance from the surrounding lots, hindering the fire's ability to spread. The last thing I need is a panicked populace caught in an uncontrollable neighborhood-wide inferno.

As I round the building, I discover that this isn't a residential property. There are few windows and no backyard. Instead, at the property's rear I find a commercial-grade AC unit and a parking lot large enough to fit a few dozen cars, though at the moment it's empty. A solitary green Toyota Camry sits in one of the spaces at the far end of the lot.

On the other side of the property I find a smaller building. A narrow walkway separates the two structures, though flames are beginning to leap from the first building to the second. 2:55, and still no sign of HFD.

I jog back to the front of the main building, feeling the heat lunge from the plastic siding that cracks and buckles, submitting to the devouring flames. The intensity of the heat is almost unbearable. I shield my face as I run, unrelenting waves of heat battering me as I charge back to my car.

The woman is waiting for me. Some mystifying sense of propriety has moved her to tie a silk handkerchief over her head, hiding the plastic curlers. Her arms are crossed. A glowing cigarette hangs from the corner of her mouth.

"Well?" she barks.

"Well, what?" I manage, still out of breath. My skin stings with the pain of a fresh sunburn. "It's a fire. Not much else to say," I mutter, annoyed at feeling obliged to answer her.

"Yeah? Well, what about the apartment in back?" the woman snaps.

"Apartment?" I gasp, feeling a sudden chill despite the heat.

"The little apartment in back. There's a man livin' in there."

I crane my neck to look back at the blaze I've just escaped. In what could've only been a minute or two, the fire has grown. The paved driveway I just traversed is now blocked by fallen scraps of smoldering debris. I fling open my car door and hit the transmitter.

"Jenny, it's me, Luke. Look, I'm at the scene of the fire and there's no sign of FD. I've been here for fifteen minutes and nothing. Where are they?"

"Unit twenty-three, copy that. HFD said it had engine trouble on the freeway. They're prepping another truck now, might be a few more minutes."

Great. Just in time to roast some marshmallows over a smoking ash heap, I think, and toss the radio back in the car.

"So this is where my tax dollars go," scoffs the woman as she leans on my door. I brush past her and race back to the flames. By the time I reach the driveway I feel as if I've plunged into a pool of fire. Inexplicable snippets of Sunday school lessons flash through my head, echoes of sermons once forgotten.

'And the devil was cast into the lake of fire and brimstone...' I try to silence the memories and focus, but they come all the same. I feel the hair on my arms singe, the skin of my face and neck stinging in the heat. I'm vulnerable and insignificant in the face of the fiery power, a wax figurine dipped into a pit of lava.

Somewhere in my mind, the preacher won't shut up. *'Where they will be tormented...'* I leap over a pile of scorched timbers and melted siding and stumble on the other side, catching the pavement in the palms of my hands. My flesh feels sticky and wilted, as if I were being melted down to my most primal elements. *'...forever and ever...'*

When I finally make it back to the rear lot of the building, I take a minute to catch my breath, my lungs filling over and over with hot air and smoke. The roof of the small apartment building is now a patchwork of flames. I edge as near as I dare and begin shouting into the fire.

"Hey, anyone in there?" I shout, barely audible above the roar of the blaze. The windows are dark and still. An odd mix of anger and relief washes over me as the thought crosses my mind that the old woman may have just been pulling my leg. Could such a small building even be an apartment? It looks more like a fancy shed with windows. An office, at the very most. The problem is that car in the parking lot. If its driver is inside...

I wipe the sheen of sweat from my face and take a step back, glancing again into the window, and freeze. There, swallowed by darkness, is the faint outline of a face. The mouth is open–screaming, probably, though I can only hear the merciless crack and hiss of fire– and the eyes, terror-filled. Trapped inside the small building is a feeble old man.

I lunge forward, baring my teeth as the heat chews at me furiously.

"You've got to get out of there! Now!" I scream, my voice weak and hoarse with the smoke. Still, he just sits there, a look of hopelessness on his face, refusing to move. I stab my index finger again and again in the direction of his door, insisting the obvious. He shakes his head slowly and raises two bony hands, his mouth opening and closing in a useless explanation.

Something is wrong. A jammed door, perhaps? Maybe he's hit his head and forgotten how to open it? Or perhaps the other side is already on fire? I watch in paralyzed horror as the old man holds a cloth over his mouth and keels over, shuddering.

Back to the door. I stand a few paces back and charge at it, wincing as my shoulder rams into the solid wood. I hear a sharp crack and feel something give, and I wonder for an awful moment if it's the door or the bones in my body. I wind my shoulder a few times, hearing a click that hadn't been there before. Bruised without a doubt, but not broken.

I resume my position, brace myself for anything, and charge again.

7:46 AM
AMY

A million awful possibilities swirl through my head as I pace the cramped kitchenette in our apartment. As usual, the cold from the night before has seeped in through the cheap single-paned windows that our landlady refuses to replace. I don't feel it today though, not with my nervous pacing and the three cups of coffee buzzing in my system.

It's a quarter to eight, almost an hour and a half past when my husband, Luke, normally gets in on Wednesday mornings. I've texted and phoned him a dozen times and nothing has gotten through. Not even Jenny, the dispatcher at Luke's precinct, has heard a thing from my husband since three AM this morning.

There's a special kind of dread that law enforcement officers' spouses have to stomach each time their partners walk out the door to begin their shift. A sick tension that never goes away. You look for distractions, and sometimes you find a way to exile the anxiety to the back of your mind, but all it takes is an unexpected knock in the middle of the night, a sudden call from an unknown number, or a husband out past the end of his shift, to turn that nagging worry into something tangible and horrifying.

I attempt breakfast but find no appetite for the scrambled eggs that quickly go cold in the frigid morning air. I contemplate a second pot of coffee but decide against it; it'll only worsen my nerves.

Finally, at just after eight in the morning, the bolts on our front door slap open. It's Luke, and I'm not sure whether to scream at the man or smile.

"Where were you?" I demand. Luke's eyes meet mine with a groggy, vacant stare.

"St. Mary's," he mumbles.

"The hospital? What on earth for! Do you have any idea how sick I've been worrying about you?"

"Look, Amy, relax. I'm fine."

"Well, what happened?" I ask, softer now, disarmed by his coolness. There are black smudges on his arms and face and he reeks of smoke.

"There was a fire."

"I heard that much, but why were you there? And why didn't you return my calls or texts? Do you have any idea–" My voice locks up with a gush of emotion and it takes everything I have to fight the tears.

"I'm sorry, Amy, I know. I know. I left my phone in my car when I got to the hospital, when I got back the battery had died."

"Hospital? I don't understand, Luke. You said there was a fire."

"There *was* a fire. Someone was trapped. I got them out and rode with them to the emergency room."

"You... Are they... Are they ok?"

"Amy, please. Everything's fine. You need to calm down. It's been a long night. Bring me that coffee and sit down and just try to relax. I'm fine."

I comply and Luke slowly goes over the events of the night. He responded to a fire and discovered a small studio apartment with an old man trapped inside. He managed to break down the door after three tries, only to discover that it had been blocked on the other side by a fallen piece of furniture. Confined to a wheelchair, the man was unable to do anything about it. By the time the fire truck finally arrived at the scene, Luke had pulled him to safety. An ambulance eventually showed up to haul him away on a stretcher, and Luke followed in his squad car.

I can only shake my head as his story comes to a close. The anger is gone; I'm just glad to have my husband home. My hands have found their way to Luke's sleeves, where they're clenched into fists so tight that he has to gently pat at them to get me to relax.

"Do they know what caused the fire?" I ask.

Luke shrugs with a sip of cold coffee. "Not yet. I think someone is there now combing through the scene, though. We'll probably know soon enough. But I'm guessing it was arson."

"Arson? You mean the fire was set on purpose? How do you know?"

"Just a hunch. When the EMTs were loading the man into the ambulance I noticed a sign on the fence. It was a church."

"Oh," I say softly. Church arson is a regular news item, along with international terrorism, school shootings, and the rest of the gamut. Our city of Haliford, Georgia, has been no exception.

"First time I've seen them go after Jehovah's Witnesses, though," Luke adds, taking another swig and nearly stopping my heart.

"What was that?" I ask.

"You know, the Witnesses. The building was one of their Kingdom Halls, according to the sign. I was just saying I think it's the first time it hasn't been the Baptists or the Catholics or one of the other mainstream churches targeted, that's all."

I have no words as I slide quietly out of my chair and across the kitchen. I busy myself with the task of warming up breakfast. Luke gets up and puts his arms around me as I fiddle with something on the stove.

"I'm sorry I worried you," he whispers into my ear.

"You... you have to be more careful out there. At least tell me what's going on so I don't worry myself to death," I beg. "This world, it's just..."

"Crazy."

"Yeah. Crazy. Baby, are you sure this isn't time..."

"Time for what?"

"You know, time to start looking..."

But Luke is already shaking his head and backing away with his palms up in the air. "No, no way," he says. "I've been with the department this long. It's a steady job. You have any idea how hard that is to come by these days?"

"But Luke," I press, "Didn't you say you were thinking of quitting? After the last incident? What more of a sign do you need?"

"First, I never said I was looking for a sign. And second, Amy, this is completely different. What happened in the pharmacy was bad, I'm not denying that. And it could've been a lot worse. But this, this was a good thing. I saved a life this morning. And I think I may have saved a spot in the precinct, too."

"What's that supposed to mean?"

"A promotion. No more running around at night getting bottles thrown at my car and worrying that some punk is going to mow me down."

"Sergeant?"

"We'll see. I'll talk with Pryce," Luke says with a look of confidence.

"Baby, that's great, and I'm happy for you. I know you've wanted the promotion for a while, but–"

"*I've* wanted? This has been *our* dream for at least two years, Amy. My salary will jump by twenty grand. Twenty grand! Do you know what we could do with–"

"It's not about the money, Luke. I'd rather have a living, breathing husband than a stuffed bank account."

"Who said it has to be one or the other?"

"You know what I mean, Luke. I'm up every morning watching CNN and it's one shooting here and another bombing there. And it's not in some faraway place anymore. It's happening right here in our backyard. My goodness, it feels like every single day people are killing and maiming each other."

"Yeah, exactly, Amy. And that's why I need to be out there. Can you imagine how bad things would get if all the officers just decided to up and quit?"

"But why does it have to be you, Luke? What about us? What if something happens out there? What if the boy in the next pharmacy aims just a bit higher? What if the last one had taken a second shot at you?"

"Amy, we can 'what if' ourselves to death here, there's no way to know what would've happened."

"Just like there's no way to know what will happen if you keep going out there."

Luke leans against the counter, closing his eyes and rubbing his temples. This isn't the first conversation we've had about it, and each time it's edged closer to an argument.

"I'm not doing this for the thrills. I don't love the risks that come with the job, and I avoid them whenever I can. You know how careful I am." Luke turns to give me an imploring stare as he jabs a finger into his chest, his concealed Kevlar vest crinkling.

"I know you're careful, Luke. It's not you I'm worried about," I sigh.

"Look," he says, planting a kiss on my nose and giving me a serious look. "If a better job comes around, I'll consider leaving the force. But until that happens, I can't turn my back on this career. This is our lifeline, babe."

His eyes are big and honest and there's nothing I can say to disagree. I nod and feel him pull me close. Despite the soot in his uniform and the smell of smoke and sweat, there's no place I'd rather be.

WEDNESDAY, OCTOBER 14

9:19 AM
LUKE

Dale Pryce sits behind his dusty green desk looking characteristically ambiguous. His head, attached to his shoulders by a thick column of muscle that appears to grow from the base of his ears, is tilted slightly to one side. A silver halo of closely cropped hair catches the morning light flitting through the office blinds.

"I assume you've seen this," Captain Pryce huffs as he spins an old laptop around on his desk for me to stare at. I feel the hot air whirring from the ancient machine's fans as he tilts the screen back to give me a clearer view.

It's the website of *The Herald*, our city's most-circulated newspaper. Our precinct and the people at this paper have had a rocky relationship over the years, and the look on Pryce's face suggests that things haven't improved with today's edition. I scroll down the page to find a picture of my own face staring back at me.

"Local cop braves blaze ahead of fire department," I read aloud, frowning as I glance over the piece. Though the hard facts are scant, I decide that the article is a fair portrayal of what happened two nights ago.

"Eva Richards. Don't know her," I mutter as I scan the name in bold type beneath the piece's headline.

"She's been in here before, though she usually knows better."

"How'd she get all the info? I didn't talk to her or anyone else at *The Herald*," I say defensively. The rusted springs under Captain Pryce's sagging office chair squeal in protest as he shifts his weight back and sets his elbows on the armrests with tented fingers.

"I know you didn't," he says.

"Oh," I say, confused. "Then what's all this about, sir?"

"PR."

"As in, public relations?" Pryce wears a blank stare, then leans forward and taps the back of the laptop with his fingernail.

"You ever do a search on the keyword 'police' on here?"

"What, the internet?"

"No, just *The Herald*'s site."

"No, sir, 'fraid not."

"Save yourself a headache. It's grim."

No surprises there. The media thrives on the foibles of the police, and our local paper is no exception. Slight misjudgments and fumbled protocol are aggrandized with drama, questionable 'eyewitness' accounts, and plenty of insinuation.

"So this is good then?" I posit.

"You bet. Best press this precinct has had in a while."

"I'm surprised this reporter didn't find a way to twist the story, make us look like the bad guys."

Pryce concurs with a grunt, sending a ripple of prickly grey flesh down his neck. I glance back down at the article, giving it a second read. I conceal a smile at seeing my smug face accompanied by such a heroic story.

"So how'd they get all the info, then? We get a new PIO?" I ask. In medium-sized precincts like ours, public information officers are the only ones authorized to talk with the press. Unfortunately, our last PIO, a lieutenant named Jerry who'd been on the force for fifteen years, was discharged after a nasty DUI incident. He'd had a few too many drinks after a double shift and had lost control of his patrol car. Unsurprisingly, The Herald turned it into a full-blown scandal that even garnered brief national coverage. Captain Pryce had been angrier at that media circus than I had ever seen before or since.

Pryce's expression sours at my question. "Nah. This wasn't a PIO," he says as if the word gives him acid reflux. "I talked to Miss Richards personally."

"No kidding?" I say, surprised. Everyone knows how much Pryce hates the press. And lawyers. And most civilians. And, well, practically anyone who isn't wearing a uniform in this building.

"I know what you're thinking. But this department needs a break. We need the public on our side for once. Anyway, Miss Richards will stop by a little later on. She wants to talk with you."

"And what do you want, sir?" I ask.

"Just stick to the facts and leave the department out of it. You were acting on your own, got it?" Pryce says, pointing a stubby finger at me.

"Yes, sir." I nod, grinning slightly.

"Now get out of my office. And I want an update after your chat with her, would you?"

Another nod. I'm almost out the door when the captain's voice comes once again from over my shoulder.

"Oh, and Harding."

"Sir?"

"I read over your report on the fire. I never condone an officer putting himself in unnecessary risk."

"Yes, sir," I say, grin fading.

Captain Pryce's hand comes up as if to swat away some invisible pest. "What you did was foolish, but that's not my point. You saved a life. In my book, that's a job well done."

I glance back into the Captain's face. If there's a smile there I can't tell, but I sense it's the nearest thing to a compliment I can hope to receive. I'm grateful.

"Thank you, sir," I say with a bow of my head. I slide out of the office back into the noise of the pen.

I return to my workstation to find Gabe leaning against my desk, grinning stupidly into the screen of his iPad. I don't even need to ask. "Local cop braves blaze ahead of fire department," he reads, his teeth smacking a wad of Nicorette. He's been trying to quit smoking as long as I've known him. We joined the force around the same time and went through academy together. Six years later, Gabe is a rank up the ladder from me and scarcely misses an opportunity to rub it in my face.

"Nice mugshot," Gabe snickers. I shrug and smile. In a precinct this size, I can guarantee the story's already made its rounds. Hiding from the limelight would be futile. Besides, there are worse things to have said behind your back.

"You already talked to Pryce about this? I'll bet he's throwing a tantrum," Gabe says with a shake of his head.

"Actually, he set it up. He was the one who talked with the reporter," I say. For a moment his jaws stop moving and his eyes narrow.

"Pryce? Pryce talked with the press?"

"Yeah, and they're sending over the reporter for a follow up."

"What?"

"That's what I said. He says we need the good press."

"The Captain said that?"

"Sure," I say nonchalantly, enjoying how this gets under Gabe's skin.

"He's gettin' soft in his old age," Gabe quips.

"Maybe. I get the feeling something else is going on, though. Did something recently happen with the department that you've heard about? Any new dirty laundry?"

Gabe leans sideways and rubs the back of his neck. "Could be a number of things," he says enigmatically. "Sergeants are privy to a lot of information that doesn't get around."

"Well, never mind. But it's an interesting tack for Pryce, in any case." I glance over at Rodriguez, who doesn't seem to be listening anymore. Something on the other side of the office has him transfixed.

"Who is that?" he whispers.

I swivel around to find a tall brunette speaking with the receptionist. The woman seems to have stepped straight out of a fashion catalog. Everything in her wardrobe–the snug cream blazer, knitted scarf, straight black jeans, and leather purse slung casually over her shoulder–belong to a class of woman not typically found in Haliford, and Gabe's shameless gawking is no surprise. She lifts her gaze from the sign-in sheet and looks in my direction, following a gesture from the receptionist. She strides over, seeming not to notice the heads that turn to follow her.

"Officer Harding?" she asks.

"That's me," I say. From her neck she lifts a plastic ID card from *The Herald* with a thumb-sized photo of her face.

"I'm Eva Richards," she says, thrusting a hand at me. I shake it delicately, as one might handle an antique, and smile faintly.

"Hello, Miss Richards. I'm Luke."

"And I'm Sergeant Rodriguez. We work together," says a voice from over my shoulder. He reaches in for a handshake before Eva can pull away.

"Nice to meet you, Sergeant. Were you at the fire too?" Eva asks, drawing a small pad from her purse.

Gabe clears his throat after an awkward silence. "Uh, no. I wasn't within the response radius, at the time." Or even on duty, I don't add.

"Oh. I see." Eva says politely with a few blinks of her long eyelashes. "So you really were on your own," she says to me.

I nod, catching eyes from several others in the den.

"If you have a moment, maybe we can chat somewhere a bit more private?" Eva suggests.

"Sure," I say, rising. I lead Eva down a hallway and past a set of swinging doors into a small break room. I sit her at one of the round tables and wander over to a vending machine in the corner. I feed it a few bills and punch the buttons, returning moments later with two cold cans of Sprite.

"So, what did you think of my piece in this morning's edition?" Eva asks. She's propped up her phone on a little stand and is arranging a pen and writing pad on the table.

"Not bad. Our Captain liked it, especially."

"Well, he was the source of the info."

"Yeah, I know. We're still scratching our heads over that one."

Eva raises an eyebrow. "What, you don't think he should've talked to me?"

"It's not about should and shouldn't, it's just not his way of doing things."

"Maybe he was feeling cooperative."

"Yeah. Maybe."

I can feel Eva studying me for a moment, but whatever she's thinking isn't verbalized.

"You mind if I record this conversation?" she asks, her finger hovering over a big red button on her smartphone's screen. I shrug.

"Guess not, but I'm not sure why you're asking me anything, to be honest. You got most of it down pat in your first story."

Eva ignores the comment and flips open her notepad. "We'll see. Let's begin, then." She taps the red button and we're off. Everything I'm about to say will be on the record and the pressure is on. It's my first interview with the press and my anxiety catches me off guard.

"Tell me about yourself," she says. It's vague, not what I was expecting.

"Excuse me?"

"Anything. What would you want people to know about you?"

"Is this, like, a personal piece? Like a profile or whatever?"

"To be honest, I'm not sure yet. It could be. We'll see what comes of the conversation."

I puzzle over this for a moment, thinking it strange that a reporter would come around fishing for stories. On the other hand, I don't really see the harm in sharing anything, and it beats filling out paperwork back at my desk.

"Well, there's not much to say, I guess. I've been with the force for six years."

"You're a patrol officer, right? Not a sergeant yet?"

"Right," I reply, doing my best to say it proudly.

"Married?" Eva asks, scribbling something on her pad.

"Yep."

"No ring?"

"Huh?"

"A wedding ring. You don't wear one?"

I look down dumbly and realize that I'm missing my gold band. An instant later I recall taking it off in the shower this morning and forgetting to slip it back on. I make a mental note to find it before Amy notices.

"Forgot it at home today," I say lamely. Eva raises an eyebrow slightly and nods slowly.

"So what made you run into the fire?" she asks. Her eyes narrow, glowing with intensity, the way sunlight does through blinds drawn halfway.

"Well, there was a man in the apartment and he seemed like he needed help."

"But why not just wait for the fire trucks to arrive, let them take care of it? That was a pretty risky thing to do, if you ask me."

"Yeah, I guess so, but I wasn't thinking of that at the time. The firefighters were nowhere to be seen. I had to do something."

"Sounds pretty brave."

Was that sarcasm? I shrug, but Eva's odd style of interviewing is beginning to unnerve me. What is she really here for? She's digging and I can sense it.

"Do you go to church, Officer Harding?" she suddenly asks.

"Umm. Church?"

"Sorry, I know it's a personal question, and you don't have to answer if you're unwilling. I'm just curious."

"No. Not for many years, anyway. My parents were Methodists, I remember going a few times as a kid. Then, I dunno, I sorta just grew out of it. I'd rather believe in things I can see."

Eva is still looking at me dead in the eyes, nodding, fully engaged.

"Are you aware that religious meetings were held in the building that burned?"

"Yeah, I saw the sign. Jehovah's Witnesses."

"Right. And I'm sure you're aware of other church burnings…"

"Sure, they're all over the news."

"Well, what do you think about it?"

There's something about the way she asks this question that gives me pause. I lean away slightly on the bench and glance around, trying to piece things together. Where is this conversation going?

The thing about good reporters–like good investigators–is their talent for asking questions. They'll calm their subject with a bunch of harmless inquiries, things that anyone could answer without batting an eye, and then *WHAM*, out of nowhere, comes a question that'll turn the subject's blood cold. If the person is hiding something, they'll flinch. It's a deer in the headlights technique I've seen a thousand times, and now I feel like the antlers are on my head.

"What do you mean, *what do I think*?" I ask calmly.

"Well, as a self proclaimed non-religious law enforcement officer, what do you think about churches being burned?"

"I think it's illegal and dangerous and people could get hurt." Safe enough.

"And why do you think it's happening?"

"You'd have to ask the arsonists."

"Have you?"

"That's not my department. As an officer, I'm usually just out on patrol, keeping the peace, writing reports. I don't investigate and I don't interrogate unless I apprehend suspects at the scene of an incident."

Eva bites her lip and frowns. This is clearly not the answer she'd been hoping for, which brings me some relief. I'm beginning to wish I'd never agreed to this interview. Then again, what choice did I have?

"Miss Richards, if you don't mind my asking, why are you really here? I'm getting the sense you're not after my life story."

That acute look in her eye vanishes instantly and she smiles. "Like I said, I'm not sure myself. I've just got bits and pieces now. I'm trying to see if those pieces fit. It might be nothing, but if there is something to this, it could be…Newsworthy."

"I'm not following," I say.

Eva leans in and presses the pause button on the recorder before continuing. "Did you know that there have been over three hundred church burnings in the last fifteen months in this country alone?"

The number is much higher than I had realized, but I manage to hide my surprise. "So? The economy is in turmoil. Crime is on the rise. People are angry and looking for a way to lash out."

Eva shakes her head. "No, these church burnings are different. Trust me, I've checked."

"How so?"

Eva pauses and raises her shoulders as if a cold draft has suddenly blown by. "I, uh… Don't have all the details with me right now."

"Yeah, but what are you trying to say? What are you on to?"

Another shake of her head and she smiles weakly. "It's probably nothing. Maybe just a wild goose chase. I thought you might have something helpful, but it looks like I've wasted both of our time."

I watch, baffled, as the woman stuffs the items back into her purse as quickly as she'd unpacked them just minutes ago.

"Look, if you think of anything, or if you come up with any ideas, call me. I've been working on this for a while and I'm waiting for a break." Eva hands me her card and strides back across the courtyard to the double doors and is gone.

FRIDAY, OCTOBER 16

10:12 AM
AMY

I flip the collar on my wool coat and cautiously eye the street as I walk. They tell me not to be too paranoid, but I can't help it; I'm married to a cop and I know better than most how easy it is to be watched these days. I take a final glance up the narrow street, checking for anything out of place. Satisfied, I dart down a gravel driveway and slip through a fence gate. I pull a key from my coat pocket and let myself in through the back door of an old house.

The tension lifts from my shoulders as I enter. The cold of a late Autumn Friday is replaced by the warm embrace of this cozy kitchen, topped with the delightful aroma of freshly baked goods. It's like coming home.

"Chelsea? Are you here?" I call out into the silence of the house. I wait for a moment, hearing the familiar pattern of creaking floorboards as my friend descends a staircase.

"Oh there you are, I was beginning to worry," Chelsea says. She brushes a few strands of grey hair from her eyes, tucking it behind her ear.

"Sorry. I would've called, but…"

"No, I understand. You did the right thing," Chelsea says, giving me a hug. "I'm just glad you're here. Hungry?" Chelsea slips on a pair of red oven mitts and fetches a metal tray of steaming chocolate chip cookies. Like everything else in the house, it appears to have been designed sometime in the fifties but has somehow maintained its original gleam. The rounded green edges and the clunky chrome dials look brand new.

"Not really, but I can't turn down your cookies," I say. Chelsea scrapes a few of the treats onto a turquoise plate on the counter. She pours two mugs of cold milk and sets them on the kitchen table beside me.

"So, how are you?" Chelsea asks between bites.

"Fine. But I feel like I should be asking you that question," I reply.

"Things have been better, but we'll make it."

"That fire…" I begin, setting down my hands and looking at my friend apprehensively. "Was anyone hurt?"

"Fortunately, no. And I suppose we have your husband to thank for that."

I nod, feeling the stir of conflicting emotions.

"How is he?" Chelsea asks.

"Oh, he's fine. Actually, he thinks he might be on his way to a promotion."

"I see. He's a brave man."

"Yeah," I say, averting Chelsea's eyes.

"So, what do you think about all this?" she asks.

"About what?"

"Oh, everything. Your husband's job, the fire. Having to sneak around like this."

I shrug. "I worry a lot." Chelsea nods, waiting.

"I know Luke wants what's best for us. He's a good provider. We've been trying to get out of our neighborhood for years now. He doesn't want to start a family in an area where all the homes have barred windows, he says. But I wish he'd find something else to do for work. Something less risky. Maybe that's not realistic with the economy like it is, but…I don't know, I just feel like the stress is eating me up."

"Have you talked to him about your concerns?"

"I've been trying, but he won't listen. Luke's a good man, but he's stubborn."

A shrewd smile makes a thin line on Chelsea's mouth and she tilts her head.

"What about Walter? What does he do for work again?" I ask.

"Plumbing, some electrical, this and that." Chelsea says. Luke would never go for that. I can be sure of it.

"It's not glamorous, but it pays the bills. The key is keeping life simple. Work is work. You said it yourself: the economy is a mess. We can't afford to be choosy about what we do for a living anymore. And we save a lot by buying second hand, trying to fix things around the house ourselves, growing our own vegetables, that kind of thing. You'd be surprised how much the savings add up."

I imagine what Luke would say if he were sitting here. To him, the dream life means a big house with enough garage space to hold a couple cars and a motorcycle. Scrimping and saving and living off the land would be a big step in the wrong direction. Still, I have lots of respect for the way Chelsea and Walter Novak live. Their lives are simple, happy, and relatively stress-free.

"You want any more?" Chelsea asks as she scoops up the empty plate from the table and turns towards the sink. I shake my head, and Chelsea tidies up quietly. She then disappears into one of the rooms for a few moments, returning with her laptop computer and a few small books. Her reading glasses, attached to a string of colorful beads around her neck, are perched at the edge of her nose.

I dig through my purse and retrieve a small tablet computer and swipe it on. I flip through the applications and enter a passcode. A series of colorful thumbnails fan out from the center of the screen and I click one. It's a black and white image of a book laid open on a table. I tap the corner of the application and slide through the contents, finding one of my previous bookmarks.

"Ok," I finally say, letting the text settle onto the screen. "I'm ready."

"Alright. I'll start with a prayer." We bow our heads and Chelsea speaks in quiet, imploring tones.

7:59 PM
LUKE

I gaze over at the flatscreen tilting downwards from behind the counter of the bar. Some news report on the Middle East is pouring out of the screen. Oranges and reds from explosion footage captured by a surveillance drone are reflected a thousand times in the mugs and glasses hanging from a rack. The smell of beer and fried food fill the stuffy space. Woozy country music spills into the air from a digital jukebox in the hall to the bathroom. A skinny bartender in a red beard and a stained college sweater polishes glasses. He glances at me a few times before nodding.

I don't care much for McCann's, but it's a popular spot for law enforcement officers and office workers from downtown. I tag along from time to time when someone offers to pick up the tab. If nothing else, it's a good place to catch up on the latest buzz.

"I know your face from somewhere, don't I?" the bartender finally asks, pointing in my direction with his chin. His voice is nasally and lathered in a thick New England accent.

"I've been in a few times. We've seen each other before. Name's Luke," I say.

"Nah, not that. I think I saw your face on the news or somethin'."

For all the good press that article has brought the department, for me it has only meant unwanted attention. After the story in *The Herald*, a few of the local TV stations took their turns shoving me in the spotlight.

"Maybe," I shrug.

"Yeah, you the guy that was at that fire." He pronounces it *fah-yah*.

"Oh, yeah. Sure. That was me," I relent.

"Uh huh," the bartender says, his expression indecipherable. "Papers said you pulled some old guy from the buildin', huh?" He sets down the glass and leans against the bar with crossed arms.

"Sure," I say.

"Well, I guess that's good. I don't condone murder." *Moidah*. "Still, I can't say I'm sad to see these churches go."

"Oh?"

"Yeah. Religion ain't my thing, ya know? Every time I turn on the TV there's some zealot blowin' himself up or beheadin' hostages. Makes me sick."

"So what, you think arson is the solution?" I grin, but my brow is furled.

"Whoa, I didn't say that. I ain't the one burnin' these places down. I'm just sayin' I'm not sad to see this country goin' the way it is."

"What do you mean?"

He shrugs. "Less religious. Last election, not one candidate mentioned their religious affiliation. You notice that? The pope, the Vatican, all that stuff rarely makes the news unless it's some scandal. People are fed up. I'm tellin' you, times are a-changin'."

I let the words hang in the air as he turns his attention back to the television set, where pictures of aircraft wreckage are strewn across the screen. The guy has a point, I guess. Something that reporter mentioned the other day flickers across my consciousness, but it's gone a moment later as a fist thuds into my shoulder. It's Gabe. He's grinning, a finger tucked under his belt loop.

"So?" he asks.

"So what?"

"The interview the other day. How'd it go?"

"It was an interview. She asked questions, I answered them."

"Yeah, I'll bet. You gonna see her again?"

I frown and swivel back to the television. "It was an interview, Gabe, not a date," I grunt.

25

"It could've been, if you'd played it right," Gabe says, chuckling as he slides into the barstool next to me. He snaps his fingers at the bartender and orders something on tap.

"For your information, Gabe, Amy and I are very happy together."

Gabe snorts into his beer, shoulders bouncing, "Luke, no one's happy."

I ignore the comment and study the contents of my glass.

"She still on you about changing jobs?" Gabe asks.

"She worries, is all. Can't really blame her. I mean look at this," I say, gesturing to the screen. A female reporter talks into a microphone, standing beside a middle school cordoned off with ambulances, police vehicles, and strands of yellow caution tape. I catch the tail end of the closed captioning, something about a homemade bomb and a disgruntled teacher. Fifteen dead, forty-five injured.

"So what, you're actually thinking of leaving the force? After this long?" Gabe asks incredulously, ignoring the segment.

"No, I guess not."

"Two words, and don't you forget them: job security. That's more than you can say about everyone else these days. Well, unless you wanna bartend. I'm sure these guys are busier than ever, helping the masses drown their sorrows."

I have to chuckle at the grim accuracy of his assessment. Silence sets in as we slurp at our mugs and let the din of dour news wash over us. A bright 3D graphic sweeps across the screen with the words *BREAKING NEWS*. The bartender saunters over and clicks up the volume a few notches.

The anchor, a young man in his thirties, sits behind the newsroom desk adjusting a lapel mike. His forehead is lined with sweat and he appears to have rushed onto the set. He holds his finger to his ear and then nods once to the camera.

"This just in: we've received confirmed reports that an emergency meeting of congress convened just this evening by the United States Senate has resulted in the passing of a bill that could severely limit the practice of religion in America. Live on the steps of Capitol Hill is our very own Gail Ling. Gail, what can you tell us about this shocking turn of events?"

The screen is split in two as another face appears in a panel to the right. A woman in a raincoat holding an umbrella and an unwieldy microphone is nodding seriously.

"Shocking is right, Danny. For reasons not yet released to the public, an emergency meeting was scheduled late this afternoon. I have confirmed that it was proposed by a member of the Senate, but in fact, both the Senate and the House of Representatives met collectively to discuss it. The proposal was voted on and passed. Now, this is highly unusual, as the passing of a bill typically takes weeks or even months to go through the proper channels."

"Truly unusual," the male anchor repeats. "Now Gail, what else can you tell us about this bill?"

"Well, Danny, we don't have all the facts yet, but we're being told that this bill seeks to limit the function of public places of worship, like churches, mosques, and synagogues."

"And do we know why?"

"I'm afraid we don't yet have all the facts. However, certain sources have told me that it is possibly connected to the earlier actions taken to limit the emigration of Muslim refugees to the United States. We do know that the bill will be sent to the President first thing in the morning, where he will either sign it, immediately making it a law, or veto it, which would send it back into the hands of Congress."

"Well, this is certainly something we'll be watching closely. Thanks, Gail."

Gail's screen disappears from the monitor and the spotlight is back on the anchor.

"With us now on the line is legal expert and CNN correspondent James Coley from Seattle, Washington. James, what can you tell us about the constitutionality of a bill like this?"

"Highly unconstitutional!" an expert says in a nasally, high pitched voice approaching hysteria. "Congress really has overstepped the line on this one. There's simply no way a president of the United States of America would sign that bill. It's unthinkable. In all the history of this country…"

The voice shrinks to a whisper as the bartender kills the volume. A few men in the back of the bar are jeering at the TV. The bartender glances over our way and jams a thumb over his shoulder.

"What I tell ya? Time's a-changin'."

I take it all in numbly, unsure what to think. Gabe is saying something about Islam but I dismiss it as I slip from my stool, fling my jacket over a shoulder, and saunter out the front doors of McCann's.

9:10 PM
AMY

I'm sitting in bed thumbing through the pages of an eBook. I've read this passage a dozen times over the last half hour, but nothing seems to be sinking in tonight. My mind is somewhere else, scampering here and there with the rest of me lagging behind. What am I going to do?

Luke will be home soon. He texted earlier this evening that he and his buddy would be grabbing a few drinks before coming home. I'm not worried. Luke's never been a heavy drinker, and he's been even more vigilant since donning the uniform. He hates corruption and hypocrisy and couldn't stand himself if he were ever hit with a DUI.

Gabe, on the other hand... I wouldn't trust him with a grocery list, much less in a scenario where alcohol is present. He and Luke have been friends for a while now, and though I have a hard time putting my finger on exactly why he makes me so uneasy, I can't shrug the feeling. Call it a woman's intuition. And there I go again, letting my mind dance around what I'm supposed to be focusing on.

Baptism. Am I really ready? Just thinking about it makes my pulse quicken. Today wasn't the first time Chelsea mentioned it. She wanted to know what's holding me back. I could think of a few reasons at the time, but the longer we talked, the more I began seeing them for what they were–excuses. The fact is, I know this is the truth, that this is what I want to do.

I first met Chelsea and her husband, Walter, in a park. It was the anniversary of my mother's death, and even though we were never really close, she left a big, gaping hole in my life. I tried to distract myself with TV, but that only led to a depressing news marathon that convinced me more than ever that the world was on the brink. I might've actually lost my mind that very day had I not forced myself outside for some fresh air.

Their smiles were what caught me. Such a simple thing, really, but it was like two twinkling stars in an endless, black sky. Just seeing their smiles gave me hope. We started talking, and we connected. In a world where most of my 'friends' were avatars that simply commented on my social media, what I had craved most was some actual human contact. Chelsea and Walter were so genuine and happy and carefree. A badly needed breath of fresh air. I asked them what their secret was, how they were so happy. 'We study the Bible,' they said.

I hadn't known how to react. No one really talked about the Bible anymore. I hadn't even seen a copy in years. Though wary at first, my curiosity was piqued, and we set a time to meet again. We saw each other a few days later in a coffee shop and talked for almost four hours. I call it The Day That Changed My Life, and it's no exaggeration. I don't mean to say that I believed everything I was hearing right then and there, but it was like suddenly new doors were opening in my mind and heart. Questions I'd been carrying around for years were finally getting answered. Why was the world spinning out of control? What was behind it all? Had we really killed God with science? What was going to happen next?

The third time we met, we looked at Bible prophecy. I could've never imagined the richness of detail and impeccability of fulfillment. Here was a book that I thought was all wizards and magic, and now, actually opening it and having it explained, I was finding out it was anything but! Why weren't more people reading this thing? We could fix the world's problems in a snap!

But no, they explained, fixing this was beyond mankind's reach. The solution to our problems had to come from a higher source. Just as a computer with a virus could not fix itself, but had to rely on a greater mind–that of a software engineer–to restore its original functionality. That was Walter's illustration, of course. A little technical for a simple girl like me, but I got the picture, and it made sense.

And it just got better and better. Each week, more and more questions answered. Where are the dead? What's God's plan for it all? Why hasn't he done anything sooner? Et cetera.

That was a year ago, and I feel like a different person now. I have a hope and a purpose. Still, I've got plenty to be anxious about. There is still Luke.

We've been together for eight years, and he's still in the dark about my study and my newfound faith. I know I'll have to come clean eventually, but it's complicated. When Luke responded to the fire at the Kingdom Hall, I thought it might be an opportunity to talk to him. Back before we started meeting in homes, I was at that exact building at least twice a week. I know the brother he saved from the apartment: back before everything went underground, he was our circuit overseer.

I frown and close down my iPad, unsure of what to do next. Chelsea and Walter have been after me for months to sit Luke down and explain everything, but I haven't found the nerve. Luke is a good, honest man, but there's no telling how he'd react if he found out I was studying with Jehovah's Witnesses, especially with the current social climate. Is this the beginning of the foretold Great Tribulation? Chelsea seemed to have hinted at it the other day. The thought is both exciting and terrifying, like climbing a roller coaster.

A knot of anxiety winds in my chest and I close my eyes to pray, asking once more for the courage needed to speak to Luke. Maybe he'll be fine with it after all? Maybe he'd even join me, one day? The sudden hope jostles me away from my prayer, a smile forming on my lips. If only!

I nearly leap from the bed as the sound of opening deadbolts echo from the kitchen. Luke is home. I swallow hard, forgetting all about the prayer, the thoughts in my mind a furious and incomprehensible jumble.

"Hey, babe," Luke yawns as he lumbers into the bedroom, hanging his jacket in the closet and disassembling his wardrobe. Hours seem to pass as he strips off his utility belt, armored vest, and various Velcro patches and pockets. I frown slightly as he removes the clip from his sidearm and flings it onto his desk.

"How was your evening with Gabe?" I ask. Luke turns to give me a brief glance and shrugs.

"Same old. A couple of beers at McCann's."

"No bar fights?" I joke, trying to keep things light.

"Nah, it was pretty quiet. Thin crowd."

"Oh," I say, desperately looking for an in. What am I supposed to say? 'Oh by the way honey, I'm studying the Bible with Jehovah's Witnesses and I've decided to become one?'

"You watch the news tonight?" Luke asks as he moseys into the bathroom and peels off the last of his clothes.

"No, anything big?" I say above the splash of water spilling into the tub.

"Not sure yet, but the news people seemed to think so. Congress passed a bill. Something about the restriction of religion." I freeze, my heart about to erupt from my chest.

"Wh-what?" I gasp, throwing the sheets off my legs and leaning into the bathroom as Luke steps in the shower.

"Yeah. It's supposed to go to the White House tomorrow, and if the president signs it, well, that's that I guess." I cover my mouth, feeling suddenly both cold and hot all over.

"I guess it's about time," Luke says from behind the curtain.

"What do you mean?"

"You know, with all these church burnings, religious terrorism. Maybe it'll help clamp down on some of that, make it safer. It'll make my job a whole lot easier, that's for sure."

I feel myself wither inside and retreat back to the bedroom. The ball of tension I've been holding inside melts in a puddle of sorrow and disappointment. Back to square one.

MONDAY, OCTOBER 19

9:21 AM
LUKE

I fiddle with the papers on my desk, looking for something to pass the time. I'm caught up on reports and not scheduled for any patrol shifts. The first few days after the fire were hectic, but since then things have cooled down. I'm old news and thankful for it. I open my web browser and peruse my newsfeeds.

The Associated Press, CNN, BBC, Reuters, and Yahoo! News are all the same. Everyone reels in the wake of The Liberation Act, the bill that turned to law with the stroke of the president's pen. Analysts, lawyers, legal experts, and politicians are all weighing in on the decision, and surprisingly, most are saying the same thing: It's about time the government stepped in and started monitoring religion.

The few dissenting voices, primarily from religious leaders and activists, seem hysterical and irrational in the light of recent news events, and if I had to guess I'd say that their ruckus will be drowned out in no time. Constitutionality aside, America's been ready for a change.

As for me, well, I'm still not sure how to feel about it all. Only time will tell if this will really solve anything, but I'm hoping for the best. At the very least, I won't have to risk my neck jumping into any more burning churches, and that's certainly a plus. I'm not much for politics and politicians, but if so many could agree on something so quickly, it certainly can't be a bad thing.

I'm shaken from my thoughts by a voice to my left. It's Cole, a rookie officer who's just been moved to our precinct from another county. "Hey, Harding. Captain wants to see you in his office."

Pryce's door is closed with the blinds open. The captain is frowning deeply and holds his phone to the side of his head. He glances at me as I knock and raises a finger in the air. I wait patiently for the call to end, then let myself in.

"Sir?" I say, standing near the door with my hands clasped behind me.

"Harding. Sit," Pryce says, a pained expression still etched into his features. I obey, my nerves buzzing slightly.

"I'll get right to the point. The Sergeant's Exam. Remind me, when did you take it?"

I look up at the ceiling as I recall the date. "I think it was about three months back, sir."

"And you've been here what, five years?"

"Six, sir."

"Why'd you wait so long to take it?"

I try not to make a face, but inside I'm squirming. I was told in this very office that no one passed the Sergeant's Exam before a minimum of five years on the force, so I hadn't bothered.

"Guess I wasn't ready for it, sir."

Captain Pryce lets out a humph and the air goes cold with an awkward silence. "You felt pretty good when you submitted it?"

I shrug to hide the truth: Absolutely not. "Okay, I guess. I'm not much of a test-taker."

Pryce leans back in his chair, the sounds of creaking metal almost deafening in the small office. He seems not to notice. "Look, Harding," he says. "The exam is important, but the score you get on the test is just one factor."

"Okay," I say, waiting for an explanation.

"The rest of it–the bulk of it–is decided by your superiors."

I'm silent as I put the pieces together.

"You're a solid officer, Harding. This department trusts you. Your peers trust you."

"Yes, sir," I say, cautiously hopeful. With his brows still furrowed, Pryce's lips part in an odd expression that I finally realize to be a smile. On the captain's face, though, it looks like something between anguish and disgust. I try to smile back, but instead only mirror the captain's grotesque expression.

"So... This means I passed?" I ask.

"You think I'd drag you in here and go through all this just to say you failed? Of course you passed."

The tension immediately releasing from my body, I sag back in the chair and smile–for real this time.

"Your new uniform will be ready in a week or so. Until then, you'll have to make do with what you've got. I'm guessing that won't be an issue."

"No, of course not, sir."

"Good. There's something else that I need to mention," Pryce says in a low tone as he leans forward and folds his arms on his desk.

"Sure, anything."

"I'm assuming you've been following the news with this whole Liberation Act."

"Yes sir."

"It's been causing some big waves. What you're hearing from the media isn't the half of it. Long story short, the federal government has been going through a major overhaul, and everyone down the ladder has been affected. That includes our precinct here."

"Yes, sir."

"Now, the feds have been very clear about what the new legislation means for law enforcement officers. None of us can be affiliated with organized religion. This doesn't mean you have to renounce God or anything like that. We're not becoming fascist here. They just don't want the men and women in uniform to be part of the major churches, get it?"

I nod.

"Now, I went back over your file, and when you first joined the force, you didn't put anything down for your religious affiliation. Is that still the case?"

"Yes, sir. I haven't been to church since I was a kid."

"Ok. That's good, then. I haven't had time to have this chat with all of the officers here but I'm not sure it'll be as easy for some of the others. Until I talk with them, I'd appreciate you keeping this between the two of us."

"Of course, sir."

Pryce nods slowly as he turns his head to gaze down the hall into the den of officers buzzing about their tasks. "I can't say I completely understand this Liberation Act business, but I sure hope the politicians know what they're doing," the captain confides with a grumble as he turns back to me. I feel the same way, but I'm unsure if it's appropriate to say so.

"Alright. You're dismissed," the older man says, shooing me away with a sweep of his hand.

Back at my desk, I quietly celebrate, wondering what Amy will think when I spill the news. With the twenty-K pay raise, I'm sure her nagging for me to change jobs will be a thing of the past. If we're careful, we could even have enough to take out a loan on a house in a couple of years. Maybe one with a small yard and a two-car garage. And then, in another year or so, we could start filling it with kids, maybe a decent-sized SUV for Amy… The possibilities are endless, and the realization that we're now one step closer to the fulfillment of dreams fills me with sweet satisfaction and anticipation.

I erase the stupid grin from my face as I notice for the first time a small yellow note stuck to the corner of my computer screen. A phone number is scrawled at the top with the words 'Rm 1109 - Mr. HARRIS' at the bottom. I dial the number from my desk phone and wait. The phone rings three times before it's picked up.

"St. Mary's Hospital, this is Margaret, how may I help you?"

"Hi, my name is officer Luke Harding, I'm returning a call..."

"Ok. Do you have an extension or room number?"

I glance back at the note. "I think it's room 1109. Mr. Harris?"

"Yes, sir. I'll patch you right on through."

There's a brief snippet of tinny smooth jazz as I drum my fingers on the desk, my mood suddenly brighter.

"Hello?" a voice says on the other end. It's frail and raspy and I don't recognize it.

"Uh, hi there. Is this... Mr. Harris? I'm Luke Harding. I'm returning a call–"

"Officer Harding! It's good to hear your voice. I suppose you might not know who I am."

"No, as a matter of fact."

"The last time we met I'm afraid we didn't have a proper introduction, seeing as you were pulling my body from a burning building." My mind snaps as the pieces come together.

"Oh! I'm glad to hear your voice. Your injuries weren't too serious?"

"Oh, some cuts and bruises, but nothing that a little time can't fix. I'm very glad to be able to talk with you."

I can't hold back a smile as I hear the warmth and friendliness exude from the voice on the other end. Of all the people I've helped and served over the years, the ones that make contact are usually looking to file lawsuits or official complaints. Gratitude is a rare thing to come by, especially when it requires any kind of special effort.

"Same here, Mr. Harris."

"Say, what do you think about paying me a little visit? I'd love to meet in person the man who saved my life. But only if it's not an inconvenience to you. I'm sure you must be busy."

"I might be able to swing by during my lunch hour, if that works for you," I say with a glance at my watch. The hospital is only a five-minute drive and there's a great hot dog stand outside.

"I promise I won't go anywhere," says the man with a chuckle.

"Great. See you then," I say, putting down the receiver and feeling even better. If there's such a thing as luck, I'm profiting from a good dose of it today.

11:12 AM

AMY

I lean against the countertop and gaze out a window into the garden. The shrubs that line the Novaks' property are thinning as the seasons shift but are still neat and trimmed–Walter's handiwork, no doubt. Skeletal branches tremble as a wind shuffles past. I hold a mug of spiced chai against my chest and sigh. Things are always simpler here.

Chelsea waits at the table behind me brewing the tea. She's been quiet until now. "So, I take it you didn't tell Luke," she says finally. I shake my head with a sigh.

"Amy, you can't keep this a secret forever. It'll eat you up."

"It already is."

"Then let it out. Sit him down and tell him the truth. He may not be happy about it at first, especially since you've kept it from him for so long, but at least he'll respect you for being honest now."

"That's so easy for you to say," I retort, unexpected bitterness tainting my words.

"I'm not saying your situation is easy. But don't forget, 'plans fail when there is no consultation.'" I quietly slip into the chair opposite her at the table and twirl a spoon in my tea.

"Did you see the news this morning?" I ask.

"Yes."

"And? What did you think?"

"It's exciting."

"Exciting? How can you feel that way?"

"Amy, prophecy is being fulfilled. Babylon the Great is finally being thrown from the beast, and we have front row seats!"

"It's hard to imagine something like this could happen in America."

"Hon, you've got to stop thinking like that. America, France, China, Afghanistan, they're all just little pieces of the same machine, and all of it is being run by Satan. Nothing is stable in this world. Nothing. Empires have toppled overnight."

"Yeah, but… I mean, this is a free country, not some communist regime. What about the constitution? Doesn't it guarantee freedom of religion?"

"Only Jehovah's guarantees are trustworthy, Amy. Never forget that."

I lean my cheek into a fist and frown. I know Chelsea is right, of course, but it's all been so sudden, so…fast. I need more time. There's still Luke.

Remembering something, Chelsea suddenly stands and steps to a drawer beside the sink. She removes a sheet of paper and hands it to me. "I almost forgot to give this to you. It's the recipe you asked for." I take the paper as an idea dawns on me. I stare Chelsea down with wide eyes and grin.

"What is it?" she asks.

"I just figured it out. I know how to talk to Luke!" Chelsea leans forward on the table, waiting.

"A dinner," I say.

"A dinner?"

"Yes. We can do it at our place. You and Walter can come, and Luke can finally meet you."

"Okay…"

"When he sees what nice people you are, I'll tell him that it's because you study the Bible, that you're Witnesses, and we'll see how he reacts. If he's ok with it, I'll broach the subject then."

Chelsea taps her fingers lightly on the table and tilts her head back. With her eyes pressed shut she makes a thoughtful noise. "And what if he reacts badly?"

"Oh, he won't, not with guests there. So, what do you think? When are you two free?"

"Amy, we'd love to come for dinner and meet your husband. I think it'd be especially good for Walter and him to get to know each other."

"Yeah, exactly! I really think they'd hit it off."

"I hope so. But how do you think it would make Luke feel?"

"What do you mean?"

"Luke may have some concerns that he will want to address with you–his wife–and only you. With other people there, it may make him feel like he's being forced into something he's not comfortable with. It is his house, after all."

"Oh, I don't think he'll mind all that."

"He's a man, Amy. He needs to feel respected by his wife, especially under his own roof. Ephesians 5:33 says that a wife should have deep respect for her husband. I believe some other Bibles use the term 'reverential fear,' so you get the picture. Don't get me wrong, I'd love to have dinner with you two, I'm just not sure it's the best way to broach this subject with him."

I sigh and lower my head. As usual, Chelsea has been able to consider things at a deeper level. It's something that's always impressed me about the Witnesses: being able to call up pertinent Bible verses at will and apply them to any manner of complex situations. Maybe I'll be able to do the same thing one day.

"Can we still do dinner, though?" I ask.

"Of course, Amy."

12:14 PM
LUKE

I hate hospitals.

Hate the smell of ultra-sterilized latex. Hate the clamor of pain and panic. Hate the withered, hopeless faces wheeled around in chairs and on gurneys. My job is to maintain order, to prevent at least a fraction of the suffering out there, but being here is a jarring reminder of how little an impact I'm actually having. I keep my head down and hold my breath as I march through the halls of the West Ward at St. Mary's.

"Can I help you, officer?" asks a gruff female voice from behind a counter. I turn to see a middle-aged woman with a heavily painted face and long red nails tapping the surface of a raised counter.

"Uh, yeah. I'm looking for room 1109. Mr. Harris?"

"Eleven-hundreds are past the West Ward, to the right," the woman says, laying out the path with a rigid arm gesture, a war general giving orders.

I thank her and trudge on, doing my best not to make eye contact with the poor souls roaming the corridors. I locate the hallway and glance at the room numbers. The door is barely ajar; I give it a light rap. A hoarse voice beckons me in.

I ease the door open to find an old man sitting upright in bed, a gauze bandage wrapped around his head. IVs sprout from spotted, gnarled hands to the metal branches of a medical rack. I barely recognize him and think I might actually be in the wrong room until he speaks.

"Well hello there, Officer Harding." He smiles, gesturing towards an upholstered chair next to the bed. Narrow shelves are littered with cards, flowers, and gift boxes. Colorful balloons and kids' drawings are stuck to the far wall with Scotch tape. A box of half-eaten chocolates and a small carton of milk sit on a movable tray in the corner.

"You must have a big family, Mr. Harris. Lots of grandkids?" I ask.

"Actually, my wife and I never had children," Mr. Harris says. I wonder if he's some sort of celebrity. Maybe it was before my time.

"Thank you for coming to see me. I know you must be a busy man."

"Eh, it was no big deal. The precinct isn't far and this is my lunch break."

Mr. Harris nods, a twinkle in his eye. "It still means a lot to me. You saved my life."

"Just doing my job, sir."

Mr. Harris turns to the other side of his bed where he rustles through the contents of a large bag. He holds a small package in his hand wrapped in newspaper and tied with string.

"This is for you," he says as he hands me the gift. "I'm sorry for the dreadful wrapping paper, but I'm afraid it's the best I could do." I carefully untie the string to reveal a framed photo. It's a picture of Mr. Harris and an older woman sitting on a park bench with large floppy hats and big smiles.

"Your wife?" I ask. A nod.

"She passed away earlier this year, unfortunately. That was taken shortly after we finished her last round of chemo. A final trip to the park," Mr. Harris explains, smile cracking slightly.

"I'm sorry," I say, almost guiltily. Harris nods gracefully, leaving me to wonder what kind of man it takes to stay optimistic in the face of such tragedy.

"Thank you. I know it's not an easy time to be in your line of work. I see the news and wonder if this world can possibly get any worse. I'm sure you sometimes feel the same. But when you feel down, I want you to look at that picture, and remember that you saved a life that night."

Maybe it's the stress of work exerting its exponential effect over time or this simple interaction with such a kind person, but I feel a tight knot in my throat as a heavy wave of emotion sweeps over me.

"Thank you, sir. This... This means a lot."

I feel my phone vibrate in my pocket and retrieve it to find a message from my wife.

Making spaghetti n meatballs for dinner and wanted to have friends over. That ok?

I reply without a second thought.

Yeah, no prob

Moments later, a response:

Thx. Love u.

I stuff the phone back in my pocket to find Mr. Harris smiling patiently. The two of us sit in silence for a few moments looking at the photo before I finally realize the time.
"I'm sorry, Mr. Harris, but I've gotta get back to the station. Busy afternoon."
"I understand."
"I really appreciate the gift. I'll stick it on my desk next to my computer. And hey, maybe I'll come back in a few days, see if you need anything?"
"That would be fine, Officer Harding."
"Ok. It's a deal." I rise, wrapping the framed photo loosely in the newspaper and heading for the door. I wonder if I'll ever actually see Mr. Harris again. I plan to make good on my promise, but he may be released from the hospital any day, and I'll have no means of making contact. Somehow it feels wrong to just leave things this way.
On an impulse, I pull my wallet from my back pocket and dig out a photo of Amy and I from our trip to Savannah a couple of years back. It's the only one I have, but it seems right as anything else. Maybe he needs to remember, too.
"Hey, um, sorry this isn't wrapped or anything, but I thought maybe you'd like my photo too," I say awkwardly. He takes it with his knobby hands, pulling it close to his eyes to get a clear view.
"What a lovely picture," he coos. "Your wife is very pretty."
"Oh, thanks."
"Come to think of it, she looks a lot like a young woman I know."

"Oh? Well, I don't think it was her. We live on the other side of town from you," I say.

"Well, how about that. They could be sisters! Her name is Amy."

1:42 PM
LUKE

I return to my desk with a bag of cold hot dogs. My encounter with Mr. Harris took longer than I expected, and now I'm forced to eat during my afternoon shift. I collapse with a frown into my chair and sift through emails. I scan subject lines but my mind wanders.

How had the old man known my wife? Stranger still, something had changed in his demeanor when I'd pressed him for more information, as if he were concealing something. I try to imagine a scenario where the two of them could've crossed paths and become acquaintances, but nothing sticks.

Mr. Harris is a bit of a mystery himself. What do I actually know about him? One: He'd been found in a small apartment on the same property as a church. Two: He isn't a pastor. I'd asked him flat out on the night we checked him in to the hospital. Three: The church property is far from our house, and the man is confined to a wheelchair. I doubt his vision is well enough to allow him to drive, so that rules out the possibility that he'd met my wife near our house. What's Amy been doing in that part of town? She certainly isn't religious. We don't even have a Bible in the house.

"It doesn't make any sense," I mumble to myself as I finish the first hot dog and toss a wad of stained foil into the trash.

"What doesn't?"

I spin in my chair to see a tall woman with crossed arms and a dark leather purse slung over her shoulders. It's Eva Richards.

"Miss Richards. What brings you back here?"

"I was in the area. You got a minute?" she asks, eyes darting around the pen. I study her a moment, pondering her motives. She hasn't written a second piece in *The Herald* since our last interview.

"I already cleared it with your captain, he said he can spare you for a bit," the woman says with a slight tap of her foot. Sure he did, I think. I decide that there are probably few men who turn Eva down, and her expression tells me she's not one to be easily dismissed. I shrug on my jacket and get up to head for the break room.

"Sure, I guess. But not too long, I've got paperwork to catch up on," I say over my shoulder.

"Yeah, you and me both. But let's take a walk instead this time. You like Bermuda's coffee?"

"Ok."

Eva doesn't say anything until we're a distance from the station. She speaks in a low voice and keeps her eyes on the pavement.

"You been watching the news?" she asks.

"Sure," I say.

"What do you think about the Liberation Act?"

"Surprising, but I guess they know what they're doing. They say it's temporary, right? Until they can get some of the extremism under control."

"You believe them?" she scoffs.

"Is there a reason not to?" Eva shoots me a side glance as we cross the intersection and enter the coffee shop. She orders a couple of tall macchiatos and clams up until the two of us are seated in a nook at the far back. She slips her business card from her purse and slides it towards me.

"I forgot to give this to you last time," she says. "You strike me as a good cop, Luke. You mind if I call you by your first name?"

"I guess not," I say, shrugging.

"Then call me Eva." I nod, but carefully withhold a smile or handshake. I'm still not sure of her angle, and until then I'm putting my trust on hold.

"Ok, Eva. Why do you say I'm a good cop?"

"Intuition. It's in your eyes. I interview people for a living, remember? I'm pretty good at spotting the slippery ones. And trust me, in my line of work I've come across my share. You can't even imagine."

"You're forgetting I'm with law enforcement. I deal with daily sleaze. I can imagine a lot."

"Yeah, maybe. I guess our jobs are similar in that way. Only, in my profession, the bad ones tend to be a bit harder to spot."

I grunt an acknowledgement and fall silent. Surely she hasn't brought be all the way out here to talk shop over a cup of coffee. I see her frown as she stirs the whipped cream in her macchiato and glances out the picture window.

"So, Luke. You come across anything?" she finally asks.

"What do you mean?"

"You know, what we talked about last time." Eva shifts her gaze around the small coffee shop as she talks.

"Well, as I remember, we talked about the church that burned. And that it wasn't the first, and that you were working on some story about it. That's all I remember."

"Kingdom Hall. That fire that you responded to was at a Kingdom Hall. The Witnesses don't like them being called churches."

"Oh. Ok. Why not?" I ask.

"I think they don't want to be seen as part of mainstream Christianity. They do a lot of things differently. You ever been to one of their meetings?"

I shake my head. "Not really one for religion, remember?"

"Right. Well, I went a few times when I was in college. In one of my journalism classes I was supposed to write a paper about them, and it turned out one of my classmates was a Witness. She invited me and we went together."

"What was it like?"

"Different… It was okay, actually. The inside of the building didn't really look like a church, more like a classroom or a lecture hall. People were welcoming. It was a mixed crowd, all ages and races, everyone dressed well. I didn't understand most of the sermons, but it wasn't ritualistic like the Catholics. They did sing some songs and have prayers, but it wasn't at all like the mass I'd been to as a kid. Lots of audience participation. Everyone had their own Bible and seemed pretty familiar with it. Even the kids could find the passages."

"My uncle used to say they were a cult," I add as I sip the foam from my mug. Uncle Jeb had been a less than savory character and I'm not sure he ever said an honest thing in his life, but I feel obliged to input something. I'm more comfortable talking now that I'm not the topic of conversation.

"Maybe. I didn't go enough to really learn much. But they seemed like good, honest, clean people. It doesn't surprise me that we haven't heard of many of their buildings burning. I think people generally respect them."

I purse my lips without saying anything. Amy crosses my mind again. Is she somehow tied up with these people? Eva keeps talking and I nod in all the right places, only hearing half of it. The conversation hits a lull and I let the silence slip in. A minute or so passes. I see Eva glance over my shoulder, hints of anxiety in her expression.

"So is that all you wanted to talk about today? Because if so…" I trail off, glancing at my watch and frowning.

"No, there is something. I've been digging."

"Is this about the church fires?"

Eva nods, takes one last look around, and leans closer. Her voice is barely audible above the din of voices and the espresso machines. "I was able to track down some info on two of the arsonists. One's a guy named Harry Levine. Here's what I found."

Eva cautiously slips a file folder from her purse onto the table and extracts a white sheet of paper. I glance at the mugshot to find a white, stocky male with short-cropped hair and a goatee scowling at the camera.

"Looks military," I say offhandedly.

"Good eye. He is. Or was, I should say. He lost a leg in Yemen. Apparently he'd wracked up some big gambling debts overseas. Online stuff. He didn't come back to the life of a war hero. His wife shortly thereafter got pregnant with their third kid. And even with his monthly CRSC–that's army lingo for Combat-Related Special Compensation–it simply wasn't enough."

"So he burns down a church?"

"Strange, isn't it?" Eva says, eyes glinting with the scent of conspiracy.

"Maybe he just wanted a way to lash out," I suggest.

"Then why a church? Why not a government building?"

"Maybe something to do with religion? Maybe he saw something when he was in the Middle East that made him angry."

"I seriously doubt this guy ran into any Baptist churches while in Yemen."

"Okay, so what are you suggesting?"

"Hold on. It gets even stranger. A week before the fire at the church, Levine takes out a loan for a car. Here's a guy who's barely getting by on government paychecks, and now he can suddenly afford a brand new Jeep. Weird, right?"

"Well, apparently he couldn't afford it, or he wouldn't have needed the loan."

"You know what I mean, Luke. A man with five mouths to feed and gambling debts and a disability doesn't go around buying new cars."

"Maybe. I don't know, maybe it was post-traumatic stress disorder." Eva glares at me with a raised eyebrow.

"Fine. On to subject number two." Eva swaps the paper on the table for another one from the folder.

"This is Frank Cardley. He was a suspect in connection with a slew of church burnings in Virginia, but was never charged."

"Not enough evidence?"

"Not enough time. He hung himself in his basement before investigators could carry out a full investigation. And by the way, there were people in some of the churches he burned. Five died."

"What's his story?"

"We'll probably never know, but it's eerily similar to Harry's. Honorable discharge from Iraq in 2009. Collects CRSC for a few years, but can't keep up with the bills."

"Gambling?"

"Amphetamines. No wife or kids, but he had a mom with advanced Alzheimer's. A month before the first fire claims a Pentecostal church and the minister inside, Frank moves his mom to one of the most expensive assisted living homes in the county. She's still there now, and the management said Frank paid five years up front, so she'll be taken care of now that he's gone."

I slurp at the puddle of cold coffee in my cup and lean back in my chair. Maybe Eva is onto something, but it's hard to see why she's getting me involved. Her tone is conspiratorial, and as law enforcement I know to be wary of that kind of thing. It's easy to draw connections and theories from scant evidence.

"How'd you get all this information?"

Eva shakes her head and stares at the table. "Sorry, can't give that up."

"So why are you telling me, then? I'm not a detective, and even if I were, this would be way out of my jurisdiction. Why not turn over this info to the police in those areas and let them handle it?"

"And what do you think they'll do? The suspects are gone, the cases closed. And no one really investigates arson with all the other things going on."

I nod. It's more or less what I was thinking. Is this really worth pursuing with real terror threats at our front door, like kids that have been converted to extremist Islam on Facebook patrolling the streets with concealed handguns and homemade pipe bombs? Should a dead arsonist really be a priority?

I say nothing but apparently my expression has spoken volumes.

"You don't care, do you?" Eva accuses hotly.

"It isn't a matter of not caring, it's a matter of not being in a position to do anything."

"Yeah, that's what the Nazis said."

"Excuse me?"

"Just following orders. Meanwhile, an entire population is exterminated."

"So what, I'm Hitler now?"

"It always starts with the small things, Luke. Look around you. This government is revoking constitutional freedoms left and right. You think it'll stop with the Liberation Act?"

I've heard enough. I put my hands up, suddenly tired of this conversation and tired of Eva. "I'm not a politician, Miss Richards. I don't make the laws, I just enforce them."

Apparently, this is the final straw. Eva stands with a flushed face as she throws the papers back into the folder and shoves everything into her handbag. She leaves without another word.

Back at the office, my mind wanders for the rest of my shift and the afternoon drags on. I don't like making people cry, even ones who call me a Nazi. She was only doing her job, after all. She's on a trail and is looking for confirmation. The more I think about it, the guiltier I feel.

I dig Eva's card from my pocket and type the cell number into my phone. A simple message will suffice. It never hurts to maintain a friendship with the press. Bad blood, on the other hand… I enter a quick text and send it off.

Sorry about this afternoon. It's been a long day. Didn't mean to upset you.

The 'long day' part is a bit of a stretch, of course. In the past eight hours, I've been promoted, visited an old man in the hospital, and sifted through minimal paperwork, but it's the only reason I can think of to justify my actions, and she'll never know the difference.

I hold my phone in my hand for a while, half expecting an immediate reply. When it's still silent after a couple minutes, I set it back on my desk and tie up the last few loose ends at work. When I finally clock out at 6:00, I've forgotten all about the text and Eva Richards.

6:40 PM
LUKE

I unlatch the door of our apartment to the familiar smell of Amy's spaghetti and garlic bread. My mouth instantly salivating, I take a deep breath and enter. Two strangers–a man and a woman–sit at the kitchen table sipping from wine glasses. I wonder for a second if I've somehow let myself into the wrong apartment. But no, that's our table, and this is our kitchen.

The man rises and extends his hand. "Hi there, I'm Walter," he says. I mutter an indiscernible response. The woman takes her turn with pleasantries; her name is Chelsea. I smile weakly and excuse myself to track Amy down. She's in the sitting room on the other side of the doorway, arranging a small plate of fruit wedges and crackers on the coffee table and humming. Some old jazz album is streaming from her tablet through the living room speakers. I flip it off as I step into the room.

"What's going on?" I demand.

Amy turns, the smile melting. "Just setting some snacks out. Did you forget about dinner?"

"What?..." I say, only now recalling the text message. I curse my bad memory. "No, I didn't forget, but who are those people?" I say with a jab towards the kitchen, not really caring if the guests hear me.

"Luke, my goodness, calm down. I said I was going to invite some friends over. And you said it was fine, remember?"

"Yeah, *our* friends. I didn't expect to come home to find two strangers sitting at our table drinking our wine."

"They brought the wine, Luke. And keep your voice down, would you?"

"I'll talk however I want in my own house. Why didn't you tell me I didn't know these 'friends' of yours?"

"I–I wasn't trying to hide anything, I just wanted you to meet my friends, is all."

"Friends, huh? Like your friend Mr. Harris?"

"Mr. who? I don't know any–"

"Donovan Harris. Old guy in a wheelchair. The one I pulled from the fire. Turns out he knows you, too. Funny how you didn't mention anything about him before. How many more secret friends do you have?"

Amy's lips quiver as tears start trickling down her face. She tries to catch them with the back of her finger but it's already too late. Her mascara bleeds. She covers her face and runs into the bathroom, slamming the door.

I stand in the middle of the living room, fists clenched. Typical Amy. I should have been the one storming out now, not her! She had no right keeping secrets from me in the first place, and then to get upset when they were uncovered! Ridiculous, and it's made even worse by the two strangers waiting in the kitchen.

I hear the soft shuffle of feet from the kitchen behind me. Amy's friends are no doubt fidgeting uncomfortably and probably hungry. Not my problem. They can feed themselves with the wine they brought for all I care. But moments later I hear the sound of coats lifted from the wall hooks and the latch slowly sliding open on the kitchen door. I wander in to find the couple leaving.

"Where are you two going?" I ask flatly.

"Oh, we can do this another night. It was really nice meeting you, Luke," Walter says as he guides his wife gently out the front door. They cast faint smiles over their shoulders and leave.

I watch as the door clicks shut behind them. Shrugging, I help myself to a glass of wine and a plate of spaghetti and collapse into the living room sofa to eat. But for the third time today, I can't help feeling like the biggest dope on planet Earth.

7:45 PM
AMY

I gaze into the bathroom mirror as makeup drains down my puffy face. How could he be so awful? What could've possessed him to say and do such mean things? I splash another handful of water into my face, trying to chase the red circles from my eyes.

My mind is a tangled mess of questions and emotions, but my body is numb and distant. How does Luke know about Brother Harris, and why does he think that we're friends? The truth is that we've only met a few times in passing; we barely know each other. Unless… I fight a shiver creeping up my spine as the terrifying thought crosses my mind that Luke might actually be investigating the Witnesses.

Or is Luke simply spying on me? But no, that doesn't make sense either. I haven't seen or spoken to Brother Harris in weeks; I haven't even been to a Kingdom Hall since shortly after I began studying. As churches around the world began to be targeted by arsonists and other extremist groups, the organization instructed us to meet as smaller groups in private homes.

All that aside, the most pressing issue is the disaster that's just unfolded with Chelsea and Walter. If only Luke knew how good those people have been to me! Their patience, concern, and support have gotten me through so much, and to be treated so cruelly by my own husband! The pain and embarrassment are overwhelming.

Perhaps Luke knows after all. Perhaps he's known all along about my secret studies with Chelsea. Maybe he even knows I'm now an unbaptized publisher. Maybe that's where the anger is coming from. I feel foolish for trying to hide it. My husband is a cop, after all. He spends his days with detectives and investigators, professionals who know how to coax confessions from suspects and conduct stakeouts and carry out all sorts of intelligence-gathering schemes. How could I ever hope to conceal anything?

I bury my face again in my hands and brace for another surge of tears. But a soft knock on the bathroom door stops me.

"Amy. You've been in there for an hour. I really need to pee." Luke's voice is still gruff but he's cooled down a few degrees. An hour. That's how long it took him to apologize! Or is this even an apology? It sure doesn't sound like it. More like I'm in his way or something. I wrinkle my face in disgust and scowl at the door.

"Amy, seriously. Open up," he says, his voice gentler now. "Or do you want me to have to use the bushes outside?" He forces a chuckle but my mood isn't ready to budge.

"Look, Amy. I'm sorry I blew up earlier, ok? It's been a long day."

"How could you be so awful to my friends?" I snap back.

"I was just… surprised to find them in my house, you know? You should've told me who was coming. It would've been different."

"Friends? Who knows now, with the way things just ended. They may never speak to me again." But even as I spit the words out, I know these aren't valid fears. Chelsea will probably text later tonight to schedule our next study and be as understanding and patient as ever.

"Can I ask how you know them? They don't seem like the gym member type."

Before I'd met Chelsea, I spent my time swimming laps and enrolling in spinning classes. But I haven't been to the gym in months. So much for the idea of Luke spying on me.

I bow my head and say a prayer. My heart is a hammer in my chest as I petition Jehovah for courage to speak the truth and wisdom to find the right way to say things. Then, after getting up and rinsing my face off one last time in the sink, I take a deep breath and unlock the door.

"Luke, we need to talk," I say. Luke wears a quizzical expression and shrugs.

"Ok. But first, can I pee?"

8:12 PM
LUKE

I observe Amy as she removes a couple of glasses from the rack and serves us some of the left over chardonnay. I decline her offer of more garlic bread and wonder if she's stalling or buttering me up before dropping a bombshell. Her tension is palpable. Amy finally joins me on the couch, takes a sip of wine, and gazes at some point on the carpet for a few moments. The story unravels slowly, how she met Chelsea and Walter in a park, how depressed she'd been that day, how badly she needed friends, how Chelsea ended up becoming the mother she never had.

I watch Amy bite her lip and half expect tears but she holds it together. Amy's mother, Diane, ran off with a man she'd met at a class reunion when Amy was only nine. The man turned out to be an abusive drug addict with an estranged family of his own, and when Diane wandered back almost a decade later with her tail between her legs, her family barely recognized her. She swore she'd given up her old lifestyle, but certain habits proved impossible to kick and Amy's father wouldn't put up with it. He filed a restraining order against Diane and she finally vanished for good. In the end, she never reconciled with her family and died alone. Amy scarcely mentions her. These are wounds I suspect will never heal.

"Well, the woman, Chelsea, seemed nice enough," I say, feeling the need to comment.

"Oh Luke, you have no idea. She's bent over backwards for me. Her and Walter both." Amy shakes her head slowly with a sip of her wine. But why? I wonder. Everyone's got an angle. What are they after?

"They don't have any kids?" I ask.

Amy shakes her head. "They have a son, I think. But he's grown and out of the picture."

"What does that mean?"

"He's just not around. They don't talk much about him. I guess they're not close." Odd. If these people are so charitable, what's the deal with their own family? Why latch on to strangers? A scam, maybe? I rack my brains for a scenario where my wife might be a potential victim but come up empty. There's a slim savings in a bank account, our ratty furniture, a few appliances. Nothing extravagant.

"Anyway," Amy continues. "I found out that Chelsea and Walter liked to read and study the Bible. Turns out they are Jehovah's Witnesses." I analyze my wife's expectant look as the pieces click together. Mr. Harris. The comment about my wife. Chelsea and Walter. All part of the same religious circle.

"How deeply are you involved?" I ask.

"I–I mean, we–Chelsea and I, and sometimes Walter–well, we study the Bible together."

"And? That's it?"

"Well, no I guess, I also go to their meetings…"

I sigh. I set down my glass and rub my temples with the heels of my hands. "Why didn't you tell me this earlier? How long have you been sneaking around?"

"It's been a while…"

"How long, Amy? When did you start?"

"Well…About a year, I guess."

"A year! What were you thinking! And you waited all this time to tell me?"

"I was scared, Luke. I didn't know how you'd react. You've always been such a good husband, but I was just worried that…I don't know. I was just worried." I finish off the wine in my glass and pour another, reflecting on the twists and turns of the day as the alcohol does its trick.

"I got a promotion today," I say finally after a long silence.

"A promotion? Sergeant?"

I nod. "Pryce told me today."

"Well… That's great news, babe. I know you've worked so hard for it." Amy reaches over to pat my arm, but I can't help but question her sincerity. She's been after me to change jobs, after all. Then again, what can she really say about it with things the way they are? She's in no position to nag.

"Yeah. He said the whole department is behind me. The new uniform comes in soon."

"That's wonderful, Luke. I'm really happy for you. And it means less patrol duty, right?"

"Yeah. But there's a catch."

"Oh?"

"I can't be religiously affiliated."

Amy's eyes widen. "It's just incredible…" she says softly.

"What is?"

"Luke, all of this, the Liberation Act, the religious violence, and now this, restricting even police officers… It's all part of what we've been studying… in the Bible, I mean…" I stare at my wife blankly. Frankly, she scares me. It's not like Amy to get excited about anything, especially religion.

"No, really babe, look at this," she continues, reaching into her purse on the bedside table and flipping up an application on her iPad. A Bible, by the looks of it. She flicks through the chapters and thrusts the screen at me. "Here, this part here. In Revelation chapter seventeen, there's this woman wearing scarlet, and she symbolizes–"

"Amy," I cut in, "did you not just hear what I said? I cannot be involved in anything religious. I could lose my job. Do you understand?"

I watch as my wife stares into my eyes sadly, the device slowly falling into her lap, and I suddenly wonder if the restrictions against religious affiliation extended to officers' families. The captain didn't elaborate. Maybe that means that Amy's study isn't explicitly forbidden. But it certainly can't be encouraged.

I lean back against the couch, wishing I could've nipped this all in the bud. Had I only known back when my wife first met these people I could've steered her away. Why take chances? After all I've done to get this promotion, why jeopardize our future with some silly Bible lessons?

Then again, how bad can it be? Amy's clearly thrilled with the friends she's found, and I can't deny that she's been happier lately. Calmer. More content, even. I finish off my second glass of wine and sigh.

"What are you thinking, babe?" Amy asks, her fingers lightly brushing against my arm.

"I'm thinking you'd better be careful. Especially with things as crazy as they are now."

"Oh, we are Luke. That's why we don't use the Kingdom Hall anymore for meetings, we have them in–" I raise my finger and shoot Amy a stern look.

"Stop. Please. No more," I say, shaking my head. "The less I know, the better."

Amy bites her lower lip and nods somberly. "Ok. I'll be careful."

THURSDAY, OCTOBER 22

10:14 AM
AMY

Chelsea sits across from me wrapped in a homemade scarf happily sipping a vanilla latte. Though she loves their coffee, she rarely splurges for Starbucks, and with the way things went the last time we saw each other, I figure that treating my friend to her favorite coffee is the least I can do.

"Thanks for not being mad about the other night, Chelsea," I say.

"Hon, Luke's reaction was understandable. I told you to come clean months ago. Did you two talk after we left?"

"Not at first. I was a wreck. I sort of locked myself in the bathroom."

"Oh, dear."

"I couldn't help it. I was just too upset. I was afraid I'd say something terrible…"

"So? Then what happened? You didn't sleep in there, did you?"

"No, he finally came and apologized."

"*He* apologized. Amy, sometimes I'm not so sure you realize how good of a husband Luke is."

"Yeah. So we talked about it all, and I told him everything."

"He knows you're thinking about baptism?"

"Well… not that part."

"So, you told him Amy's edited version of everything."

"I'm working on it. I feel pretty good about myself for finally saying what I did, you know?"

"But only after it came to a confrontation. You've got to be more proactive about these things, Amy. You need to earn his trust and respect."

"You don't think he respects me?"

"Put yourself in his shoes. You're out doing a stressful, dangerous job every day, doing your best to support your family, and suddenly you find out about a secret life your wife is living. How would you feel?"

"You make it sound like I was doing something illegal."

"Studying the Bible may very well be illegal someday soon. Isn't attending meetings at the Kingdom Hall already illegal?"

"That's not what I meant, Chelsea. I'm saying that studying with you isn't a bad thing."

"Not to you and I. But being empathetic means seeing things from someone else's point of view–in this case, Luke's. He's a police officer, Amy. His job requires him to uphold the law, whether we agree with it or not. It can't make him feel good that his wife has been doing something contrary to what he stands for."

"So what am I supposed to do?"

Chelsea gives me a long look for a moment, wheels turning.

"I'd say you could start by meditating on what Jehovah inspired Peter to write in First Peter chapter three, verses one and two. Let's look it up."

Chelsea glances around us to make sure we're not being overheard as I navigate to the verse and read it softly.

"In the same way, you wives, be in subjection to your husbands, so that if any are not obedient to the word, they may be won without a word through the conduct of their wives, because of having been eyewitnesses of your chaste conduct together with deep respect."

"What do you get out of this verse?" Chelsea asks.

"That actions speak louder than words," I respond.

"Good. What actions?"

"Being kind, I suppose. The first verse mentions being in subjection. But I can't do everything he says just because he's my husband. You just said that studying the Bible might soon be illegal, but we'll still be doing that."

"Certainly. There's a line there, and this scripture isn't telling you to cross it. But notice that verse two uses the phrase 'eyewitness of your chaste conduct'. That might seem like a strange way to phrase it. When you hear 'eyewitness', what do you think of?"

I take a moment. "Someone at a crime scene, maybe? A person giving testimony in court?"

"Yeah, those situations come to my mind, too. An eyewitness is someone who is willing to speak about something they've seen personally. They're convinced of its veracity, and so they testify. That's how Luke needs to feel about you. He needs to be convinced of your fine conduct, your chasteness, your deep respect. That requires much more of you than just admitting the truth when cornered."

No one speaks another word for a few moments as I process what Chelsea has just said. As usual, the scripture makes sense, and Chelsea has been able to penetrate the surface where I'd been looking.

"So I need to show him more respect," I finally say, my voice barely a whisper.

"That's the idea, hon."

FRIDAY, OCTOBER 30

1:58 PM
LUKE

I hold the glossy pamphlet in my hands and inspect the cover carefully. In the picture, two police officers–one male, one female–are decked out in full riot gear, cradling automatic rifles with one arm and saluting with the other. An enormous American flag waves in the air behind them. 1033-DEFENSE LOGISTICS PROGRAM is plastered front and center in bold yellow type.

The DLP is nothing new. It's a federal program responsible for transferring billions of dollars worth of excess military equipment to local law enforcement agencies, often with little or no charge to the police departments themselves. In some of the bigger cities–Chicago, New York, and Los Angeles, where terror threats and heavily armed gangs are common–the DLP allows civilian agencies access to high-powered rifles, grenade launchers, armored vehicles, sometimes even military-grade helicopters. But even the smaller outlying precincts have benefitted from the program with plated body armor, tear gas, and other weaponry previously available only to special tactical units.

Years ago, the liberals made a huge fuss over what they liked to call 'the militarization of police,' though the program managed to survive. It only took a slew of terrorist plots foiled by well-armed metropolitan police forces.

I glance around the den to find most of the officers thumbing through the same pamphlet. Obviously, each desk received a copy, but why? Our precinct is only mid-sized, about thirty officers. It's hard to imagine us qualifying for the program, though one could hope. Safe is always better than sorry. What's the point of armed police if the average Joe can outgun us for a few hundred bucks on Ebay? It makes no sense.

I tuck the brochure away in my desk drawer and stretch. It's been almost a year since the incident in the pharmacy, but there's still a tightness in my right triceps. I doubt the muscles and tendons will ever return to normal. It could've been worse, of course. The bullet missed the carotid artery in my neck by centimeters. Just a bit higher and I would've been a black and white photo on the front page of *The Herald*.

I think back to that fateful night the call came in. It was just after 11:00 when the dispatcher announced a 10-47, robbery in progress. All nearby units respond. I was there first.

The kid was only sixteen. Red hoodie, baseball cap, shaking an aluminum bat at the pharmacist behind the counter. The pharmacist's hands up, trembling, pleading. They made eyes on me at the same time, and in an instant everything came undone. The flash of silver from the kid's back pocket. The explosion of glass as the bullet shattered the front door. Sudden, searing pain in my upper arm.

I kept my balance somehow and returned fire. Three rounds before the perp hit the floor. Despite the daggers in my arm, I would live to tell the story. Not so for the boy in the hoodie. He left the pharmacy on a stretcher, his body draped in a white sheet. The EMTs pronounced him dead before he even reached the hospital.

His name was Kyle. He'd been after a bottle of Oxycontin. To this day I don't believe he was a bad kid. Just desperate.

My attention drifts back to the DLP catalog. Would things have been any different had I been in military-grade combat gear that night? Maybe holding a riot shield, armed with tear gas? It's hard to imagine Kyle taking the shot under those circumstances. Then again, who can predict a user?

"How's the arm?" Gabe asks as his desk chair skids across the floor. I'm rotating my cuff in alternating circles, an exercise I've repeated thousands of times since physical therapy.

"No more pain, but it gets stiff sometimes."

"Too much desk work, man. Welcome to the life of a sergeant," Gabe snorts as he gooses me in my good shoulder. It's true. Now that I've climbed ranks, I spend most of my time in front of a computer looking over reports from the officers I supervise. Ironically, the office work is taking a physical toll.

"Death by paperwork," Gabe sighs, as if reading my mind.

"You get one of these?" I ask, holding up the pamphlet.

"Yeah. The whole department got 'em."

"What's up?"

"Looks like the captain's been trying to pull some strings. The Defense Agency sent the info. I think Pryce is working his way through the forms now." I nod, mulling it over.

"So I guess you already heard about the new religious policy around here, huh?" Gabe asks, picking his teeth with a fingernail.

"Sure," I say, remembering something. "Wait. How does that work out for you? No more Sunday mass with the fam?"

"My abuelita won't be too happy about it when she finds out, but I don't expect the rest of them to raise too much of a fuss. They're not happy about the church closing, of course, but they've been too scared to go recently anyway. They'll get over it."

"And you?"

"What choice do I have, man? Give up the job?" Gabe leans forward a little, and in a lower voice, says, "Anyways, it's not like they can make me renounce my beliefs. They just don't want to see their officers formally involved in religion. I get it. So I ditched the cross." Gabe says, pulling back his collar at the neck.

I nod. "You know much about Jehovah's Witnesses?" I ask, trying not to sound overly interested.

Gabe makes a face. "Not really. My ma always said they were dangerous. We'd hide as kids when they came knocking."

"You ever talk to them?"

"No. I had a classmate back in high school who was a Witness, I think. Didn't seem like such a bad guy, but we never saw him much after school. He was quiet, kept to himself. Pretty square. Wouldn't do the holiday stuff. You know, a few years ago, we had a family in our church that talked to the Witnesses. They told me about it once after mass. They said they were studying the Bible together, and that they were learning all kinds of stuff. Seemed excited about it, but I couldn't understand half of what they said. I just told them to be careful. And then, one Sunday, they weren't there, and never came back to our church. Our priest made a big fuss over it during one of his sermons. So no, I've never talked with the Witnesses. I never wanted to risk anything that would take me away from my church and my family."

I resist the urge to point out the irony of his comment given the current policy change.

"Why you wanna know?" Gabe asks, slipping a pack of gum from his pocket and sliding two sticks into his mouth.

"No reason," I say, avoiding my friend's stare. "Actually, you remember that fire from a month ago?"

"Yeah, sure."

"It was a Kingdom Hall. Where the Witnesses meet."

"And?"

"I just got to wondering about them. That's all."

Gabe smacks his gum and frowns. "Ok, buddy," he says as he walks off. Dumb, I know. Despite his rough edges, Gabe is not one to miss the details. It's foolish to put myself in danger by snooping around.

My mind jumps again to Eva. I'm sure she knows a lot more about all of this than I do. She's been on this trail for who knows how long. I decide it's probably worth trying to meet her again. If she's willing, that is. Things could've gone smoother last time we talked. Still, prying her for info will be much safer than picking the minds of other officers.

I'm shaken from my train of thought by a sudden flurry of activity. The dispatcher, Jenny, is running from one of the back offices with a yellow pad in her hand, the headset still on her ears as the loose cable whips at her side. Officers are looking around, turning to each other and asking questions, startled. Jenny's a pro, but she's clearly panicking now.

"Listen up," comes a booming voice from down the hall that can only belong to Captain Pryce as he lumbers into the pen. "We've got a situation. Bomb threat and possible hostages. We need to get eyes out there. I want all units that aren't in the middle of something crucial out there ASAP. We'll organize you en route. Go!"

More commotion as coats are lifted from chairs and items are hoisted onto officers' bodies.

"Captain? Where we headed?" asks a voice amidst the sea of confusion.

"Decker Street and Coldwell Avenue."

Everyone's movement slows by a fraction as we process the location in our minds. Decker and Coldwell. The megachurch.

2:41 PM
LUKE

I screech to a halt behind a barricade of crisscrossed squad cars, lights flashing, radios chattering. Someone flags me into position and I park. Captain Pryce is right behind me. He explains that they've set up a small command unit in the parking lot of a bank across the street. A handful of officers have been sent out to extract civilians from nearby buildings and evacuate everyone from the scene.

Five officers with automatic rifles are making a circle around the captain. No one speaks, but the expressions say plenty. Pryce's breathing is labored and irregular; it's the most rattled I've ever seen him. Despite the uniforms and special ops weaponry of the huddled officers, they aren't soldiers. No one expected to end up here this morning while they were munching on cereal with their kids and feeding the dog. I'm sure it's precisely these kinds of ordinary family moments flicking through their minds right now.

"Brief them, Ben" Pryce mutters curtly to Lieutenant Lorrace as he goes to retrieve something from the trunk of his car. Lorrace nods and glances into the eyes of each of the armed officers as he speaks.

"The call came in a little less than an hour ago. Apparently one of the church members is upset over the recent legislation. He's demanding the right to worship freely with his family. An eyewitness said he was rambling off excerpts of the constitution before we showed up. He's wearing some kind of vest, claims it's rigged with explosives. He says that if his demands aren't met, he'll hit the trigger."

"We know for sure he's not bluffing?" one of the officers in the circle asks. His name is Mike. He joined the force a year before me. As far as I know, he only started training with our department's tactical ops unit a few months ago.

"We snapped some photos and sent them to ATF," explains Lorrace. "They had one of their bomb techs take a look and he said it was impossible to tell, but they could very well be live pipe bombs. Anyone with an Internet connection can learn how to rig an explosive these days. We can't take any chances."

"What are his demands?" one of the ops officers asks. Her name is Selena and she's the unit's ace sharpshooter.

"He wants the law reversed, of course." Heads with dire expressions lower around the circle.

"Who are the hostages, sir? They look like just kids."

"Yes, that's right. He's got four children with him. We don't know whose they are, but we're assuming they're his."

Soft groans erupt from the group; one of the officers appears faint. His face is pale and he keeps swiping it with a damp handkerchief. Captain Pryce returns with a plastic tube he's pulled from his trunk. He uncaps it, unsheathes a large map, and spreads it out on his hood.

"Ok, listen up. We're here," he growls, marking a red X with a marker near the intersection of Decker and Coldwell.

"The church is here." Pryce circles it unnecessarily. The building is the largest structure on this map and clearly labeled with a black cross and the name *St. Peter's Episcopal*. It's unmistakable.

"I want eyes here, here, and here," Pryce is saying, making small check marks at several strategic locations. The captain gestures to three of the officers and they nod an acknowledgement.

"I also want two snipers, one on the roof of the bank and one on the deli, here. I'm sure I don't need to remind you to stay out of sight. I don't want him spooked."

"The rest of us, sir?" I ask.

"We'll form a command team here and communicate with the eyes up top. I want you all to stay close. And I want information on our bomber. Who is he? Does he have a record? And find out who the kids are. If they aren't his, you'll have to track their parents down." I'm lightheaded at the mere thought of that phone conversation but acknowledge the order all the same.

"Lieutenant, you're in charge of these officers. I don't want any shots fired unless it becomes absolutely necessary, do you understand?" Lorrace nods, the muscles in his jaw tight and bulging.

"Ok, let me go talk to this clown," the captain grumbles. And with that, Pryce strips off the top half of his uniform and shrugs into a faded grey college sweater. Georgia Tech, go Yellowjackets. The wardrobe change is an odd thing to me until I see him on the monitors from the command center. I get it. He's no longer Captain Pryce, chief of police, but Dale the Neighbor. Just your average good Samaritan from down the street. Nothing to make a guy with a death wish nervous.

I pull my attention from the screen to reacclimatize myself with the surveillance van. I was trained on this equipment but it was months ago. My eyes crawl over the controls and dials as I try to remember how it all works. A technician hands me a white earbud and I stick it in. I can hear heavy breathing. The captain.

On the wide steps leading to the front door of the massive church, a man in a wired vest stands with an arm wrapped tightly around the shoulders of four children. The youngest are hysterical, wailing and pleading, but none of them dares to move away.

"Not another step!" the man screams, waving something in his other hand. It's connected to his body by a pair of black and red wires, some sort of remote. I know the eyes must be scrambling above us to zoom in and take snapshots that will then be analyzed by technicians from a bomb squad a few towns away. The captain stops in the middle of the road looking amicable and harmless.

"You got it. I'll stop right here." His voice is almost unrecognizable from the one he'd been using to give orders moments ago.

"My name is Dale," says the Captain with a friendly wave.

"What do you want?" the man snaps.

"Well, let's start with your name, if that's all right."

"Why do you care?"

"I just wanna talk to you. That's it. I thought maybe if we knew each others' names–"

"You don't care about my name! You don't care about any of this!" I can hear Pryce's even breathing in my earpiece. If he's nervous, I can't pick it up.

"I can see you're upset. Care to tell me why?"

"Why do you think? They've taken everything from me!"

"Can you tell me what you mean? Who's they?"

"Them! The powers that be! The system that controls it all!" The man's hand is flailing again, pointing to the buildings around him. "They control everything, and I'm sick of it! And they're controlling you, too." Pryce nods calmly.

"I'm sorry they've taken so much from you. But do you really want to hurt the children?" The man looks down, blinking a few times as if he's forgotten he isn't standing alone on those steps.

"I know how it looks," the man says, his tone softening just slightly. "But this is more merciful."

"What do you mean?"

But the man doesn't answer. His jaw is clenched and his head is shaking back and forth. A single tear slides down his cheek. Captain Pryce turns away slightly from the steps and begins scratching his face. The microphone we strapped to his wrist is now in position for him to send us a message. He speaks in a low, quick voice: "Get me intel on this man NOW."

"Find me the number of the pastor of St. Peter's," I say to the man on my left. The officer flips open his laptop and scrolls through an online phone listing. He rattles the numbers off as I press them into my phone.

"Hello?" says a gruff voice on the other end.

"Yes, is this Emmett McCallister? From the Episcopal church?"

"Well, not anymore. Who're you?" grumbles the voice, clearly annoyed.

"My name is Luke Harding, and I'm a sergeant with the local police department. We've got a situation that we need your help with."

"Yeah?"

I lay out the scene, mentioning only the most crucial of details, afraid to waste even a second.

"Oh, Lord in heaven," sighs the voice when I've brought him up to speed.

"Mr. McCallister? Do you have any idea who this could be?"

"Matthias Ward. That's his name."

I scribble the name frantically on a pad of paper and pass it to the officer with the laptop. "Any details you can share with us that might help?" I ask.

"I'm afraid he's not stable," McCallister says with grave certainty.

No kidding. "Any idea why?"

"Life has not been kind to that one. His wife died of cancer last summer. She fought it for years. Matthias had his own battle–with the insurance company. They paid out almost nothing. That poor family…"

"They have kids? Can you tell me how many? And about what age?"

"Three. Two boys and a girl, all about the same age, maybe spread out a year or two."

Four kids on the steps means one belongs to someone else. My stomach twists into knots. Our situation has just become that much worse.

"…All in elementary school. I don't know their exact ages. We're a big church, you see, and sometimes hundreds–"

"Yeah, can you tell me about his work? Would he have any knowledge about building a bomb?"

A pause on the other end as the pastor thinks. "Oh, I suppose he might. I believe he was on the police force for years before the family moved here. Somewhere up north. Baltimore, maybe? DC? I can't recall…"

I cringe. It doesn't get much worse than an ex-cop turned terrorist.

"And do you have any idea what he might be acting out against now?" I ask. There's a scoff on the other end.

"Oh, sure. He's mad about that awful new law. The family was getting a small cut of the collections our church took in each month. It wasn't much, you know, just something to help them get by. Now that the church is closed and the federal government has seized our accounts, there's nothing left for them. I've tried talking with him, but he was furious. Seems like he finally snapped." The pastor chuckles humorlessly, his voice becoming accusatory, as if somehow I'm responsible.

I consider asking him to come down and talk with our bomber but decide against it. If he's hostile on the phone, there's no telling what he'll be like in person. It could push Matthias in the wrong direction. I thank Mr. McCallister and he says nothing in reply before hanging up.

I speak quickly into the transmitter, feeding the vital details directly to the Captain's earpiece. The image on the feed zeroed in to his position shows him wrinkling his brow slightly and dipping his head a centimeter or so in acknowledgement. It's enough, and it only confirms what I already knew. It's time to change tactics.

4:28 PM
LUKE

"You ready to talk yet, Matthias?" Pryce shouts. He's been standing in the street now for almost two hours. The roads going off in each direction have been blocked off, but it hasn't prevented several news vans from squeezing onto the scene. Camera crews are setting up and training their lamps on reporters on the sidewalk. I half expect to see Eva Richards out there among them, but so far no representatives from *The Herald* have made an appearance.

"How d'you know my name?" the man shouts back. He's sitting on the steps now, the children still within arms' reach. The smallest one, probably only five or six, has his head cradled in one of the older girls' laps sleeping.

"I did some research," Pryce says, shrugging. His voice is cooler now, more authoritative.

"I didn't see you go anywhere. You wired?"

Pryce pulls the earbud from the side of his head and lifts it up for Matthias to see. "Of course. We both know how this works."

"Should we get rid of the press?" I ask Lieutenant Lorrace, who now stands behind me studying the screens before him with one hand clenched in a fist at his chin.

"No, they're good where they are. This guy wants to be heard, let him. Get him to think his words are reaching the ears that matter."

I nod. It makes sense. "Were you able to get in touch with the Senator?" I ask. This had been one of Matthias's requests from early on, and Pryce had promised him they'd try to get him a phone conversation.

Ben Lorrace shakes his head. "Can't get past his secretary. She says he's in some meeting. It better be important," Lorrace fumes.

"So, I guess you know all about me, then," Matthias yells from the steps. Pryce shrugs.

"I know your name, and I know you've been through a lot. But I still don't know you. What's going on Matthias? Talk to me."

"I already told you, they took everything."

"I remember that part. But why do this? Why hurt those children?"

"I won't let them take them from me."

"You mean the government? You won't let them take your kids?"

"Yeah."

"They won't."

"What? What do you mean?"

"You were a cop in Baltimore?"

"DC."

"Yeah, ok. So you ever heard of the Maryland LEO Pension Fund? It was put together for law enforcement officers who worked near the capitol. I guess they thought it was a riskier city to work in, with all the terror threats and everything. They never told you about it?"

"No."

"Well, then you need to make some phone calls. I'm sure there will be something there for you, once they find out about you being a single dad and a widower. Especially after that fiasco with the insurance companies."

Matthias's eyes are a thin line as he weighs the captain's words.

"It'll never work. Not after this. I'll go to prison."

"Not if you end this now, Matthias. Call it off. Let the kids go. No harm done."

"And I'll never get help from the government. They won't give me a dime after they see this."

"They'll have to. People will be in an outrage when they hear your story. They'll put pressure on the government until you get taken care of. The power of democracy," Pryce says with a sweeping gesture towards the news vans.

Matthias glances over at the reporters waiting hungrily down the road and seems to consider the offer. The cameras are rolling, capturing his every move. It's his stage, and now he knows it.

Screeching tires. A car pulls up behind the police barricade and a couple jumps out. They're hysterical, wailing and pointing to the steps of the church. The line of policemen converge and try to block the road, but they move too fast. They squeeze past the cars and run directly for the church, screaming.

"Madison! We're here! Daddy and Mommy are here!"

I feel my whole body go numb. The parents of the other kid have arrived. Perhaps they've seen the news footage and recognized their daughter. On the screen, two officers attempt to hold the wife back.

"Get these people out of here now!" Pryce screams without the aid of the microphone.

More police jump in to contain the couple. The wife is out of control, her nails clawing at the officer's faces. Someone manages to get handcuffs on her, which only infuriates the husband. When he starts swinging punches, the officers mace him.

The children on the steps are now awake and watching the scuffle with large, terrified faces. But worst of all is Matthias. The hint of calm that had settled in during Pryce's dialogue has vanished. He's once again edgy, panicked, and dangerous. He stands, raising his arm into the air. Everyone holds their breath.

The next few moments are a blur as the oldest girl slips out of Matthias's grasp and makes a run for it. She bounds down the steps, tumbling into the curb but catching herself with lanky, outstretched arms. Her sneakers dig into the pavement and she's up and running, moving like a wild animal.

The other kids are alert and restless now, perhaps contemplating bolting themselves. But the girl was older, faster. They wriggle around listlessly as Matthias reaches for their clothing and tries to corral them again. Without the oldest there, his primary source of cover is gone.

"If you can get a clean shot, take it," Pryce says into his mike.

A single crack into the evening air, and that's it. Matthias spins sharply to one side and crumples backwards onto the steps. The children scatter, the air filled with the patter of small feet and shrieks of fear. Officers from a dozen concealed locations now materialize, weapons drawn, scooping the children into their arms and withdrawing instantly back to the shadows. Matthias is writhing on the steps in an unnatural position. Our eyes on the roof zoom in, and we confirm the bomber's only taken a shoulder shot. He'll live.

With the children at a safe distance, two more officers approach the steps. Pryce inches in another fifty yards behind them. One of the officers kicks at Matthias's shoe to see if he is conscious, and when he barely moves, they lean in closer to get a look at the damage. A team of paramedics who've been waiting nearby rush in with a gurney, and just as they all gather in a frantic knot on the steps, it happens.

It is the sound of utter destruction. Metal crumbling, glass shattering, the obliteration of stone and concrete. All packed into a single, explosive surge. My world is an orange fire filled with a million searing daggers.

SUNDAY, NOVEMBER 1

8:09 PM
LUKE

I open my eyes to the cold metallic glow of a hospital ward. Machines beep and whir at my sides. The overhead lights are dimmed but still manage the pallid glow of the unwell. I wonder what time it is and move my head, searching for a clock. A dull, throbbing pain in my neck and shoulders tells me this is a bad idea. I guess it doesn't really matter anyway.

I try to move my hand to my face but find it impossible. I don't think I'm paralyzed, there's simply no strength left. I note an intravenous line tethered to the back of my other hand like a refueling pump. A sedative cocktail, no doubt. I take it as a positive sign that I've figured this out; at least my brains are intact.

I wriggle my fingers against a series of rectangular buttons on the side of the bed and give one a push. A nurse shuffles in a few moments later and swings away the curtain shielding my bed. I try to say something, only to find that my tongue, like every other muscle in my body, is feeble and useless. A muffled gurgle is the only sound to make its way past my lips. The nurse steps forward, presses her hand against my shoulder, and begins to scrutinize the machines suspended above my bed. She jots something on a clipboard before finally speaking.

"You've been out for a while, Mr. Harding," she says, shaking her head. "I'm guessing you probably don't remember much of it."

She pauses to study my reaction. She's right, I think.

"Well, there was an explosion… You were hit with some shrapnel." Another pause. I stare at her blankly.

"You took a lot of it in the arm, neck and face. Fortunately it was nothing that'll cause permanent damage. It's a wonder it missed your eyes. The doctors say you are a very lucky man." I glare back at the woman, wondering if she knows how idiotic that assessment seems right now.

"Your wife is waiting outside. I think she's pretty eager to get in here and see you. Is that ok?"

I give her the best nod I can muster. She acknowledges it and hurries out. A few moments pass and Amy's face appears at my bedside. She smells warm and flowery, and suddenly the sterile ward is alive with her color.

"Oh my God, Luke!" she exclaims with a gasp. She rushes to my side and collapses, draping her body over me. I ignore the pain of the physical contact and enjoy her warmth.

"I can't believe this, Luke... Are you ok? Can you talk?"

I attempt using my vocal chords again, and this time I'm nearly intelligible. "Mmm... ngg...okkg."

"You were in surgery for seven hours, do you realize that? They said they extracted over fifty pieces of glass from–" Amy stops suddenly, a hand rising to shield her mouth. "But they say you're going to be ok. Dr. Adams even said it should heal up without any major scarring." Scars. That's the last thing I have on my mind. At this stage, walking and talking would be a big accomplishment.

"I'm just happy you're ok, babe," Amy says, squeezing my hand.

"Wwgghat... day?" I whisper. The sound is low and raspy, a stranger's voice.

"Today? It's Sunday. You were checked in two days ago, right after the... the incident. Around 7:00."

I struggle to recall all the events but it's too jumbled in my head. I recall us responding to the scene of an incident. A shooting? A robbery? I seem to recall a church.

"I came over as soon as I got the call from Lieutenant Lorrace. I'd never heard him so scared in my life. I thought the worst had happened to you... Like those others." I frown at my wife, not understanding. Others?

"The two officers who were trying to arrest that man... They... Didn't make it." I close my eyes and force myself to remember. More snippets come back. There was a panic, people running around. Something loud. Fire and glass.

"Hey, how's my buddy?" says another voice from the doorway. I glance over to find Gabe walking in. His arm is in a sling around his neck, but otherwise he looks ok.

"The blast knocked me over and I sprained by wrist. I'll live. How you holdin' up?" He's smiling but he's not himself somehow.

"He can't really talk right now, Gabe. Must be all these drugs they're pumping into him," Amy says bitterly.

"When's he gonna be out of here?" Gabe asks.

"Maybe a couple more days."

"Oh, ok."

"Prryss?" I struggle to ask. They stare at me blankly before understanding dawns on them.

Gabe gives me a somber look before responding. "Cap's alive, but he's worse off than you. A chunk of concrete caught him in the arm. Almost bled out in the parking lot. The doctors had to amputate at the elbow." He bows his head and looks away. He's angry, I realize. Amy glances at him suddenly, her mouth hanging open. Apparently this is news to her, too.

"If only I could just go back and finish that scum off before he had a chance to pull the trigger," Gabe growls, his eyes like stoked coals. The nurse enters the room, glancing briefly at my two visitors before giving me a nod.

"You've got another visitor here, Mr. Harding. The name is Richards. Are you up for it?"

The name conjures up Eva's face. Why is she here? She can't expect an interview, can she? I can barely state my name, let alone give a statement for a newspaper. And what difference would it make? It all suddenly seems so trivial. News reports, interviews, conspiracies, all of it. Who cares? The nurse leaves before I have a chance to respond.

"We'd better give him some space," Gabe is saying to my wife. "Why don't we grab something in the cafeteria. You want anything, Luke?"

I give a slight shake of my head, all inklings of an appetite killed off by the bad news. I watch as the two leave quietly down the hall.

When Eva enters a few minutes later, she's clutching a small bouquet of flowers in one hand and her purse in the other. She sets the bouquet down on a table at the foot of the bed and then stands at my side assessing the damage.

"So, who were you trying to save this time?" she asks with the slightest of smirks. I groan, not in the mood for humor. "I heard about Officers Cole and Stenson on the news. I'm so sorry. The bombing is all anyone is talking about, even the big networks…" Her voice trails off as she notes the distance in my expression. I'm totally apathetic to whatever's dominating the airwaves, and she senses it.

"Look, I'm not here for your story, Luke. I just wanted to pass something on, something important. I wanted you to hear it from me before the press descends on you. And trust me, they will. I counted six vans with reporters and camera crews milling around outside."

"What?" I ask in a voice still hoarse but stronger than minutes before.

"I did some research on the bomber, Matthias Ward. You know he was a cop before?"

"Yeah."

"Did you hear why he quit that job?"

"Dunn really care," I mumble.

"Well, apparently there'd been all sorts of internal issues with him in the department. Some thought he was unstable. Later, he moves down here. I think he wanted a fresh start. He gets a job working in a post office. He's there for a couple of years, probably for the health benefits. At the time, his wife has stage three colon cancer. The insurance company refuses to cooperate; they say it's pre-existing and not coverable, et cetera et cetera. Well, she finally dies and Matthias is stuck with the kids." I'm half listening as she rattles on, wondering why she thinks I need to know any of it. Frankly, I'll be happy if I never hear the name Matthias Ward again.

"Flash forward to about eight months ago. Matthias decides to sign up for a church membership at St. Peter's Episcopal and takes the kids with him faithfully every Sunday."

"I know, I talked to the pastor," I say, surprising myself with a nearly normal voice. Maybe it's the mental focus.

"Yeah, so did I. He said the family was getting a portion of the donations."

"Right."

Eva's face flashes with a wry smile and she shakes her head slowly. "But church membership at St. Peter's for a family of four isn't cheap. If my sources are correct, it would've been over four hundred dollars a month for Matthias and the kids. I doubt the church would've then turned around and given him that money back, plus a little extra."

"What're you saying?"

"I think Matthias was there for something else. He may have even been a plant." I close my eyes and let out a heavy sigh. I'm not in the mood for Eva and her conspiracy theories.

"It fits the pattern, Luke. I think Matthias was hired by the same people that rounded up those arsonists."

"Eva, stop. Please. I don't want to have this conversation now. People are dead."

"Yeah, and they'll continue to die if something isn't done soon. These are contracted attacks, Luke. Something bad is going on and I believe it's going to keep escalating."

"Then go to the police."

"You *are* the police."

"Not the police you need. If you really think something this big is underfoot, you need to talk to the FBI." Eva averts her stare for a moment, a shadow settling over her expression.

"I tried."

"And?"

"I went to them months ago. I... I don't trust them, Luke. That's why I came to you. When I saw that you'd saved someone from that fire, I knew I could trust you." I take a deep breath and try to process everything, but my mind moves in slow motion.

"So what's your theory, then? That Matthias–an American, and an ex-cop–was hired by some terrorists to bomb a church, and kill himself and his children in the process?" Eva's shaking her head.

"No, the kids were never meant to be hurt."

"How can you even know that?" I say, flustered. Eva gives me a cold stare and pulls something from her purse. It's a flash drive with something scribbled on the top in black marker.

"What's this?" I ask.

"I went through all of the footage from the news crews at the scene and put the video together. I want you to have a look, tell me what you think."

"Now?"

"No, but don't let it wait too long. I feel I'm running out of time."

"Okay, fine. I'll take a look."

"Do it at home, make sure you're alone."

"Sure, whatever," I say, alarmed by the paranoid look in her eyes. Eva turns suddenly as my wife walks into the room, a can of soda and a cellophane-wrapped sandwich in her hands.

"Who are you?" she asks Eva.

"Hi, my name is Eva Richards. I'm a friend. You must be Mrs. Harding."

"That's right," Amy says with a suspicious edge. "I'm sorry, but I don't think my husband is able to talk with you right now, not in this condition."

Eva opens her mouth as if to explain, but stops herself. "You're right. I'll be on my way." Then, to me, "Rest up, Officer Harding."

THURSDAY, NOVEMBER 12

3:21 PM
AMY

All my worst nightmares materialized last Friday when I got the call from Luke's precinct. I must've been the only one in all of Haliford who hadn't been glued to their TV or radio as the incident at St. Peter's Episcopal unfolded. I could barely comprehend the news. My husband? At the scene of a suicide bombing? He'd make it, they said, but I still had no idea what I'd find when I raced over to the hospital.

That was nearly two weeks ago. Since then, Luke's been at home recuperating. Half of his body is covered in black and purple bruises from the trauma caused by the blast, and much of the rest of him is still wrapped in gauze and bandages. He takes ibuprofen with his meals to mitigate the pain and ampicillin in the morning to prevent infection. With time, I know these wounds will heal. What really worries me is his mind.

I guess it shouldn't surprise me that the man who I've been nursing back to health feels like a different person. He speaks little, usually only to mention some item he's running short on as I'm scampering out the front door on a grocery run. He spends his days wrapped in a blanket on the couch, surfing channels, soaking in a dozen networks' analyses of the attack. The reporters and camera crews have finally stopped sniffing around our apartment for morsels to include in their coverage.

Overnight, Matthias Ward became a household name. His family members and old colleagues have been rounded up and placed on couches and interviewed until there's nothing left to say. Everyone's sentiments have been the same. Matthias was a family man, a hard worker, a decent father. How he could've lashed out is beyond anyone's understanding.

Even more startling than this is how quickly the media has denounced the event as an example of 'Christian extremism'. Some predict copycat incidents, especially in the Bible-thumping South where we live. A number of politicians have suggested stronger preemptive measures against ex-churchgoers with a history of activism.

And there my husband sits, expressionless, soaking it all in. What is he thinking? Is he just trying to make sense of it, or is he angry? I enter the apartment after picking up a few bottles of Gatorade and Cheetos and he's in his usual position slouched against the sofa. I slip into the living room and flick off the TV. He doesn't seem to notice.

"You were gone a long time," he remarks offhandedly as I set his groceries on the coffee table and remove my jacket and scarf.

"They didn't have any of the blue Gatorades. I asked one of the guys stocking the shelf and he was able to grab a couple from storage."

Luke looks up at me and I'm sure it's the first time we've made eye contact in days. "Thanks," he says, and I can tell he means it. I lean down to kiss him on the side of his face that still looks normal and gently run my fingers through his hair.

"Any new developments?" I ask, gesturing towards the blank face of the TV. He shrugs.

"So," I say tentatively, "today is Thursday… Usually I meet with Chelsea today. You mind if I make you dinner a little early?"

"Oh," Luke says with a strange look, as if suddenly remembering something. I wonder if he's forgotten all about Chelsea and Walter and my studies. He frowns as he pieces it together. "How are they?"

My face lights up and I allow myself a little hope. "Oh, they're good. They keep asking about you. Chelsea offered to bake you something. How does that sound?"

"You guys meet once a week?" Luke asks.

"It depends. Sometimes two or three times, though last week we didn't study, with everything that happened, of course."

"What do they do for work?"

"Chelsea sells things online–antiques and other knickknacks she finds and restores. Most of it comes from garage sales. And Walter does a little bit of everything. He's a handyman, I guess. Why?"

"Just curious."

I pause, folding a brown shopping bag against my chest as I study Luke's expression. "Does it worry you that I spend so much time with them?"

"How could I not worry?"

"What do you mean?"

"I don't know a thing about them. And I don't know anything about the Witnesses. I mean, I probably shouldn't even be agreeing to let you get wrapped up in all of this."

"The Witnesses are the most peaceful people I've ever met, Luke. They actually practice what they preach. Their families are happy and close, they respect each other, and they never condone violence."

"What about now?"

"What *about* now?"

"Now that the government is limiting their freedom to worship, their right to religious assembly? Will they still be peaceful?"

"Yes."

"You say it like you know, but how can you? What do you really know about these people?"

"What do *you* know? Have you actually taken the time to understand them, or are you just making assumptions about us?"

"'*Us*'? So you're one of them now?"

"Luke, I can understand that you're worried. A lot of people say negative things about the Witnesses. The same things ran through my mind when I first met Chelsea and Walter. But then, after we started talking, I found out that most of what I'd heard was lies. People blindly repeating stuff they'd heard from someone else."

"So what are you saying, that I should start studying with the Witnesses?" Luke says with a derisive laugh.

"It wouldn't hurt. You're a cop, aren't you? Investigate," I say, trying my best not to sound snide. I peck him again on the cheek and start thinking about dinner.

MONDAY, NOVEMBER 16

1:57 AM
LUKE

Sleep evades me. I hear the explosions at night behind closed eyelids, feel the glass from the surveillance van's windows slicing into my skin. I spend hours after dark waiting for the drowsiness but it never comes. I'm up and walking around the apartment, as if maybe I can tire myself out and force my body to rest. On the worst nights I leave the apartment building and go for a walk in the dark. I carry my sidearm, of course, but I'm not really worried. Facing off with a suicide bomber sort of makes everything else in life less scary.

The air tonight is cold and crisp, tainted with burning coal from a factory on the other side of town. It's all surreally comforting, and my mind goes elsewhere, and before I know it I've walked almost three miles. I find myself crossing the street, heading as if by migratory instinct to McCann's. The neon sign is still lit even at this late hour, and I decide I have a taste for something greasy.

A solitary man in a dark felt hat bites into a hamburger. He's sitting by himself at the far end of the bar and doesn't seem to mind the ketchup drooling onto his fingers from the overstuffed burger. Taking a few steps closer, I realize that it's our captain, Dale Pryce. He's in a thick, wrinkled overcoat and faded corduroys, and I can't help thinking back to the getup he'd been wearing when he first tried to talk down Matthias. It's the first time I've seen him since the incident.

I'm unsure if Pryce will be in the mood for conversation, but with us two being the only patrons at this hour, ignoring him might be worse. We've known each other for six years, after all.

"Hey there," I say casually, sidling up to his barstool, hands deep in my pockets. The captain looks me over for a long moment before speaking.

"Harding," he says tiredly.

"I think this is the first time I've seen you in here," I say.

Pryce shrugs. "It's the only place that makes decent onion rings after midnight."

"You can't sleep either." He shakes his head slowly.

"Well don't just stand there, have a seat."

The grill cook on duty doesn't seem pleased when I put an order in for chili cheese fries and a strawberry milkshake, but he complies all the same, and before long the Captain and I are churning our way through thousands of calories in quiet misery.

"You been back to the office yet?" Pryce asks when our plates are emptied but for streaks of grease, crumbs, and condiments.

"My first shift starts in a few hours. My injuries aren't so bad. But the doctors wanted me to rest."

"Looks nasty enough," Pryce says, tilting his head to glimpse at the scars on my face.

"You coming back any time soon?" I ask hopefully.

"Yeah, s'pose so. Not doing anyone any good sitting around all day eating junk food, that's for sure."

"I think you've done enough good for a lifetime, sir."

Captain Pryce makes an unpleasant face and shakes his head. "Two of my officers died in that blast. So you can take that praise and stick it someplace else."

"It wasn't your fault, captain. And think about those kids. They're alive because of you."

"And scarred for eternity. You expect them to grow up and have a normal life after seeing something like that? And what about Cole's kids? You know his wife's pregnant with their third? What about them?" I hadn't known, and now there are no words of comfort left.

"How does a man do something like that? How does he bring three innocent children into this world and one day decide to wipe their lives out? Wasn't he supposed to be *religious*? What was he learning in that church?" Captain Pryce's voice rises and trembles. He clutches a dirty napkin in his remaining hand with blanched knuckles.

"I don't know. Maybe he just went crazy," I offer.

"Everyone's excuse. You know, I've been watching the news the last few days. I never have any time at the office, but now it's all I do. And it finally occurred to me, religion is all the same."

"Yeah?"

"It doesn't matter if it's Al Qaeda or ISIS in the Middle East or the Army of God in Russia or disgruntled Christians in our own backyard. They're all the same. When they're angry, they want blood, and they do it in the name of their deities to make it seem ok. These people have no conscience, no moral inhibition when they think they're on their way to martyrdom."

"They do seem dangerous," I relent, as it dawns on me that I've gradually been led to the same conclusion.

"And then I'm thinking, if a single father of three can build a bomb and kill himself, two policemen, and two EMTs, what happens when we face a whole army of them? What happens when they decide not to announce their intentions first, and instead just opt to walk into a football game or a bus station and just BOOM!" Pryce slams his fist on the bar, rattling the silverware and nearly tipping my milkshake.

"I don't know," I say weakly.

"All I can say is, we need to get a handle on this before it gets out of control. We need to start taking offensive action here, rather than just sitting around waiting for the next threat. I'm sick of waiting."

The Captain's eyes bore into mine, looking for confirmation, but I feel cold inside and offer nothing. What could possibly be said to extinguish the man's anger or soothe his pain?

"I guess... We just have to take one day at a time," I say lamely. Frowning, the Captain sighs. He stands, fishes a twenty from his pocket, and tosses it next to the plate.

"See you at the office," he grumbles as he lumbers out the door and into the night. I watch the door swing shut, as if holding out the blackness of the dark world beyond. How much longer can it go on like this?

I brush my fingers along my face, feeling the sandpapery scabs left by the glass shards from a bomb that killed two of my friends. I guess that nurse was right after all: I'd gotten off easy. So where's the gratitude? There is only numbness. It spreads over my body like an enormous callus until there is nothing else.

I dab absently at the puddles of condensation seeping from the sides of my glass onto the cigarette-burned wood. I feel my phone vibrate twice in my pocket and know it must be Amy, probably waking in the middle of the night and worrying when the other side of the bed is cold and empty. I slide the phone from my pocket and glance at the screen.

It's Eva.

3:44 AM
LUKE

I push through the glass doors of the motel lobby and find myself in a room that reeks of old cigarettes and mildewed carpet. A dusty grandfather clock, likely the only thing of value in the whole place, clunks out a steady rhythm in the far corner. The only other sound is a rasping, choking noise coming from somewhere behind the front desk. I approach it to find a man with a balding head of wiry grey hair asleep in an office chair with his feet crossed on the counter.

I tap the rusty service bell. When this fails to wake the man up, I reach out to shake his leg.

"Hey buddy, I need some help," I say. The man's eyelids flutter open, widen for a moment, and then narrow again.

"Who're you? And what in the world happened to your face?" he whines. His voice is high and strangely accented.

"It's not important. I'm looking for Agnes. Know her?" The man studies me cautiously, moving nothing but the eyes in his sockets.

"I might. Who's looking for her?"

"Mr. Sprite," I say uncomfortably.

"Yeah, right. Ok, Mr. Sprite. Room 212, on the right."

"Thanks." The man mumbles something under his breath as I exit the back door and climb the outdoor staircase. I glance over my shoulder a few times as I've been instructed and knock three times when I find the door. I see a shadow pass over the peephole and the door swings open just enough for me to slip inside.

Eva's hair is damp and messy and she wears a tattered white hotel robe and slippers. The smell here is the same as the lobby, though tinged faintly of cheap hotel soap and shampoo. She offers coffee and I accept, feeling the full weight of the hour on my eyelids. Now that I need to be up and alert, my body's ready for bed. Figures. Eva pours me a cup from a French press and collapses into a dirty recliner on the far side of the room. I sit on the edge of the bed, waiting.

"So, what's the emergency?" I ask. Eva gazes blankly at a wall, seeming to miss the question.

"Thanks for coming," she finally says. "I'm sorry for getting you involved, but I literally had no one else to call. Even my colleagues at *The Herald* won't return my messages."

"Why? What's going on?"

"Did you watch the video on that USB?" she asks.

"Yeah," I say. "It was interesting."

It's an understatement, but I'm still not totally sure how I feel about the footage. Somehow, Eva was able to piece together video from the live news feeds that show exactly what happened on that fateful afternoon at the church. From the angle of one of the cameras on Coldwell Road, it's clear that Matthias prodded the oldest away from him when her folks showed up, and that he let the other children out of his grasp minutes later. Seems they were just there for show after all.

"You're still not sure if you believe me," Eva says.

"I'm not sure what the video proves, Eva. Maybe he had a change of heart. I don't see how you can tie it in to everything else." She looks at me with sad eyes for a moment and then bows her head.

"I guess it doesn't matter now anyway," she says quietly.

"What do you mean?"

"I'm done. It's gotten too dangerous."

"You mean your story?"

Eva glares at me. "What else?"

"Look, why don't you start from the beginning? Tell me how you got involved. I'm sure it can't be beyond fixing."

"Fine," Eva says. She rubs her temples as she speaks.

"It all started when I got this anonymous tip via email about a year and a half ago regarding the church fires on the West Coast. I didn't pay much attention to it at the time because, let's face it, no one in Haliford County really cares about what happens out there. I set it aside and forgot about it until months later, when we started seeing similar incidents here in the South. I responded to the email, trying to get some more info, but they all bounced back. Apparently the account had been deleted by whoever set it up.

"In my line of work, that's not particularly strange. We're always getting false tips, kids pulling pranks, people that just want some of the limelight. No big deal. But this email was different. I just… got a weird feeling from it."

"What did it say?"

"The entire message was just one sentence: 'Church burnings are organized, contracted.' That was strange enough. But then, under that sentence, was a seventeen-digit number."

"A number?"

"Right. Too long to be a phone number, even an international one. Obviously not a social security number, or a postal code, or any kind of address. Which left only one option." I consider it for a moment and then frown with a shake of my head.

"A bank account," she says.

"Oh."

"Of course, I knew it could be a wild goose chase, some kid typing random numbers to waste my time, but I started poking around anyway.

The number, it turns out, was real. It was a Bank of California account. And guess who the holder was?"

"One of the arsonists?"

"Harry Levine, whom I told you about before. So I followed that trail for a while, and found out about the money transfers, and everything that had happened shortly before he'd burned the church. Weird, but by itself, not conclusive. But then, a few weeks after I'd found all that out, I get another anonymous email. This time from a different account, and the message body is just a number. A *new* number. I go through the same routine, and again, it's a bank account linked to someone, this time in Washington State. Same story. Guy gets a bunch of money wired to his account, then he goes off to burn a mosque."

I hold my hand up to interrupt her. "Sorry, just a quick question. How did you get the information about the bank transfers and account holders? Isn't all that private?"

Eva gives me a coy grin from the corner of her mouth. "Sorry, can't say."

I sigh. There are a number of ways she could've done it, but none are strictly legal, and it's probably best she keeps her criminal escapades from her law enforcement friend, even if what she's doing is in the name of the common good.

"So how many cases have you come across, then?" I ask. She looks at me grimly and shakes her head.

"Half a filing cabinet full."

My eyes widen and my head is spinning. "And where are you keeping all this stuff? At work?"

"No. The filing cabinet is at my place. But tonight, when I got in, I found my apartment had been burglarized."

"Burglarized?"

"They took the files, Luke. All of them. They must've been watching my apartment and knew when I'd be out. I'm guessing it was a team of people. It would've been way too much for one person to handle. It was *organized*."

I can hardly believe what I'm hearing, but at least the secrecy of our clandestine meeting now makes sense. She may be paranoid, but she's got solid grounds for it. Even her bizarre instructions for me to give my name as the type of soda I'd bought her the first day we met makes sense. She trusts no one. Well, no one except me.

"I guess you haven't filed a police report yet."

"Wouldn't do a lick of good, Luke. They only stole a bunch of paper, after all, worth nothing to anybody but me. Well, me and whoever took them. And in any case, the papers don't really matter that much to me."

"Oh?"

"I've got backups. And I've got a contingency plan in place, if anything happens to me. I'm fearful for my safety, Luke."

I start pacing the motel room, the gravity of the situation landing heavily on my shoulders. In some way, Eva feels like my responsibility now. I wish there was a way for me to offer the protection of the police, but there's nothing in place for something like that. And there's no way she can hole up in my apartment.

"You have a place to stay?" I ask.

"I've withdrawn enough cash from my bank account, so I can stay here for a while. It's cheap enough."

"Ok, good. You need to be careful, though. If you *are* being watched, and they're as good as you say, they may know that you're here."

"Yeah, I thought of that. I'll call Doug in the morning and have him buy me some hair coloring and clothes."

"Doug?"

"The guy at the front desk."

"Oh, right," I say, realizing that a guy like him will probably jump at the chance to run errands for a rare and attractive guest such as Eva. I glance at my wrist, mortified to find that it's nearly five AM. I don't feel the least bit drowsy, thanks in part to the strong coffee and the mental strain.

"You'd better go," she says, seeing my expression. "You work tomorrow?"

"Yeah. I'll call you in the morning to make sure you're ok."

Eva shakes her head. "No, you'd better not. I'm going to dump this SIM card and switch to a new number. I'll call you. Address me by the name I gave you earlier, ok?"

"Agnes."

"Right. It was my grandmother's name."

"Got it." I walk to the front door and open it as Eva calls from over my shoulder.

"And Luke? Thank you for coming and listening. You've been so sweet to me. I really appreciate it." Rising on her long legs, Eva strides across the room and gently kisses my cheek.

"Yeah. Right. No problem," I say awkwardly. Then, after wishing her a safe night, I slip out the door and back to my Charger.

6:30 AM

AMY

At 6:30 AM every morning, the cheap plastic clock on our bedside table comes to life with an odd sound that's part rattle and part bell and fully annoying. The snooze button on top is usually silenced as Luke's fist comes slamming down. We groan at the light streaming through the blinds and fight for a few extra minutes under warm sheets. But not today.

The bell-rattle lasts for a full minute before I finally unwrap the pillow from my head and reach over my husband's lifeless body to pound the clock into submission. I stare quizzically at Luke, who seems not to have heard the alarm at all. This is a good sign, I figure. Maybe he's finally catching up on his sleep debt. I roll out of bed and head for the kitchen to tackle breakfast.

It's another half hour before I finally hear the stirrings of life from our bedroom. I've put on one of Luke's favorite oldies records to coax him out of bed–Sam Cooke's *Greatest Hits*–and I'm swaying my hips and singing into a spatula covered in scrambled eggs when he finally stumbles into the kitchen.

"You're always, you're always, you're always, o-o-on my mind," I coo at him, managing to elicit a smile.

"Haven't heard you sing in a while. I think you missed your calling," he teases.

I toss my hair over my shoulder with an exaggerated flourish and bat eyelashes at him. "Why thank you. Breakfast is ready, my dear. Hungry?"

He nods, but seems distracted. Did I say something wrong? It's been hard these last few days, knowing what I should and shouldn't do and say. I don't want to push him, but at the same time, we can't live in the shadow of tragedy forever.

"Oh," I say, pouring Luke a glass of orange juice, "just remembered–the front door was unlocked when I got up this morning. Did you forget to lock it last night?"

Luke frowns for a moment before answering. "Oh, sorry, yeah. Must've forgotten. I couldn't sleep, went out for some food."

"When did you get in?"

"It was... pretty late. Ran into Pryce."

"As in Dale Pryce? Your Captain? What was he doing out there?"

"He couldn't sleep either, I guess."

"Did you talk?"

"Yeah. He's angry."

"What about you?" I ask nonchalantly.

"I'm ok, I guess. It's all still on repeat in my brain. But I'll make it."

"Good," I say with a smile, resisting the urge to say a lot more. I lean forward and peck him on the cheek, but he tenses. He's got that strange look in his eyes again. I wonder if I'm pushing him too hard. I wish someone would just tell me what I'm supposed to do.

"Good eggs," Luke says, staring into his plate. "Thanks."

I nod and smile, and a few minutes pass before either of us speak again. Luke's got his phone on the table and he keeps checking it, probably to avoid conversation. I amble around the kitchen, wiping away the grease on the counters and stovetop.

"So, how do you feel about your first day back at work?" I ask.

"Not sure yet. I guess I'm looking forward to seeing everyone."

I nod, my mind going through all the colleagues that I've met there over the years. Sanders. Johnson. Odewald. Liezek. Then another face suddenly pops into my head. "Hey, by the way, Luke, I've been wanting to ask you something."

"Yeah? What's up?"

"Who was that woman who visited you at the hospital? Richards, right? Is she a cop?"

I turn to see Luke reach for his glass of juice, and gulp down the entire thing before answering. "She's a reporter. Works with *The Herald.*"

"A reporter? Was she there to interview you?"

"No. But she interviewed me before. She wrote that piece about the fire."

"So why was she at the hospital?"

"She had some interesting information about the explosion. She's been working on a story and... Well, she just wanted to fill me in."

"Oh. She's pretty. I'd kill for legs like that."

"Oh? Didn't really notice," he says before shoveling a pile of bacon into his mouth.

"I'll bet Gabe is all over her."

"Maybe, I think he's mentioned something once or twice," Luke says, bringing his plate to the sink and heading for the bedroom.

"Oh, and that reminds me," I say.

"Yes?"

"It's about Chelsea and Walter."

"Ok."

"I was kind of wondering if, maybe sometime, we could have them over again. I feel kind of bad about how things ended last time."

"Uh. Yeah, sure babe, that's fine," Luke says quickly as he goes to get dressed.

8:30 AM

LUKE

A few of my colleagues nod solemnly as I enter the station's front doors. My face is still a mess. I could be a villain in a horror film. But I'm not ashamed of it. It only feels right to have some scars to show for everything that happened. I pause as I pass the framed, frozen smiles of Cole and Stetson, faces wreathed in miniature flags and flowers on the brick wall beside our pen.

It's good to be back. If nothing else, it's a place to commiserate. By the same token, I'm thankful for the distraction that Eva has become. Keeping her safe is still at the front of my mind. By now she's probably had Doug fetch her breakfast and ditched her old phone and is working out a way to get in touch. I can only hope she won't keep me waiting.

I spend the rest of the morning wading through a mountain of police reports and making phone calls. Since the explosion at the church, the application paperwork for new equipment through the Defense Logistics Program had sped through the tubes, and I've been tasked with the job of getting the right signatures and filing everything through the proper channels. I even chat briefly with our mayor, who assures me we'll get everything we've requested.

If all goes according to plan, our department will receive a few palettes of military-grade firearms and an armored personnel carrier, the kind that SWAT teams frequently use. If you'd asked me a month ago, I would've said it was overkill for our little precinct, but now I'm wondering if even this will be enough.

We're not alone. Since the bomb, there have been a slew of similar incidents across the country. Many don't escalate beyond the anonymous-threat stage, but a couple in Oklahoma and Indiana were almost exact copycats of Matthias. The cops didn't take their chances.

Both bombers were shot and killed on the spot before the news vans even showed up.

On Capitol Hill, some lawmakers are suggesting even stronger actions against ex-churchgoers, including state-sponsored surveillance. News stations have dubbed it 'America's Anti-Holy War'. The voices in opposition are few and far between.

I think back to the conversation Amy and I had this morning and shake my head. I wasn't thinking clearly when I agreed to meet with her friends again, that's for sure. The truth is, I want nothing to do with the Witnesses or anyone else tied up with churches and religion, and I'd be surprised if anyone in this office feels differently. The more I think about Christianity and its flagrant opulence and rampant sex abuse, the more confidence I have in the direction our government is going. Constitutional or not, these reforms are going to save more lives than anything else the administration has done in years.

It's nearly half past noon when I finally break for lunch. I scroll through the alerts on my phone looking for something from Eva, but there's nothing. The stirrings of dread begin gnawing at my stomach. I try to silence it with a couple of hot dogs soaked in mustard and sauerkraut from my favorite sidewalk stand, but when another forty-five minutes roll by without so much as a text, the dread has nearly turned to panic. I hop in my Charger and speed off in the direction of the motel.

I find Doug in the same position he'd been in the night before, slumped in his chair, sleeping with his feet propped on the counter. I pound a fist once to rouse him, and he wakes with the same sour look.

"You again. What do you want this time?" he snarls.

"The woman in room 212, you hear anything from her today?" I ask. Doug pauses for a long while, looking me over in my uniform.

"So you're a cop, huh?"

"No, I just wear this for fun. You gonna answer my question or not?"

"Depends. What's it worth to you?"

"What?"

"You think you're the first man in a uniform I've seen come through here? Keeping secrets is hard work, you know? And now you come looking for information, and you expect it'll come for free?"

"You know what kind of charges you could face for trying to extort a law enforcement officer?" I growl. Doug shrugs, unintimidated.

"Probably nothing worse than you'd face at home when your wife finds out you have a pretty little thing locked away in some ol' motel," he replies with a snicker. He points down at the counter where my hand is still clenched in a fist, my wedding band in plain sight.

"It's not like that, you—"

"Yeah, yeah, sure it's not. It never is."

"What do you want from me?"

"Well, for starters, you could pay for her room last night. The number your lady friend gave me for her credit card bounced back this morning."

"Fine," I growl, tugging my wallet out and handing the man my Visa. Doug flashes me a smile and turns to process the payment.

"Thanks for your business. I hope you enjoyed your stay. Oh, and by the way, 212's been quiet all morning," Doug says with a wink.

I brush through the back door and climb the stairs, leaping up the steps three at a time, feeling more anxious by the second. I jog down the walkway, glancing at the numbers. 209… 210… 211… Then I come to a stop, turning to look at the room. The door is wide open. Bed sheets and pillowcases lay in a pile in a corner. The smell of bleach is almost overwhelming and someone inside is humming.

"Hello?" I call out, rapping against the open door. The humming stops abruptly and a middle aged Hispanic woman emerges in a stained apron and rubber gloves.

"Ah?" The woman says in surprise, then rattles off something rapidly in Spanish. I raise my hands, trying to slow her down.

"The woman, in this room. Where is she?" I ask. The housekeeper frowns and shakes her head. I clench my teeth and do my best to summon my mostly forgotten Spanish.

"La mujer? Donde esta?" I attempt, pointing at the floor. The woman's face finally registers something.

"La mujer? No está aquí. No está," she says with an exaggerated shrug and a shake of her finger.

Not here? But why would she leave? And why would she do anything without letting me know first? I sit on the edge of the bed and mull it all over as the housekeeper returns to her chores. She shoots me a few wary glances at first but quickly ignores me.

I try to reassure myself that there's probably a reasonable explanation for this. Maybe Eva got tired of being cooped up in a grimy motel room and went out for breakfast and fresh air. Maybe

Doug from the front desk made a move and she decided to switch motels.

I survey the room once more. Everything of Eva's from the night before–suitcases, garment bag, a couple pairs of shoes–are nowhere to be seen. I poke around the room looking through drawers and under the furniture, but there's simply nothing left. Not a single trace of the woman who'd been here only hours before. Clearly, wherever's she's gone, she's gone for good.

I'm shaken from my thoughts by the touch of the housekeeper's hand on my shoulder. I turn to find her dangling a small black piece of plastic from a string between her fingers. She asks me something that I can't understand and motions for me to take the object. I grab it from her and turn it slowly in my hands. I twist one edge slightly to reveal four gold prongs; it's a USB thumb drive.

Apparently Eva has left something behind after all. I want to ask how and where the housekeeper had found it, but I've used up all of the Spanish I know and I doubt Doug will be any help as a translator, so I simply make a grateful gesture, pocket the drive, and leave.

1:57 PM
LUKE

Back at the station I slide the flash drive out from my pocket and study it carefully. It's a Sony Micro Vault, an older model from the looks of it. Most current flash drives on the market are 64 gigs and up; this one's only 4. I uncap it and nudge it into the side of my laptop. It takes a second for the drive to appear on my desktop as "ER's Flash".

I click open the drive and explore the nested directories and files. It's all very well organized, just as I'd expect from Eva, though I can't make sense of a thing. Each folder has been labeled with a cryptic string of numbers and letters. I check the creation dates and find that the oldest files go back a year or so and the newest ones are from just days ago. I open one at random and find it packed with text documents. I try to open one but a password locks me out. I close it down to inspect the other files, most of which are mp3s. Audio files, but of what? Music?

I drag one of the mp3s from the folder to the audio player on my computer. Before it starts, it displays the playtime: twenty-seven minutes. I plug in my earbuds and turn the volume up. My pulse quickens in anticipation.

It's an audio recording, outside noises, kids laughing, cheerful voices coming and going, a barking dog, the whine of swingset chains. A park. Then something else, louder and closer. A man's voice. He speaks in short, terse sentences.

"Where you want me to start?" he asks, barely audible over the squeals of a few children running past, their feet scuffling along a gravel path.

"Wherever you feel comfortable," says a familiar voice. Eva is calm, reassuring.

"It's complicated," says the man, his voice dropping out again. Eva waits, says nothing.

"We shouldn't be talking like this, out here in the open," the man says, agitated.

"We both agreed this was the best way, Frank. We're safe here."

"Safe. Yeah, thanks for the reassurance. You're clueless, you know that? We're not safe anywhere. Not in our houses, not on our phones. Certainly not here."

"We're not safe from whom, Frank?"

"You think this is a game, don't you? Well, they sure don't."

"I never said it was a game. But if we don't talk here, today, I can't do anything to help you."

"And what, you think writing some article in a newspaper is really going to help me? You're dead wrong."

"Words are powerful, Frank."

"Yeah, not as powerful as you think."

"Then why meet at all? Why are we here?"

"I'm not here for me, lady. I know my neck's already on the chopping block. I can feel it. Blade's comin' down any second, time's just tick-ticking. I'm just here to set the record straight. Expose them."

I stop the recording as a body flops into the empty chair beside my desk.

"What's that?" Gabe asks. He's chewing the end of a taco that I recognize from a Mexican restaurant at the corner of the street across from us.

"Nothing much," I shrug, pulling the buds from my ears and tossing them on the desk.

"You seemed pretty absorbed."

"Yeah, well, just something to do with a case I came across."

"Right," Gabe says. He tosses the last bit of the tortilla into his mouth and brushes his hands off on his pants. "Hey, by the way, you still seeing that girl from *The Herald*?"

"I was never 'seeing' Eva, Gabe. She stopped by a couple of times with some questions, that's all."

"And? You two still in touch?"

I shrug. "From time to time."

"Yeah well, next time you see her, pass my number on, would you?"

"Yeah, right. I'll be sure to do that."

Gabe smiles widely and saunters back to his corner of the pen. I wait until he's gone to drag another audio file dated several weeks ago into the player.

The background noises here are different. Hollow and hard and mechanical. I hear the pitch change as the sounds bounce around. Cars passing, I think, perhaps on an overpass.

"Ok, start when you're ready," Eva says. Her voice is soft and cautious.

"I'll tell you what you want to know, but I want my personal details left out of it," says a man.

"That's fine. I'm not here to expose your identity. Why don't we start with your time in the Middle East? How long were you there?"

"Two tours, total of seven years."

"Can I ask about the nature of the operations you were involved in?"

"I was part of a black ops unit that would track down and eliminate hostile targets. I won't be any more specific than that."

"No, that's fine. What happened when you came home?"

"Shortly after the end of my second tour, I was approached by this guy from a private security firm. Basically their company was hired by all sorts of wealthy people to protect their assets. Sometimes that meant guarding things, like houses or boats or cars, and sometimes it meant protecting people. It was standard private sector security stuff. Nothing out of the ordinary. I took a few jobs when I needed the money. That went on for a year or so.

"Then, one night, while I was doing security detail for one of these millionaire playboy's parties–I think he was a sheik or something–one of the guests had too much to drink and crashed their Lamborghini. It came through a wall just a few feet from me. The car was doing nearly fifty miles an hour when it hit. Thankfully it missed me, but some of the flying rock shards caught me in the leg and abdomen. It took the doctors more than twenty-four hours to perform the surgery that saved my limbs–which was paid for by the contract, of course–but I could never work private security again.

"The problem, of course, was that that was my only skill set. I was raised on military bases as a kid. My mom and dad were both Air Force. I signed up for the Army when I was nineteen, and that became my life."

"So what did you do for work after the injury?"

"Nothing for a while. I lived with a friend and his wife for a few months while I tried to figure things out, but that didn't really work out. I finally got a job at a grocery store. It was barely enough to pay my rent. I was miserable."

"Is that when you met Mr. Donner?"

"That's correct."

"What can you tell me about your encounter with him?"

There's a pause before the man speaks again. "Mr. Donner was fairly straightforward with his offer. He said that he had a job for me that would pay well, and that my limited mobility wouldn't pose any problems. I was doubtful, but he assured me he'd pay if I could get the job done, and he had confidence I could handle it. He had me sign a NDA before he'd give me any more details. That made me nervous, I guess, but at the time I was in sore straights and badly needed the cash."

"And what was the job?"

"He handed me an envelope with some photographs of a building and an address, and told me, in so many words, to demolish it. That was it."

"Didn't that strike you as odd?"

"Sure, but you don't get how desperate I was. I was behind on rent at the time, could barely afford to keep the lights on, and the economy was in the dumps. This felt like some kind of miracle."

"So you took the job."

"I did, and I got a stack of cash in an unmarked envelope as promised. It was two grand, more cash than I'd seen in months. We met again in a few weeks, and he gave me a new target. This went on for a while."

"All churches?"

"Mostly. Catholic, Baptist, Methodist, you name it. A mosque or two in there somewhere too."

"And you didn't have a problem with these 'missions'?"

"I had my misgivings, but at this point many of the buildings were either abandoned or in disrepair. Few seemed to be in regular use. Their congregations were dwindling. I'd usually burn them at night, when no one was around."

"Did you have any idea who Mr. Donner was working for?"

"I thought he might actually be working for the churches, trying to make them money on insurance claims, but those suspicions eventually went away."

"Why?"

"Because one day, when Mr. Donner handed me a new list of targets, the pictures didn't contain buildings. They contained people."

THURSDAY, NOVEMBER 19

5:49 PM
AMY

I'm in our cramped kitchen adding radish slices to a salad, the final touch for tonight's meal. The oven is just about done with the main course and our little apartment already smells like ricotta and Italian spices. Lasagna's a pain and I can rarely muster the patience, but it's Luke's favorite dish and tonight must be a success. I've thought of nothing else all week. The fact that Luke even agreed to this at all was a surprise, but that's just how he is sometimes. I've lost count of how many times I've prayed for everything to go smoothly, but Chelsea says that prayers are like coats, and you just keep putting them on until the cold goes away, so I close my eyes once again and repeat my petition.

Chelsea and Walter Novak arrive a few minutes later. They've brought another bottle of wine, this time a burgundy that Walter has specially selected to pair with the lasagna. He explains that the acid of this type of red wine helps to cut through the flavors of cheese in the dish. I nod as if I understand, but it's all way over my head. The Novaks may live simply, but they're by far some of the classiest friends I've ever had.

Chelsea helps out around the kitchen, getting the table set and starting on the dirty oven pans while Walter tends to the wine. He's very methodical about the whole process–he's even brought along a funny looking device that apparently airs out the wine to enhance the flavor. When everything's set on the table, Walter suggests that we say a prayer now to avoid causing Luke any embarrassment later. I agree gratefully, but before Walter can say another word we realize it's too late. The locks on the front door are sliding open. Luke is home.

He enters the apartment and I can immediately sense his discomfort. Chelsea and Walter are gracious as always, though, and Luke seems to relax a little after everyone has been reintroduced.

"Did you want to change, babe?" I ask as I begin cutting the lasagna on the counter.

"Nah, I'm good like this," Luke says coolly.

"So, tell us about your work, Luke," Chelsea beams, handing my husband a glass of wine.

He rattles off some statistics in response: how long he's been on the force, how many officers work at his precinct, how much paperwork his desk job involves.

"He just got a promotion, actually," I add as I remove my apron and sit at the table.

"Oh? I'll bet it had to do with that man you saved from the fire. That was quite heroic," Walter says.

Luke shrugs, "Any officer would've done the same thing. It was all reflex and training."

"Well, whatever you call it, we're grateful. Donovan Harris is a good friend. We've known him for years," Chelsea says.

"Have you gotten a chance to meet him, Luke?" Walter asks.

"Yeah, a few weeks ago Mr. Harris called me and asked me to come by the hospital. He seemed… nice."

"I'm glad you paid him a visit. I'm sure it meant a lot to him. He wouldn't have liked it if he hadn't had the chance to thank you face to face."

With all of us seated at the table and a meal steaming in front of us, I wonder anxiously what will happen next. I exchange quick glances with Walter and Chelsea and they seem to sense the unspoken question. Walter turns to Luke and smiles warmly.

"Luke, typically before we eat a meal, my wife and I like to say a prayer. Would that be ok with you?"

Luke shrugs indifferently. "It's your religion, do what you like."

"Very well, thank you," Walter says.

I can feel my pulse throbbing in my eardrums and can barely focus on anything Walter is saying. I can't help but obsess over what must be going through my husband's head.

I open my eyes to find that Luke has already served himself to a portion of lasagna and doesn't seem very engaged. I try to not let it bother me and soon Walter and Chelsea and myself are talking about something we saw recently on the news. The president has been giving speech after speech decrying the rising wave of religious violence, and it's clear the nation's patience is wearing thin.

"This just goes to show how important it is to show respect to the superior authorities," Walter says with a pointed glance at Luke, and I realize that everything we've been talking about is for my husband's benefit. They want him to know we aren't a threat. We're not extremists. Luke doesn't appear to pick up the cue.

"So Luke, how are the officers in your department faring since the attack?" Chelsea asks. It takes a moment for Luke to process the question. He glances at me before answering.

"We lost a couple of good men in that blast. Our department was shaken up by it, but we're resilient."

"I saw on the news that one of them had a wife and kids. It's just awful," Walter says.

"Jared Cole. He was a good cop. A good man."

"Luke's captain was seriously injured as well. They had to amputate his hand," I say. I catch Luke's glare from across the table. Maybe this isn't public knowledge. I bite my lip and offer an apologetic glance, deciding to keep myself out of the rest of this conversation.

"Oh! That's just horrible. This world is just a mess, isn't it?" Chelsea says as she shakes her head and frowns at us.

"Well, that's why I do what I do. Try to keep the mess at bay," Luke says.

"Well, we all appreciate the work you do, Luke. And we're very cooperative whenever we come across law enforcement," Walter chimes in.

"You two often have run-ins with the police?" Luke says with a sardonic smile. The question is posed in an ambiguous tone somewhere between accusation and playful banter, and none of us quite knows what to make of it.

Walter chuckles. "No, I suppose we don't. But I was talking about Jehovah's Witnesses in general."

"Oh?"

"Sure. We abide by local laws and always show respect to those in charge, and that includes the men and women in uniform."

"I guess you're trying to assure me I won't have to respond to another bomb threat with one of your people on the other end, huh?"

"Luke," I say in a mildly scolding tone.

"Sorry, I have nothing against your people. I just feel like I've been watching an endless stream of news and police reports involving religious violence. I have a hard time believing that your churchgoers are any different. No offense."

"None taken," Walter says easily. "Trust me, I've heard much worse."

"You've said worse," Chelsea says, shaking her head with a laugh.

"What does she mean?" Luke asks.

"I wasn't raised as one of Jehovah's Witnesses, Luke. In fact, neither was Chelsea. We met in high school, and when she went off to college, I signed up for the Air Force."

"You were in the armed forces?"

"17th Air Division, Desert Shield."

"You fought in the Gulf War?"

"Fought, not so much. Our division was in charge of refueling active-duty units. We didn't do much else, other than sit around the base drinking and gambling."

"And then you came home and became a Jehovah Witness?"

Walter smiles. "It wasn't so simple. Chelsea and I had been dating long distance while I was on tour. The Witnesses knocked on her door one day and she said she had found science and didn't need God. They asked why she thought the two were mutually exclusive and she didn't know the answer. They ended up talking for over an hour and she realized there was a lot she didn't know about the Bible. She agreed to study it with them and liked what she learned. When I came back from duty and found out, I was furious. I prohibited her from seeing them anymore, or else our relationship was over."

"Why were you so angry?" I ask. It's the first time I've heard the story from Walter's side.

"Well, like anyone else, I'd heard nasty things about the Witnesses. They let their kids die rather than getting blood transfusions, wouldn't celebrate holidays or birthdays, wouldn't serve their country, and so on. All negative stuff."

"Was any of it true?" Luke asks.

"Well, like most prejudices, there's always a thread of truth somewhere, but there's also a lot of blind emotion mixed in to make it seem worse than it is. But it took me a while to see all that. In the meantime, I put the woman I loved through a lot of heartache."

I glance over at Chelsea, who smiles through faintly glistening eyes.

"So what changed? Why didn't you break up with her?" Luke asks.

"I guess I came to my senses. Does it really make sense for a man to leave a woman who is honest, respectful, and loving? I mean, regardless of her beliefs, isn't her personality what really counts? The other thing was, I started observing the marriages of my buddies–the ones I'd been in the Gulf with–and they were all the same. Ruined one way or another, sometimes by alcohol, sometimes by drugs, sometimes by another woman, or even another man. And I began to realize that I didn't want that. I did a lot of thinking about life and what's important in it, and I came to the decision that I wanted her, Witness or not."

"That still doesn't explain how you became a Witness yourself, though," Luke says.

"I suppose it doesn't. However, I believe there's still a cheesecake on the counter, and to be honest I'd rather hear the story of how you two met than listen to myself talk. What do you say?"

Luke glances at the counter and nods. "Yeah, ok, that's fine," he says, standing and fetching some desert saucers as the three of us exchange hopeful glances.

10:23 PM
LUKE

Well, that didn't go as planned. I thought I had the whole thing figured out: I'd gather some intel while trying to get to the bottom of the Novaks' relationship with my wife. I'd pry without being too nosy and begin the task of opening my wife's eyes. I even kept my uniform on just to make the distance between us clear. I figured the Witnesses were like most other churchgoers: more or less good people, but going along with their religion for the sake of tradition. Now I'm not so sure.

In the end, we spent about two hours talking, and I was surprised to find that it was past ten o'clock when we finally wrapped up. Amy doesn't say much as she clears off the table and tidies the kitchen. She tells me to jump in the shower first, that she'll finish up the dishes on her own, and I comply. I'm exhausted after my first day back at work and still processing the events from this evening.

And as for Eva, well... To be honest, I'm at my wit's end with that woman. First she drags me out to a motel in the middle of the night, scares me half to death with her girl-on-the-run routine, and then vanishes into thin air... I never asked to be a part of her mess but I'm invested in her plight all the same and now I'm totally in the dark. The audio clips I heard back at the office only fuel my anxiety. My curiosity about what she's been digging into is eating away at me. I feel her obsession gnawing at my own bones now.

When I step out of the shower I hear Amy calling my name. I'm still dripping wet when I poke my head from the bathroom and reach for my phone from her hands. It's buzzing with Gabe's name on the screen.

"Yeah? What's up?" I say, trying not to get water on the device.

"Luke," Gabe says flatly. "Turn on the news. Now. Channel 7."

I stumble into the living room, stumbling over my towel as I try to dry myself off while walking, and flip on the television. Footage of a smoldering car wreck circled by police cars and fire trucks. No ambulances. In the corner of the screen, a still photo of a young woman's smiling face. My heart stops. It's Eva Richards.

I jam my finger into the volume button, hoping to dismiss my fears. I must be misreading this.

"...was found at approximately 6:30 this evening by a group of local teenagers, who reported seeing a large fire near the exit ramp of the highway. The fire department was able to extinguish the flames, and the remains of a single person were recovered. Although the coroner has still been unable to positively identify the body, police have determined that the vehicle was owned by a young female reporter working at The Herald *named Eva Richards. Her employer confirmed that she had not reported for work for the last couple days..."*

My stomach twists in horror, my body suddenly light and weak and cold. I slide into the couch with a hand on my forehead. The report cuts to a segment of an earlier interview with the local chief of police, a man whom I don't recognize. He explains that Eva's car had been found in a county to the north of us.

"While we're still conducting an investigation into the cause of the accident, judging from preliminary evidence, we believe the driver lost control of the vehicle, whereupon the vehicle left the road, was overturned, and ignited. Unfortunately, we believe the driver was killed in the fire, and we do not currently suspect foul play."

The cameras cut back to the news anchor, who continues the story. I can hardly breathe. My mind is reeling. Eva? Dead? But how? I saw her–*talked* to her–just a few days ago. How could something like this happen? And why had she been driving so far out of the county? And why had she not contacted me like she'd promised? Why had she been so stupid? I shake my head, feeling myself grow angrier and angrier with the woman that burst into my life so suddenly and slipped away with the same unexpectedness.

There's no way I'll be able to sleep tonight, I realize, as Amy lathers lotion on her face and arms and slips into bed. When she asks what I'm doing still up, I tell her I've just thought of some work I need to get done for the office. I get up and wander around the apartment for a while until she falls asleep. I find myself an hour later still sitting on our living room couch in the cold darkness. I'm holding Eva's flash drive in my hands, turning it over in my fingers and wondering what to do next.

I'd only known Eva for a month. We met a few times, but the effect she had on me is undeniable. As a man who firmly believes in fidelity, I was never tempted to step beyond the boundaries when it came to our relationship, but had I met Eva when I was still single, it's not difficult to imagine a romance might've budded down the road.

I think back to the first time I met her at the station. It was easy to admire her; she was determined, sharp, intrepid. When I saw her that last time in the motel, it was like looking at a shell of the former woman. She was jittery, paranoid, ready to run. A hunted animal.

It's difficult to ignore the fact that this small piece of plastic in my hands may be her untold legacy. And I, its keeper. I go over to my desk and slip the USB into my laptop. It mounts, and as I stare at the words "ER's Flash" on my screen, I feel a chill go up my spine.

Then I get to work.

I begin by browsing through the info labels on each of the folders. There are a total of 217 files on the drive. I'm guessing most are text documents, and if Eva was as fastidious as I think, I'm betting that most of these files are password protected. The rest, most of which seem to be audio files, I hope to access without problems. I copy all of the contents onto my hard drive and begin reorganizing everything, putting all the audio files into a single folder. When this is done, I import these files into my audio player. The software tells me that the total playtime is 1,232 minutes. About twenty hours' worth.

Between work and sleep and everything else, this will probably take me the better part of a week to get through, especially if I'm meticulous about documenting everything. But I don't have a choice. Suddenly it's all that matters. If I've failed at keeping Eva safe, at least I can embark on the task she'd set out to accomplish.

I take a deep breath and attempt to decipher the file names.

190804HA01
190907HA02

200119JLP01

I bring up the info pane again for each of the audio files to check the modification dates and make my first discovery. The first six digits of each folder are simply the date. YYMMDD. Easy enough. August 4th, 2019. September 7th, 2019. January 19th, 2020. The letters after the date are more curious. Is it a code Eva had come up with to organize the interviews? Perhaps an abbreviation based on the location of the interview? Or the name of the interviewee?

I drag the first audio file back into my music player, insert my earbuds, and listen carefully. Sure enough, throughout the interview, Eva calls the man by his first name, Harley. I make a notation on a text file in my computer and turn up the volume. Like the other files I heard back at the office, there's an unmistakable discomfort in the man's tone. The volume of his voice constantly drops and peaks as he shifts around uneasily. Perhaps he's watching his back.

I go through the files in order, making little notes as I listen. In many of the interviews, Eva asks the same questions; her subjects make the same dodges. Why had they even agreed to these interviews in the first place? And how had Eva managed to track them down? From what I can piece together, many of these people had been approached by an organization through different people but had been contracted for similar jobs.

But what disturbs me most is the way the interviewees describe their meetings with the agents who'd been sent to recruit them. These agents were precise, well informed, and highly organized. They operated with the professionalism of a criminal organization but without the telltale signs of such. They met potential contractors in broad daylight, in public areas. How could they afford to be so brazen? They acted as if they had nothing to fear.

I glance at the blinking clock in the corner of my laptop's screen. It's already past three in the morning and I'm beginning to feel it, but my brain doesn't want to stop unraveling the mystery. I close down the audio player and open my web browser. I only need to type in "f" and it can already read my mind. Good ol' Facebook.

I was a lot more active on the site years ago, before I started working on the force. I log in and am unsurprised to see that I have hundreds of unchecked messages and alerts. I brush past them and do a user search. I enter the city, name, and all the other details I can think of. It doesn't take long to track her down.

Eva's profile pic is a photo of herself smiling with a Boston terrier in her arms. I scroll down to find a few dozen eerie messages from friends who've heard the news. The notes are heartbreaking. I scroll back up and click through to her album. She was only twenty-nine. A tear leaks from my eye and I squeeze it away with a knuckle.

I nearly jump as I feel a hand on my shoulder. I turn to find Amy looking down at me and my laptop with a sleepy frown.

"Luke? What are you doing up…?"

"Just some research," I say, honestly enough.

"What time is it?" she asks, yawning.

"Late. I'm going to bed," I say, leading my wife gently back to the bedroom. I'm asleep before my head hits the pillow, though my dreams are anything but restful.

TUESDAY, NOVEMBER 24

10:09 AM
AMY

My thoughts are a disorganized jumble in my head. I don't know how to feel, what to do. I've always trusted Luke. We've known each other for almost a decade, and nothing's come between us. But lately... I've been having doubts.

It started with that woman at the hospital. Luke had acted so strangely, especially when I questioned him later. It's not hard to tell when your man is being dishonest with you, and I saw all the indicators. I gave him the benefit of the doubt at the time; he'd been through so much trauma, so I wasn't about to pry.

I didn't mention it to anyone, not even Chelsea. But as I sit in her kitchen waiting for her to gather her materials for our study, I realize how badly I need to talk about this. I need to know what I'm supposed to do. Just the thought of losing my husband is terrifying. And if we're not together, how will he ever make it through the end?

And now I'm crying.

Chelsea enters the kitchen and stops abruptly at the sight of me with my hands over my face, quietly sobbing. She pulls a chair to my side and tries to console me. "Amy? What's going on? What happened?"

I realize how strange this must all look to her. Moments ago we were enjoying her homemade macaroons–a small celebration of how successful our dinner together last week had been. Luke had opened up and Walter and him even seemed to hit it off. Five minutes later, I'm bawling inexplicably.

I decide to let the anguish and confusion just run its course, and Chelsea, in her typical motherly fashion, forces nothing. She rests my head on her shoulder and doesn't say a word. There are more tears here than normal, and I begin to suspect that there's a lot of pent-up anxiety waiting for a release.

I've got a small mountain of crumpled tissues in my lap by the time I've finally regained composure. Chelsea, still silent, is gently patting my shoulder and watching her husband bag dead leaves outside.

"I'm sorry," I finally manage with a pathetic whimper.

"It's ok, those weren't our only tissues," Chelsea says, and I can't help but laugh despite everything. "Do you want to talk about it?" I nod, and she cleans up the soggy tissues as I clear my throat and try to figure out where to start. I decide to cut right to it.

"I think Luke might be having an affair."

"What?" Chelsea gasps. She's frozen in the corner of the kitchen holding a trashcan in one hand and my mess of tissues in the other.

"I caught him the other night looking at this woman's Facebook photos. I've seen her before, too–she came to visit him once in the hospital. She even brought flowers."

Chelsea slides back into her seat, looking at me intently. "Have you talked with him about this?"

"No."

"You need to talk with him, Amy. Before you get all caught up in this. It could be a misunderstanding."

"A misunderstanding? Chelsea, he was sneaking around on his computer checking some woman out at three in the morning!"

"Oh dear," Chelsea says, putting her hand on her forehead.

"I should've seen this coming. I feel so stupid," I'm saying. "He's been so distant lately. We're such different people. That's why he agreed to the dinner, and that's why he doesn't mind me studying. He's found someone else!"

"Stop, Amy," Chelsea says. The sharpness in her voice catches me off guard. "Don't act like your marriage is already over. It's not. *Talk* to him."

"And what if he just keeps lying about everything?"

"Amy, it's like you've already sentenced him in your mind. At least give him a chance to explain himself. I know how much you love him, and he seems to genuinely care about you as well. Men like that don't cheat."

"And if he *is* cheating?"

Chelsea shakes her head, her eyes misting slightly as she stares into mine. "We'll cross that road if and when we come to it."

WEDNESDAY, NOVEMBER 25

8:05 AM
LUKE

The entire precinct is in a frenzy. Officers scramble around with boxes of manila folders stuffed with reams of paper. There are faces I don't recognize in here too, their stares carefully surveying the chaos. It doesn't take long to figure out where they're from. Dark suits and dark blue windbreakers in this line of work can only mean one thing: FBI.

I spot Pryce scowling from the entrance of the hallway, his bandaged stump of an arm still hanging in a white sling. I make my way over to the captain quickly, nearly colliding with a female agent carrying a cardboard box full of files. Her snakelike eyes flash me a threatening look and I half expect a forked tongue to extend from her lips as she hisses me out of the way.

"What's going on here?" I ask, sidling up to Pryce's side.

"The feds have decided we have a leak," he growls.

"A leak?"

Pryce jerks his head in the direction of his office and the two of us enter and close the door. Standing behind his desk, he swivels his laptop around to let me look at the screen. I glance at the familiar logo of two globes suspended in an hourglass and realize I'm looking at the homepage for the notorious Wikileaks website.

"Nearly 800 files were uploaded over the weekend. No one knows where they came from but there are some references to Haliford. Apparently it's tied to our police department. The feds put two and two together and here they are."

"When did they arrive?"

"I was here at six thirty; they'd already let themselves in."

"They can do that?"

Pryce shrugs. "Who knows? Laws change overnight." How true.

"So what were the leaked files about?" I ask.

"What, you think I've had time to comb through it with these snakes in our living room?"

"No, I guess not. May I?" My hands hover over the keyboard of the laptop and note the captain's curt nod of approval. I do a quick site search for our city. The first few results that spill onto the screen are unrelated articles leaked from the Syrian War, all of which mention some soldier with the same last name as our municipality. But further down the page, I see it.

RE: INVESTIGATION INTO ANTI-RELIGIOUS ARSON

I click the hyperlink as the hair on the back of my neck stands on end. The document that loads on the screen is riddled with odd symbols, numbers, and indecipherable strings of letters, making it all appear to be some sort of gibberish spit out by a malfunctioning computer. It seems the letters are a form of shorthand, and the symbols are inserted to denote dates and timestamps.

I read over a paragraph in the middle of the document carefully.

%101419"" 8th mo. resrch church arsn, seek advc from Haliford PD. Dead end. Subj not clear w/ MO, INT. ""

I feel a knot forming in the pit of my stomach. All of this points to Eva. Somehow, from beyond the grave, she's leaked the files she'd collected during her yearlong investigation. Maybe it's the 'contingency' she'd mentioned in the motel last week. An automatic email forwarder in the case of her sudden disappearance? Prior instructions given to a trusted friend? I have no way of being certain.

Then I wonder if any of this will somehow trace back to me. Pryce, Gabe, and a handful of other officers had known about my first interview with Eva. I'd given her nothing—I'd *known* nothing, but if anyone had been following or watching us or if Eva had included my name in any of the leaked files, I could very well find myself the prime suspect in a federal investigation.

"Find anything?" Pryce grumbles from the window of his office where he stands picking at the blinds and watching the disarray outside. It takes me a moment to register the question.

"Yeah. Looks like there's a reference to our PD."

Pryce spins around with a look of fury and is instantly on my side of the desk seething at the screen. He scans the text and takes just a fraction of a second longer than I to make sense of it.

"This is from that reporter, *Richards*, isn't it?"

"I think so," I say cautiously.

"Well, then why are the feds at our throats? Why not go after the reporter? Heck, bury the whole paper in agents for all I care. Why come after us?" Pryce fumes.

"They can't," I say quietly.

"They can't *what*?"

"They can't go after Eva. She's dead." I explain the story as I heard it on the news. Pryce furls his eyebrows and lets out a soft groan. There's nothing I feel like saying in response. Pryce studies me for a few moments before he returns to his weathered green chair with a grunt.

"Anything else you want to tell me about why these people are raiding our precinct?" he inquires with a shrewd stare.

"Sorry?"

"I know you two were in contact, Harding. I saw the day you left with her, and Rodriguez told me she paid you a visit at St. Mary's. If there's something I need to know, you'd better come clean now."

My voice catches suddenly as if my neck is held fast in a noose. I try to speak but my tongue is dry and stiff. There are no words, and all I can do is slowly shake my head.

"No, sir," I manage.

"You're saying you didn't divulge any classified information, ever, to Miss Richards?"

"No, sir," I repeat firmly. "She wanted to know if I had information and I told her I didn't. I knew nothing about her investigation at the time."

Pryce frowns in a way that nearly stops my heart. It's the look a man might give to an animal about to be euthanized. But something tells me the worst is yet to come.

The next hour drags on in quiet agony as I sit at my desk and fight the urge to crawl over the Wikileaks documents Eva posted. Did she mention me by name? I'd like to think that she considered me enough of a friend not to indict me, but what can I really be sure of? It's clear to me now that she put the story before everything, even her own life. Why should I expect preferential treatment?

Still, whether or not she mentioned my name matters not. Eventually the feds will realize she'd talked to me, and I'll get sucked into their investigation all the same. My concentration is broken by a sharp rapping of knuckles against the corner of my desk.

I look up to see a man in a dark suit. His eyes narrow slightly as he looks down at me and motions for us to take a walk. I hear another set of footprints behind us, and in the glass of the hallway windows catch the reflection of a second federal officer a few paces behind me, his thin windbreaker bunched at his side around a clearly visible sidearm.

I wonder frantically how this will this affect my standing in the station. My promotion? I'm well aware that my superiors could just as easily revoke the uniform after this fiasco. But under those personal fears is another layer of questions that I can't quite get past. Why are these agents here? As a law enforcement officer myself, I'm fairly clear on the scope of FBI operations, and I know that they tend to move slowly on lower priority investigations. It's hard for me to imagine what could've brought them to our little precinct here in Haliford with such speed and show of force.

As I enter the interrogation room, I'm struck by the irony of it all. I think of how many times I've been the one leading a suspect through these same doors to an interrogation. Most perps are handcuffed as they take the walk to the hot seat, but the especially cooperative ones get to move without restraints. Is that what I am now? A suspect? My pulse quickens as I'm seated in a chair bolted to the ground. Things do look different from this side of the table. The double-sided mirror. The bright lights. Purposefully menacing.

The agent sits opposite from me. He takes his time sorting through papers in a folder and booting his laptop. It feels like an hour has gone by before he finally acknowledges me. He nods and smiles, but his eyes are cold, two black steel bolts screwed tightly in metallic eye sockets.

"You thirsty? Want a coke? Coffee?" he asks.

"Coke is fine," I mutter. The agent snaps his fingers and I can hear feet patter to silence in the hallway outside. They've at least left the door open, which I appreciate.

"I'm sorry to have to do this, dragging you in here and making it seem like a... I don't know, some kind of *criminal investigation*. But unfortunately it's one of the best places for a conversation like this."

I shrug, pretending not to be bothered by the setting, though I suspect this room was chosen exactly for its connotations.

"I'm Agent Logan Meade. You're... Luke Harding, correct?" the man says, frowning at papers from my file. "You've been with the department for what now, five years?"

"Six."

"Six, right. My mistake," Meade says with a cocky expression. The extra year makes no difference to him. He's a typical federal agent, a class above local law enforcement.

"I'm a sergeant with the department here," I say.

"Yeah, I noted it in your file. Recent promotion?"

"Yeah."

"I see. Congratulations," Agent Meade says flatly.

"Yeah, thanks. Mind if I ask what this is all about?"

Agent Meade studies me for a moment, a predatory grin forming on his lips. His voice is nonchalant but the ferocity in his eyes is unambiguous. "You've heard about the leaked documents, I assume?"

"Sure, the Captain mentioned it to me this morning."

"Yeah, well, it's causing a nightmare for the Bureau. Apparently some of the things mentioned... Point fingers in our direction. It's all very conspiratorial, of course, cloak and dagger nonsense. Speculation and hearsay, like someone was trying to write a spy novel. But here we are all the same, doing clean up."

"What do you mean, pointing fingers?" I ask coolly.

"Apparently, someone anonymously leaked files that suggest the U.S. government is connected to these church burnings."

And there it is. This was what Eva had been hinting at all along. It's the terminal point of a trail of clues she'd been following for months. I had sensed it as well, but of all the evidence I've seen, there's been nothing nearly as incriminating as what this federal agent has just offhandedly mentioned. If only Eva could be here now to see this.

"Have you seen the files, Luke?" Meade asks as he sips from a silver thermos.

I shrug. "I got a glimpse in Pryce's office this morning."

"And? Any idea where they might've come from?"

I weigh my possible responses carefully, acutely aware that every second of silence has the potential to make me look guiltier. But then it occurs to me that bringing up Eva's name can do her no harm.

"There was a reporter that came around here a few times, she might've had access to some of that info."

"You got a name?"

"Yeah, I think it was Eva. Eva Richards."

"Think? So you didn't like, know her well or what? Did you guys ever talk?"

I swallow hard, back at another crossroads. "Yeah, we talked. She interviewed me once or twice."

"She interviewed you?"

"Yeah. I'd been at the scene of a fire, rescued an elderly man from a church. It was in the papers."

"Uh huh. So that was it? You had no further communication with her?"

A pause. "I may have run into her occasionally after that, but I wasn't able to give her any more information."

"Be more specific. What kind of information?"

"Info on the church arson. That was the story she was after."

"Didn't you say she was after your story?"

"Yes, she was. But she was also working on something bigger."

"Go on."

"It was… something on a national scale."

"Having to do with church arson."

"Right."

Agent Meade takes a moment to make a note in his legal pad. "How many times did you and Miss Richards meet?"

"Just a few."

"Give me a number, Luke. Was it two? Three?"

"We talked a couple times, and she came to see me once in the hospital."

"Hospital, huh? Sounds like you two were close friends."

"Not really. Like I said, she was just after information for her investigation."

Meade pauses to stare at me hard, his eyes a narrow, oily slit under dark eyebrows. "That's an interesting word, officer."

"What is?"

"You said *investigation*. So it wasn't just some fluff story."

"I don't know. She never let me in on the details. But I knew she was digging."

"Fine. Anything else she might've mentioned to you when you two talked?"

I shake my head vigorously. Maybe too much. "She had been doing some research but didn't share a lot of it with me. I think she wanted me as a source of more information, but when I didn't have anything to give, she gave up."

Meade scribbles something on his pad again.

The questioning wraps up a few minutes later, and I'm left with the impression that my role in their investigation is over, but as an officer of law enforcement, I know this is just the beginning.

5:45 PM
AMY

"Brothers and sisters, are you keeping on the watch? As the scene of this world continues to change, rest assured that it will align with God's purpose to bring an end to false religion once and for all. As students of the Bible, we know that it is Jehovah who 'puts it into their hearts'. Does this mean that the Great Tribulation will only bring hardship for those who belong to Satan's system? To answer, let's turn to our Bibles in Matthew chapter twenty-four..."

My mind wanders as the program continues. I saw it last week after my study when I was at Chelsea's. She and Walter were particularly interested to see if the broadcast was going to formally announce the beginning of the Great Tribulation. Everyone suspects that it's already begun, but our organization has been cautious to label it. According to Walter, the brothers may be waiting for something more significant to happen on a global scale, since the attack on Babylon the Great comes from the image of the wild beast, the United Nations, and not just the government of a single nation.

I still find the symbols and prophecies in Revelation difficult to grasp, but Chelsea and Walter have been patient, explaining things simply and even helping me to put together my own timelines for personal study. Regardless of my limited grasp of everything right now, it's exciting to be living through such a clear fulfillment of Bible prophecy.

Still, I can't help but feel distracted by an equally pressing issue in my life: my marriage. I glance at the kitchen door leading in from the hallway, knowing that as soon as it swings open I'll be faced with the task of confronting Luke. It can't wait any longer, though I still don't have the words. How could I? Until just a couple of weeks ago, I thought our marriage was just fine. I look back at the screen, tuning in long enough to catch the following:

"What kind of tribulation can we expect to face? Well, in the first century C.E., what trials did Christians fleeing Jerusalem have to face? The material sacrifices were many. They would've had to leave behind homes, businesses, material possessions. Many likely faced opposition from unbelieving family members..."

Footsteps in the outside hallway come to a halt at our front door and I realize that Luke is home. I turn and take a deep breath. There's a loud thud on the front door as someone knocks.

"Who is it?" I yell, startled.

"FBI. Please open up."

FBI? Is this a joke? I wonder if it's Gabe out there and he's expecting to catch Luke at home. I angrily lean into the peephole to find two strangers in black jackets looking back at me impatiently. One of them holds a golden badge to my eye

"Give me a minute," I say, going through the five-step process of unlocking our front door. A man and a woman step inside.

"Can I see some ID?" I ask. They exchange a glance before allowing me to inspect their badges.

"We're with the Federal Bureau of Investigation, ma'am. You're the wife of Officer Luke Harding, is that correct?"

"Has something happened to him?"

"No ma'am, I can assure you he's perfectly safe. However, his precinct is currently under an investigation. We're here with a seizure warrant…" The man pauses slightly as his partner produces a notarized document from a jacket pocket. "Are you familiar with this?"

"It means you're here to take something," I say with a quick glance.

"That's right. We won't be but a minute. Perhaps you can show us where Luke keeps his laptop computer."

I nod hesitantly. I'm violated by this intrusion, two strangers walking into my apartment and taking whatever they want. Worse yet with me leading the way, giving the grand tour. I point out Luke's desk as we enter the living room. The man walks over, yanks cables from the walls, and throws everything into a black duffel bag. The woman looks around our apartment smugly while she waits. It unnerves and angers me.

"Is that all?" I ask irritably when Luke's computer is packed away.

"That should be it, yes," says the man. He hands me his business card before he leaves. "If you or your husband wish to get in touch, here's my number."

I take it from him and, without a word, escort them to the door.

6:37 PM
LUKE

I come home to a quiet apartment and find leftover meatloaf wrapped in foil on the stove. I warm a slice in the oven and collapse onto the sofa. I've barely slept the last couple of nights and it's finally catching up. Even caffeine and adrenaline have their limits. I'm halfway through my dinner when Amy enters the kitchen quietly and takes a seat. She's got a funny expression on her face. I ask her what's going on.

"Some people came by here today," she says, crossing her arms and staring at the floor.

"People? What do you mean?"

"They said they were with the FBI." That's all it takes. My mind is reeling again. This nightmare never ends.

"What did they want?" I demand, knowing full well what the answer must be.

"They took your computer," Amy says. I curse loudly and slam my fist on the table, startling her. I shake my head and cover my face. It's the worst possible news.

"What's going on, Luke?" she pleads. "Are you in trouble?"

"Maybe. I don't know," I groan.

"What's that mean? Have you done something wrong?"

"No, I haven't. They may think I did, but I haven't. I just talked to a reporter a few times, and now they think I'm somehow mixed up in this mess."

"What mess?"

I sigh. There's no real harm in letting Amy in on everything, though it's anyone's guess how she'll react. I decide to take my chances.

"There were some leaked files posted online. The documents incriminate the government for some of the arson attacks on churches around the country." I glance up at Amy. She seems to be frozen, her mouth open, eyes staring off into space.

"So it was all a set up, then… Just to get that law passed!" she says with a strange look.

"I… I don't know about all that, but I guess anything's possible."

"Why did they come here, though? How are you involved?"

I take a deep breath and pause before answering. "I talked to the reporter who leaked the documents. They must think I know something."

"Do you?"

"Only the little that the reporter gave me."

"Did you have any of it on that computer?"

My head drops and the next word takes tremendous courage to utter. "Yes."

"Oh, Luke... But what does that mean? Can they come after you? Can they come after us? Can you be... charged with anything?"

"No, I don't think so. I don't know. All I had were some files. I knew so little about her investigation. I can't see how that could be a crime..."

"*Her* investigation?" Amy asks, her voice taking on a new quality.

"Yes, *her*. Eva Richards, that reporter from *The Herald* I told you about."

There's a long silence before Amy asks, "Was she the woman who came to see you in the hospital?"

I nod, surprised that Amy remembers this detail. "Yeah, that's right," I say.

"Are you still in contact with her?" Amy asks.

"No," I say simply, trying my best to avoid reliving a tragedy that's still heavy on my conscience.

"So what happens next then?"

"I'm not sure, babe," I say shakily. And I mean it.

THURSDAY, DECEMBER 3

12:30 PM
LUKE

As the days pass things gradually return to normal. The feds are gone along with reams of paper, but on the plus side no one's been indicted. The clock keeps ticking and we're busy with our jobs. More and more, the news is dominated by reports of religious violence, both in the US and abroad. Russia, France, Australia, the UK, and a handful of other Western countries have followed America's lead and begun limiting the practice of religion. Surprisingly, the public's response is overwhelmingly positive. Like Matthias, there are those who try to lash back, but most seem content to privatize their worship or give it up completely.

Although my laptop is still in FBI custody, it brings me some relief that they haven't come back with cuffs and a warrant for my arrest. I'm not sure what they could charge me with, but as a law enforcement officer I know that sometimes the pressure to bring in a conviction can overshadow justice, and Eva's untimely death has denied them of this so far.

The air outside has less of a bite to it than the last few days and I feel the need to stretch my legs. I hike to my favorite hotdog stand and order the usual. I'm just about to bite into one of them when I feel a tap on my shoulder. I turn to see a familiar face and freeze.

"Hi, Harding," says Agent Meade. "Let's take a walk."

I follow begrudgingly, knowing I have no choice. Meade knows it too. I'm sure he enjoys it.

"You done with my computer?" I grumble.

"Just about. Found some interesting stuff on there."

I refuse to reply.

"You could be arraigned for obstruction of justice, Luke," Meade says with a frown. He plays the considerate friend now. Just trying to look out for me.

"That's a stretch and we both know it," I say.

"Maybe, maybe not. You did withhold evidence. You also lied to a federal officer."

"Check your transcripts. I answered all of your questions with the truth."

"Not the whole truth, Harding."

"Enough to hold up in court," I say.

"You sure about that?"

"Look, you know I wasn't feeding her any confidential information. No laws were broken. The only reason you even showed up at our precinct was because we were mentioned in some of her notes. That's it. You're grasping at straws and we both know it."

"And yet, we found your laptop with her USB in it. Odd, don't you think?"

"It was given to me by a housekeeper from the hotel she was staying at. Go interview her if you want. I brought it home and looked at the files because I was curious, ok?"

"Ok," Meade says with a shrug and a cold smirk. I wait for a new line of questioning but he remains silent. We're a block away from the precinct when he stops and opens his shoulder bag. He pulls out my laptop with a tangle of wires and hands it to me.

"So that's it, then? Are we done here?" I ask. Meade is studying me with his hands in his pockets.

"Yeah, I think so," he says. But as I turn to leave, he thinks of something.

"Oh, one more thing, Luke. One of the agents that confiscated the laptop noticed something in your apartment that I've been meaning to ask you about."

"Yeah?"

"He said that when he entered your kitchen, he caught a glance of your wife's iPad."

"So?"

"She had it opened to a religious website–a video streaming site used by Jehovah's Witnesses. Is your wife a Witness?"

"No," I say, but Agent Meade gives me a cold stare that demands details.

"She's got some friends who are Witnesses, I think."

Meade pauses for a moment, looks around, and then nods. "Ok, just wondering. Have a good day, Luke."

We go our separate ways. I hope it's the last I'll see of the creep for a long, long time.

FRIDAY, DECEMBER 4

10:05 AM
AMY

A huge weight has been lifted from my shoulders. Cliché, I know, but true! All the anxiety of the last week spent worrying about whether my husband was hiding some dark secret from me has melted away. Chelsea was right; a little communication goes a long way. I'm so thankful, in fact, that today I've brought her a present: five pounds of organic flour I bought online. (I'm not sure what organic flour even is, but I'm sure Chelsea will find a use for it.)

I've stopped sneaking to and from their house. I figure that since my husband knows about me studying with Chelsea and doesn't seem to mind, there's no reason to keep being so secretive. The air is still biting today, but I sense that the coldest part of winter is yet to come. I don't mind the nippiness in the air. Today it makes me feel alive. I smile as I get off the bus and stroll towards the Novaks' home.

As I approach, I notice Walter installing a row of steel cages over their windows. I recall him mentioning a series of burglaries in the neighborhood. He waves at me from a ladder as I cross their driveway and enter through the front door. Chelsea's got her iPad set up on the counter in the kitchen and is watching live coverage of some riot in Europe. I catch a glimpse of a man with a bloody nose being dragged by his arms into an armored van by a SWAT team before Chelsea pinches the window away.

"Hey hon," she says. She pours a cup of fresh coffee from a French press and adds the right amount of cream and sugar. I'm spoiled here, I know.

"What was that all about?" I ask, nodding at her device.

"More of the same, I'm afraid," she says with a sigh. "The few that are still holding on to their religious identity are getting pushed closer and closer towards extremism. An ex-deacon in Germany was caught stockpiling grenades in his church. They think he was planning to bomb a police station in Paris."

"Just crazy," I whisper.

"The brothers were right to give us the instructions when they did about holding our meetings in private. Cautious as serpents, right?"

I nod, looking over at the blank screen as if it had something more to offer. "How long do you think this will go on?" I ask.

Chelsea takes a deep breath and mulls over the question with a sip of her coffee. "It's impossible to know. Jewish Christians fleeing Jerusalem had to wait four years before the Romans returned to finish their city off. It could be a long time for us, too. Or it could not be. We really have no way of knowing."

"But the Great Tribulation has begun?"

"It does fit with what we've been studying all these years, but I'm sure the organization wants to be certain before any grand announcements are made."

"It doesn't seem like it could be anything else to me."

"Me either. But does it really matter?"

"What do you mean?"

"I was baptized in the early seventies, when I was in my twenties. I've waited for decades for the end to come. I'd always hoped I'd see it in my lifetime, but it wasn't my main motivation for serving Jehovah. I served him because it was the right thing to do. Time makes motives manifest, you know." I feel like Chelsea is referring to something specific, so I press her for more details.

"In the seventies and eighties, some of our brothers and sisters grew impatient. They felt like they'd been promised something that hadn't come. They wanted the end *now*. They weren't willing to go by Jehovah's timetable. As a result, they fell away. Some even resorted to abusing the friends who remained faithful."

"Why would they do that?"

"Their heart conditions were manifest over time. They weren't in it for the right reasons, you see? For those who were serving Jehovah because they truly loved him out of an unselfish heart, the date of Armageddon didn't matter. It was going to come one day sooner or later, so why get upset if it was a little later? But for those who lost their patience, well, they resembled certain groups of people in Bible accounts. Can you think of who?"

I smile at Chelsea's ability to take my question and turn it into a Bible lesson. I do my best but after a minute of racking my brains I give up.

"Think of the Israelites."

"Ok."

"Imagine the scene. Here they'd just been released from cruel Egyptian slavery by Jehovah's miraculous hand. They saw his blessings on his people and his power in splitting the Red Sea. There was no question who the true God was. And yet, just weeks after their deliverance, do you remember what they complained about?"

"Wasn't it the food?" I venture. Chelsea smiles in affirmation.

"That's right. They actually thought back to the food of Egypt, the meat and bread and onions and watermelons! They totally lost sight of the fact that the blessings ahead were sure to come. All they needed was a little patience. Instead, they disrespected God's representatives, thereby disrespecting God himself. Jehovah put up with it for a time, but eventually it cost many of them their lives.

"It's the same for those who leave the organization now because they feel the end is taking too long to come. Truth is, the organization doesn't have any more say over when Armageddon comes than Moses did over when they got to the Promised Land. Their job is to keep us focused on the work at hand and get us there in one piece, whether that's sooner or later than expected."

"And so that's why it doesn't really matter to you if this is the Great Tribulation or not."

"Don't get me wrong, I'm almost certain that this is the Great Tribulation, and that's exciting and monumental and I'll never forget it. But even if it's not, I'll still be here, serving Jehovah, as always."

It suddenly occurs to me that from the moment I heard about Congress passing a bill to limit the public practice of religion here in America, I'd never even considered the possibility that this *wasn't* the Great Tribulation. Many of the friends I've talked to since then have assumed the same, that this was the first strike against Babylon the Great. But Chelsea's determination despite her uncertainty is inspiring and I'm forced to consider what condition my faith will be in if this turns out to be something else. I also have renewed confidence in the organization for being so cautious with labeling these tumultuous times.

There's some noise from the living room as Walter enters the front door and shuts it behind him. He stows the ladder and tools in a narrow closet under the stairs and comes into the kitchen for a cup of coffee.

"How's the study going?" he asks.

Chelsea summarizes our conversation while Walter nods thoughtfully and bites into a blueberry muffin on the counter. Judging from the look Chelsea shoots him, I assume it wasn't meant for him.

"You all done installing those security cages?" Chelsea asks. Walter nods as he fetches a jug of milk from the refrigerator.

"How's Luke?" he asks, taking a seat.

"Pretty good, actually. Things have calmed down some. We're back to our old routine, more or less."

"I gotta say, it was nice getting the chance to talk with him that night at your place. He reminds me a lot of myself, back when I still thought I could fix this mess."

"I think you left an impression on him," I remark.

"Oh yeah? Did he mention something?"

"No, it's just a feeling I get. Call it a wife's intuition."

"So he's still ok with you coming here and studying and everything?"

"Yeah, I think so. It hasn't really come up."

"What about the other officers at his station? How much do they know?"

"I… I don't know. Luke hasn't mentioned anything. Why? Is something wrong?"

"Maybe it's nothing…" Walter says, frowning at the table.

"Walter, what are you talking about?" Chelsea asks.

"Well–and again, maybe I'm just being paranoid–but the last couple of times you've come here, Amy, I noticed a car pull up a few houses down and wait at the curb. I can't make out the faces, but it seems like there are a couple of guys in there, just sitting around."

"Walter, don't scare her," Chelsea says in a chiding tone.

"Amy, you know I wouldn't say anything just to frighten you, but maybe you can ask Luke about it. It could just be a coincidence. Maybe it's all unrelated. But we do need to stay alert. Especially since we're having the meetings here."

I nod, trying my best to look calm, but my insides are anything but.

"Are they still out there now?" Chelsea asks, looking in the direction of the street.

"Yeah. The last couple of times they've arrived a few minutes after Amy's gotten in, and they leave soon after she does."

"Maybe we should just call the police," Chelsea suggests, but Walter and I are both shaking our heads.

"No, I'm not sure that's a good idea. From the looks of them, they might be *with* the police. I think it's best if Amy just talks first with Luke, see if he knows anything. Maybe your husband is just looking out for you," Walter says to me.

As I leave that afternoon, I try to resist the urge to look at the car on the other side of the street, but my curiosity gets the best of me. With a glance I see it's a black Buick. In spite of the tinted windows I can make out a figure in the driver's seat. He's holding something to his ear, maybe a phone. I force my gaze back to the sidewalk in front of me and hurry to the bus stop.

MONDAY, DECEMBER 7

1:15 PM
LUKE

After all that's happened in the last few months, I was beginning to worry that I'd never get back into the old rhythm of life. According to a local news bulletin, the government has seized over 100,000 religious properties in the US. What was originally purported by congress to be a temporary measure appears to be rather permanent.

Some of the confiscated properties have already been auctioned off or demolished, leading some to move their activities into private homes. While this isn't yet strictly illegal, it's certainly out of the question for law enforcement. Word has been going around that two officers from another precinct who were caught attending family churches were immediately dismissed.

It's still hard to wrap my mind around this kind of thing happening in this country, but I guess desperate times beget desperate measures. I think this nation has scarcely seen it worse than it is now. Everyone's looking to turn the page on history, and maybe these restrictions will get us there.

In spite of all the recent upheaval, things at the precinct have settled into a kind of altered normalcy. I doubt it'll ever go back to the way it was before, but we're resilient and I expect we'll acclimatize in time.

Pryce is more or less his old self, though he's quieter these days. On the plus side, he's more protective than ever of the officers under his watch. Bullet-resistant vests are mandatory for all officers on patrol and our armament continues to bulk up.

Today, as I pull into the parking lot behind the building after my lunch break, I see the captain barking orders at a couple of cadets unloading black plastic crates from an armored truck. I park my car and jog over to the men, helping them haul the half dozen or so cases through the back doors and into the gun locker. Everything will need to be meticulously catalogued and checked for safety, and I'm betting Pryce has got these two rookies pegged for the job. I try to give them a bit of encouragement as I leave them to their task.

"Are those what I think they are?" I ask as Pryce examines the electronic lock to the gun locker.

"Yeah. DLP finally came through. How about that," Pryce grunts, referring to the order he placed with the Defense Logistics Program back in October.

"What'd they send us?"

"Everything we ordered, believe it or not. Flash grenades, AR-15s, M4s, and enough riot gear to deck out the whole crew. And the Lenco BearCat outside is ours, too," Pryce says with a glance over his shoulder. When I realize he's referring to the armored personnel carrier that the crates were delivered in, I let out a high whistle. Its armor plating is enough to withstand anything we're likely to come across in this county, and looks to be tough enough for an actual battlefield. It would've been a much safer command center than the flimsy surveillance van we camped out in during the bombing at the megachurch. Judging from the bitterness in Pryce's voice, he's thinking the same.

It's staggering to think that we've received all of this free of charge. I'd guess the carrier alone would run a couple hundred grand. There's simply no way our little precinct would've been able to purchase it on our own. Of course, it's also unlikely we would've received so much as a single crate of ammunition had it not been for the tragedy at St. Peter's Episcopal that killed two of our men and created a public outrage in our favor.

I think for a moment on what Amy suggested the other day, that somehow all of these events are part of some larger conspiracy. Whatever Eva had been investigating had obviously been headed somewhere dangerous and it's impossible not to speculate. I'm convinced the FBI knows more than I ever will, and I find it difficult to believe that Eva's death was an accident. I have to keep telling myself to let it go but I can't. The seeds of suspicion have been sown in my mind and abandoning her fight makes me feel like a coward.

Since Eva's 'accident' happened over county lines, it was outside of our jurisdiction. I doubt the investigators had known much about her. Had it been in our territory, things could've been handled differently. I might've even been able to get a peek at the evidence. Then again, what difference does any of it make? She's gone and she isn't coming back. She died in that fire and almost took my career with her. Move on, I keep telling myself.

Of course, that would be a lot easier were it not for the conversation Amy and I had a few days ago. She said she's being followed, that she'd spotted two men in a car watching her come and go. I told her to ignore it, that it was probably nothing. But my wife isn't stupid, and neither am I.

Why are they watching her? If I happen to have the misfortune to run into Meade or any one of those goons, I'll be sure to ask. I'm certainly not about to make any phone calls to poke around. I'm not sure if my post here at the station could survive another run in with the FBI. It does make me wonder, though, if Amy and I need to have another chat about her Bible study.

WEDNESDAY, DECEMBER 9

9:49 AM
AMY

Every Wednesday morning at approximately 10 A.M., I get a text from Chelsea. It's a code that contains my arrival time and location for the meeting that afternoon.

Hey Amy, our friends are coming here on flight DE0405. Don't forget!

Their house at 4:05 PM. Got it.

Meeting days are always hectic. Now that the groups are even smaller (rarely more than nine or ten), we all have plenty of opportunities to comment, so thorough preparation is a must. The student parts have been reduced since there aren't enough people to care for everything every week, but I still end up with at least two assignments per month.

Tonight I've got the four-minute *Return Visit* on the second part of the meeting. Even though we're not on a stage and the audience is a bare minimum, it's still nerve-racking. Chelsea says it gets easier with time, but I doubt I'll ever achieve her level of poise.

I'm in our kitchen going over my notes as I wait on a casserole I've prepped for dinner. Another five minutes and I'm out the door hurrying to the bus stop. Ever since spotting the mysterious black Buick, I've been extra cautious going to and from the meetings. I even bought myself a double-sided jacket and a couple of hats at the local thrift store. I slip into one of the bathrooms at the strip mall by the bus stop and change every now and again. I can't be sure it's having the desired effect, but it calms me some to know I'm making an effort.

I'm on the Novaks' front porch at precisely 4:05. Chelsea answers the door in an apron and I slip in.

"Any strange cars today?" she asks as I hand her my coat and scarf. I shake my head. In spite of all the trepidation we felt when we first went underground with the meetings, it's all begun to feel very normal. The parts are, for the most part, the same as when we were in a Kingdom Hall. We dress about the same, though the sisters have been reminded to go easy on the makeup and perfume so as not to attract too much attention. For the same reason, we come in pants and change into skirts after arriving. We also lug around items to suit the occasion. Sometimes it's a dinner party and we all bring a covered dish, sometimes we're carrying instruments to a music party. We have assigned times for arrival and a designated departure order, and obviously we're careful about clapping and singing, but other than that, it still *feels* like a meeting.

I've gotten a bit closer to the others, too. The small group setting means we get to spend more time socializing, and there are usually snacks and desserts served afterwards. The meetings are basically little spiritual parties and I love them.

My part goes ok. I get lots of compliments when it's over, but I feel like I was probably speaking too fast and I know I missed one of my lines. It's amazing to me how natural Walter and Chelsea and the others are when they give parts. It all seems so effortless. I know they've been doing it for years, but still. It's really impressive.

Chelsea's baked a chocolate cake (my favorite), and once the meeting's over and we've all changed back into more casual clothes, she divides it up. A little boy named Matthew hands them out on paper plates. He's five or six and is the son of a couple in our group, Marc and Ashley.

"I liked your talk," he says as he holds out a slice of cake for me. His two missing front teeth have given his adorable lisp the slightest whistle and I can't hold back a smile.

"Well, thank you very much, Matthew."

"My dad says your husband is a policeman. Is that true?"

I nod. "Yep."

"So, does he have a gun and stuff?"

"He does indeed," I say, wrinkling my nose.

"Oh. Is he not allowed to come to meetings, since he has a gun?"

I blush slightly and have trouble answering. His mother is at our side in an instant, blushing. She gives her son a scolding look but it doesn't seem to register.

"I'm sorry, Amy. It really was an excellent part though."

"Oh, thanks," I say. "And don't worry about it. I wish my husband could be here, too. Maybe one day, huh?" I say to the boy. He smiles and grabs a piece of cake for himself and disappears. Ashley and I make small talk for a minute or so, but it's a bit awkward. I hate making these people feel guilty about saying or doing the wrong thing around me, questioning whether they should mention Luke or not.

Things have improved lately, though. It was a lot worse when I first started attending. When the friends found out I was married to a cop, it made people anxious. It wasn't until Chelsea sat me down and explained things that I finally understood. There had been a lot of tension between the police and Jehovah's Witnesses in other cities and some people just assumed that cops everywhere were the same.

I find a seat on a couch near the fold-up podium and enjoy the double fudge chocolate cake. As always, it's breathtaking. An elderly sister keeps me company for a few minutes. Her name is Doris Harvey. She was widowed years ago when her husband died of a stroke. It was long before I knew Chelsea and became a part of this congregation, but I hear his name mentioned often. Like Luke, her husband was an unbeliever. He even opposed her for some time before finally softening. At the time of his death, he was an elder in our congregation. Doris offers a few words of encouragement and pats me gently on the knee as we chat.

Suddenly, we freeze as the sound of a loud banging comes from the front door. We've rehearsed for this scenario, but it takes a moment for us to spring into action. The few remaining theocratic books are stuffed into bags or drawers and the folding podium is shoved under the couch. Walter answers the door to reveal a man standing on the porch. I've seen him before. He's usually out trimming his hedges or washing his car a few doors down.

"Hi there, Ron, how are you?" Walter asks cordially. The man is frowning and glances past Walter to get a look at everyone inside.

"You havin' a party over here or somethin'?" The man asks.

"Just a few friends. They're actually getting ready to leave. What can I help you with?"

"Well, one of your friends is parked right in front of our house."

"Oh? Are you sure? What kind of a car is it?"

"An old Ford Taurus. Navy blue, big dent in the door."

"I'll move it for you right now," Walter says, already making his way over to Doris. She hands him her keys with a look of embarrassment.

As the door closes, everyone in the room breathes a collective sigh of relief. The law is still unclear on the consequences if we were ever caught having religious meetings in a private home, but no one wants to find out. Chelsea looks especially frazzled as she sends me off. I know it must be hard doing these things in their home. We hug goodbye and I'm swallowed by a gust of cold night air.

1:20 PM
LUKE

I'm sitting in one of the corner booths of Bermuda's drumming my fingers nervously on the table while I wait. I had a feeling Agent Meade wasn't done with me. When I started my shift this morning, I found his email waiting for me in the internal system our PD uses for communication. The fact that the feds have access to these private accounts only added to my unease. Meade told me to be here at half past one, so here I am.

I wonder if Meade has summoned me here for something specific or if he simply enjoys yanking my leash as he pleases. It's puzzling, too, that he didn't simply march into our precinct and demand another session in the interrogation room. The fact that he's chosen such a casual setting for our third meeting is actually even more worrisome.

He slips through the front doors right on time, his head dipping between his shoulders like a vulture eyeing carrion. A wiry grin splays across his face when our eyes make contact. He strides directly to my table and sits.

"Meade," I say with as much civility as I can muster.

"Luke, thanks for coming. How are things?" he asks, setting his briefcase on the table and folding his hands on top. I shrug.

"Back to normal, more or less. You?"

"Oh, busy, busy," Meade says with calculated ambiguity.

"Why are we here?" I ask.

"What, no small talk? I drive all the way down here from my field office and that's all I get?" I give Meade a droll look and sigh. "You've got a real attitude on you, officer. If I remember correctly, I did you a huge favor last time we met."

"A favor? You barged into my home and stole my computer."

"And returned it even after finding some rather incriminating evidence. I could've made things real bad for you."

"Yeah, well, thanks a lot for not extorting me," I sneer.

Meade's eyes narrow and he gives me a cold stare, but he's still smiling. "You know," he says, "with all that's going on right now, law enforcement has been given a certain amount of... *autonomy* that we didn't enjoy in times past."

"*We?*"

"Yeah, we. Think about it. The cops around the US, including your little precinct, outfitted with military weaponry and advanced tactical gear. Can you imagine the fuss, the protests, the liberals, had this happened a decade ago? Now, nobody cares. They see armored police vehicles patrolling their neighborhoods and they smile and wave. People want peace. People want order. They don't mind the cavalry in their backyards."

"And what does this mean for the FBI?"

"We're still on the federal leash, but things have been lightening up. Especially since the Liberation Act, of course."

"Yeah, some would say that it was the federal government behind the events that led to that legislation," I say, an edge in my voice. It's reckless trying to spar with a federal agent like this, but I don't regret the jab and Meade isn't riled.

"By 'some' you mean your reporter friend, huh?" I shrug. "Look, I'm just a field agent, I don't know the whole picture. Maybe she was on to something, maybe not. But it's ignorant to think that America doesn't wage internal wars."

This is a more significant admission of guilt than I expected and I'm left without words.

"But that's beside the point, Luke. Don't forget, we're on the same side here. We want the same thing: safe families, safe communities. Sometimes, that requires doing difficult things. I'm sure that's something you can understand."

I listen to Meade's words carefully and realize that he's staring at the spot in my arm that was struck by a bullet. Apparently he looked deep into my file.

"Ok," I say dismissively. He gives me a look before pulling a folder from his briefcase. He sets it on the table and frowns at me.

"I'm sorry to do this to you, Luke."

He opens the folder to reveal two eight by tens. I can tell from the blurred foreground that they were taken from a concealed location, and my heart sinks when I recognize the two people in them. It's Eva and I, the night before she went missing, when I went to her motel room and heard her story.

In the first shot, I'm on the edge of her bed while she sits in a chair wearing a robe. It doesn't look good, but the second photo is much worse. It was taken at the moment Eva gave me that kiss, and from the angle of the shot it looks like a lot more than a peck on the cheek. Both have white time stamps in the corner.

"You were watching us," I mumble.

"It's my job, Luke. It's what I do. Watch. Listen. Collect intel."

"So when you questioned me that day at the station…"

"Yeah, we already knew you were helping her."

"But why do you still have these photos? Why show me now? What does this accomplish?"

"The FBI wants to make you an offer."

"An offer?"

"We want you to help us with something, and in return, we'll be sure these photos don't get into the wrong hands."

"The wrong hands? You've already seen them, what other hands are there?"

"Well, your wife, for one."

"But… Eva and I weren't having an *affair* or anything. I was just trying to keep her safe. You had a photographer there, you know what happened."

"But Amy wasn't. And if she were to see these pictures, she'd assume what any wife would." Agent Meade's eyes crawl over me as his words sink in. I feel my fists and teeth clench tight.

"This is blackmail," I say, my voice trembling.

"Just a bit of leverage, Luke. Like I said, I'm sorry."

"What do you want?" I ask through gritted teeth.

"I'm glad you asked. You see, you're in a very unique… position."

"How."

"Well, your wife, Amy, is affiliated with Jehovah's Witnesses."

"You've been watching her."

"Is it that obvious?"

"She spotted a car with tinted windows across the street from a friend's house. I told her it was nothing."

"Rookie agents. They belongs behind a desk," Meade hisses with disgust. "In any case, we know your wife is affiliated."

"And?"

"And you know about it. And she knows you know. That makes you ideal."

"Ideal for what?"

"Ideal for collecting information."

"Wait, you expect me to spy for you?"

"To put it simply, yes. You see, the Witnesses are a shrewd bunch. They're not like the Catholics or the Methodists or whoever. They're not vocal politically. They're not militant."

"Then why spy on them?"

"Well, Luke, we believe there are no less than one million practicing Witnesses in this country alone. We think they took their activities underground well before the Liberation Act went into effect. They're organized, and somehow they've kept one step ahead of law enforcement this whole time. We want to know how."

"Don't they have a website or something? Why not just go online and read up?"

"They don't post anything sensitive there. It's all stuff meant for the public. The amount of traffic on their websites is enormous, by the way, which tells us just how active they are despite all the legislation."

"I can't believe this," I say, putting my face in my hands.

"We'd send one of our agents in, but it's tricky. We've had a few people approach known Witnesses in public places and ask for Bible studies, which is usually how the Witnesses find new recruits, but in every case so far it's failed. Our agents were too pushy, I guess. It scared them off. You're a better man for the job. You're already where we want you."

"What will you do with the information you get?" I ask.

"That's not really my call, Luke. Believe it or not, I'm a low rung on a tall ladder. I just write reports and pass them on to my superiors."

"And if I refuse?"

"You won't," Meade says without even looking at me. I consider Meade's offer for a moment as I glance over my shoulder out the window and into the street. I'm trapped. Everything he's said for the last two minutes is meant to give me the impression that I have a choice, but we both know that isn't the case. Either I take this or my marriage with Amy is over.

"Can I accept this on a condition?"

"You're not really in a position to be bargaining, Luke," Meade says with a chortle.

"I want immunity for my wife. Whatever happens, she goes free."

"I'll pass it on, but I'm not making promises, you understand?"

"No, I don't understand. If you can't guarantee this, why would I help you? Either way I'll lose her."

Meade is forced to admit that I have a point. He smirks and gives a slight nod. "Fine. Your wife's record stays clean."

"Ok," I say, taking a deep breath. "How do I begin?"

10:13 PM
AMY

It's actually happened! Jehovah has answered my prayers! I never, *ever* thought that things could happen so quickly, but now that I've seen it with my own eyes, it's nothing short of miraculous! Where to start...

Today is the day I'll never forget. When Luke came home he was like a different person. His mood towards the end of the week typically ranges from slightly irritable to outright foul. By this point he's been through all kinds of drama at the office and can bristle at the smallest things. Today, though, he was calm and quiet. Even asked how my day was. We ate dinner over pleasant conversation. I felt so good that I suggested we open a bottle of wine, and Luke agreed.

We cuddled on the couch as we worked our way through the bottle. I haven't felt this close to Luke in months, maybe even years. He really opened up about some of the things he's been going through at the office: the pressure that's come along with his promotion, the rigors of training with all their new equipment, and the endless paperwork he has to deal with as a sergeant. Maybe it was the cabernet that loosened his tongue, but he just kept talking and talking.

I sat there, elated, and tried not to interrupt. But nothing could've prepared me for what came next. *He asked about Chelsea and Walter!* I was stunned. Speechless! I nearly spilled my wine. Then I wondered if I'd had too much. When he repeated the question I mumbled something incoherent. He said he thought that they seemed like nice people, and that he was actually happy for me to have such good friends. I could've died right there in his arms!

My mind was a mess at this point. I felt like I'd been given a golden opportunity and didn't want to blow it, so I said a quick prayer and gently suggested that we all get together sometime for dinner, that they really liked Luke and wanted to spend more time with us. I held my breath as I waited for a response. And to my intense, unimaginable delight, he said yes! *YES!*

Can it be? Is this the beginning of a new Luke? I was to excited, so utterly thrilled, that I called Chelsea as soon as Luke had slipped into the shower. She was just as happy, and the planning began immediately. We decided to schedule a Sunday dinner at their house. We both agreed it's a more relaxing environment of the two homes, and this way Luke will get a chance to see some of Walter's handiwork.

I really think those two will become friends. Oh, I just can't wait to see how things turn out!
Thank you Jehovah!

SUNDAY, DECEMBER 13

6:15 PM
LUKE

The Novaks live in a quaint, two story bungalow. They've maintained the house well, and the result is a stark contrast to the surrounding dilapidation. Being this close to the city, the property value must be sky high, and I guess that most of the neighbors know their houses will eventually be demolished when they sell. Until that day comes, many seem content to let nature take its course. Most of the yards are clogged with weeds. The houses themselves seem to frown with age, their sagging eaves and crooked window shutters gazing sadly at the cracked macadam.

Walter and Chelsea's house is an exception. A low stone wall encircles the property. The hedges, though mostly bare for this time of year, are trimmed and neat. The house looks freshly painted. Even the loose gravel driveway seems to be groomed. I also note the window cages, which appear to be new. Having patrolled this neighborhood and come face to face with some of the characters behind these doors, I find it prudent. I wonder if Walter owns a gun?

Hidden sensors capture our movement as we let ourselves in through a wrought iron gate in the wall, and a line of lights beside the walkway flickers on. I spot a blurred figure in the frosted glass windows beside the front door as it swings open. Chelsea and Amy squeal in unison and embrace each other like long lost relatives. Walter appears in the foyer next to them, smiling. He's wiping his hand on an apron with faces of cartoon dogs and cats. The whole thing is like something out of a Lifetime movie with Martha Stewart in the director's chair. I find it so absurd that I actually chuckle. In all my years on this planet, I've never seen such happy people. I'm suddenly wary, remembering what Meade told me: *these Witnesses have consistently evaded detection for months.*

I enter the house as Walter takes our coats and get my first good look around. Part of me is doing this for the FBI investigation, but I have to admit that I'm curious, too. What is this place where Amy spends so much time? What's the draw?

The Novaks' home is small and well decorated without feeling kitschy or cluttered, something all too common for sixty-somethings living on their own. I once responded to a domestic dispute in this very part of town where a couple had started throwing punches when the wife swore her husband had pawned off one of the gnomes from her collection. An entire *room* of their house was literally crammed full of small ceramic dwarves.

    This, though, is nice. They've even got a taste for art. There's a cool wire sculpture of a lion's head on one of the side tables in the living room and a few abstract paintings hanging on walls. One in particular catches my eye and I pause for a moment to try and interpret it.

    "You like art?" Walter asks. I shrug.

    "I like looking at it. I wanted to study it in college, actually."

    "Oh? Where'd you go to school?"

    "Just a small state university in Tennessee, nearby my hometown."

    "I take it you didn't pursue the art degree."

    "Nope. My mom refused. I had an uncle who was an artist. Ended up on the street for a few years. He's in a ward somewhere now. My mom thought criminal justice was more promising. I went along with it and here I am." I let out a soft sigh and the two of us continue to gaze at the painting. "So, are you two collectors?" I ask.

    "You mean the art? Oh no, it's just a hobby for us. I do a little sculpting in my spare time and Chelsea likes to paint."

    "You mean you two did all these?"

    "No, not all of them. Some we purchased. A few were trades. Chelsea and I used to do little art market displays, and sometimes other artists would come by and make an offer. It was fun."

    "Sounds like it. I guess I can look forward to retirement," I say.

    "I never have. I like keeping busy."

    "You still work?"

    "Sure."

    "Something to do with the military?"

    "Oh no, those days are far, far behind me. I'm sort of a handyman now. I fix things around the house, do some plumbing or electrical when there's a need, that sort of thing. And once in a blue moon we sell a painting or two."

    "That's it? It's enough for all this?" I ask with a quick glance around the house.

    "Chelsea occasionally deals antiques online, but for the most part that's it. We live simply. We purchased this house in the '80s when property was cheap, and the mortgage's been paid off for years. We save money by doing our own gardening and we try to make what we can ourselves rather than purchasing. The savings add up."

I'm nodding thoughtfully but have a hard time swallowing it. I make a mental note to explore this topic further, as it might be a clue to something else.

Walter disappears for a moment behind a corner and returns with two glasses. He hands me one and I take a whiff. It's scotch, and I can tell immediately not the cheap stuff.

"This is incredible," I say after the first sip. It's warm and slick and layered with flavor. "What is it?"

"25-year-old single malt Scotch. Glenmorangie. Not sure if I'm pronouncing that right though. It's a little out of my league."

"You and me both."

Walter chuckles and retrieves the bottle for me to inspect. "Some friends of ours work near the stills in Scotland and brought us a bottle. Not bad, huh?"

"Yeah," I say, and it's an understatement. Once I'm done with this glass I'll probably never be able to enjoy another glass of anything else. There's a voice calling from the kitchen and Walter is whisked away. I'm left to my own wiles as I wander around the halls looking at things. Other than the art, I find a collection of foreign trinkets on some of the shelves. They look African, or maybe South American. Other than art and knickknacks, the house is decorated with numerous framed pictures. I spot a younger Walter and Chelsea with a little boy. I assume this is the son Amy once mentioned, and I make a second mental note.

I finish off my drink just as Amy appears in the hallway. She's beaming, obviously thrilled that I'm here and not being a total jerk. She loops her arm in mine and leads me towards the dining room.

"Pretty cool place, huh?" she whispers into my ear. I nod. I've never been in a house like it before. Though the place is small, it's clear that Walter and Chelsea have lived a full life together.

The table is set with a spread of steaming dishes. I spot a pot roast, candied yams, roasted corn, stuffing, and a salad sprinkled with blue cheese. It's enough to make my knees wobble and I grab a chair to steady myself. Just like the last time we ate together, Walter asks if I mind him saying a prayer and I give my consent.

It's a strange feeling being around people praying again. It's been years since I went to church or even thought seriously about God or religion. It just never appealed to me. Not even as a kid. One day in

Sunday school when I was about eight or nine, the teacher insisted I recite the 'Our Father' prayer. I refused; I just didn't get why it was so important.

"Why would God want to hear the same prayer over and over again?" I asked her. She sneered at me in response.

"Who are you to question God!" she snapped. Even at that age, I'd decided that if I wasn't allowed to question something, it wasn't worth my time.

Half of my brain is replaying that memory while the other picks up bits and pieces of Walter's prayer. It's not the 'Our Father', and I'm pretty sure he isn't reciting it from a prayer book. He talks like he's actually speaking to someone real, someone whom he respects and cares about. He even mentions my name. I glance over at Amy, but she's got her eyes closed like the rest of them. I patiently wait for Walter to finish, and when he does we all dig in.

"How is everything?" Chelsea asks after I've cleaned my first plate off and lean in for seconds.

"It's amazing, Chelsea. As always," Amy says.

"Thanks, hon," Chelsea says, brushing Amy's arm. "Luke, you need anything?"

"No, I'm good. Thanks," is all I say.

I realize it's been a long time since I've enjoyed a dinner like this. There was a time, when I was small, when I could look forward to the holidays for this kind of thing. But then my Dad found a younger woman. There was a divorce; our family was split down the middle. And big dinners together–along with just about everything else–were suddenly a thing of the past.

I realize Amy is nudging me and I turn to look at her. She's smiling.

"Walter asked you a question, babe."

"Just wanted to know if anything exciting happened at work lately," Walter says from across the table.

"Exciting?"

"Yeah. It's not often we have a police officer over for dinner."

"Oh. Well, not really," I say. My mind drifts from the conversation a bit as the three of them discuss people I don't know. There are also a lot of terms I can't quite comprehend, and I begin to wonder if the Witnesses have their own coded language. Perhaps that's one way they've evaded the law all this time.

"So," I finally interject as their conversation hits a lull. Chelsea is opening the oven removing something that smells like desert and Amy is collecting dishes from the table to make room. "It's just you two? No kids?"

I notice Chelsea pause momentarily as she lifts a pair of well used oven mitts from a wall hook. Walter glances over to her and then back to me with a smile.

"We have a son, actually," Walter says mildly.

There's a crash on the tile floor as Chelsea drops a knife. It flings bits of fruit goo onto the cabinets and she apologizes.

"A son? Does he live around here?" I ask.

"No, I'm afraid not," Walter says with a frown. "At least, he wasn't living around here last time we saw him. He moves around a lot."

"When was that? I mean, the last time you saw each other?"

Amy turns from the sink where she's washing dishes to shoot me a warning look but I ignore it.

"Oh, I suppose it's been five or six years now," Walter says with a strange distance in his eyes. I wait for him to continue, but there's nothing. What could cause a couple to be so caring and generous to strangers and yet barely communicate with their own son?

"I hope you like peach cobbler," Chelsea says as she sets a steaming plate in front of me. I take a few bites and decide to let the topic rest.

"So Walter, I think last time we had dinner you didn't get to finish telling your story," Amy says from the counter. She's done with the dishes and returns to my side to pick at my plate of cobbler with a tiny fork. It's always the same with women. They never want their own portion but they'll eat most of yours. I nudge the plate in her direction and she immediately holds her hands up. Oh no, of course she couldn't. She just wants a *taste*. I glance at Walter and he chuckles knowingly.

"Right, my story. You still interested, Luke?" he asks.

"Sure," I say, shrugging. I'm frowning at my plate, where half of my cobbler has already vanished.

"I believe last time you asked how it was that I went from opposing my wife to joining her. Well, I can tell you that it didn't happen overnight. I'd heard so many negative things about the Witnesses that I refused to consider the other side of the argument. The result was, I'd treat all the Witnesses I came across terribly. I once spotted an older lady on the street handing out *The Watchtower* magazine. I pretended to be interested. She handed me one and I tore it up and threw it right in the trashcan beside her. I was a real knucklehead back then.

"It's amazing, though, how your life can get flipped upside down in an instant. One night, while I was driving home from work, it started raining really heavy. I mean, it was just coming down in sheets, and I couldn't see a thing. I veered off the road and hit the embankment. The car flipped on its side and skidded about two hundred feet across the pavement. My briefcase, which had been sitting in the passenger seat, flew through the windshield and was discovered by the paramedics another hundred feet from the vehicle. That would've been me, too, or at least pieces of me, had it not been for my seat belt."

"Oh Walter, don't be so gruesome," Chelsea says with a distasteful look.

"Were you hurt?" I ask.

"Oh sure, I was battered to a pulp. Both legs broken, my neck fractured in four places, and I almost lost a finger. I spent four months in the hospital. Because of the neck injuries, some of the doctors thought I might be paralyzed. It was the scariest, most helpless feeling. It takes a man's dignity away like nothing else. I didn't even feel like a person any more."

I realize I'm nodding along as Walter is speaking. I went through some of the same things while in the hospital, and I was only there for a few days.

"Anyhow, I had a lot of time to think while I was laid up in that hospital bed. Couldn't do much else, really. I worried about everything. What would I do for work if I couldn't walk again? At the time I was privately contracting as a test pilot for military prototype aircraft. There was no way I could do that without my legs. Sometimes the stress of it all just broke me down. I'd cover my face with a pillow and wish I could just die.

"But Chelsea was there right by my side the whole time. She never seemed to worry about the future, never seemed to even think of leaving me. She kept saying we'd get through it together, that everything would work out. I wondered where this strength was coming from. How was she, this quiet, reserved little thing, able to keep it together, when I, a rugged military man with years of intense physical and psychological training, was collapsing from the sheer pressure?

"Then there were Chelsea's friends. The Witnesses. The very people I'd viewed as my personal enemy combatants. They came and visited me. They brought flowers and cards and balloons. They brought me food when Chelsea was unable to. They'd sit and chat with me when I allowed them to. These people who I'd done everything to resist–they just wouldn't give up on me. And where were *my* friends? Where were the guys that I'd served with overseas, or the ones I'd risked my life for flying aircraft? In all those weeks, I think I got three phone calls. That was it.

"So there I am, both my legs strung up in casts, so pathetic that even my old buddies can't take a day off to come see me, and these droves of strangers are coming in day after day to wish me well. To cook me meals. To write me little cards. That kind of thing, it…"

Walter's draws a ragged breath, his voice catching. He pauses a moment, eyes closed tightly as he holds a fist to his mouth. He takes a deep breath to regain his composure, and says, "That kind of thing changes a man. My whole life I thought I knew who I was and what I wanted. But when I lost it all, that's when I found what I really needed. There'd been a hole in my life all along and I'd been trying to fill it with personal accomplishments, the acceptance of my superiors, badges and honor. But in the end, it did nothing for me. *Nothing*. I finally realized it wasn't the life I wanted."

"So you became a Witness?"

"Well, not right away. I still had concerns, you see? Those things I'd heard about them were still rattling around in my head. I needed to understand what the truth was. But now I was willing to ask. And that made all the difference."

We all seem to let this soak in as the room fills with silence. The pan of cobbler at the center of the table holds one last piece and Chelsea wastes no time shoveling it onto my plate. Since I barely had two bites the first time around, I'm happy to oblige.

"So," Amy says eyeing my cobbler, "how long did it take you to actually start studying with them?"

Walter glances at Amy, then back at me. "Perhaps we can delve into that chapter over a future dinner," he says. "Besides, it's a clear night, which means conditions are perfect for me to show Luke the balcony."

The two women nearly applaud this suggestion, though I have no idea what he's talking about. Still, I'm curious enough to follow behind him as he trudges up the stairs to the second floor.

Like the downstairs, the area here is artfully decorated and well maintained. There's an old cherry secretary desk by an arched windowsill and a couple of old upholstered chairs. It all belongs to some bygone era, and yet still merges seamlessly with the modern art strewn about the walls. Walter leads me through one of the doorways and past a sliding door onto a small balcony. He pops open a closet and produces a heavy looking telescope. He extends the tripod and sets it on the center of the deck. He pulls a small sheet of paper from his pocket and mumbles something to himself as he twists and turns various knobs and dials.

"Take a look," he finally says.

I lean down and peer into the eyepiece expectantly. It's been years since I've looked into a telescope. My field of view, however, is black. I shift my angle to see if that clears anything up, but the view remains completely blank.

"See anything?" Walter asks.

"A whole lotta nothing," I say.

"Well, somewhere in that tiny dot of space, lies a planet known as Kepler-452b. Heard of it?"

I back away from the telescope, shove my hands in my pockets, and shake my head.

"Scientists discovered it a few years ago using a powerful telescope orbiting us in space. They say it's the most Earth-like planet found to date. It's just a bit bigger than this planet, and they think it may be habitable. Problem is, it's one and a half thousand light years away."

"Interesting."

"NASA spent over half a billion dollars building this particular telescope and shooting it into space for the sole purpose of finding other Earth-like planets. But we still have no way to get there, or even determine if they're really habitable. This seems to be a recurring pattern with us humans. We spend so much time and money looking for the next great thing that we fail to appreciate what's right in front of our eyes, what's right under our feet."

I nod thoughtfully and stare up at the sky. The stars are especially bright tonight and the view is stunning.

"You know," Walter says softly. "I wanted to share this with you because it's a lesson that I learned late in life. Unlike those scientists at NASA, I like looking at the stars to remind myself of how precious what we have now is. Had it not been for my accident, I may have never seen how fortunate I was to have a wife like Chelsea. You're a better man than me, Luke. You already value your wife. I can see it in the way you speak to her, in the way you treat her."

"Thanks," I say awkwardly. Walter smiles and pats me on the shoulder.

"Never forget that like this planet, our wives are a gift. And they're one of a kind."

THURSDAY, DECEMBER 17

8:15 AM
AMY

Every Thursday, Chelsea swings by to pick me up at the corner of our apartment block. By 8:45 we've got our coffee, and we head off to wherever the meeting for service has been scheduled for that day. Today it's at Brother Colson's house. He's been a Witness for ages, they say. A bachelor all his life, he lives by himself in an old condo not far from Walter and Chelsea's place.

I hear a muffled buzz as Chelsea presses a button on his door. We wait a few seconds as he makes his way over and opens it up. He nods without a word and we slip in. Chelsea's got a small paper bag of groceries in one arm and she sets it on his dining table. As an extension of the Liberation Act, this week the government recently banned all private religious gatherings, meaning this clandestine meeting for service is strictly prohibited. If anyone were to show up uninvited, we could claim–honestly–that we were just bringing groceries to an elderly friend.

The few chairs and sofas are occupied by a handful of friends. We acknowledge each other with hushed greetings. I know they must've arrived much earlier than us but they don't seem impatient. Some are holding paper coffee cups just like Chelsea and I and making quiet conversation.

"You see the news last night?" a sister whispers. Her name's Janice. She moved to our area from Nebraska to be closer to family. Now that we're so close to the end, many have made similar migrations, giving up homes and jobs and old congregations.

"No, what was it?" Ashley asks. Her son, Matthew, is wriggling uncomfortably in his puffy down jacket but knows to keep quiet.

"A bunch of Witnesses in Canada were arrested and sent to prison. The police found out about their meetings."

"Oh, that's terrible. This was on the news?"

"Yeah. They really twisted it, of course. Made us look like a cult or something," Janice says angrily. Ashley frowns and wraps her arms tighter around her boy.

"Ok friends, it's time," Brother Colson says. There're seven of us here today. Not a huge crowd, but difficult to explain if we have unwanted visitors. As the brothers have repeatedly warned, one nosy neighbor is all it takes.

"Today, I'd like to talk about ways we can introduce our website to those who might be interested. As you know, the homepage of JW.org has been redesigned to feature the *Warning* video. Many have already seen this video on the Internet and on TV, and we want to stress the importance of its message while still seeking out honest hearted ones. Any suggestions?"

A few hands go up and Brother Colson motions at Sister Bailey.

"I like striking up a conversation with people and then asking what kind of social media they prefer using. Then I tell them that a friend of mine recently messaged me with a link to this website. I try to gauge their reaction and share an article I think they might like. Then I point out the video."

"Fantastic," Brother Colson says. He's got an iPad balanced in his lap and seems very comfortable with the technology as he nimbly swipes his fingers this way and that to bring up an application. A few other hands are still up, and he calls on the next one.

"I've found it helpful to print out a few of the articles for families and couples and keep them in my purse. When I run into someone who seems friendly, I tell them I recently made copies of an article for a friend and have an extra one if they'd like to keep it. If they seem favorable, I'll then share the video." Ashley says.

"I like that. Very prepared," says Brother Colson. "Now, just as a reminder, there's some things we want to watch out for when preaching informally. As the recent letter we received from the branch stressed, it would be wise to avoid drawing immediate attention to ourselves as members of an organized religion. So how might we respond if someone asks about our religious affiliation?"

Chelsea raises her hand. "I've found that it's easiest to say that I enjoy reading the Bible, since that's still legal to do. I won't mention that I'm a Witness unless they ask specifically."

"Very cautious, Sister Novak, thank you."

Brother Colson gives a few more suggestions before saying a brief prayer and sending us out. Chelsea and I are assigned to a shopping mall. It's an easy place to talk to people, and Chelsea seems to know all the tricks to starting conversations. I'm excited for our day to begin as we pull up in a parking space at the Grand Avenue Plaza.

We take a moment 'casing the joint' as Chelsea jokingly calls it, spotting a few women by themselves sipping coffee or checking messages on their phones. We seat ourselves on a bench next to a woman browsing Amazon products on her tablet. I catch a glimpse of a page full of remote controlled drones and mini HD cameras.

"Excuse me, do you know if there's free Wi-Fi here?" Chelsea asks. The woman looks up, startled, but disarmed by Chelsea's friendly smile.

"Uh, yeah. It's a little slow, though," she says. She opens her device settings and shows Chelsea the name of the network.

"Thanks," Chelsea says. She pulls her tablet from her purse and links it to the free Internet. "Whew, you weren't kidding. This is like dial-up."

"Yeah, it's terrible. I can barely load these images," the woman laments.

"Holiday shopping?" Chelsea asks.

"Yeah," the woman says.

"How's it going? Got everything picked out?"

"Eh, you know how it is. Kids always want the newest stuff. It used to be cheap, when they were still little, but now all they want are gadgets, and they're just outrageously priced. Even the online prices are crazy."

"How many kids are you shopping for?" Chelsea asks. She's turned slightly to face the woman.

"Three. The youngest is twelve, the other two are in high school now. Fifteen and seventeen."

"Wow. Those are tough years."

"Tell me about it."

"It's not an easy world to raise kids in," Chelsea says with a sigh. I sense her testing the waters, seeing how the woman will respond. When she doesn't, Chelsea sips from her coffee and says nothing for a few moments. "Things were simpler years ago, weren't they?"

"I don't know," says the woman with a shrug. "Probably. I don't think about it much."

"Well, I I guess I have been around a bit longer than you. It feels like we've got a lot more stuff than we did years ago. More clothes, more accessories, more gadgets."

"That I'd agree with."

"It's funny though, it doesn't really feel like it's made our lives all that much better." Chelsea says the words thoughtfully, as if it's a conclusion she's just now come to. The woman wrinkles her brow and then turns to face her.

"I'd agree with that, too."

"Maybe it's just me getting older and all that, but I find myself thinking more and more about what the important things in life are. Do you do that too?"

The woman pauses for a moment before smiling. I marvel at the way Chelsea has gotten this complete stranger to open up in just a few short minutes.

"You know, it's funny you should bring that up, because just now, before you sat down here, I was thinking about that very thing. I was looking at all this junk on Amazon thinking, 'who really needs this stuff? Is it really going to make my boys happier?'"

Chelsea chuckles. "That's the same thing I try to ask myself whenever I go shopping. It's helped me to really simplify my life. No more worrying about debt and loans and all that other stuff. It's such a weight off the shoulders."

"Sounds like the dream life," says the woman wistfully.

"You know, it kind of is. Actually I was just reading this really interesting article about how to cut back on spending and still enjoy life to the full. Let me see if I still have it..." Chelsea opens her album and quickly brings up the screenshot of an article she's saved to her photos. It's from one of our *Awake!* magazines a few years back. The woman leans in for a closer look.

Chelsea refers to a few of the points and briefly mentions the fact that some of the quotes are from the Bible, but says nothing more. The woman seems interested, so Chelsea sends her the screenshots wirelessly and they appear seconds later on the screen of the woman's device.

"You come to this mall often?" Chelsea asks as she starts to pack her things back into her purse.

"Yeah, but usually only on the weekends. Just to get away from the craziness at home."

Chelsea makes a sympathetic face. "You poor thing. Yeah, I like coming here as well. Have you tried the pretzels in the food court?"

"Um, no, actually," says the woman.

"I'll tell you what, next time I'm headed this way I'll let you know. We can meet at the pretzel cart and I'll treat you to one."

"Oh. Um. Ok, sure," says the woman, her face showing a look of pleasant bewilderment. "But how will you let me know?"

"You have iMessage?" Chelsea asks. The woman nods, and moments later they've exchanged contacts. "My name is Chelsea, by the way. And you?"

"Melissa."

"Well, it was nice meeting you, Melissa. I've got to run now, but I'm looking forward to that pretzel."

"Yeah. Thanks. Me too."

We wave goodbye as Chelsea and I whisk ourselves away to another part of the mall. Chelsea's got her phone in her hand and is madly typing away in a password-protected app that tracks her return visits. We've been instructed by the branch to do this instead of keeping physical paper records.

"Alright, I think I got everything," Chelsea mumbles as she closes the app down and shoves the phone back into her purse.

"Well done," I say softly. We admire a shoe display through a store window for a few moments and then mosey past.

"Thanks," says Chelsea. "She seemed like a really nice woman."

"What'll you talk about next time?"

"We'll chat a little, then I'll ask if she read the article. You know, try to feel her out a bit. Then I'll mention the website and the video."

I nod as I rummage through a bin of discount socks in a plastic tub beside a vendor's cart. I decide Luke could use a pair, and I purchase a few for a great bargain. Chelsea has taught me it's best to buy something small here and there when we do informal witnessing at malls like this. If anyone catches on to what we're really doing here, it'll be the vendors. Maintaining a good relationship with them can go a long way.

We walk from the sock dealer to a pair of escalators and take the slow ride up. As we do, we spot two men pointing at something in our direction. One is a security guard, and he moves quickly towards us. He climbs the escalator two steps at a time and is directly behind us in no time. The walkie-talkie he holds in one of his hands is exploding with static gibberish.

"Excuse me, ladies," he says from a couple of steps below us. We shuffle to one side to let him pass and his head shakes slightly. He frowns and looks us directly in the eyes. "Actually, I'd like you two to come with me," he says.

12:14 PM
LUKE

I pull up to the parking lot behind McCann's a little after noon. Gabe's squad car is the only other vehicle in the lot. I wonder at how empty the place is as I push through the front doors. The lunch crowd during weekdays here is never large, but today it's practically deserted. I spot Gabe at the booth farthest away from the bar and slide in. He's studying the laminated menu with a frown.

"They're out of burgers," he grumbles.

"Out of burgers? How does that happen?" I ask.

"It's this cow flu everyone is freaking out about. Even McDonald's stopped serving beef."

"It's that bad?"

"You been living under a rock, man? It's all over the news."

"Haven't been watching the news much. Been kinda tied up with other stuff."

"Yeah, you look it. Like your head's not in the game."

I begin to say something, but am interrupted by a large woman who appears suddenly at the edge of our table. She's smacking on a wad of gum and wearing a stained apron with a metal clip that says *Sandra*.

"You two 'bout ready to order?" the waitress asks. We settle on soup and sandwiches. Sandra turns and disappears into the kitchen.

"So what's going on with you?" Gabe asks, sipping from his ice water.

"Just got a lot of stuff going on."

"Like what? Issues with the new recruits? Not settling well into the sergeant's uniform? What is it?"

"No, that's been fine. Work's been ok. Just… life, you know how it is."

Gabe studies my expression and I glance away, locating the flatscreen television perched above the bar. As usual, it's turned to the news, where drone coverage from the scene of a massive flood in Asia is plastered across the screen. I can make out the white tips of gushing water as it moves over the few obstacles swashing above the tide. The top of what looks like a school bus and a green tin roof rush by in the current.

"Is that fed still after you?" Gabe asks quietly. I shoot him a quick questioning glance.

"How did you know?"

"He came by the station one time when you were out, asked for your personal records."

"And you handed them over?"

Gabe looks down at his water, frowning. "Didn't like it, but I don't think I had a choice. So, what does he want with you?" Gabe asks.

"It's complicated," I say.

"But, you're not like in trouble with them or anything, right?"

"No, I guess not," I say weakly.

"Well shoot, man, that doesn't sound very reassuring."

"I can't really talk about it. But basically, I'm being forced to cooperate with them on something."

"*Forced?*"

"Yeah. Like I said, it's complicated."

"Huh," Gabe says, giving me a strange look. I can sense his need to pry, but he decides to let the issue drop. Our food arrives a few minutes later. Our expectations weren't high so we're not disappointed. We eat in silence as a news anchor rattles off a barrage of headlines. Waves of racial tension spreading across the country. Unemployment higher than it's been in decades. Schools in the UK closed after a slew of bomb threats. Chinese economy continues to implode. More corporations to shut their doors as their fleet-footed CEOs head for the hills. There's some update on the bovine flu as well, but I've tuned out.

"Crazy times, huh?" Gabe says with a glance over his shoulder at the TV screen. "That's why I'm glad I'm not on patrol so much these days. I'd rather be stuck behind a mountain of reports than have to deal with all the insanity out there, you know?"

"Yeah," I mumble. I turn my attention to my food and refuse to glance again at the TV.

"By the way, you heard about this Zeke Brady guy?" I shake my head.

"He's an ex-cop from Seattle. Started a Facebook group for neo-anarchists. Seems like he's got a huge bone to pick with the government. The group got a few thousand members within the first two months it was up, but people started posting threats to federal buildings, so Facebook shut them down. Apparently they've found some other way to continue communicating. They've been protesting across the country."

"Sounds like another home-grown terrorist group."

"We'll see. Lotta ex-cops and ex-military on their side. It's scary, man. Thank god for the DLP package, right?"

"Yeah, I guess," I say.

12:30 PM
AMY

I find myself alone in a small room behind a metal desk buried in papers and computer monitors. Cables snake from the back of their screens around the desk like roots holding an old tree in place. A large man in a bulging security uniform has his cellphone to his ear as he eyes me suspiciously from across the desk. He jots something down on a notepad and grunts a few times in acknowledgement. He finally ends the call and slaps the phone down on a stack of papers. He glares at me for a few long moments before saying a word. My heartbeat is pounding behind my eardrums and I think I may be on the verge of fainting. I rattle off a dozen quick prayers and try to look unfazed.

"What's your name?" the man finally asks, crossing his arms and leaning his elbows on the edge of the table.

"Amy," I say, my voice a feeble squeak. He writes this down on his pad and my heart thuds even harder. Any minute now and I'll be on the floor.

"Last name?"

"Harding," I say. He jots this down too. I expect two police officers to burst from the doors any second to haul me away in handcuffs.

"This your first time to Grand Avenue Plaza?" he asks, pen at the ready.

"No sir, I've been before."

"Can you remember the last time? What day was it?"

"I… I don't really remember. Maybe a couple of weeks ago?" I say.

"You come alone?"

"No."

"Who were you with?"

"A friend."

"Your friend have a name?" he asks, sounding irritated.

"Sorry, yes. Chelsea. Chelsea Novak." He writes this down too, and I feel like I've just betrayed her.

"Either of you have records?"

"Excuse me?" I ask softly.

"Rap sheets. Criminal records."

"No sir," I say.

"How well do you know your friend?"

"Well enough. What's this about?" The man studies me with narrowed eyes for a few moments before replying.

"We had a vendor complain today. Said he's seen you two at the mall on several occasions, that you usually sit on a bench nearby, browse around in a few stores, and then leave. Their store has had a history of missing merchandise and he put the pieces together." My mouth is open wide but there are no words. I'm too shocked to even think of a reply.

"Do I really look like a shoplifter?" I gasp. He responds with a scoff.

"You think all shoplifters look the same? I've seen all types and all ages, lady. Some are even rich. Just do it for the kicks."

"Well that is not me, and it's not my friend, either!" I say, feeling my body begin to go hot.

"You mind if I search your purse, then?" he asks with a cocky look.

I shrug, tossing my bag onto the desk. He glances into it cautiously, as if he might find a grenade. He pulls a pen from his pocket and uses it to sift through the contents. It's a full minute before he slides the purse back to me.

"Satisfied?" I snap.

"You got lucky," he says with a shrug.

"What does *that* mean?"

"We got you before you got your goods today."

"Excuse me?"

"Look, lady, I have no way to prove anything, but we both know you and your friend aren't just window shopping." This shuts me up, and I hate how he misunderstands the guilty look on my face.

"I... I... Can't two people just hang out at the mall anymore?" I say weakly.

"Sure, but not here. Next time you two want to hang out, I suggest you do it somewhere else. You're not welcome here anymore, and neither is your friend. I catch you here again and I'll file a formal complaint with the police. You got me?"

With nothing to say, I nod and rise slowly from my chair. A security guard escorts me down a back hall and through an exit to the parking lot, where Chelsea waits. Her arms are crossed but she seems collected. We walk silently to her car and drive a few blocks before saying anything.

"That was really scary," I finally say, my voice shaking.

"It was a close call," Chelsea says, her voice low and serious. "But it could've been a lot worse."

"Why are people so suspicious of everyone these days?" I ask.

"It's to be expected. It's the end of the end. No one knows how to act, or who to trust."

"I hate this world," I say, leaning back against the headrest and staring out the window.

"You and me both, hon," Chelsea says.

"So what do we do now?" I ask.

"We'll just have to find someplace else to go. And preferably someplace with good pretzels."

WEDNESDAY, DECEMBER 23

1:49 PM
LUKE

Only a year ago, I'd drive by this park to the sounds of children and the cheerful squeals of seesaws and merry-go-rounds. All that's gone now, replaced by the dismal caw and cackle of ravens picking at a heap of garbage and the rattle of wind through skeletal trees. Ever since the city cut spending on the parks department to boost law enforcement, places like these have become breeding grounds for all sorts of riffraff. Long gone are the children and women and yapping terriers. Welcome to the graveyard of innocence.

It's been two weeks since I last spoke with Agent Meade, and I'm here to update him on my findings. Truth be told, there's little to say. I did what I could that night at the Novaks' but didn't come up with anything out of the ordinary. I thought of trying to arrange another meeting with them but felt it'd seem suspicious, especially given my initial reluctance to even be around them. I have to take it slow if I expect to learn anything, and the FBI should understand that, shouldn't they? I flip my collar to shield myself from an icy breeze and hear a familiar voice.

"How are things, Luke?" Agent Meade says as he eases down next to me on the bench. He takes a deep breath, apparently not minding the exposed pile of trash lying just a few yards from us. "Fine, just fine," I mumble.

"Well, that's good. And the wife? How's Amy doing?"

"Can we skip all this, Meade? I know you don't care about me or my family."

"Don't care? You've got it all backwards, Luke. I care very much about you and Amy. It's my job to care."

I shake my head and clench my teeth. "Whatever, man."

"Have you forgotten our agreement, Luke?"

"No, of course not."

"Well that's good. Because the future of your family kind of depends on it."

"How can you be so sure? I know my wife. She'd believe me if I told her the truth. Pictures or not."

Meade snickers with the shake of his head. "Harding, with pictures like I've got, I could wreck a perfect marriage. Now, what do you have for me?"

I take a deep breath and speak slowly. "She's studying the Bible with some Witnesses named Chelsea and Walter Novak."

"Yeah, we know that much. What else?"

I shrug. "Walter's a repairman, Chelsea sells antiques."

"And?"

"That's all they said. It's only been two weeks, Meade. We talked once."

"You have to do better than that, Harding. Give me something to work with."

"They're cautious. They don't tell anything to just anyone. And it probably doesn't help that I'm a cop. They've got their secrets."

"Oh?"

"Yeah, like their son. I get the feeling they're estranged somehow. I don't know, something just seems... *off*. When I tried to bring it up in conversation, they changed the subject."

"Don't bother with him. He's a dead end," Mead says flatly with a wave of his hand.

"Oh?"

"Kid's a dropout, hangs with a bunch of his friends in Almead. He doesn't know a thing."

"You know him?"

"Sure, we tracked him down weeks ago. He's had run-ins with the law. Name's Jesse. You got anything else on the parents? Did they mention any other names at all? Or discuss their organization?" I think for a few minutes. There were some names mentioned, but nothing is coming to mind. I shake my head.

"What about their meetings?"

"Meetings?"

"Yeah. We think they've been having illegal meetings in their homes, but we don't have any proof."

I think back to a few months ago, when Amy first revealed that she'd been studying with the Witnesses. She had briefly mentioned meetings before I stopped her, not wanting to get myself involved. Now I wish I'd let her talk. Or do I? As Meade pries me for information, I find myself hesitant to comply. Walter and Chelsea don't seem like bad people, and I can't understand what threat they could possibly pose to the government at this point.

"Witnesses aren't like the other churchgoers, Luke. They're smart. Resourceful. They know how to stay under the radar. We track their messages and phone calls and come up with nothing. That's one thing we want to know: Who's training them? They're not like the others. These people operate like professionals."

"You track all that?"

"Of course we do. Easier than it's ever been. We've got *carte blanche* on surveillance. Makes the Patriot Act look like child's play."

I feel a chill go up my spine as a sharp December wind snaps through the trees. I jam my hands in my pockets and pull my jacket in tighter.

"You really think the Witnesses are dangerous?" I ask.

"If I had to guess, I'd say these people are planning something. Maybe a terrorist attack. We want to know about this, too, of course. And where their intel is coming from. It seems they were prepared for the Liberation Act even before it went into affect. They sold a bunch of properties, started dividing some of their assets. We think they went underground months before congress passed the bill. Now you tell me, how is that possible?"

"Maybe they have people on the inside," I mutter.

"Maybe, but the Witnesses say they aren't political. In some countries they'd rather get tossed into prison than vote."

"You said before that there are about a million Witnesses in the country, right?" I ask.

"We're not sure. That's another one of our big questions. According to their own public records, it was around a million before last year. But that could be an exaggerated number. A lot of churches used to do that. They'd count ex-members and spouses; some even counted the deceased. On the other hand, it could also be a low-ball figure. If they were as prepared as we think, they may have been leaking false numbers for years."

"Oh," I say quietly. I find it hard to believe that Amy's friends belong to the kind of organization that Agent Meade is describing, but I admit that I know very little about any of it.

"Look, Harding, you need to pick up the pace on this," Meade says impatiently as he rifles through his jacket. He pulls out a small plastic device and hands it over to me.

"What's this?" I ask.

"It's a wireless remote microphone. We call them WIRMs. It's got a mini USB connector on the side." Meade points to the port and then presses a small rectangular ridge with his fingernail. "Press here to start recording. It can hold about eight hours of audio. Clip it under your lapel and it'll pick up whatever's happening around you."

"You want me to record my conversations with them?"

"Yes, Luke," Meade says irritably as he brushes something from his coat and stands.

"But it's not like we see each other that often," I protest.

"Then figure out a way to see each other more."

"How am I supposed to do that?"

"I don't know, maybe ask them if they'll study the Bible with you. We're done here for now." Meade grabs his bag in his gloved hand and starts off for the path. He stops a few paces in and turns back to me with a stern look.

"And Luke," he says, "don't disappoint me next time. I don't like going away empty handed. Oh, and Merry Christmas."

Meade walks away, sending the ravens into a noisy panic of flight.

THURSDAY, DECEMBER 24

AMY
9:41 PM

Luke cycles through channels distractedly as I browse the latest downloads on the new encrypted JW Library app. Although our website has finally been blocked, mirror sites have sprung up all over the web, and the updated app can automatically connect to the one with the least traffic.

I grab the newest *Watchtower* and *Awake!*, both of which feature cover articles on the end of the world. The Watchtower features an especially sobering picture of a submerged city with buildings toppling in flames as people scramble atop vehicles and billboards. Years ago this might've seemed overboard, but these days it could be the front page of the morning newspaper.

Luke finally settles on a late night talk. A deadpan comedian is doing a monologue on the cow flu epidemic. His jokes elicit a few scattered laughs, but even that jaded studio audience seems to find his comedy in poor taste. The death toll in Asia is somewhere around 20,000 and the casualties are gradually climbing here in the States. Yesterday the FAA started grounding some international flights, but it all seems like too little too late. Between this latest virus and the Ebola-N outbreak last year, it's a wonder there's any air traffic at all.

The comedian's bit finishes without so much as a chuckle from my husband. Luke's been very quiet lately. Distant. Distracted. I chalk it up to work pressure. As the economy continues to spiral and unemployment reaches new heights, crime just keeps worsening. Looting and armed robbery don't even make headlines. My only way of knowing it's happening at all are the sudden business closings all over town. Convenience stores are open one day only to be abandoned the next, their windowpanes rimmed with jagged glass teeth, their insides littered with garbage, as if they've been hit by small tornadoes in the dead of night.

There are more police cars patrolling the streets than ever before, many of them driven by frightening faces I've never seen. Luke, fortunately, spends most of his time at his desk, and is now tasked with overseeing the newcomers. He complains often about the stress of his promotion, but frankly I think he's happy to have the job. He'd never admit it, but he's scared. He doesn't want to be out patrolling anymore.

I flip through the *Watchtower* I've just downloaded. A small box on one of the pages catches my eye. It's entitled *Do You Have a Go Bag?* and includes a list of suggested items to include in an emergency evacuation pack. Some of the things are obvious: a waterproof flashlight, a tent, batteries, matches, water purifying tablets, sleeping bags, bottled water. Others–a laser pointer (green), N95 respirator dust masks, a 50-ft nylon rope–I wouldn't have thought of. My pulse quickens a bit as my eyes scan the list. I can't help but think of a movie Chelsea and I watched recently on our website, the one where the Christians in the first century fled to the mountains as the Roman armies withdrew from Jerusalem. *Will that be us?*

I glance at my husband, who's clearly bored with the talk show. The audience is rolling with laughter as the host and his comic guest throw cream pies at each other. Distractions, all of it, I realize. It's all been manufactured to keep people from seeing the real urgency of the times. I'm suddenly anxious. I wonder how much time we have left. How much time Luke has. He glances over to me now, catching my gaze before I can look away.

"What?" he asks, flipping off the television.

"Nothing, babe," I mumble. He leans his head back against the couch and stares at the ceiling.

"What are you working on over there?" he asks.

"Just reading some magazines," I say. Luke is silent. "It's about disaster preparedness," I add, hoping to pique his interest.

"Oh? What's it say?"

"There's a list here for an emergency bag. I was just wondering if we already had most of this stuff."

Luke scoots across the couch and leans over to squint at my screen. He nods as he scans the list.

"Not bad. And no, we don't have half the stuff on this list," he finally says.

"What do you think? Should we check online?" I ask. Luke shrugs.

"It's up to you, babe. But that list is missing one thing I'd never leave home without."

"What's that?"

"My sidearm."

I study his expression and can tell he's serious. It's not hard to see things from his perspective. According to a recent news article I read, there are enough guns in this country to arm half its citizens (including children). It's a scary thought. I glance over to the desk where Luke keeps his gun and feel goosebumps wash over me.

"So is this the kind of thing you study at your meetings?"

"Our meetings?" I ask.

"Yeah. You mentioned them before, that you were having meetings, but doing it safely…"

"I thought you didn't want to know about any of that," I say warily.

"I'm not asking for details, I'm just curious, is all."

"Why?"

"Amy, I'm gone most of the day. When I walk out that door I have no idea what's going on here, what's going on with you."

"You think we have meetings *here*?"

"No, I don't. I mean, I hope not. That could get me in a lot of trouble."

"Well, we're not. I'd never do anything like that without asking you first."

"Yeah, well, that's good to hear," Luke says tiredly. I could kick myself for being so defensive with him, but I find his sudden interest unsettling and I'm unsure how to react.

"I'm sorry," I say softly, rubbing Luke's hand. "I didn't mean it. The laws have become so strict recently, and we've had to be cautious."

Luke looks my way with a blank stare and finishes off the last of his beer. "There's just so much I don't know about this life of yours, Amy," he says with a sigh.

"What do you want to know? I'll tell you whatever I can."

"Do the Witnesses believe in the end of days?"

"Um… Can you be more specific?" I say, trying to gather my thoughts. Am I actually hearing things correctly? Is Luke actually taking an interest in the truth?

"You know, like the rapture or whatever. Good people get taken up to heaven, the bad ones go to hell. That kind of thing."

"No, we don't believe in the rapture. And we don't believe in hell. And as for heaven, not all good people go there. The Bible says that only a set number of people get to go to heaven, and that number is 144,000. That number appears in the Bible a few times in Revelation, I believe, and we know it's not just a symbolic number because–"

Luke shakes his head and raises his eyebrows. I've messed it up. I bite my lip and give it another try.

"Sorry. No, not everyone gets into heaven. But the Witnesses do believe we're living in the end. I don't think we call it the end of days, though..."

Luke's brow is furled as he mulls this over. I wait patiently, but my insides are bubbling over with things to say. Scriptures I want to point to. A dozen articles and chapters in books to lay it all out for him to see. I desperately wish Chelsea and Walter could somehow materialize out of thin air. They'd know what to do, what to say. They'd keep their cool. Actually, they'd probably just ask a question.

"What do you think?" I attempt.

"About?"

"About the state of the world? What do you think will come next?"

Luke takes a deep breath and picks at a loose thread on our couch with a fingernail. "I don't know. Doesn't seem to be getting better."

My chest aches and I realize I'm holding my breath. I've been waiting for a long time for this opportunity and it's all I can do to not throw my arms around his neck and start kissing him.

"You know, Luke... What's happening around the world, all this stuff with governments versus religion... It was foretold in the Bible. Very specifically."

Luke's face is blank as he looks into my eyes. "Foretold?"

"A long time ago. The Bible said that world governments would suddenly attack false religion and strip it of its wealth and position. We've known this for a long time..." I say.

"What do you mean, you've *known*?" Luke asks.

"That governments would turn against religion. The Witnesses have been preaching it for years."

"So the Witnesses were prepared, then," Luke says with a strange look.

"Yeah," I say.

"How did they prepare?"

"Well, we did our best to strengthen our faith in God. We trusted that the direction would come at the right time, and that we would be protected."

"Protected? How?"

"By our organization, by the brothers. They've always been there to give us the right direction at the right time."

"Like what? What kind of direction?"

The questioning unnerves me again. It's as if Luke is prying for information out of more than just a desire to satisfy his curiosity. Am I just being paranoid?

"Maybe you should talk to Walter about some of this," I finally say. I expect Luke to shoo the suggestion away, but instead it seems to intrigue him.

"Yeah, maybe. I could go for that," he says.

SATURDAY, DECEMBER 26

LUKE
6:29 PM

    I got my in. It wasn't all that hard, either. Amy was the one to bring it up, and all I had to do was nod my head in the right places and seem interested. She and Chelsea had everything planned within a day, and now here we are, driving down the boulevard to the Novaks' bungalow. I catch Amy trying to hide the smile that keeps creeping onto her face from the corner of my eye. I know she must have high hopes for me, that I've come to see the world through her eyes, and that I'm ready to give her religion a chance. It doesn't feel good stringing her along like this, but what choice do I have? I'm doing this for *us*.

    We don't talk much in the car, a few scattered comments about the weather and the traffic. It snowed a couple of days ago and just about threw the city into a panic. We're too far south to ever get serious snow, but these last two years have brought freakish weather. The temperature drops and spikes as it pleases and no one knows what to expect anymore. Most of the snow has begun melting and collecting on the dirty lanes' shoulders like clumps of wet coal. I hear the hiss of our tires as we slip onto a side road and gun it up the hill.

    I've got the recording device clipped under my jacket's collar. What did Meade call it again, a *WIRM*? I'm not sure how much it'll actually be able to pick up, but I'm not overly concerned. I have no desire to make Meade's job any easier. Hey, maybe if I fail enough times he'll just give up and forget about me. Or, we could win the lottery.

    We finally get to the house. It's a little before seven and we get the same warm welcome from Walter and his wife. We're ushered into the dining room and discover another elaborate spread. It's the one thing I've been looking forward to all day. When it comes to cooking, I've learned that Chelsea doesn't disappoint.

    The evening goes on more or less as it did last time. The meal is eaten mostly in silence. You don't ruin good food like this with too much conversation. The three of them discuss a thing or two, but I sense some restraint, like they're trying not to annoy me with prattle I don't understand.

"So, Luke," Walter finally says from across the table. The girls have gathered our plates and begun cleaning the kitchen. "Amy said that you had some things you wanted to ask."

If only he knew. A dozen questions come to mind. *Where are their meetings held? Who's in charge? Where do their orders come from? How are they communicating?* I can't ask any of this, of course. I'm the concerned husband, I remind myself. It's something Walter will relate to, something that won't seem out of place.

"Yeah, Amy said something about being prepared for disasters," I say. Walter nods, waiting for the question. "I'm curious what you two have done to prepare. And what, exactly, you're preparing for."

"Oh, I see. Well, yes, Chelsea and I try to be prepared in case of emergencies. We have a couple of bags always at the ready in case we have to evacuate."

"Evacuate?" I wonder aloud. Geographically speaking, we live in one of the safer parts of the U.S. No fault lines, no coastal areas prone to flooding or hurricanes, too heavily wooded for tornadoes.

"Sure. We're not just thinking of being prepared for natural disasters. Man-made disasters are just as common."

"Like?" I ask dubiously.

"Suppose a power plant has an incident. Maybe there's a fire. Or maybe something happens to the highways, blocking off our food supply for a few days."

"And there's been lots of looting on the news," Chelsea chimes in.

"Ok, so you're survivalists," I say, imagining a propane generator tucked away somewhere and a closet full of guns and ammo. But Walter only smiles at me and shrugs the assumption away.

"No, nothing like that, Luke. Our ultimate trust is placed in our God, Jehovah. We have confidence that he can protect us better than we ourselves."

"Isn't that a contradiction, though? You say you trust in God, but you've stocked up on supplies."

"We're not really *stocked up*. We've got enough to last us a few days in case of an emergency, especially in the event that we'll suddenly have to leave everything behind."

"And how likely do you think that is? That you'll have to leave it all behind?"

Walter shrugs again. "Who knows? But we believe that *the shrewd one sees the danger and conceals himself.*" Walter says this in a way that makes me think he might be quoting from something, but says nothing to explain.

"So is this common, then? Do most Witnesses prepare for worst-case scenarios?" My question elicits a frown as Walter leans back and takes a deep breath.

"Do you really think it's a worst-case scenario, Luke? Or do you think that the time we're living in is prone to upheavals?"

"I'd like to think I'm making a difference with all those hours I put into this community," I say defensively. The words sound hostile but I lack the emotions to back them up. I can't disagree with Walter and he probably knows it.

"I'm not trivializing the work you do, Luke. As I said once before, I'm grateful for law enforcement. If it weren't for people like you, I have no doubt that things would be much worse. Still, you must admit that things are worsening, and not just here in Haliford. The whole world feels it. When we first moved into this house in the '80s, we could leave our back door unlocked. We knew our neighbors. We felt safe. Crime was always something that was happening on the *other side of town*. Thirty years later, we've got cages on our windows and motion sensors all over the property. At night, we barely feel safe leaving the house to get something from our car in the driveway. From where I'm standing, we're already living in a kind of worst-case scenario."

I think to the apartment Amy and I have been renting since shortly before we were married. It's a good two notches below this neighborhood in terms of desirable real estate, with gunshots and ambulances a regular part of the background noise. The lowlifes seem to steer clear of me somewhat because of the uniform, but even that won't protect me forever, not with the level of crazy that people are climbing to these days.

"The Witnesses are not paranoid, but we are prepared. We're taught to be," Walter says.

"Taught by whom?"

"Taught by the Bible."

"The Bible tells you to prepare a bag with nylon rope and dust masks?" I say, laying it on thick.

"The Bible encourages us to keep an eye on the times. It gives some clear signs to look for to know what period we're living in."

"So it tells you when you have to grab your stuff and run away from your house?" I say, my tone softened.

"Actually, there are Biblical accounts that describe exactly that. But if and when those pertain to our circumstances, we will have to wait and see. We don't spend too much time worrying about it."

"Well, that's good, because in the case of the manmade disasters you mentioned, I doubt that grabbing a bag with some bottled water and canned goods and running away would be safer than just staying put in your own home. People panic easy. It would be chaos outside."

"Interesting. So it sounds like you've given this scenario some thought, too," Walter says.

"It's part of *our* training. We study mob psychology in the academy, what happens when society starts breaking down and people go nuts. It's pretty scary how fast things can go to pot." Walter is nodding thoughtfully but says nothing.

"Still, whatever happens, it'll all come down to firepower. If you want to talk worst-case scenarios, I say invest in a well-stocked gun locker with plenty of ammo. Food won't do you a lick of good if you can't protect it from thieves." I watch Walter's reaction carefully, seeing if he'll take the bait. He is military, after all. He's probably been trained on more weapons than I can identify, and it'd be foolish for him to not keep a few around for safety's sake.

"I used to think the same thing," he says finally, glancing down at the back of his hands. He runs a finger along a groove in the wood grain. "The problem with weapons is, they can be used *against* you just as well as they can be used *by* you. It all depends on whose finger gets to the trigger first. And in a world where so many people have guns, not having one makes you much less of a target."

"So you're saying you've got nothing stashed away in this place somewhere?" I ask a little impatiently.

Walter shakes his head. "I haven't owned a gun in years. Haven't needed one."

"But you were just talking about how bad things are getting, how dangerous people are becoming. How can you leave it all up to chance?"

"I'm not leaving it up to chance. But a gun is no guarantee either."

"Ok, fine. Let's say there's one of these man-made disasters. Chaos everywhere. People start freaking out, looting each other's homes, setting things on fire, the works. Cops don't show up for their patrols. Everything's insane. You're saying you wouldn't want a gun at your side?"

"No, I wouldn't. Let's analyze that scenario you've just described. So you've got looters going around breaking into shops and stores and stealing what they can. Eventually that runs out. So where do they end up? They go door to door. And it's not just one or two people. In actual cases of societal breakdown, gangs form. That means when the people come knocking they come in groups; they're more effective that way. And you can bet *they're* armed. So they find you in your home, and it's just you and your gun. Maybe you shoot and wound one or two of them, but you can bet they'll return fire. And now they're angry; they won't stop 'till you're dead. So, how much safer did that gun make you?"

"So what are you saying, then? Just let them come in and take everything?"

"Absolutely. I would lock myself in a closet with my wife and let them ransack the place. They can have whatever they want. I don't care. My life and Chelsea's is all that matters."

Chelsea brushes up past us in her apron with a round platter topped with a chocolate cake lathered in pink icing. Despite being stuffed from the meal, my mouth is watering again.

"Sorry to interrupt your conversation, boys. Sounds pretty heavy," she says, setting the cake onto the table and licking a bit of icing that's smudged into the back of her knuckle. Walter thanks her and she leans in to kiss him on the forehead. She takes a moment to glance at the two of us before fishing a board game out of a cabinet drawer and heading into the sitting room with my wife.

We're quiet for a few minutes as we savor the cake. "You know, you remind me a lot of myself, Luke," Walter says without looking up from his plate. "Back when I was in the Air Force, I thought I could rely on myself for everything. That was part of our training, really. Learning to look out for number one. But as I got older, I learned that that kind of thinking just isn't practical or realistic. We're just not big enough to meet certain problems we face. We have to rely on something bigger than ourselves."

"God. Right?" I say.

"I take it you don't believe he exists, do you, Luke?"

"I don't really think about it. Never really had a need to. Never saw the point. Maybe one day I'll change my mind."

"I know I did."

"Yeah, I can see that."

"You want to know why?"

I shrug. "Sure."

MONDAY, JANUARY 11

10:12 AM
AMY

The tang of yeast hangs in the air of the deli as I warm my hands on a Styrofoam cup. The heaters in here are cranked up to full blast but the cold gusting through the front doors with the entrance and exit of each customer effectively negates it. Chelsea sits next to me in the booth, skimming over the latest news on a mirror site of JW.org. Over a hundred counties have now officially banned the activities of our organization, though in some of these places our website continues to function normally. The Great Tribulation is in full swing.

We've been sitting here nibbling on pretzels and sipping coffee waiting for Melissa, the woman we met at the mall a few weeks ago. I'd figured it was a lost cause after we were banned from Grand Avenue Plaza, but Chelsea managed to find this deli and somehow persuaded the woman to come out and meet us.

Melissa finally stumbles through the front door at ten thirty. She peels off her down jacket and gloves and stuffs them into the bench across from us in the booth and plops down beside them. Her cheeks and nose are bright red from the icy weather outside, but I also note the dark blue discs under her eyes, which I attribute to the fact that she's raising three boys.

Chelsea orders her a latte and a pretzel and sets them in front of Melissa, who flashes the older woman a look of gratitude. We make small talk for a few minutes. We commiserate about the cold and the traffic and the flu.

"So how were your holidays? Were your kids happy with the gifts?" Chelsea asks. Melissa pauses for a moment before tearing a bit of pretzel off and sticking it into her mouth.

"Oh, I suppose so. The youngest one for sure. He was so excited about the hoverboard that he took it outside that morning and rode it down the road. I guess he hit a patch of ice, because he came home with a sprained wrist. We spent the rest of Christmas morning at the clinic getting him fitted for a brace."

"Oh, poor kid," I say. Melissa shoots me a look, as if she's surprised to learn that I can speak. Chelsea encouraged me earlier to try to be more a part of their conversation, but the result of this first attempt isn't encouraging.

"Boys will be boys," Chelsea says with an easy laugh. "My son was just the same. For a while it seemed like we were at the hospital every other week for casts or stitches or slings."

"Oh, you have a son?"

"Yeah. He's grown now, of course."

"Oh, I see. Sorry, I kind of figured..." Melissa gives Chelsea an embarrassed look and glances back and forth between the two of us. My face goes red with the realization of what she was going to say.

"Oh, no, we're just friends," Chelsea says, coolly as ever.

"Right, of course. No, I'm sorry. I mean, not sorry, it's nothing to be ashamed of if you guys were, you know... But whatever," Melissa says with a dismissive shake of her head. She gulps down a bit of her latte and takes a long stare out the window as we wait for the awkwardness to pass.

"So, are your boys still on winter break?" Chelsea asks.

"No, and thank goodness for that. Don't get me wrong; I love my kids, but after two weeks having them lounging around the house playing video games, it gets old. I finally have the place to myself again."

"Spoken like a true mother." Chelsea smiles.

"So how were your holidays then? You have a big family thing?" asks Melissa.

"Actually, no. My husband and I don't celebrate Christmas. But we did get to spend some time together since his work was so slow that weekend. It was nice to have the quiet time."

"No Christmas, huh? That must be nice, not having to worry about holiday shopping," the woman says wistfully.

"It is. I've kind of always felt that the holiday season brings people more stress than joy. What's supposed to be a happy time ends up being a burden, especially financially."

"Oh, absolutely. You know, I actually have friends that took out a loan from a bank just to buy gifts for their kids this season. I told them not to do it, that the kids would just have to understand, but they insisted. I guess they couldn't deal with the pressure they'd face from the rest of their family if the kids went empty-handed. And with the interest rates as high as they are! Can you imagine?"

"Wow, that's really sad," I say, and this time Melissa's look tells me she agrees.

"I've always thought that gifts should be given out of joy," Chelsea says, and Melissa nods. "It reminds me of something I read recently." Chelsea's voice trails off as she fishes her iPad from her purse and taps the JW Library app. She navigates to 2 Corinthians 9:7 and highlights a section of the verse with a finger before sliding the tablet across the table. Melissa leans over and reads the words quietly.

"Is this the Bible?" she asks, her expression slightly shifting.

"Yeah. I like this verse because I think it really captures the essence of what gift giving should be about. Giving freely when we want and not when others expect us to. I think of myself here. If it was me, and I was waiting all year for a particular day because I knew my husband was supposed to give me something special, and when the day rolls around all he's gotten me are some flowers, I'd be disappointed. Maybe even a little angry. But if, one day when I wasn't expecting it, he bought me those same flowers, it'd put a smile on my face. That's the beauty of giving without compulsion."

"Makes sense. But try telling that to three teenage boys," Melissa says.

"Oh, I can only imagine."

"So," Melissa says, lowering her voice as she looks between the two of us. "You're Christian?"

"I like to live by the principles here in the Bible," Chelsea says nonchalantly. "What about you, Melissa? Do you have a faith?"

Melissa shrugs and gazes into her coffee. "I dunno. Used to like going to church when I was a kid, always thought about returning one day, but looks like that opportunity is gone now."

"What do you mean?" I ask.

"What, you haven't seen the news in the last six months? Churches are all but extinct."

"The Bible isn't," Chelsea says.

"Not yet, but maybe one day it will be. Everything's changing so quickly in this country. These riots, religious bans. It's like we're living through one of those dystopian novels. What was it, *1984*? Anyways, I don't really know anything about the Bible. It's been so long since I went to church. And plus, I don't even know if I believe in God."

"You sound like me when I was your age," Chelsea says.

"Oh?"

"When I was younger, I always sort of had this feeling, this inkling that God ought to exist, but I had no proof. I didn't think anyone did. I wasn't particularly interested in the Bible or religion."

"But you read the Bible now."

"I do. Eventually I met someone who really understood it, and used it to explain a lot of interesting questions for me. I realized I had lots of misconceptions about it, and eventually I came to see it as something very different from what I'd first thought."

"So, how do you see it now?"

"I really believe it's the inspired word of God."

Melissa's eyes narrow slightly as she leans back in the booth and closes her eyes. I hold my breath as I wait for her next words.

"You two are Jehovah Witnesses, aren't you?" she finally says.

"Yes," Chelsea says calmly.

"I recognized that Bible app you just used. Been seeing that logo everywhere with that video everyone's talking about. What's it called?"

"*A Warning Message*?" I say hopefully.

"Yeah, that's the one."

"And? What did you think?"

"You people have some nerve, posting stuff like that. It's fear mongering," the woman says angrily. My heart sinks. "My littlest one saw it and couldn't sleep that night. Kept saying something about God and Armageddon."

"I can understand how you feel, but the fact is–"

"The fact is that we're done here. I have no idea why you people dragged me out here, but I want no part of this," Melissa says, gathering her items quickly into her arms and pushing out the front door, leaving her coffee and half eaten pretzel.

LUKE
10:20 AM

It's been three days since I stuck the WIRM in a P.O. box as instructed. Agent Meade called me this morning; he wants to meet again. It's too cold to be outside, so I sit in my car in a parking lot and wait. The strip mall attached to it is all but abandoned; half the shops have succumbed to either looters or the economy and shelled up their windows with plywood. A homeless man throws an empty beer can at my car as he wheels his shopping cart past. He yells something, too, but I can't make out a word of it with my heater going at full blast. It seems like there are more homeless on the streets every day and I feel for them, especially with this harsh winter weather.

I've had a lot on my mind ever since that last dinner at Walter and Chelsea's. I hadn't been prepared for Walter's scientific explanation for his belief in a God. The evidence he presented left me with even more questions. I'd never really understood evolution when I was in college, and the way Walter dissected and refuted it made me realize there was a whole lot left unsaid in those textbooks. According to Walter, there's even more evidence for the existence of God to be found in the Bible itself. Though I'm skeptical, I wonder why we weren't taught any of this in Sunday school.

Half an hour passes before I finally spot a black SUV slithering into the spot beside me. Meade rolls down his window and gestures for me to get in. I can tell from a glance he's not happy about what he heard on the recording device. I cling for a moment to the hope that maybe it failed completely, but Meade's next words indicate otherwise.

"What was this?" he says with a sneer as he flicks the WIRM at me. It ricochets from the window before disappearing somewhere beneath the seats. "I thought we were clear last time that I needed something *solid* to work with. I end up sitting through three hours of you two talking about what, *natural disasters* and *God*? Are you playing games with me, Harding?"

"Look, I'm sorry. The opportunity didn't come up. I tried, but we didn't get around to it."

"*Didn't get around to it?* You kidding me? Three hours and you're telling me you couldn't think of something?"

"I tried asking my wife about their meetings. It's not on the recording. She gave me nothing, and said I should talk to Walter. These people are careful, Meade. They probably know your people are onto them."

"And how would they know that?"

"They're smart. They've been trained."

"We *know* they've been trained, Luke. It's the *somehow* that we sent you to investigate. And so far you're zero for two. I've got a hole burning in my pocket where the evidence we have against you is just waiting. I'm getting tired of sitting on my hands."

I've heard this rhetoric before, and each time it's lost a bit of its sting. Maybe Meade senses he's losing leverage.

"So what happens, then? If I give you the info you're looking for, what do you do with it?"

"Not my job, Harding. I'm just here to get intel."

"And you're the only one on this? For an operation that seems so important, you must have other sources."

Meade gives me a long look before scowling. "Stop worrying about my job and focus on yours."

The homeless man from the parking lot hobbles our way, his wobbling cart towed in his wake. Meade lets him get within a few feet before leaning into his horn. Startled, the man falls over, toppling the cart and sending his few possessions scattering along the macadam. Meade chuckles, clearly pleased with himself.

"The Witnesses aren't bad people, you know," I mutter. "I don't see why you're targeting them."

"Jehovah's Witnesses are like all the rest, Luke. Put them under a little pressure and they'll either give in or turn against you. It's a basic fight or flight response."

"Well then, there you have it. They've chosen flight. Why not just let them be?"

"Because we're not the weak country we used to be, making laws and then not enforcing them, or giving in when the people have their say. We're fighting the banks, for once, going after corporate corruption like never before. This is a new America, Luke, and you should be proud to be a part of it. The government has finally got the bite to match the bark, and we're it. We are securing a future that our children will feel safe growing up in."

I silently let the words wash over me as I gaze out at the empty parking lot and darkened store windows. The homeless man reloads his cart with tarps and tattered blankets and glares at us. Is this the new America Meade is talking about?

"I don't have kids," I finally mumble.

"Your loss. I have three. And I expect my government to take action to protect them."

"And you really think removing religion is the way to do that?"

"Of course *you* don't, Luke. But I've seen things that would change your mind. I wasn't always an FBI agent. I served my country overseas. Had a chance to get a close-up view of what religion does to people. Muslims, Jews, Christians, they're all the same. Killing in the name of their gods. Wreaking havoc for their so-called *faiths*. I thought what I was seeing was just in the Middle East, that for some reason we'd found a way to reconcile our differences here in America. Then I came home and woke up."

"You mean terrorism?"

"Yes, but not the kind you're thinking of: jihadists in masks running around with AK-47s and taking hostages. It's terrorism on all levels. Christians burning crosses in the name of Christ. Black ministers stoking the fires of racial hatred. Baptists protesting at gay funerals and weddings. Terrorism has many faces. And I'm sick of it."

"Ok," I relent, "But if you take religion away, something will just come up in its place. People will always fight about something."

"No, Luke, you're wrong. Not like religion. Nothing has the power to warp minds and divide communities like religious brainwashing. In all the history of man, nothing has caused more war and suffering. It's time for a new era."

"And you're going to change it? By locking people up and closing churches?"

"You seem to think I'm the only one on this crusade. If only you knew how many senators, politicians, intellectuals, ex-Presidents–"

"But the presidents were all churchgoers themselves," I blurt out. Meade shakes his head and grins, but he seems to simmer from within.

"In the past, maybe. Recently, it's just been something said to gain support at the ballots. Truth be told, most are as secular as myself. Trust me when I say that in ten years, all the churches will be gone."

Ten years. It's difficult to imagine, but I have no reason to doubt him, judging by the swiftness of the Liberation Act and how it's upended the entire religious spectrum in just a few months.

"So what happens to the couple, then–Walter and Chelsea? After I get you the info you're after, where do they end up?"

"Why do you care?" Meade snivels.

"They're friends of my wife. It won't be easy for her if something happens to them."

"They'll be booked, spend a little time in jail. It'll be on their record, then we let 'em go, under one condition."

"What's that?"

"That they renounce their religious beliefs."

"That's it?"

"That's it. Otherwise we'll keep them till they do. In any case, they're not the big fish we're after. We want to know how they're connected. Obviously, the Witnesses are still functioning as an organization, and that's something we won't tolerate."

"Don't they have a headquarters or something?"

"Of course they do. We shut that down weeks ago. There's no one there now, just a bunch of empty offices and factories. But apparently, they're still operating, and we need to know how. This has become a top priority of national security."

"Ok, I'll look into it," I finally accede.

"You'd better. This is your last chance, Harding."

I nod, frowning.

"And by the way, don't assume that the worst that will come of your refusal to cooperate is some incriminating photos of you and another woman finding their way to Amy."

I'm shaking my head, not fully understanding.

"Little slow on the draw there, Harding. Not sure how you ever made sergeant. You're about as dumb as they get. The audio recording you gave me. It's evidence."

"Evidence?"

"Against you. If you fail me, we'll make sure your captain gets a copy. Once he finds out you're affiliated with a religious group, well, I'm sure your marriage will only be one of your worries."

Meade leans across my lap and flings my door open. I step out in a daze, his threat still sinking in.

"Now get out of my car and get me that intel," Meade growls as he starts his black SUV and roars away.

AMY
11:37 AM

"I'm sorry," I say quietly as Chelsea and I sit in her idling car, the heater struggling to warm it up.

Chelsea allows a cautious smile. "We gave her a chance. That's all that matters."

"It seemed like things were going so well at first."

"Perhaps there's still time for her to change. Keep her in your prayers."

"Do you think anyone is responding positively to the message?" I ask.

"I have no idea, hon, but I like to hope. Maybe inactive ones will see it and have second thoughts. Maybe new ones will be motivated, too. It's hard to say."

"The end feels so close, Chelsea," I say.

"It is. But until the organization tells us to stop with the preaching, we've got to keep positive."

I think over Chelsea's words as she eases her station wagon from the lot and stops at a red light. Rain from the previous night has frozen with the sudden cold, and the road is covered in frosty patches of ice. Chelsea cranks the heat to full blast and I feel my feet slowly thaw in their boots.

"So, what's the plan for the rest of the day?" I ask, fingers hovering over the vents. The hot air streaming between them feels marvelous.

"Let's head back to my place. I noticed this morning there were a bunch of updates to the news section on the app. I'm curious to see what's happening with our brothers in Hong Kong."

I nod thoughtfully, looking forward to getting out of the cold. The latest broadcast emphasized the need to pray specifically about our brothers undergoing various trials around the world. Chelsea and I have gotten into the habit of checking the site weekly, making notes of all the events, and then praying about them together after our study.

The light turns green and Chelsea presses gently on the gas, letting the wheels find traction as we coast into the intersection. We hear the spin of rubber on ice as the vehicle behind us tries to accelerate too quickly. Chelsea throws a quick glance at her rearview mirror.

"These roads are pretty sketchy today," she says anxiously. "I hope Melissa takes it slow on her way home."

I nod in agreement and glance out my passenger window. There's a green pickup truck speeding in our direction. Through its windshield, I see the driver, a man in a white beard, raise his eyes from the cell phone in his hand and panic. He drops the phone and grips the wheel tightly in both hands as all four tires lock. The bed of the truck fishtails left and right, but the vehicle continues to move our way, skidding across the slick ice.

Chelsea turns to look and the two of us scream. There is no time to react, no time to move out of the way. A powerful explosion of glass erupts from the side of the vehicle as the pickup slams into us and everything goes black.

LUKE
11:39 AM

I sit awhile alone in my car wondering what comes next. The homeless man has found some scraps of cardboard and has made a sort of sleeping bag from them. The temperature is far below anything bearable and I pity him. I remember a fleece blanket in my trunk and drive over. His hands shoot into the air as soon as he spots my car. He's trembling when I open my door, and I can't tell if it's from fear or cold. I grab the blanket and hand it to him.

His face explodes in a web of wrinkles, deep grooves cut into the skin and accentuated by a buildup of dirt and sweat. He thanks me softly with a mouth devoid of teeth. He throws the blanket over his head and burrows beneath the boxes as I drive away.

It's nearing lunch time but I'm not hungry. My mind keeps going back to Meade's threats. I've never felt so helpless. He's got enough leverage against me to completely derail my life. My marriage, my career, my future. It's all in his hands. I have no choice but to comply. I need to get whatever information I can about the Witnesses and extract my wife and I from this situation as soon as possible. There's simply no other way. I don't like the implications this has for Walter and his wife, but I simply have no choice.

I feel my foot go heavy on the pedal and scold myself, forcing myself to slow down. I pull to a stop at a red light and notice a couple of cars skidding a few feet into the crosswalk. The roads blister with black ice; there will be plenty of accidents today. I flip on my console, eager for a distraction. Sure enough, there's been a collision on Raymond Avenue and Vonn Parkway, less than two miles from me. I inform dispatch that I'm on my way and hit the sirens and flashers.

The cars ahead of me wiggle their way onto the shoulder lanes as I slip past, careful not to cause an accident of my own as I risk the intersection against the light. I keep my speed well below the limit and approach the scene.

A green pickup truck spews a charcoal column of smoke from beneath its crumpled hood. The other vehicle, a maroon station wagon, has fared much worse. The right side is smashed and tattered beyond repair, a sea of glass shards splattered about the wreck. The driver of the pickup is on his cellphone babbling incoherently. A thin line of crimson runs down the side of his head but he's oblivious to the injury.

I approach the other vehicle carefully, looking through the shattered window to see if anyone's inside. When I see them, my heart stops.

MONDAY, JANUARY 11

7:03 PM
LUKE

I try to ignore the plastic tubing coming from my wife's head and the patch of hair they had to shave away to insert it. A neck brace keeps her locked in place. Her right leg, which was shattered on the truck's impact, is elevated and cocooned in a cast. A web of pipes and wires stream from her nose, mouth, and hands. It's as if Amy is so frail that she would simply fall apart if it weren't for these machines. My hands ache to reach out and touch her, to somehow pull her back to consciousness, but I'm too afraid of hurting her. I grip the edge of her mattress and lower my head in defeat.

I was twenty-three when Amy and I met. I'd just finished my degree and marriage was the farthest thing from my mind. I was perfectly content with the idea of eternal bachelorhood. But Amy changed all that. We first met at a dinner party of a mutual friend, Hector. Amy was friends with Hector's sister and he was interested in her. Hector had thought the feelings might be mutual, but after just a few minutes of observing the two of them, it was clear that the romance was one-sided. Amy was too sophisticated for him. While the other partygoers discussed the latest trends and music and movies, Amy's mind was elsewhere, and eventually she disappeared completely.

I found her lying on the back deck staring up at the stars. She said she'd always wanted to study astronomy but didn't have a knack for the science behind it. She hoped to visit space someday and see if Earth was really as beautiful as the pictures made it seem. She had so much on her mind. She worried about the GMOs in her food and the way cotton was harvested by children in Bangladesh. She complained about the corruption of megacorporations and the greed of politicians.

I'd never met anyone who cared so much about so much. She had the motivations of an activist but couldn't decide what to do about it. She liked that I wanted to be a cop and said she'd probably be doing the same thing if it weren't for her aversion to guns. We gazed at the stars and chatted for almost three hours. When we finally went back inside, nearly everyone had left or passed out. Hector was milling around picking up trash with a plastic bag in his hand. He gave me a defeated smile when he saw Amy and I together, as if he'd known all along it would come to this. Amy and I helped him clean up and left at two thirty in the morning. We exchanged numbers and were engaged within six months. We were married a year later.

It was never a fairy tale marriage, but it's been close. Amy's always stood by me, supported me, and respected me. I can't hold back the tears as I clench my hands together and press my forehead into them at the side of her bed. I can't bear the thought of life without her. Walter knew what he was talking about. Amy was my star. My one in a million.

A plastic printout of Amy's MRI hangs from a railing above the foot of her bed. Some nurse has stuck a few sticky arrows to the film strip indicating where the brain swelling is worst. The surgeons put a tube in my wife's head to help drain the fluid and reduce the inflammation. No one seems to know when she'll wake up. Comas are unpredictable, they say. It could last hours, it could last days.

It could last the rest of her life.

I retreat downstairs to the cafeteria as night settles in. I have no appetite, but I force myself to eat anyway. I grab a small plastic dish of tossed salad covered in cling wrap and a baked potato. I dine by myself at a round table beneath a television set spewing an update on the North Korean missile crisis. *'On the Brink?'* teases a headline at the bottom of the screen. For some reason it makes me angry, but I continue to watch.

I shovel the tasteless food into my mouth as I stare numbly into the screen. They briefly mention Zeke Brady, the anarchist ex-cop Gabe mentioned a few weeks ago. He's in police custody after being charged with plotting the assassination of a Senator. His supporters, who call themselves 'zekes', are up in arms over what they believe is a federal conspiracy to frame their leader. I watch, detached, as they wave a giant black flag with a painted red 'Z' at one of their rallies.

I'm suddenly too tired to care anymore. I throw the half-eaten tray of food into the garbage and wander the corridors. I find myself in the underground parking garage, where a uniformed guard smoking a cigarette nods in my direction. There's a firearm strapped to his side and I wonder when they started arming these people. Maybe after that shooting in Miami? I can't remember and don't bother to try. It's all bad news, everywhere I look, everything I think and feel.

I meander back through the corridors to the wing where Amy sleeps. There's a voice I recognize down the hall and I track it down. I peek into one of the rooms and glimpse the back of a grey haired man hunched over a hospital bed. It's Walter.

I stand there quietly for a few moments, watching him as he strokes his wife's head. She's unconscious, though she seems to be breathing on her own. There are bandages on her face and arms, but the rest of her body is shielded from my view. She doesn't look as bad as Amy, though. Walter seems to sense my presence. He turns to look at me. Dark skin circles his eyes and his smile is a thin wire.

"Hi, Luke," he says softly. I nod. Walter glances back to his wife before grabbing his coat and motioning for us to leave the room. He shuts the door as we exit.

"How is she?" I ask.

"Hit her head pretty bad on impact, but the doctors seem to think she's through the worst of it. How's Amy?"

"Still unconscious," I say, unwilling to call it a coma.

"They'll need lots of rest," Walter says with a tired look. "We've both got a long road ahead of us."

"Yeah," I say, sinking heavily into a bench in the hallway. I suddenly feel frail and exhausted, as if the blood's been drained from my body. I rub my face in my hands, working the circulation back into my brain. Walter sits next to me and says nothing as the hospital sounds wash over us. A doctor mutters something quietly to a nurse behind the counter. Someone fills a plastic pill bottle. A stack of blood packets are loaded onto a cart and wheeled through a set of swinging doors.

"We'll get through this, Luke," Walter says with a hand on my shoulder. I nod slowly, appreciating the support more than I'm willing to admit.

FRIDAY, JANUARY 15

10:22 AM
LUKE

The days tick by at Amy's side as I hope for some sign of improvement, but there's only the sound of the ventilator disturbing the still air, causing her chest to rise and fall. The swelling in her brain is down, says the doctor, but there's no telling how long it'll take before she wakes up. The coma must run its course. He encourages me to stay by her side and talk to her as if she can hear me; for all we know, she can.

After four days I've finally had enough of the waiting in stuffy hospital corridors and call in to the office. Pryce tells me to come in when I can but I'm not sure how to respond. I haven't felt much of anything since the surgeons told me that my wife might never wake up. I head home for a long shower and fall into my uniform. I'm on the clock shortly after one in the afternoon, and the others trickle in the office as their lunch breaks come to a close. Gabe offers to take me to the firing range and I welcome the distraction. There's a stack of reports waiting for my review but I can just as well do them on my laptop at Amy's side.

Gabe and I drive across town to Lizzie's, a firing range run by the widow of a cop who was killed in a firefight with a couple of teenagers a decade ago. It's ironic, I think now, that his framed picture hangs above a glass cabinet full of the kind of weapons that killed him. Gabe signs us in for two M4 carbines and a case of twenty magazines, thirty rounds each. It's enough to keep us busy for at least a couple of hours.

M4s are one of the automatic weapons our precinct received as part of the Defense Logistics Program, and each of our officers is required at least ten hours of range time with them before taking them on patrol. Breaking this rule could result in disciplinary action by the department, though with all the precinct's current chaos I doubt anyone's keeping track.

Gabe barks something into a walkie-talkie hanging from a hook. A teenage boy in a red baseball cap emerges from behind a dirt hill fifty yards in front of us and sets up a couple of wooden targets. He vanishes a moment later and gives the go-ahead through the radio. Gabe slips a pair of reflective goggles over his eyes and squeezes the trigger. The barrel snaps back with a crack and a flash as a round hurtles through the air. It nicks the wooden target and sends a shower of splinters into the air.

Gabe smiles as if this was intentional and nods for me to give it a go. I set the stock against my shoulder and squeeze the trigger. The kickback's minimal as the round exits the barrel at three thousand feet per second. With targets only half a football field away, the impact seems almost instantaneous. The dust settles from the target, leaving a clearly visible hole in the right shoulder.

"Not bad, Harding," Gabe mutters as he shoulders his weapon and prepares to outdo me. He squeezes off three shots in rapid succession, but only two make their mark.

"You're slipping, Rodriguez," I tease humorlessly. Gabe makes a face and keeps firing. It feels good, being here out in the open, firing at targets with my buddy. The cold soaks through my gloves within ten minutes and I feel my toes going numb, but I don't mind. So much of me is numb already, what's a few extremities?

"So, what do you think of the M4?" Rodriguez asks as we dismantle and clean the weapons two hours later.

"It's smooth. You don't realize its power when you're firing," I say, admiring the rifle as Lizzie grabs it and slides it into a locker beneath the front desk.

"Same thing I thought. Been out here five times this month. You know the department pays for this?"

"Since when?"

"We got a memo a week after the crates came in. They want us all trained, ASAP. There's been a huge push to get us up to speed on all this stuff."

"Not just the carbines?"

"Everything. Grenades, tear gas, the works. You didn't read the letter that came through?"

"I've had a lot on my plate."

"Huh. Yeah. Well, it's a good excuse to get out from under all that paperwork, huh?"

"Sure. I wonder what the push is for, though."

"Just beefing up security, I guess. The National Guard can't handle it all, that's my guess. I read online this morning that in this country alone, there have been more riots this year than the past decade. It's crazy, man. Gotta arm the police, you know?" Gabe flashes me a smile as he flexes one of his arms.

"Yeah, I guess. Still, it just seems a little... Overkill."

"Overkill? You serious, man? You know how many registered M16s and AKs there are in the US? Way more than the cops can keep up with, that's for sure. What we got through the DLP isn't enough. Too little too late. You should know, man. You took a bullet to the arm last year. Can you imagine what that punk would've done if you'd showed up with an M4? Probably wouldn't have ended with you in the hospital."

"He was a kid, Gabe. High on Oxys. He wasn't thinking straight."

"Yeah, well, whatever. If I had a say, we'd have all gotten automatic rifles years ago. Before the Liberation Act, before the church arson, before all the riots. But better late than never, right? *Right?*"

6:39 PM

LUKE

At the end of my shift I grab a burger and head back to the hospital. I pause at a gift shop to buy a bouquet and wonder if somehow Amy will have found her way out of the coma. Maybe she'll be sitting up in bed smiling with a tray of food in front of her. Maybe that awful ventilator will finally be turned off and I'll get to hear my wife's voice one more time.

I leave the elevator with a quickened pace as I catch the sound of soft voices coming from Amy's room. I expect to find a group of nurses and a doctor huddled over her bed, but instead find a young couple with a small boy sitting at my wife's side. They glance at me awkwardly as I enter. I glance quickly at the face in the bed, making sure I've got the right room.

"Can I help you?" I finally say to the man. He rises quickly and introduces himself.

"I'm so sorry, we didn't mean to intrude. My name's Marc, and this is my wife, Ashley, and our son, Matthew."

"Ok. Do we know each other?" I ask suspiciously.

"No, not really. Though we've heard a lot about you. We're friends of Amy's."

"Oh."

"We, uh... We also know Chelsea and Walter."

"Oh. So you're Witnesses." Marc and his wife exchange anxious glances and nod slowly.

"We're so sorry about everything," the wife says to me.

"Yeah, me too. How long have you been here?" I ask.

"Only thirty minutes or so. Our son, Matthew, kept begging us to bring him for a visit. He wanted to see Amy. They're good buddies," Marc says with a sad look, gazing down at his boy. "Why don't you show Mr. Harding the card you made, Matt?"

The boy glances up at his father, as if the request doesn't make sense to his little brain.

"It's ok, Matt. He's Amy's husband."

Matthew blinks a few times, beginning to understand, and walks over to the table at my wife's side, where he grabs a small card and hands it to me shyly. On the front of the card, he's drawn a small child with yellow hair holding the hand of a tall woman at his side. There's a waterfall behind them and a few wild animals in the background. On the inside of the card, scrawled in wandering red crayon letters, are the words:

Dear Amy,
I really miss you. I am sory about your acident. I hope you can get beter soon so we can play more chekers and go to paradize together.
Your frend, Matthew

"Matt likes to draw cards for our friends from time to time, and he insisted he do one for Amy and deliver it tonight."

"Thanks, Matt," I say to the boy, who stands quietly behind his mom's shoulder. "I'm sure Amy will love it."

"Any news on her progress?" Marc asks.

"No one seems to know for sure. It's just a waiting game for now, hoping she'll come out of it soon."

"For what it's worth, you two are in our prayers every night," Marc says.

"That goes for a lot of our friends, Luke," Ashley says with a pained look.

"Thanks," I say.

There's a few moments of silence as Marc and his family gather their things. Before they leave, Matthew runs to my wife's side, bows his head, and says something in a quiet voice. It's a prayer, I realize.

Their son is saying a prayer for my wife.

"It was nice to meet you finally. And sorry again for barging in here without calling first," Marc says.

"No, it's fine, I don't mind," I say.

"Well, maybe we could get your number, then? I think some of the other friends would like to come by, to bring her little gifts and what not. We'd love to make you a meal, too, if you need. We could let you know beforehand…"

I shrug and fish my name card from my wallet. I point out my cell number and they thank me. We wave goodbye and soon I'm alone in the room with the ventilator. I pick up Matt's card in my hands and weep.

WEDNESDAY, JANUARY 20

10:19 AM
LUKE

The next few days are a blur. I'm in and out of the office, keeping my head down as much as possible as I churn through reports and file paperwork. Our station is still on an aggressive hiring campaign, and I'm assigned a handful of interviews with potential recruits. What used to be our parking lot is now occupied by a cluster of trailer offices set up to house everyone.

Frankly, some of these new guys scare me. I can't be sure of their motives, but I doubt they're here to serve the public. I suppose the promise of job security is what brings most of them around. A few are war vets. These men show up knowing how to run the guns and the vehicles, and their attitude suggests that our training and operational protocols are beneath them. They pass all the tests, of course, but the realization that they will soon be armed officers patrolling the streets under my watch is unsettling to say the least.

With the first new wave of recruits, Captain Pryce and some of the senior officers shared my concerns. Now they're too preoccupied with getting everyone organized and trained and tending to the rigors that come with the badge. If anything, they seem grateful for the extra help. The fact of the matter is, the push to hire more officers goes past our rank. It's nation-wide. More spending to local law enforcement is a federal mandate. From Honolulu to Anchorage to New York City, police departments everywhere are bulking up on manpower and firepower.

I still patrol from time to time, but with the workload around here I'm mostly at my desk. This is a good thing; I'm more than willing to leave the heroic fire rescues and pharmacy shootouts to other officers. Not that I mind the occasional patrol shift. Getting out of the pen clears my mind. And with all that's gone on recently, this is one thing I badly need.

As usual, my thoughts drift to Amy. I wonder if she'll ever open her eyes again, or if I'll simply have to accept this as my new reality. She's finally off of the ventilator, but the doctors cautiously warned that it's no sure sign of recovery. It's terrifying to think I may have to watch the woman I love grow old in an eternal sleep.

Chelsea's a little better off. She's in and out of consciousness, but it'll be some time before she can return home. She still hasn't spoken, and the doctors are unclear if there's been any permanent brain damage. This is perhaps the only possibility more frightening to me than never seeing Amy wake up: having her wake up as a different person. I try to shake the disquiet from my mind but it's impossible. The anxiety weighs me down like an anchor.

At half past ten, dispatch reports a domestic disturbance in the Pylons. It's only a mile from my present location and I respond. When I arrive, an adult male and female are shoving each other on the front lawn of a dilapidated apartment block. A couple of onlookers take swigs from beer bottles and chuckle to themselves, welcoming the entertainment. My flashing lights and siren send them reluctantly back to the shadows, but the couple seem not to notice.

My backup arrives within a few minutes of my arrival and we're able to separate the two. The male suspect is bleeding from what looks like fingernail scratches to his face and there's a fresh bruise on the woman's neck, but otherwise the two are unharmed. We separate them and take their accounts of what happened before booking them. The other two officers place them in the back of their squad cars and haul them off to the station. They'll be released tomorrow and I try to ignore the nagging suspicion that we'll be back soon.

In my car, I jot some notes for the report I'll have to write back at my desk. It's still well before noon. I think back to last October, when I was called out to this very neighborhood to respond to a fire and wonder what the lot looks like now. I decide to drive by.

It's all pretty much as I'd expected. The lot has been bulldozed over and is surrounded by a chain link fence topped in loops of barbed wire like a giant, menacing slinky. A plastic sign has been zip-tied to the fence explaining that the property has been reclaimed by the city. A phone number is posted for potential buyers. I highly doubt that they'll get any bites, not in this neighborhood with its houses of boarded windows and sidewalks sprouting more vegetation than the front lawns.

I wonder if our neighborhood will look like this one day, too. The demographic is about the same, as is the crime rate; we hear our neighbors fighting and crying and screaming all the time. We know they're using, too. Most mornings we have to step around shards of shattered beer bottles and other paraphernalia just to leave our apartment.

My mind jumps to Walter. Despite his wife's injuries, he manages to keep his hope for a better future, just like the little boy with that card. Are they all just ignorant? Have they just chosen not to see how bad things are becoming? The more I learn about these people, the more I wonder. *Could the Witnesses really have some master scheme in place?*

Still, despite my growing doubts, there's one issue that sticks in my mind: Walter and Chelsea's estranged son. I recall what Meade mentioned, that he wasn't worth pursuing, that he didn't know anything. But whether that was regarding his parents' faith or the Witnesses secret activities, I can't be sure. In a way, I realize, I've embarked on my own investigation, and while its subject is the same as the FBI's, my motivation is different. For me, it's personal; I'm not out to hurt anyone.

I boot up the Toshiba on my dash and do a quick name search. *Jesse Novak.* A loading bar slides across the screen as the databases of nearby precincts are scoured for any relevant information. There's a direct hit.

And a mugshot.

From the long hair and scraggly beard it's impossible to tell if the face is the same one I saw in the photos at Walter's home, but the birthdate seems to fit. He's only a month younger than myself. The rap sheet is short but telling. He's had a couple DUIs in the last five years and was once hit with possession of narcotics. He's no career criminal and I'd be surprised if half the adults his age in this county are any cleaner. Still, given his family background, it's odd.

The most recent address on record is just east of the Pylons in Almead County. It's not in our jurisdiction, but I'll chalk up my visit to a personal matter if it ever comes to light. The GPS software leads me to a trailer park full of campers and doublewides. A handful of kids in puffy jackets and rollerblades swat at a tennis ball with chipped hockey sticks and barely notice the squad car as I slip past. I weave in and out of cramped alleys and finally track down the unit. I wedge my car between two trailers and rap my knuckles against a flimsy aluminum door at the warped landing of some wooden stairs.

A young woman with greasy blonde hair and facial piercings opens up and looks me over before speaking. "Yeah? What's up?" she asks.

"Hi. My name is Luke. I'm looking for a man named Jesse Novak. You know him?"

"Maybe. What do you want him for?" she asks, pulling the door close to her side.

"He's not in trouble or anything," I say quickly as she eyes my uniform. "I'm here on personal business. Just want to ask him a few questions."

The woman studies me carefully and swigs from a soda can, in no rush to comply. She turns her head and calls over her shoulder. A few moments pass and a man appears in the doorway. His appearance has changed little since the mugshot. Except now the eyes are set deeper, perhaps, and there seems to be a new tattoo creeping up from beneath the collar of his shirt.

"Yeah? What do you want?" he grumbles wearily.

"Hey," I say in my least antagonizing voice. "I just wanted to ask you a few things. You got a minute?"

"What about?"

"Your parents."

A puzzled look comes over his face briefly, then disappears with a shrug. The door gapes open with a squeal and he gestures in the direction of a small dining table and folding chairs. The woman has retreated to the corner of their double wide, where she's curled up under a blanket and jamming her fingers into an Xbox controller. The clatter of machine gun fire ricochets into the kitchenette until Jesse shouts at her to turn it down. He sits across from me at the table and rubs his eyes with the sleeve of his shirt.

"My parents, huh? They in trouble or something?" he asks.

"Actually, your mom was in a car accident," I say.

"An accident... She ok?"

"She will be. She's recovering in the hospital now." I let this sink in as Jesse rubs circles into his temples with his thumbs.

"So, you guys don't talk much, huh?" I say delicately.

Jesse shrugs. "They call from time to time to check up."

"You see them often?"

"Nah. It's been years." I nod. This confirms what they told me, at least.

"So you know them? Personally?" Jesse asks.

"They're friends of my wife," I say.

Jesse's eyes narrow as he mulls this over. "Friends, huh?"

"Actually, your mother is studying the Bible with my wife, Amy."

There's no reaction to this at first, but then Jesse smiles. "So that explains it, then."

"What do you mean?"

"Why you came looking for me. You want to know about the Witnesses."

I consider ways to dodge the question, but can't see a reason to. "Yeah, that's it, more or less," I admit.

Jesse shakes his head and looks up at the ceiling. "I can't believe this," he says with a scornful laugh.

"So what can you tell me? Why did you guys drift apart?"

"I just ended up… Going my own way."

"Why? Are the Witnesses… You know, hiding something?"

"Nah, man, they're exactly what they seem."

"They seem like good people," I say, challenging him to refute me.

"They are. They're… They've just got rules about stuff."

"Rules? What kind of rules?"

Jesse avoids my gaze and nods to the center of the table, where an ashtray lies full of cigarette butts.

"No smoking? Is that one of their rules?" I ask.

"Yeah, that's one. No smoking, no…" he pauses, looking over my uniform carefully. "No other stuff."

"Drugs," I say, like it's no big deal. "You can't do drugs if you're a Witness."

Jesse gives me a harsh look and I raise my hands with a look of innocence. "I'm not here to investigate you, man. I just want to know about these people my wife spends so much time with."

"Whatever."

"So is that why you left the church? Because you couldn't do… the stuff you wanted?"

"It's not a church, but yeah, that's it, pretty much."

"And you were a member before, then you left?"

"Nah, that's not how it works. First you have to be a publisher. It means you have to go out in the ministry, going door to door, preaching to people and stuff. I got that far. I used to go out when I was just a little kid. But then, when I hit my teens, I just… I just didn't take it any farther." I note the change in Jesse's expression, as if a shadow has fallen across his face, and I catch him glance momentarily at the girl on the couch.

"You ever think about going back?"

Jesse looks at me. There's a long pause before he answers with a shrug. "Yeah, man. I've thought about it," he says softly. "They used to come around, too. Back in the day."

"Who?"

"The Witnesses. They didn't know who I was, but they'd come knocking from time to time. Used to hand out invitations to conventions every summer."

"Conventions?"

"Yeah, big meetings. Thousands of Witnesses from all over the place. They have them every year. Or, they used to. Who knows what they're doing now, with the ban and everything." Jesse bites his lip at hearing himself say this and makes an expression I can't decipher.

"That's actually one of the things I'm trying to find out," I say cautiously.

"What do you mean?"

"I'm curious if they're still having meetings, how they're organized, and all that."

"Why?"

"I just want to know. For my wife's sake. To make sure she's safe, you know?"

Jesse peers carefully into my eyes as a smirk creeps onto his face. He's shaking his head as he looks at me now. "Nah, man. That's not it. You're on an investigation. Aren't you? You're trying to figure out how to nab them."

I try to brush it off with a laugh, but Jesse won't let it go.

"That's it exactly, isn't it? You've been sent to spy on them, and you thought I'd give them up. Well, you can forget it. I may not be a Witness now, and I may never become one, but I'd never sell them out."

"Now listen, Jesse," I say, trying to calm him.

"No, *you* listen. I may have drifted far from the person my parents thought I'd become, but I never forgot the things I learned when I was a kid, man. I'm no Judas. And if that's the game you're playing, you'd better get ready for what's coming." Jesse stands suddenly from the chair and pulls the door open, making it clear that our visit is over. I try to find words, only to come up empty. I give a defeated nod and slide back out into the cold air to begin the drive back.

FRIDAY, JANUARY 22

7:35 PM
LUKE

Sleep is impossible. I miss Amy's voice. I miss reaching over and feeling her in the bed beside me. In the last few days I feel as if I've lost everything. Visiting Jesse was a stupid move. All it'd take is a phone call to his Dad and I'd lose them, too. And what would Meade do if he found out I was carrying out a personal investigation? What is there to stop him from ruining my name at the department? I don't doubt for a moment that he'd do it. There's a vindictive streak in him, and maybe that's not all.

I'm back at the hospital the next day. I check up on Amy, but there's nothing to report. She's stable, the doctors say. She could wake up any day but it's unwise to get my hopes up.

I wander across the ward to Chelsea's room. She's conscious, though she doesn't seem to recognize me when I enter. A young man is sitting at her side, and he turns to greet me. One look at his clothes and his haircut and I know he must be a Witness. I wonder if this is one of their rules, too–always be clean cut, clean shaven, and well-dressed. Chelsea gives the man's arm a gentle shake as I enter.

"Chad, can you remind me who this young man is?" she asks him.

"Sorry, I don't know him either," Chad replies sheepishly.

"Ah, that's ok then. Can I help you, sir?" Chelsea asks. It pains me to see that blankness in her stare, but maybe it's for the best, in the end. *If only they could all forget me and what I'm about to do.*

"Hi, I'm actually looking for your husband, Walter. Is he here?" I ask.

"He's in the cafeteria," Chad says with a worried look at my uniform. I thank him and head for the elevators.

I find Walter huddled over a wilted club salad stuffed into a flimsy plastic container. His eyes are closed and I figure he must be praying. For his wife, no doubt. I can barely stand myself as I take the empty seat beside him and wait for him to finish. He smiles at me but I catch the deep lines in his face and wonder if perhaps he's been sleeping even worse than myself.

"So, how's Chelsea?" I ask.

"She's recovering. It'll be a long road yet, but I have hope. The doctors have given me some exercises to perform with her. With time, perhaps the memory gaps will begin to fill in."

"Well, at least she's up," I say hopefully. Walter turns to me with a look of sympathy.

"Amy will wake up, Luke," he says.

"How can you be so sure?"

"Because I believe what the Bible says. There is a bright future waiting for us."

"Heaven."

"No. Right here on the Earth. God intends to undo all the wickedness we're seeing."

"How?"

Walter takes a bite from his salad before answering. When he does, he leans in closely and speaks softly. "With a war."

My blood turns to ice. This is it, I realize. He's about to tell me what I've been after–what the feds have been after–all this time. *The Witnesses are preparing for war.* The realization turns to sad dread in the pit of my stomach. I didn't want it to come to this. I'd hoped that Meade and the FBI had been wrong about these people. They had seemed so different, so sincere. The disappointment weighs heavily on my shoulders as I slide a finger into my pocket and flick the switch on the WIRM recorder.

"A war?" I ask, knowing that Walter's next words will incriminate both him and his wife. I hope that one day I'll be able to forgive myself for doing this to Amy's friends.

"Yes. A war that will be fought once and never repeated. It'll crush the tyranny we see going on in every country around us. It'll bring an end to corruption and injustice and usher in a new era of rule."

"A war for peace," I say with a nod. "And you're preparing for this war?" I ask sadly.

Walter's smile shifts slightly as he gazes into my eyes. "Why, yes. But not to fight in it." The conversation halts as I struggle to process this.

"The war will be fought directly by God's heavenly armies and Earthly governments that oppose his people. We will not need to fight."

"You're telling me that as a veteran from the Gulf War, you're going to stand by and watch from the sidelines when you could be involved?" I ask.

"This won't be like any war before it, Luke. This will be the one to end them all." Walter pauses as an older couple wobbles past. He turns back to me when they're out of earshot. It's clear this is not a conversation he wishes to be overheard.

"You said something about governments opposing God's people," I say.

"Well, yes, it's happening right now. Our work is being banned across the globe, our people have been harassed. Many have been arrested, and some killed."

"How do you know?" I ask.

"We're a brotherhood, Luke. We keep tabs on our family."

I want to press the matter, but something stops me. Meade will have a fit when he hears this conversation. He'll wonder why I missed a perfect opportunity to ask how the Witnesses are communicating. But I can't. In spite of all the leverage the FBI has against me, something deep within me stirs, warding me off my questions and this investigation as a whole.

I can't go on. I'm now convinced that Walter and Chelsea and the others I've met–from the grateful Mr. Harris to the kind friends who brought cards and flowers–are no threat. When I first donned my officer's uniform six years ago, these were the kinds of people I swore to protect. They're not extremists or vigilantes. They simply want to serve their God and live out their lives quietly. What kind of government would want to stop them? The thoughts in my head come like a deluge, and as they've washed over me, I'm left with the beginnings of a new resolve.

I look back at Walter, who's been watching me thoughtfully this whole time. He takes a deep breath before speaking.

"Do you know why I have so much faith that God's war will be the war to end them all?"

I shake my head.

"In every war mankind has ever fought, there were always those who slipped through the cracks. After World War II, thousands of Nazi war criminals fled Germany. Some retreated to the shadows, but others rose to very prominent and prosperous positions. And I can assure you, there were other men, just as evil as those Nazis, who were never forced to flee at all, simply because they were on the winning side.

"Man can't really *win* wars. It's never just the good guys versus the bad. It's much more complicated than that. To really end war, you need to be able to read *hearts*. Each and every one. And then you need to eliminate the bad ones, regardless of where they live or what they look like on the outside. This is beyond the ability of humans."

"But not beyond the ability of God…" I conclude softly. Walter gives a slow nod.

"You have a lot of faith," I say.

"I do. Jehovah has helped me many times personally, and he's always been the Protector of his people. He's very real to me, and he's very real to your wife. Do you know what she told me, the last time we spoke?" I shake my head slowly.

"Her greatest wish was that Jehovah would become real to you, too. She loves you so much, Luke. Every time she'd come to our house, she'd talk about you and how good you were to her. Chelsea and I felt like we knew you long before we'd actually met you. More than anything, Amy wanted the two of you to come out of this together."

"Out of what?"

"The end of the world," Walter says seriously.

"The end of the world?"

Walter nods somberly and pulls his phone from a jacket pocket. He gestures for me to take his earbuds and plays me a video. The beginning is a newsreel mash up of everything's that's unfolded in the last few decades. The atomic bomb. Vietnam. Bloody riots. The cold war. 9/11. Ebola-N. The bovine flu. Earthquakes and tsunamis and landslides. Famine in Africa. Fade to black, and then a soaring vista above a windswept beach. Perfect crystal water, children playing in the sand. Deer running through mountains. People singing around a campfire, a vast web of stars stretched far above.

"But how will it all be possible?" asks a voice. *"The wicked must be destroyed!"* Grey images flashing, politicians washing blood off their hands, grinning. Obese businessmen swimming in piles of cash while explosions erupt outside their glass towers. Tanks funneling endlessly out of factories, bombs falling from the sky, soldiers screaming and firing. A glowing sword descends from the sky and the screen fills with fire.

"Only Jesus Christ, supported by an angelic army, can bring this about, and he will, in the coming War of Armageddon. The question is, 'Where will you stand?'"

I can hardly breathe as the video fades to a close.

"Surely you don't think what we're seeing in the world is normal, do you?" Walter asks as I remove the earbuds. I have no response.

"Open your eyes, son. The economy is in a meltdown. The richest people on the planet have vanished, supposedly to wait out the coming storm. This flu is wiping people out left and right. We've had more earthquakes and hurricanes in this year alone than the last five combined. Mankind is in panic mode."

My eyes wander to a TV monitor hanging from a pillar in the cafeteria, where a scrolling marquee reports on a media blackout that's plunged parts of Asia and all of the Middle East into virtual oblivion. The closed caption links this to the uprisings on the Chinese-Pakistan border and the subsequent Internet takeover by the Chinese government.

"It's easy to think things are always worse overseas, that they won't catch up to us here in the US, but that's an illusion, Luke. You said it yourself: the government has cut spending to almost every department in order to bolster law enforcement and the military. That's a sure sign of a scared government. Americans are the most armed populace on the planet. When the panic hits…"

"Ok, enough, I get it," I say, the fear stirring in my veins.

"I'm sorry, Luke. I'm not trying to scare you. I just want you to pay attention to the bigger picture."

"And then what? And what for? To live in paranoia? Build a bomb shelter under my house and hunker down for the apocalypse? What am I supposed to do?"

Walter takes another deep breath. He appears anxious about what he's about to say.

"Quit the force, Luke."

"Quit? My job? Are you serious?" I say, scoffing.

"Hear me out. You don't want to be one of the ones in uniform in the coming days. Trust me on this, Luke. Get out while there's a chance."

"And then what? The economy's a mess—you said so yourself. How would we survive? And with all these hospital bills!"

"I talked with Chelsea before the accident. She agreed that you two could live with us. Money would be tight, but we'd get by. Many of our friends have had to do the same. We have to stick together to weather this storm. We can help you."

"But… It's… There's just no way."

"Luke, listen to me," Walter says gravely. "There's going to come a time when the police won't be able to do a thing to maintain the peace. Even the military won't be able to stop it. It's already happening around the world. And it's even worse than what we're seeing on the news."

"Worse? How do you know? How much worse?"

"Like I said, we keep in contact with our brothers around the world. I can't say much more, but it's bad. Several governments have already been toppled. It's a mess."

I look back to the screen and wonder over the media blackouts. Walter is still looking at me when I bring my gaze back. There's an expectant intensity in his eyes. I know he's waiting for a response.

"Let me at least think it over, ok?" I mumble numbly. He doesn't relax much. There's a vibrating noise, and Walter reaches into his pocket for his phone. He glances at the screen, his expression immediately melting away.

"I–I'm sorry, Luke… I… I have to take this," he says, nearly overturning the table as he stumbles out of the chair. He retreats quickly to a far corner of the cafeteria, but I can still make out the first words he speaks as he scrambles to take the call.

"Son? Is that you?"

SATURDAY, JANUARY 23

7:53 PM
AMY

A dark blue haze engulfs me. I'm vaguely aware that I'm horizontal but can't guess why. It feels as if someone is knocking a bowling ball repeatedly against the side of my head when I realize that the pain is coming from within. The room sways as if we're on a ship in rough seas. I try to focus and feel the pressure of needles stabbing at the back of my eye sockets. Everything aches. My lower half is totally immobilized. The strength in the rest of my body has been completely drained; it takes enormous effort just to wiggle a finger. Something is terribly wrong with me.

My eyes wander downwards to find a needle taped to the back of my hand. To my right, a metal bar rises from the floor where a clear plastic bag hangs above me leaking fluids into my system.

So I'm in a hospital. But why? I struggle to remember, but it's hopeless. The mere effort fatigues me and I give up.

With my poor eyesight and the lack of light, I can only make out shapes and shadows. I scan from right to left, and then I spot something odd: a figure sitting in the darkness. I part my lips to speak, feeling the skin crack and tear at the corners of my mouth. My throat and tongue are parched to the point of excruciation, the skin inside like sandpaper. I can only utter a dry, hoarse moan.

The figure rises anxiously, and I can see now by the long straight hair and slender shape that it's a woman. She moves silently to the door and is gone. I keep watching the door waiting for the figure's return, but the longer I stare the more convinced I become that I've simply imagined it. My head is still spinning and nothing makes sense.

I shut my eyes and feel the weariness pull me back into the darkness.

8:09 PM
LUKE

Walter's hushed conversation with his son seems to go on for an eternity. It doesn't look good; Walter's got a hand over his face and appears to be shaking. I realize that nothing good can come from my being here and so I grab my jacket from the back of the chair and go for a walk to clear my head.

I peek into Amy's room; nothing's changed. There's an odd smell in the air though, a light women's perfume. I attribute it to one of the night shift orderlies and withdraw to the hallway. I roam around aimlessly for a few minutes, nodding to the orderlies and nurses I pass. Most of them know my face by now and shoot me brief glances of recognition.

A young receptionist behind the counter is staring bug eyed at her computer screen. From the audio, it seems to be a homemade video from one of the recent riots. People are shouting and guns are going off in the distance. The noises rattle from the speakers and tumble through the stark, sterile halls.

There are rapid footsteps behind me, and I step to the side of the corridor to let them pass, expecting a nurse with armfuls of medical supplies. Instead, it's a woman in civilian clothes. Her long bangs cover her eyes and she stares at the floor as she walks. She's gone a moment later, but as I turn to head back to Amy's room, there's the sound of crunching paper beneath my shoe.

When I inspect it, I find that someone has scribbled the following message:

Luke, meet me in 10 minutes. Level C. White Tacoma.

I hurry to the walkway from the west ward and ride the elevator down to the carport. I get off at the third level and meander through the mostly empty lot. I find the Tacoma at the far back behind a green concrete wall. With a glance over my shoulder I realize that it's one of the few spots hidden from the domed security camera overhead and I'm guessing this isn't a coincidence.

I approach the vehicle cautiously from the rear, my academy training kicking in on instinct. I briefly consider returning with my squad car and firearm, but decide against it. I can see through the rear window that there's only one person inside–the driver. I approach the passenger's side door and hear it unlock with a *thunk*. I reach for the handle and slide inside.

The woman with the long bangs from the hallway sits in the driver seat and says nothing. She won't even turn to look at me, but it doesn't matter. I'd recognize those eyes anywhere.

It's Eva Richards.

She's dyed her hair black and let it grow out a little and seems to have lost a lot of weight, but it's definitely her.

"You're alive," I say dumbly as the shock subsides.

"It wasn't easy, finding the time and place to talk to you. Cameras just about everywhere. When I found your wife was in the hospital, I figured this would be the safest place to meet. I waited in the room for an hour, but you were nowhere to be found."

"That was clever, with the note."

"It was the only way I could think of where we wouldn't be seen talking to each other. And I couldn't text you, of course. They're monitoring everything," she explains, her head still facing forward as her eyes dart from mirror to mirror. "I'm taking a huge risk meeting you like this, but I felt that I had to do something. You helped me before, and now I'm returning the favor. But just this once. It'll be too dangerous to try again."

"What's going on?" I ask.

"You're working with a federal agent on a case, right?" she asks quickly. I'm not supposed to talk about it, but my silence is as much confirmation as she needs. "The guy you're in contact with. He's tall, jet black hair, creepy eyes, right?"

"Agent Meade," I mumble.

Eva scoffs. "He's dangerous, Luke." I'm not surprised to hear this, but I wonder at the effort she's gone through to pass this message along.

"I did a lot of digging when I was still at *The Herald*. He's almost impossible to track down. There're so many contradicting reports about his past, and I think it's been done purposely to muddy the waters. But what I do know is that he goes way up the chain of command."

"Funny, he told me he was a nobody."

"I'm sure he's told you a lot of things. Good luck separating fact from fiction."

"I thought he might've been the one that killed you, actually," I add.

"I'm sure it would've crossed his mind if I hadn't beat him to the punch. The wreck and fire were staged, of course."

"How?"

"Not incredibly difficult, but the planning was pretty meticulous."

"I can only imagine. So you'd been planning it for a while, then," I say, feeling a mix of irritation and amusement. "You could've told me first, Eva. I was worried sick. I thought I was partly to blame."

"I'm sorry, but it was the only way. Trust me, I considered every possibility, but it was too dangerous. I couldn't risk telling *anyone*. If the feds suspected anything they would've just kept looking until they'd found me. As it is, my skin is crawling half the time. I constantly feel eyes watching my back. I can barely sleep or eat."

"But if you knew you were going to run off why did you call me the night before?"

"I just wanted to be sure you were on my side. Originally I planned to keep working on the story, once I could stop running from them. I thought you might be able to help me. But then... It just got too crazy."

"So how'd you do it?" I ask. Eva smirks slightly, though her eyes are still glued to the mirrors.

"The first thing was setting myself up financially. I had to slowly siphon enough out of my bank account to set up a second life. It was done over a period of months. I wasn't sure if they were watching my bank account, but I certainly wouldn't put it past them. Anything sudden and they would've known what I was up to.

"Then I had to get myself a new driver's license. That part was surprisingly easy. I met up with a kid I found online and he had one for me in a few days. Then I set the day for the wreck. I knew, when I met you at the motel that night, that it would have to be soon. The feds had ransacked my place and it was just a matter of time before I was in custody or dead. And with all the latitude the feds have been given regarding interrogation practices, I would've preferred the latter.

"I had the spot picked out for the crash in advance. I purchased an electric scooter and parked it under the bridge as a getaway the day prior. I loaded the backseat of my car with a few milk jugs of lighter fluid and lit the upholstery on fire. Then I tied the gas pedal down and let it crash over the embankment."

"And the body?"

"A cadaver. I had a friend at the morgue. I paid her well and she didn't ask questions." A few moments of silence pass as I mull over all she's telling me.

"Sounds like you thought of everything. So why are you back?"

"To tell you that whatever deal you have going with that agent, get out of it. Cut your ties. Run away if you have to."

"Run away? My wife's in a coma fighting for her life. How am I just supposed to up and run?"

"I don't know, but you have to think of something. Whatever promises he's made you, he's lying. There's a pattern with him, where he makes these deals with people, and then in the end, once he's got what he wants, he burns them to cover his trail. He's ruthless, Luke."

I mull over this for a moment, hearing echoes in Eva's words of what Walter told me just a minutes ago.

"And what about you?" I ask.

"I've made some contacts who own a small compound upstate. They're stocked up with weapons and plenty of resources and I convinced them that with my knowledge of government and politics, I have something to offer. They're willing to take me in."

"A compound?" I ask warily.

"They're preppers. Survivalists. They've been working on this camp for years and covertly recruiting online." I close my eyes and shake my head silently. For the first time, Eva turns to stare at me, a scalding look in her eyes. "What?" she asks, her voice on edge.

"It's just all this talk about the end of the world… Do you really believe it?"

Eva pauses long enough for me to see just how much the last few weeks in hiding have aged her. Long creases line her face and eyes. Gaunt cheekbones jut from her features and cast deep shadows over her cheeks. "I don't know, Luke, but I've never seen anything like this. I'm terrified."

We gaze out the windshield at the still parking deck for a few moments without speaking. "Well, I appreciate the warning," I say softly.

"I had to come back. I know you risked a lot, helping me like you did."

I nod. Eva glances at her watch. "I'm sorry, but I've got to go. The longer I stay here…"

"No, no, it's fine," I say. "I understand. Thanks again."

Eva gives me a somber look. "Take care of yourself, Luke."

"You too."

I exit the car and watch her drive off and I know it's the last time I'll ever see Eva Richards.

MONDAY, JANUARY 25

1:47 PM
LUKE

I fiddle with the WIRM in my pocket as I sit at my desk sifting through paperwork. It's been two weeks since my last run-in with Meade and it's just a matter of time before he appears again. I shake the thought off as I stare at the papers in my hands, a psychological evaluation from an army doctor for one of our recent recruits. Discharged from the military in 2016 after a 'stress-related episode,' though due to clearance regulations the report is littered with chunks of blacked-out text. I can barely make heads or tails of it, and that in itself is disconcerting.

Years ago, we would've thrown an applicant like this right out the window. No precinct in the county was willing to take its chances with volatile officers; no one could afford the liability. Now, though, weapons experience and military training trumps all else.

Even so, I'd prefer the opportunity to interview this particular candidate personally before signing my approval on these forms. I decide to run it by the captain first, and stuff the papers into a folder as I hike it to his office. When I enter, Pryce is gazing tiredly at something on his laptop.

"Something wrong?" I ask.

"More of these media blackouts. Now it's starting in Europe. Half the world has gone dark," he grumbles with a furrowed brow.

"You think it's serious?"

"I think the governments are in a panic. You heard about the protests at the capitol?" I shake my head.

"Apparently some hackers have leaked evidence that the blackouts aren't originating abroad. The news coverage is being blocked out on our end."

"Here? Like, America?"

"That's the story, anyway. People are angry. They're trying to figure out what's going on. Lots of conspiracy talk. Some of the buildings in Washington have already been attacked."

"*Attacked?*"

Pryce nods gravely and turns his laptop around for me to see. A series of images reveal a fiery and chaotic scene. Plumes of smoke and tear gas rise from a crowd of angry, masked rioters.

"This is insane," I mutter under my breath.

"It'll spread, it always does," Pryce says. "Maybe they knew this was coming. We got this today from the DOD." Captain Pryce pulls a small sheaf of papers from his printer's tray and slides it across the table to me. It's an official document from the Department of Defense branded in bullet points and bold text. The header is enough to send a ripple of goosebumps over my arms and neck:

GUIDELINES FOR TEMPORARY SUSPENSION OF CIVIL LIBERTIES

"What is this?" I ask uneasily as I scan the pages.

"They want us to prepare for the institution of martial law."

"Martial law? But that's not our call."

"That document explains it," Pryce says, wagging a finger at the desk. "There's a contingency plan in place for us here, in case the National Guard is unable to assist. We'd be on our own, in that case."

"They think it'll get that bad?"

"Apparently, in many countries, it already has."

I sink heavily into the chair across from the captain and try to process everything I'm hearing. "So what do we do?" I ask.

"We prepare for the worst. We suit up and hope to weather the storm."

I stare down at the folder in my hands, which I've forgotten all about. It'll be no use bringing this up now, I realize. We'll need as many officers as we can get, checkered past or not. Then there's another realization.

"That's a lot to ask of our officers. They'll be going head-to-head with the citizens of their community. But what happens if they aren't up for it? What if they leave their post?"

"That's covered in those pages, too. Not pretty. They're calling it *desertion*, and it carries a prison sentence."

"A prison sentence? They're threatening the officers into staying?"

Pryce shrugs, but I can tell he isn't any more pleased about it than myself. "That's the idea, I guess."

"I can see this going downhill quickly," I mutter.

"And we have to prevent that from happening." Pryce pauses and leans back in his chair, staring at me intently. "We've known each other for a while, Luke."

"Almost seven years."

"In that time, you've given me no reasons to doubt your loyalty to that badge and all it represents."

"Thank you, sir."

"I need to know that you're solid, Luke. We'll get through this, but only if we hold ranks."

"Yes, sir." Pryce nods with a grunt and breaks his gaze to stare out his picture window into the den of officers.

"Your wife holding up ok?" Pryce asks absently as he leans over his desk and reaches for the papers I've set down in the folder. I watch him perch a pair of glasses on the rounded, speckled ridge of his nose and sign his name messily on a few of the forms.

I consider sharing some of my anxiety, but I hesitate. I'm unsure of how much Pryce really wants to hear of my personal life. Deep creases etched into his face tell the story of a man under immense pressure, concerns bigger than a rookie sergeant with a sick wife.

I've never been fooled by his callous exterior. Deep down, I know how much he cares about the officers under his command. He takes seriously his responsibility to get them home safely after each shift. But his concern can only stretch so far. What happens in our private lives, so long as it doesn't affect our performance and the safety of ourselves and others, is beyond his realm of supervision. I don't blame him, but this sudden realization saddens me, and I can't explain why.

"She'll be ok," I say simply with a thin smile. Pryce doesn't acknowledge me until he's signed all the relevant forms and handed the folder back to me.

"Good to hear," he says. "Now get that recruit in here ASAP and see how well he handles an M4."

I say something as I excuse myself and find my way back to my station. My phone buzzes as I plop into my seat. It's the hospital.

1:47 PM
AMY

I open my eyes to a warm yellow glow. Afternoon sunlight bleeds into the room around me. There's still that throbbing pain at the back of my eyeballs and I have to squint against the light, but I'm worlds better than the last time I awoke. I can wiggle my fingers and toes a bit more vigorously, but the dull pain coursing through my body tells me it'll be a long road to recovery. My right leg is still hanging in its cast, the looseness of the plaster an indication of just how much weight I've lost in here.

I glance around the room for a call button. I finally find it with wandering fingers at the side of my bed. I press a button and hear the ding of an electronic bell from somewhere in the wall.

A woman in lavender scrubs shuffles in. Her eyes and mouth go wide as she sees me, and she rushes back into the hallway. She returns a few minutes later, followed closely by a tall woman in dark slacks and a white lab coat.

"Well hello there, Mrs. Harding. It's good to see you're finally up," she says proudly with a grin. It takes all my effort to respond but my voice is raspy, the words indecipherable.

"Take it easy there," she says in a motherly tone. "You won't be able to talk for a while. You haven't drunk anything in weeks." Weeks!

The doctor slips what looks like a remote control from a slot at the side of my bed and holds it close to my face. Under the call button are two buttons: *YES* and *NO*. She slips the controller into my right hand.

"We can use this to communicate until you've got your voice back. I just want to ask a few questions and see how things are coming along, ok?"

YES.

"Good. First, are you in pain?"

I think for a minute. *NO.* The throbbing in my eye sockets has subsided some, and so long as I keep still, the rest of my body seems to be ok.

"Good. You're pretty tough. You've been through a lot. Do you know why you're here?"

NO.

"Mm-hmm," the doctor says with an arched eyebrow. She proceeds to tell me about the accident and my injuries and coma. She's gentle and considerate about everything, a parent softening bad news for the ears of a child.

"I'm sure this is very frightening for you, but I want to tell you that you're recovering well. And you're finally conscious, which is very promising."

Questions race through my mind. *How long will I be in here? Where is Luke? Was he in the car with me?* I shudder at the thought and struggle to speak again, but it's hopeless. The doctor places a hand on my shoulder and glances at something behind my bed. She tells me to conserve my energy and leaves, promising to check back in an hour. The nurse appears at my side with a cup embedded into a plastic tray hanging from the side of my bed. She pushes a straw between my lips and orders me to take small sips. It's barely enough for two mouthfuls, and my throat aches for more when I'm done.

I become antsy as I wait for the doctor to return, but when she finally does, my eyes light up. At her heels is the man I love. *It's Luke!* He rushes to my side, slipping his strong, warm hands around mine and squeezing tightly. I've never wanted his arms around me so badly, but I see restraint in his eyes; he doesn't want to hurt me. My husband's eyes are misting as he says my name over and over, the sweetest sound I could ever hope to hear.

"I was so worried, babe," Luke says, swiping at his damp eyes with a shirtsleeve. "They said you might not wake up. The doctor said you don't remember much of the accident, huh?" Luke says, looking down at the controller in my hand.

YES.

"You were in an intersection. Another driver hit a patch of ice and slammed into your car. You were in the passenger's side, the side that got hit. Chelsea was driving," Luke says. My eyes go wide with dread.

"Don't worry, she's ok... For the most part." I frown.

"She's got some memory loss. The doctors aren't sure if it's temporary or not, but they're hoping for the best. But the important thing is that you're both alive. We can work through the rest of this together." Luke leans forward to kiss my forehead and brushes a strand of hair from the side of my face, tucking it behind my ear.

The moment is lost as the sound of heavy footfall echoes through the corridors. The door to the hospital room swings open as two men in navy blue windbreakers and matching baseball caps enter. They stand at either side of the doorway as another man enters. He wears a dark suit and a wrinkled trench coat nods in Luke's direction. The men in jackets lunge at my husband and wrestle him to the ground. The doctor enters and protests loudly, but the man in the suit pushes her out and shuts the door without a word. He kneels beside my husband, whose hands are now cuffed behind his back.

"Luke Harding, you're under arrest," he says with a grin.

3:14 PM

LUKE

"On what charges?" I demand.

"Conspiracy to commit treason, among other things," Agent Meade says. His two goons make a big show of peeling me from the linoleum floor and turning me to face Amy. I can barely bring myself to look into her eyes.

"I'm sorry we had to do this here, in front of your wife, sergeant," Meade says with mock sympathy. "But as you know, the law knows no boundaries."

It's the last straw. I can't help myself. With the two federal officers still clutching my arms, I swing my legs up and plow my feet squarely into Agent Meade's chest. There's a flash of surprise in his eyes as his body propels backwards. He tumbles into a dolly of medical supplies and sends the items scattering.

The doctor's face appears in the window of the door, yelling something. One of the agents glares at her and she storms away angrily. Agent Meade actually chuckles as he rises from the ground and brushes himself off. "Nice, Harding. We can now add assault to a federal officer to our charges."

I don't care. I'll do it again, I think. Maybe I'll aim higher this time. I glance at Amy. There are tears in her eyes as she watches helplessly. As much as I want to keep fighting, I can't. Not like this. Not with her here.

I bow my head dejectedly and feel a sharp pain race across my body, like lightning in my veins. I convulse in breathless agony and collapse to the floor. I glance up to see one of the agents grinning at me, a Taser in his hand. I watch as blue sparks flicker from the silver contacts. I groan and attempt to move, but the electrical charge has rendered my muscles completely inert.

"It's too bad your wife had to see that, too," Agent Meade says, shaking his head. "Now, will we have any more problems, or can we do this the civilized way?"

I say nothing as the agents drag me out the door and into the elevator. I'm still wincing from the shock of the Taser and can't quite control my legs as they toss me into an unmarked SUV. Someone pulls a black sleeve over my head and shoves me down. I lie there in a dazed, dull pain, half expecting another go of the Taser or worse, but instead I hear the doors slam shut as the driver steps on the gas.

"Why?" I finally manage to ask, coughing, air struggling its way back into my lungs. The muscles in my chest and abdomen ache as I breathe and it's much worse when I speak.

"Because you didn't hold up your end of the deal," Meade says.

"I did what you asked!" I say, hating how desperate and vulnerable I sound.

"Did you? Then why is it that we're still no farther along on our investigation than when we first contacted you, hmm?" Meade slams a palm against what sounds like the steering wheel and makes a hard right turn. I nearly tumble from the seat, bashing my skull against the handle of the door.

"Where are you taking me?" I ask, masking the pain as best I can.

"Somewhere far from here," Meade says.

"To do what?"

"To give us the information you agreed to give us."

A sharp and sour smell fills my nostrils as a cold, wet cloth presses against my mouth. I try to wriggle away but it's pointless. My last memory is the scent of strong chemicals and the squeal of impatient tires.

4:29 PM
AMY

The next hour passes in frantic confusion. Nurses and doctors are in and out of my room, retrieving items from the ground as I struggle to understand what's just happened. A perplexed security guard is brought in and surveys the damage, wandering off moments later to check the CCTV tapes. Someone refills my water cup and I gulp it down, feeling my throat open a little. My voice is still a thin whisper, but at least I can talk.

I ask a nurse to make a call, and within minutes Walter arrives from the other wing of the hospital. He's thrilled when he sees me sitting up in bed, but his expression quickly changes as I struggle to tell him everything. It takes great effort just to get the words out. My tongue and lips move numbly and awkwardly, as if I'm speaking for the first time.

Walter orders me to calm down and relay all the details to him clearly. Tears begin welling in my eyes from the fear and frustration.

"They took him!" I say, gasping through sobs. The exertion of the last hour has burned through the traces of whatever drugs they've pumped into my system and the pain is returning with a vengeance. Still, it barely registers over the panic.

"*Who* took him?"

"They were police, I think," I say, forcing myself to think clearly.

"Police? From Luke's precinct?"

"No, no, I don't think so. I didn't recognize them. And they didn't look like regular cops. One of them was in a suit. They hurt him, Walter! They hurt Luke and handcuffed him!"

"Ok, ok. Let me just think for a second," Walter says. He puts his fingers to his temples and begins pacing the room. The orderly who was sent in to clean up after the scuffle glances at Walter with annoyance and lets herself out with a snort.

"Why do you think they took him?" I ask softly.

"I have no idea, Amy. Everything is… happening so quickly. Luke's not the first to be arrested."

"What do you mean?"

"There have been a few others. None in our congregation, but in some of the others… It's happening."

"You think this happened because of us? Because he was associated with us?"

"It's possible. I hope that's the case. If it is, Jehovah will see to it that he's taken care of."

"What does that mean? You're not saying… We're going to help him, aren't we, Walter?" Walter gives me a long look before glancing at his wristwatch and frowning.

"Amy, something's happened." I wait as Walter agonizes over his next words.

"What?"

"This morning we received a message from the branch. The information was to be conveyed to every congregation member."

"What message?"

Walter looks over his shoulder and lowers his voice. "It contained specific instructions for our evacuation," he says.

"Evacuation?"

Walter nods. "The instructions were very explicit. Our congregation, along with a few others, are to head to a secret location. A safe house, if you will."

"When?"

"No later than midnight tomorrow."

I gasp. "Midnight! But what about Luke?"

Walter shakes his head sadly as a single tear strays down his cheek. "I'm sorry, Amy. There's nothing we can do but pray. It's in Jehovah's hands. We have to trust that he'll know what to do."

"No... *Please*, Walter, there must be something!"

"It's out of our control, Amy," Walter says firmly.

"We can't just give up on him! He was coming around Walter, I could feel it! He just needs more time!"

"I'm sorry, Amy, but–"

"What about the officers at his precinct? What if we contact them? Maybe they can help!" Walter's mouth opens as if to object, but he stops himself. Another glance at his watch. And then a slight nod.

"Ok, that's an idea. We can try that. But we need to leave as soon as possible."

I have Walter grab my phone from my purse. The battery is dead and it takes him a few minutes to round up a charger and another few to get it back to life. I skim through the contacts until I find a name I never thought I'd be asking for help.

Gabe.

7:02 PM
LUKE

I come to in a bleak concrete cell. A row of overhead halogen tubes cast stale white light into the small space, aggravating my throbbing head. A single steel door with a three-inch square window is the only way in or out. The window appears to be blacked out with some kind of paint.

My hands are still cuffed behind my back, though they've swapped out the steel cuffs for plastic zip ties. They're cinched so tight that my hands are cold and stiff from the lack of circulation. The ties are connected to a short length of chain attached to the floor. Movement is painful and difficult. The slightest twist of my wrists drives the edge of the plastic ties deeper into my skin.

It's impossible to tell the time in here. There's no natural light, no clocks hanging on the bare walls. This is intentional, of course. Disorientation is part of the mind game. I've heard about federal prisons like this before, along with the horrors of water boarding and sleep deprivation. Just reading about them is harrowing enough; being here in person makes my skin crawl with morbid anticipation.

As my head clears and my eyes adjust to the light, I realize how empty my stomach feels. I wonder how long it's been since eating lunch back at the station before I got the call from the hospital. It seems like days ago, but I'm guessing it's only been a few hours judging from the intensity of the hunger pangs.

Is it within their legal bounds to withhold food from a prisoner? It's best not to think about it, just as I resist the urge to speculate what horrors await me in this awful, dank cube.

I think about Amy, how scared she must be through all of this. That's what makes me the angriest, really. It was so cruel, so unnecessary, for Meade to make her witness all that.

I can't help but think back to Eva's warning the other night. *She was right.* And I'm not the first. The reminder twists my stomach in knots. I look again at the stark space around me, sick with the speculation of how many others suffered a similar fate at Agent Meade's hands.

Suddenly there's a groan of scraping metal as the door yawns open. Meade's got a manila folder in one hand and a folding chair in the other. He sits down a couple of feet in front of me and smiles.

"Holding up ok, Harding?" he asks.

"Why are you doing this to me?" I ask pitifully.

"You're taking this far too personally, Luke. This isn't *me* against *you*. This is your country taking necessary actions to protect its interests."

"What interests?"

"Peace and security. The eradication of religious sects."

"What does that have anything to do with me?"

Meade looks at me dubiously before scoffing. "Really? You're going to play dumb? We both know you were cooperating with the Witnesses. You were bound by law to take action against them, and instead, you aided them. We have all the evidence right here," Meade says, waving the folder in the air. "You want to look at it?"

"You put me up to it, Meade. I was working for you. I wouldn't have gotten involved if it weren't for you."

"And yet, before we met, you already knew your wife was affiliated with the Witnesses, didn't you?"

"It wasn't illegal at the time for an officer's family member to be affiliated with a religious group," I say.

"Yeah, that's a good defense strategy. You can try that at your hearing. We'll see how it pans out."

"Why are you doing this to me? What benefit is it to have a law enforcement officer in a prison like this?" I'm nearly begging now, but I don't care anymore. I need to get out of here. Meade's cold eyes suggest terrifying things.

"Good question. And it's one I'm willing to answer, because I want you to know how serious your government is about enforcing its laws. That's the beauty of this Liberation Act. It's streamlined everything. The red tape is gone. The bureaucrats are finally at bay. We can do what we need to ensure order. You could've been a part of that, too, Harding. Too bad you chose the wrong side."

"So that's it, you're just doing this to punish me? To show how much clout you have?"

"Well, that's part of it. I won't lie, Luke, there's nothing I enjoy more than seeing swift justice carried out. Especially against traitors like yourself." Meade leans back in his chair and cracks his knuckles. He glances up at the corner of the cell, and I notice for the first time a small black dome jutting from the ceiling.

"What's the other reason?" I ask.

"Well, I'm not the only one who has a say about what happens to you. Homeland Security has been working closely with us to gather intel on the Witnesses, and they believe you know more than you've given us."

"And?"

"And they want you to share it with us," Meade says.

I shake my head and let out a chortle. "Really? You expect me to cooperate after *this*?"

"They do. They've got quite an offer, too."

"An offer? What offer?"

"It's very simple, Luke. You cooperate, and in return, they agree not to throw Amy into a cell just like this one."

There are no words to express my anguish. I shut my eyes and lower my head. He lets out a little laugh, letting it all sink in slowly, before rising and exiting the cell with his papers and chair.

"I'll give you some time to think it over, Harding. See you next time."

The door groans shut and all is silent.

7:30 PM
AMY

Walter lifts me delicately from the hospital bed and sets me into the wheelchair. It's the first time I get a good look at myself and I hardly recognize what I see. I've lost at least a quarter of my body weight and barely have the strength to sit upright. Walter props me up with pillows and wheels me down the hall.

The corridors are surprisingly full for the late hour. Some halls are lined with stretchers and wheelchairs of the infirm. I ask Walter about it and he briefly mentions a bad flu going around. An orderly we pass in a doorway hands us a couple of masks and tells us to keep them on when outside of the room.

Gabe is waiting for us at one of the round tables in the dining area as we approach. He's frowning at a news segment covering a series of fires downtown. I only catch a glimpse of the headline–something about riots is scrolling by too quickly for my tired eyes to capture. He finally sees us and gives Walter an odd look before letting his gaze fall on me.

"Wow," he says. "You look awful."

"Thanks," I say dryly.

"So what's up? You said it was an emergency," Gabe says with a glance at his watch.

"It's about Luke. Something bad has happened to him."

Gabe crosses his arms and glances back and forth between the two of us. "Oh yeah? What?"

"I think he was arrested. The men who took him didn't look like regular police. They said he was involved in some kind of conspiracy... For treason."

Gabe's eyebrows raise slightly and he scratches the back of his neck. "Treason, huh?"

"Do you have any idea what they were talking about, or where they were from?" Gabe avoids my pleading stare to glance back up at the TV for a few moments.

"I can't say for sure, but I definitely think Luke was wrapped up in something."

"Did any of this have to do with that reporter?"

"Yeah, maybe. I dunno. Luke didn't tell me much. The FBI raided our office a couple of months ago. They questioned him. It had to do with some leaked information. The investigation sort of died out after a few days, but they kept in contact with him. Luke never said anything, but there were all kinds of rumors going around the office. Someone had seen him with one of the agents in a park. It wasn't really our business to butt in. The feds hate it when local law enforcement encroaches on their investigations. I figured Luke was working with them on something, I even asked about it once, but he was pretty tight-lipped."

"And you didn't think to say something to someone? To me?" I say angrily.

"Look, with all that's been going on lately, we've all been a little tense, ok? You have no idea what it's been like around the station lately."

Walter puts his hand on my shoulder and gives it a gentle squeeze.

"Officer, is there anything we can do to help Luke?" Walter asks.

"Who're you?" Gabe asks with a snort.

"A family friend," he says. "Name's Walter." He reaches a hand out and Gabe shakes it reluctantly.

"Look, I don't know nothing, but it sounds like Luke got wrapped up in something bad and the feds got onto him. They're probably the ones who took him into custody."

"Is there a way to contact him?" Walter asks.

Gabe shakes his head, "Nah, I don't think so. You'll just have to wait. He should be able to call. Then again…"

"Then again, what?" I ask.

"Well… Laws have been changing. The FBI's limitations have been totally redefined. They aren't bound by the same rules we are. They can take suspects into custody for all sorts of things. No lawyers, no trials, nothing."

"Do you know where they might be keeping him?" Walter asks.

"My guess would be the FBI field office in Atlanta, but there are a couple of closer resident agencies in neighboring counties. He could be in any of those places."

I place my head in my hands. It feels hopeless.

"Look," Gabe finally says, "I gotta run. I'm sorry about Luke, but I'm sure he'll be fine." I look up to see him smiling at me, but it gives me little hope. He gives Walter a curt nod and walks briskly back to the elevators.

8:00 PM
LUKE

I sit on the cold, damp concrete slab of the cell floor and listen to the groans of my empty stomach. I assume it's nighttime, or perhaps early morning, but I'm neither tired nor alert and I can't tell if I've slept. I suppose it could be the anxiety keeping me awake.

Hunger and cold are the only sensations that register. My wrists have stopped aching; the lack of circulation to my hands has numbed everything below my elbows. There's a metallic groan as the door swings slowly open. A man in military fatigues enters.

"Try anything stupid and you'll regret it," he says with a sharp look as he pulls a knife from his back pocket and snips the zip ties off.

The muscles in my shoulders protest painfully as I slowly swing my hands into view. My wrists have been worn raw, though it'll be a few minutes before I can feel their sting. I knead my forearms gently to get the blood flowing as the man leaves without another word. The door slams shut, and a few minutes later a small slot at the bottom slides open. A metal tray of food clatters along the floor and my mouth waters instantly.

It's not much–a few slices of bread and two cold hard-boiled eggs– but I scarf it down without a second thought. I wash it down with a cup of heavily chlorinated water and feel my energy gradually return. My wrists are burning now, but at least my stomach is placated. I stand slowly and begin to explore the room. My knees pop with the effort, pain shooting through my thighs as my legs unfold.

I get my bearings, studying the tinted dome in the corner of the ceiling, which is certain to house a camera monitoring my every move. There's the steel door, of course, which I've been staring at now for hours, and a closer inspection reveals nothing new.

I sigh, imagining Amy's fright. At least she has Walter, I think, and I'm comforted. He's been like a father to her this whole time. I'm ashamed for ever trying to betray him, but what choice did I really have?

The faint sound of voices leaks in from the other side of the door, which opens again to reveal two new faces. One man wears a dark blue military uniform, his face pinched in an eternal scowl. The other appears to be a doctor of some sort. He leans down and shines a flashlight in my eyes, mouth, and ears, and then jots something on a clipboard before nodding to the military man. He shoots me a final, nervous expression as he leaves the room. Something about his expression makes my hair stand on end.

Agent Meade enters next, pushing a cart full of tangled wires and electronic equipment and he closes the door behind him.

"How was the meal?" he asks cheerfully as he and the other man sit on folding chairs.

"Delicious," I say.

"Well, we do make a point of caring for our own," Meade says with that devil's grin. The other man frowns at him and then stares at me.

"I'd like to introduce you to George. George, this is Luke."

I give the man a cautious nod. I might as well be greeting a piece of stone. He is completely motionless as his eyes bore into me. He doesn't even seem to be breathing.

"George here works with Homeland Security. He identifies threats, investigates them, and takes the appropriate action. He was one of the men who asked for you to be brought here. I, of course, was against the idea. I didn't like the thought of a friend of mine ending up in a place like this," Meade says with mock sadness as he looks around the cell. "Anyway, I guess by now you've probably figured out what's going to happen next."

"I'm guessing it has something to do with that machine," I say, trying to keep my voice level as I look at the cart overflowing with wires.

"That's correct. I don't like having to pull this thing out, but I have to admit, it gets results," Meade says, sighing. I swallow hard as I glance into George's eyes, two smoldering pieces of coal, but there's no salvation there.

"Interestingly, once upon a time this thing was actually illegal. In 2008, when all those leaked documents made their way to the Internet after Guantanamo Bay, Congress stepped in and labeled it cruel and inhumane. Unfortunately for you, that decision was overturned a couple of years back when terrorism spiked." Meade is smug as he lets the words sink in.

"The good news is, *you* have a choice. We don't have to use this today, or ever. But we need the information you were supposed to give us."

"Why? Why are you after these people?" I ask. The question elicits a raised eyebrow from George.

"Because they're breaking the law, Luke. In the last few months, this government has effectively stopped the practice of religion, and we believe the nation is better for it. But somehow, the Witnesses have managed to continue their operations."

"They're not bad people," I say softly. "They're no threat to anyone. Why not just let them be?"

"*Let them be?* And what kind of government would that make us, Luke? We pour hundreds of billions annually into maintaining a first class military. Our intelligence agencies are second to none. Our police are more armed than any other paramilitary organization in the world. And we can't handle a single religious organization? What kind of message does that send to the rest of the world?"

"So that's what all this is about? Saving face?"

Meade chuckles a little before responding. George remains stoic.

"Of course not. Actually, this goes beyond just the government of the United States. Believe it or not, this directive comes straight from the U.N. Security Council. They've put a deadline on the eradication of Jehovah's Witnesses, and that deadline is almost up."

"This is happening around the world?" I ask. Meade nods proudly.

"So as you can see, there's really no other options available to you. Whether you help us or not, the Witnesses will soon be a thing of the past."

George stops glaring at me for a moment and motions impatiently with his head to Agent Meade. Meade nods and walks over to the far end of the cell, where he tugs at a metal panel in the wall. It extends as a narrow slab just big enough for a body. Without warning, two soldiers enter the cell and forcibly heave my body onto the slab. Rigid nylon straps are pulled tight around my ankles, thighs, shoulders, wrists, and forehead. The soldiers disappear as George dons a pair of gloves.

He swabs a cold and pungent liquid onto a few spots on my exposed skin before affixing something to the wet points on my chest, arms, and thighs. It's sticky and metallic. I shut my eyes tightly.

"Last chance," Meade says as George wheels the cart over to the side of the bed.

"Even if I knew anything, I would never tell you," I say softly. Meade nods once as George pries my mouth open and stuffs a rolled towel between my teeth. There's a low hum as the machine is switched on and I brace myself for what will surely be the most horrendous moments of my life.

10:15 PM
AMY

Walter wheels me into the elevator and down to the lobby. I'm sure my doctor would have a fit if she saw me checking out so soon, but the chaos engulfing the ER spills quickly into the rest of the hospital, and no one notices us exit the ward.

Bloodied gurneys line both sides of the hallway on the first floor. Several patients moan in agony, many of them covered in gruesome burns and bandages made hastily from torn bits of clothing.

"What happened?" I ask Walter, my voice trembling. For a moment I meet eyes with a man pressing his fingers to a gaping, ragged wound in his shoulder.

"Rioting. It's happening all over the country. We need to get out of here, and quick. This whole area is going to start looking like a war zone," Walter says anxiously as we rush out the front doors into the cold night. The air is filled with the wail of sirens and a hint of smoke. Walter quickens his pace and finds his truck at the far end of the parking lot. He fumbles for his keys and helps me into the front seat.

"Keep your head down. Whatever happens, do not open these doors unless you see me. You got it?" he says sharply with a finger pointed at me. I nod, frightened beyond words.

"I'm going back up to get Chelsea. Sit tight," Walter says before shutting the door. He folds up my wheelchair and sticks it in the bed of the truck and jogs back into the hospital. An ambulance nearly runs him over at the front doors. EMTs swing open the back gates and unload a gurney with a small child. I look away quickly.

I lie across the front seat, trying to ignore the awful sounds swirling in the air outside the truck. Occasional gunfire peppers the air, followed by scattered screams of panic. I squeeze my eyes shut and stick my fingers in my ears, but it's no use. It's as if the noise is emanating from within my head and nothing will keep it out.

I say a prayer to calm my nerves. A sudden blast rocks the truck and I peek out the windshield to see a row of cars burst into flames. A man with a bandana tied around his mouth lights a piece of cloth jutting from the end of a glass bottle and tosses it in my direction. The glass shatters on the ground as a plume of fire erupts into the air just a few yards from the truck. I fall back against the seat and pray again, feeling the heat from the fire gradually warm the interior. My heart is racing.

There's a bang on the driver's window and I scream. I look out to see Walter holding Chelsea in his arms and I lean over to unlock the door. He puts her in the backseat and straps her in before quickly starting the car and backing out of the space. There's a screech as his tires peel against the pavement and we shoot into the road.

The traffic lights are out, and Walter slows the truck slightly as he approaches the first intersection. A group of people in masks are throwing bricks through the glass windows of an electronics store and clambering inside, shouting with crazed glee as they loot and pillage.

"When did all this start?" I ask, my voice shaking as I take in the chaotic scene.

"The first riots started a couple weeks ago, but they've spread quickly. The police are doing their best, but they can't keep up with it. They're completely outnumbered."

I think of Luke, in custody, and wonder for the first time if maybe it was for the best. I turn around to look at Chelsea. Her head sags and bobs with the movement of the car. She appears to be unconscious. Maybe drugged.

"Is she ok?" I ask Walter.

"It's just the sedatives in her system. She'll be like this for another few hours, I think, then she should be ok."

"It's good to see her," I say softly.

"Yeah. At least we're all together. We should've left earlier, though. We're cutting it very close."

Walter swerves hard to avoid a barricade in the middle of the road. Things quiet down some as we hit the outskirts of the city. Apparently we're not the only ones evacuating. We spot dozens of other cars loaded up with belongings as people flee the city. I wonder where they're all headed.

The highway traffic is thicker than usual for this time of night, but we make good time as we head north on I-85. I lose count of the number of ambulances and police vehicles that pass us. Walter is careful to stay well within the speed limit, although I can feel the urgency in his driving. He shoots constant nervous glances into his rearview mirror as we crawl up the interstate. Suddenly, he yanks his cellphone from his jacket pocket and hands it to me.

"Alright, I've made up my mind," he says. I glance at him quizzically. "Do a search for 'FBI Field Office' and get me those directions."

"We're going there?"

"We should be passing close by. If it looks safe, we can at least stop and see."

Walter glances over as I beam at him. I lean into his shoulder and wrap my arms around him. "Thank you. Thank you so much," I say.

"Don't thank me yet, Amy. There are no guarantees."

11:24 PM
LUKE

I guess I blacked out. Everything from the last day is an incomprehensible blur. I consider the possibility that I've died and gone on to the next life, but the slightest movement of my shoulder sends a fresh streak of pain through my body and that hopeful notion is instantly dismissed.

What did I tell them? How long did they question me? Only bits and pieces of the interrogation come back, but it's a senseless jumble of sounds and sensations. The only clear memory is the pain.

I'm laid out flat on my back on the cold metal slab, a cadaver awaiting cremation. I lift my head gently from the table to get a look at myself. It's not pretty. The spots on my skin where the electrical contacts were taped are covered in puffy wet blisters. The skin in some places has actually been burned so badly it's flaking away. I look at my wounds with curious detachment, not quite grasping that it's my own body I'm seeing. I realize that I'll always bear the scars of this horrific ordeal.

That is, if they don't kill me first.

As the mental fog clears, I begin to recall some their questions. They wanted to know who was in charge and how the Witnesses were communicating and convening. It's almost amusing how this untrained band of Christians has managed to evade the authorities for so long. If I remember correctly, I had asked the interrogators some questions of my own. The answers hadn't been forthcoming, but I learned as much from their silence as I would've had they come out and told me everything.

It seems that Walter and the rest of them were telling the truth: the Witnesses are harmless. This is in contrast to so many other churchgoers, many of whom took up arms to protest their suspended freedoms when things first started going downhill last year. Walter doesn't even own a gun, for goodness' sake.

All of this is preemptive.

I can't help thinking about my own precinct. How much does Pryce know? I suppose it's possible that he's too low on the ladder to have the whole picture, but I guess it doesn't really matter. I may never know the truth. Like Eva said, the waters are intentionally muddied. At some point it'll be impossible to separate fact from fiction, to know who's really pulling strings. Does it really trace all the way back up to the U.N., like Meade had claimed, or was that just another strand in his web of deceit?

I close my eyes and delicately cover them with a hand. The muscles in my shoulder quiver and scream with the effort, but it'll be the only way I can sleep in here. The halogen bulbs embedded in the ceiling are on and brighter than before. The game now is sleep deprivation, just one more tactic to get me to crack. That my government is capable of such things against one of it's sworn officers should enrage me, but I'm far too tired to summon the indignation.

With time my mind finally succumbs to the fatigue and my body relaxes. The pain is almost tolerable as my consciousness slips away. But all that is shattered as music is suddenly pumped into the room. It's heavy metal, screeching electric guitars and pounding drums, all designed to push me closer to the brink. My eardrums buzz with the assault and my headache returns in full force. I jam my fingers into my ears and try to will the sounds away, but it's futile.

It's the last straw. I feel my chest heave involuntarily as hot tears sting my eyes. The weight of defeat is unbearable. I'm not nearly as strong as I thought. All that experience on the force, all that psychological training, and they've broken me in less than a day. How could I be so weak?

And all the while, the domed eye watches me from the corner of the ceiling, recording it all. They've won. I give up.

"I don't know anything!" I scream. The exertion sends waves of pain cascading through my body, but I ignore it as I continue screaming. I can almost feel my mind slipping away. The pain is submerged under a wave of hysterics.

I'm a victim of their game. I'm cracking.

I force myself to calm down and shut up. *Why? How did I get here? Is God punishing me?*

Maybe He really is out there and the Witnesses have it all right. Heck, maybe that's why the feds haven't been able to nab them yet. And if that's true, and I've been trying to sell them out... I almost laugh at the thought, yet I can't seem to shake the feeling that I've been on the losing side of an uphill battle for a long time.

As suspicious as I always was of Chelsea and Walter, it's impossible to ignore how peaceful things were when we were together. And the conversations I had with Walter, though few, stick in my mind. Even now, despite the screaming guitar chords hammering against my skull, his words come back to me.

"Imagine a cell phone plan that offered worldwide on-site emergency services. No matter where you were or how dire your circumstances, your call would be taken and responded to. Now imagine it was free. That's what prayer is."

I think back to the few prayers I heard Walter say before meals, remembering how freely he spoke. I figure that'll have to do, since I can't remember any of the formal church prayers I learned as a kid. I shut my eyes and clench my hands together and hope that God, if He's up there, won't mind me saying this one half naked while laid out flat on my back.

It's awkward at first, like cold-calling a friend you haven't seen in years because you need a favor, but it's my last hope and I force myself to persevere. I begin with the apologies.

I'm sorry for giving Amy a hard time when I found out she was studying with the Witnesses. I'm sorry for being so cold to Chelsea and Walter when they were only trying to help. I'm sorry for trying to pry the Witnesses' for their secrets...

The list is long, but I do my best to get it all out.

After a while, the words become more natural. It almost feels like I could be talking to someone sitting in this room, someone right beside me. I unload everything that's been weighing me down for the past few months. My anxiety with the new recruits at the office, my concerns with the decline of society and the government's constant encroachment of civil liberties. It's not the country I thought I was defending when I signed up for the force all those years ago, and I'm not sure it's where I want to be now. It certainly hasn't protected *me*, has it?

When I start talking about Amy, the tears return. The idea of her being held in a cell like this, going through any kind of interrogation, is unbearable. I pray that whatever happens, God keeps her far from this place. I thank Him for getting her through her coma. I pause as I come to the end of my prayer, wondering if I even deserve to ask to be saved. I decide it's too unlikely to even bother mentioning, and plead again for Him to keep Amy safe. And Chelsea and Walter too. They're good people, and if I never get out of here alive, I know they'll adopt Amy as their daughter. I suppose, in a way, they already have. I decide to thank God for this, too.

I finish the prayer and open my eyes slowly. The lights are still glaring down from above and the music is as loud as ever, but somehow the room looks less threatening. I feel calmer, at peace. I shield my eyes with the crook of my arm and manage to drift off.

11:47 PM
AMY

It's almost midnight when we pull up to the Atlanta FBI Field Office. I expect we'll have to turn around when we spot a guard booth at the entrance, but it's empty and the gate is open. We drive in slowly, scanning the premises. There are a handful of buildings on either side of the road. They're five or six stories tall with wrap-around mirrored glass windows on the upper floors and chunky concrete pillars at their bases. None of them looks like a prison. Were it not for the official FBI seal we passed out front, I would've just as soon guessed that this was a business park.

We coast southwards down the narrow road, flanked on either side by neat rows of towering, bare trees. The road dead-ends in a parking lot. Despite the late hour, there are a few dozen cars scattered about. Walter finds a space away from the nearest building. I turn back to glance at Chelsea, sound asleep and snoring.

"You wait here, I'll see if there's a front desk or something," Walter says without looking at me. "Keep the doors locked."

I nod and activate the electronic locks as he closes his door, stuffs his hands into his jacket, and strolls quickly towards the rotating glass door. The reflective glass hides him from view as soon as he enters. I wish Chelsea were awake. She'd know what to say to calm me. The thought that Luke might be nearby has me buzzing with nervous energy.

I glance around, noticing at once the security cameras perched like vultures on the overhead light posts. I watch as one of the lenses rotates eerily my way.

There's a sudden *bang* from the rear of the vehicle. I jump with a gasp and whip around in my seat. A bright light is flashed directly in my eyes, followed by the bark of a man's voice.

"Ma'am, I'm gonna need you to get out of your car slowly with your hands up," orders the voice. I raise my hands immediately and watch as the beam of light travels across the cabin. The man comes around to my passenger side window and taps the glass twice with the edge of his flashlight. The light makes it hard to see, but the firearm in his hand is clear and cold.

"I need to unlock the door," I say loudly.

"Use one hand and do it slowly," he says with a warning tone. He eyes the cast on my leg as the door eases open and motions for me to stay in my seat.

"What's her deal?" he asks, gesturing towards Chelsea sprawled out on the backseat.

"She's on heavy medication. We just left the hospital. We were in a bad car accident a few weeks ago."

"Uh huh," the officer says as he shines the beam in my eyes. "You drove here?"

"No, sir. Another friend of ours drove the three of us."

"Where is your friend now?"

"He went into that building over there," I say.

"Why? What are y'all doing here?"

It takes me a moment to think of the right response. "Checking up on a friend."

I expect a barrage of questions but the officer just glares in silence. A moment later he calls for backup into a microphone hidden somewhere on his wrist.

"I'm sorry, sir. I didn't realize we were breaking any rules coming here. The guard shack out front was empty, so we just drove in." The officer gives me a strange look and then turns away to say something else into his mike, but it's too muffled for me to hear.

A second officer arrives in an unmarked car. He slings an automatic rifle over his shoulder and extends a long pole with a small angled mirror attached at the end. He makes sweeping motions under Walter's car, apparently looking for hidden weapons or explosives.

The first officer looks me over suspiciously while the other conducts a thorough search.

"Your friend, the driver. What's his name?"

"Walter Novak," I say without hesitation. And just as I do, I see him walking back towards the car, alone, and my heart sinks.

"Can I help you, officers?" Walter asks as he approaches the vehicle with his hands raised. The two officers whip their weapons in his direction and order him to freeze. They ask a few questions and even frisk him, but when their search turns up nothing, they seem to relax a little.

The officers finally agree to let us go, but as Walter enters the driver's side and pulls out his keys, the unthinkable happens. A loud crack of gunshot splits the air. The officers begin shouting as they duck for cover behind their cars.

We spot the van as it barrels towards the parking lot. The top half of a body is sticking out form the top of the roof, holding something up to his face. The object lights up with an orange spark as he fires a second round. I hear the bullet embed itself into the metal of one of the unmarked police cars.

Walter doesn't wait for the third shot. He jams his keys in the ignition and floors it, racing to the far end of the parking lot away from the gunfire. Several more shots ring out behind us as we speed away. The sounds are much closer, the federal agents returning fire.

The men in the van holler and shriek with laughter as they race down the road, seemingly oblivious to the bullets whizzing their way. A cloud of yellow fire erupts from the ground as an explosion goes off. Streaks of blue flame creep along the pavement as the fireball dissipates high in the air.

"How are we going to get out of here?" I ask, terrified, as I watch the mayhem unfolding in our rearview mirrors. There's only one road in and out of this lot, and it's currently blocked by armed madmen. Walter still has us pointed in the opposite direction, but we're quickly running out of room to run. A handful of heavily armed officers spill from one of the building's side doors as we speed past. They take up positions behind trees and parked cars and join the fray.

Walter rounds the end of the parking lot, getting us as far from the rattle of automatic weapons as possible. A spotlight from somewhere high up floods the parking lot with a focused beam of light and centers itself on the attackers. I can see them clearly now. There are four men in total. Bandanas are tied around their heads and they're covered in some kind of armor. Their van appears to be reinforced with heavy metal plating, and each of them is firing a weapon. On the side of their vehicle is a large, red spray painted 'Z'.

"Who are these people?" I ask, terrified.

"I'll explain later. Right now, I need you to hold on to something and make sure your seat belt is on."

I turn around quickly in my seat and buckle in as he activates the 4x4 drive on his steering column. I brace myself by pressing against the headboard as Walter rambles up the sidewalk and onto a small paved footpath. Spindly shrubs scrape noisily against the sides of his truck. He grits his teeth as we charge up the hill. We plow across a small lawn bordered by low bushes and bound ahead.

We dodge trees and benches and eventually make our way back onto the main road. We've cut around the flying bullets, but it's still only a few dozen yards behind us. If the attackers have backup, we'll be right in their path.

Walter floors the gas as the screams of injured men fade in the distance. We fly past the abandoned guard shack and slip back onto northbound 1-85.

TUESDAY, JANUARY 26

7:42 AM
LUKE

There's an odd smell in the air when I open my eyes. It's faint, a mixture of gasoline and gunpowder, I think. The heavy metal is gone, and the only sound in my cell is the faint echo of voices from outside in the hall. They seem to be arguing, though I can't make out any of the words.

When the door creaks open I struggle to prop myself up on an elbow. It's Meade, and he's not happy. I brace for the worst, and the dark thought crosses my mind that this may be the day they kill me. Without a word, he motions to a man behind him who enters the room and unshackles my legs. They cuff me and slip me into laceless sneakers.

"Get up and follow me," Meade growls. The skin beneath his red eyes is blue and puffy.

I emerge from my cell to a concrete hallway. The narrow space is lined by other steel doors which no doubt lead to more chambers, and I wonder momentarily if any are occupied. I refuse to consider the fact that one of them may be holding my wife.

Agent Meade leads me silently up a set of concrete stairs and into another hallway flanked by floor-to-ceiling windows. Strangely, a few are badly cracked and one is missing completely. On the other side of us is a huge room of computer desks, bulletin boards, and stacks of boxes. Dozens of agents scramble around the space, packing items into plastic crates and yelling at each other. We descend into a parking lot where a black armored van idles, engine rumbling. Two armed men fling the back doors open and Meade shoves me in.

As we drive off, I glimpse out of the back windows at the parking lot. It's a war zone. Broken glass and brass bullet casings are strewn across the macadam as far as the eye can see. Fire damage is everywhere. Men and women in white gloves photograph an area where the charred remains of a vehicle is surrounded by what can only be dead bodies draped in white sheets.

"What happened here?" I ask incredulously. The guards scowl at me before pulling the black sleeve over my head. They push me against the wall of the truck where I sit on a narrow bench. I wince in pain with every dip and bump in the road.

When we get on the highway we hit traffic, forcing us to slow to a crawl. Drivers around us are on laying on their horns, screaming, shouting profanities. I can hear the two guards mumbling something to each other. Their voices are tense and agitated.

"I swear, if I see any of those Zekes, I'll shoot first."

His partner grunts in agreement. "I heard they hit a couple of other field offices in the South. Seems coordinated."

"I can tell you one thing, I don't like sitting in traffic like this. Easy target for anyone camped out on an overpass."

"You think they'd just take shots at us like that?"

"Who knows? Everyone's lost it. They don't even care if we're armed."

The conversation stops as they move around the vehicle, presumably keeping a lookout through the tinted security windows. One of them finally sighs in frustration.

"I-85's gonna be like this for miles. We'll be stuck here for hours."

"I wonder where all these people are headed..."

"Probably don't even know themselves. They just want out of the city, not thinking it through," he scoffs.

"Yeah, seems like it. Don't blame 'em, though. Hard to believe this is really happening, man. Your family alright?"

"Yeah, I sent them down to Florida last week. Got an aunt down there who lives out in the boonies. Told 'em to hole up till this blows over. You?"

"My ex won't return my calls. She has the kids. They should be ok if they stay put. Both my boys know how to handle a .35 and I know the house is well stocked. Heck, I used to own it." The man lets out a disdainful chuckle.

A momentary silence is shattered by the crack of a high-powered firearm. We hold our breath waiting for the impact but it doesn't come. I can hear one of the guards fumbling with something. When he speaks, I realize he's talking into a radio.

"Was that what I think it was?" he asks tensely. A pause. Meade's voice responds form the other end.

"Yeah, someone pulled a gun about ten cars up. I don't have a line of sight on them anymore. Keep your heads down, this could get ugly." The guard copies this into the radio and I can hear the two men check their rifles. They say nothing, but their breathing quickens.

"I wonder how many of these drivers are armed?" one of the guards says. When the second shot rings out it's accompanied by screams. I can only imagine the chaos outside as people must decide whether to remain in their vehicles or abandon them on foot.

Car doors opening. Feet rushing past. More gunfire. More screams. Some of the bodies bang against the outside of our van as they stream by. I think I hear a few people stumble and fall, and I try not to think of what will happen to them.

"We should be out there helping them," I say.

"What did you just say?" one of the guards hisses at me.

"People are going to get hurt. We should be helping them."

One of them orders me to shut up as he jabs the butt of his rifle into my chest. Despite the tough guy routine, there is fear in his voice and the gunfire continues.

Meade revs the engine and attempts to ram the cars in front of us. The three of us are thrown to the floor on impact. I hit the side of my head on something hard as I go down. He must be attempting to squeeze by on the shoulder lane, but he gives up after a few minutes of spastic driving. The smell of burning rubber seeps into the cabin. Meade's voice crackles through the guard's radio a moment later.

"Alright, we're gonna have to suit up. Full riot gear."

"Sir, it's literally a constant flow of people out there, we'll never be able to fight past them."

"Go with the flow of human traffic. We'll head southbound. I'm calling a local sheriff to meet us at the on ramp."

The two guards grumble as they suit up in the cramped space. One of them tugs the black hood from my head and gives me a bitter look. "I'm taking this off because I don't want you slowing us down. Keep up and don't try anything stupid."

I nod obediently and for the first time grasp the scale of panic outside the van. A thick sea of terrified faces rushes by without end. Some hold screaming children in their arms. Others wander by aimlessly with blank expressions, as if the panic is too great to process.

It's insanity, joining the mob like this, and the two guards seem to realize it. They cast wary glances at each other as they fling the doors open and climb out. As soon as we exit the vehicle we're sucked into the strong current of moving bodies. A few people shoot us nervous glances but most don't seem to notice.

The two guards cut their way through the crowd to the right shoulder lane. I can see now that we're on an overpass. About thirty feet below us lies a river. Thin patches of ice line the banks. We pause for a moment to regroup as Meade brings up the rear, eyes never leaving me.

"So how far is this exit?" one of the guards asks as he checks his rifle. The other guard is eyeing the crowd warily. An occasional shot of gunfire rings out, forcing us to brace harder against the pushing bodies as they try vainly to quicken their pace.

"Couple miles. We need to keep moving," Meade answers. The guards grunt in accord and turn to move, just as a man reaches out from the crowd and grabs one of the guard's rifles.

"Hey!" the officer shouts as he tries to yank it free. The man's grip is strong, and he's pulled from the crowd with the motion. He snarls at the guard and wraps a second hand around the firearm, doing his best to wrestle it away. The second officer moves in quickly and attempts to pry the man off, but a woman launches from the fray and claws at his face with a snarl. The guards do their best to fight them off, but a frenzy has set in. Meade stares at the crowd in disbelief, his mouth moving without words. He shoulders his weapon and pulls the trigger.

For a split second, everything seems to stand still. The bodies stop moving, the faces frozen as their minds process reality. The woman collapses, her arms dropping away lifelessly from the guard. The man who attacked first charges at Meade, screaming with hysterical rage.

I back away slowly from the scene. The waist-high concrete wall is just behind me now, and I lean into it. It's a crazy idea, but it's my only chance. I hear a shot ring out as I swing my legs over the wall and plummet headfirst into the icy water below.

8:10 AM

AMY

I wake in the parking lot of a rundown Texaco. My teeth chatter in the cold. Walter snores loudly in the driver's seat, his feet propped up on the dash. Chelsea is still laid out on the backseat, sleeping soundly under Walter's jacket. I dig through my purse to locate my phone, but the battery's dead. According to the clock on the dash, it's a little after eight.

I can't remember dozing off the night before. Walter had insisted we drive as far as possible while the traffic was still light. I remember getting on the highway after that terrifying attack at the FBI building, but I must've fallen asleep soon after. Snippets from yesterday's events littered my dreams. Sounds of gunfire and explosions, screams from the hospital ward, Luke's arrest. There must still be a way to help him, but my mind can't focus enough to think of it.

I stretch and yawn, my breath puffing condensation into the air. I swipe away some of the moisture from the glass windshield to get a clearer look at the gas station. Little maintenance appears to have been done in the last decade to keep it up. I almost wonder if it's been abandoned, until I note the price of gas and a pile of empty Mountain Dew cans. I rub my shoulders to keep warm and consider waking Walter when I suddenly scream.

An oversized German shepherd is reared up on the outside of my door. He's snapping and snarling through barred teeth. If it weren't for the glass, I'm sure he would've taken a chunk out of my arm. The noise stirs Walter to his senses and he rubs his eyes for a moment, collecting himself.

"How long did we drive last night?" I ask as I eye the dog nervously, fully expecting it to break through at any moment.

"Only a couple of hours. I was starting to nod off, and thought I'd just take a quick nap. I set my alarm, but…" Walter digs through his coat pocket in the backseat to retrieve his cellphone, only to find it as lifeless as mine. "Well, that explains it."

"Do you know where we are?" I ask. The dog's paws are still up against the glass, but it's stopped barking for the moment. It retreats suddenly to the back of the building. Walter leans over the seat and extracts a map from the glove compartment. He unfolds it on his lap and runs his finger along the yellow line of I-85.

"Should be around here somewhere," he says, tapping a small dot on the map. It's a small town I've never heard of far beyond the state line.

"And how much further?" I ask, a shiver running up my spine.

"We can be there before noon if we hurry."

"Ok. Just one little problem," I say sheepishly. Walter looks at me questioningly. "I've gotta use the bathroom."

Walter grimaces as he looks down at the cast on my leg. Then he freezes. Standing just outside the truck is a tall man in a puffy coat and dirty jeans. In his hands, he holds an old shotgun, and it's pointed straight at us.

Walter's hands go up slowly, palms out.

"Whoa there, bud. You gon' wan' stop raght there," the man drawls.

"We don't want any trouble, sir," Walter says calmly.

"What y'all doin' sittin' up in this truck? You been here all naht," the man says, his eyes darting back and forth between the two of us.

"We were driving last night up from the city and got tired. We didn't expect to stay overnight. I apologize. Is this your property?" Walter asks, lowering his hands an inch or two. The man studies us another moment before speaking.

"Been havin' nothin' but trouble here with out-of-towners. Looters came through coupl'a nahts ago. Had to turn Rowdy on 'em, but it was too late. Ransack'd my store." Apparently hearing his name, the German shepherd appears from behind the building and sits at his master's side.

"I'm sorry to hear that," Walter says sincerely. "I can assure you, we're not here to bring you any more trouble. The missus here just needs to make a trip to the little girls' room."

"*Missus*? You two married? Looks young enough to be yer daughter."

"No," Walter says, managing a chuckle despite the gun pointed at his belly. "She's just a friend. My wife's in the backseat, sleeping."

The man mumbles something under his breath before motioning towards the store with his gun. "Go on, then. There's a restroom in the back. But if I cetch you two stealin' anythang, Rowdy here's liable to take a chunk outta yo' leg. Y'hear?"

We nod and Walter grabs my wheelchair from the back and helps me into it. The man seems puzzled over my injury but doesn't ask any more questions. I see him peek into the vehicle curiously a few times as Walter wheels me away. When we're done, Walter packs the wheelchair and me back into the car. The man is sitting on an old tree stump chewing on a handful of tobacco.

"Thanks for that," Walter says, offering his hand. The man eyes it for a minute before taking it and shaking.

"Where're y'all headed, anyway?" he asks.

"A little town near Greenville, South Carolina."

"Hope y'all not thankin' of takin' the interstate," he says with a grunt.

"Why not?"

"It's all clogged up. Had a whole bit on it in the news this mornin'. Folks've started leavin' their cars and walkin' it's so bad." Walter glances off in the direction of the highway and frowns.

"Thanks for the tip," he says. The man nods and spits on the ground. His dog walks over and sniffs it curiously.

"Y'all watch yo' backs out there," he says as he looks ominously down the road. "Folks a'int the same these days."

Walter and I thank him again and head off down the road in a cloud of dust.

8:15 AM
LUKE

The water is so cold it nearly takes my breath away. I fight the urge to gasp as I plunge below the surface. A lung full of this water is all it would take to kill me. I force myself to keep calm and surface. Though my hands are still handcuffed in front of me, I'm able to find purchase on a metal handhold jutting from one of the pillars of the overpass. The interrogation from the night before and the unimaginable cold have sapped most of my strength; it takes all I've got just to hold on.

I brace my legs against the concrete pylon and push myself towards the east bank of the river. If my captors chase me, they'll have to fight the torrent of bodies on the overpass, get off at the next exit, and comb through the wooded area around the river. I've got an advantage, but it's not much and I can't waste a second.

My muscles are numb and stiff and my teeth are chattering uncontrollably as I reach the riverbank. Fatigue is next, and it takes every ounce of remaining strength to force myself to stand and press on. It's difficult to think clearly as I analyze the situation. I'm covered in mud, shivering fiercely, and handcuffed. I come to the terrifying realization that I'm experiencing hypothermia. I need to keep moving, and follow the river north.

My body fights me all the way. The muscles in my legs and feet feel swollen and sluggish, and it's an act of sheer willpower to resist the urge to lie down and rest. The thought of Amy keeps me going. I mull over the conversation of the two guards in the back of the van. I wonder if my wife's ok, if she's still in the hospital, or if Walter managed to get her out somehow. I'm safe for the moment, but Meade could just as easily sic a pack of agents on Amy as leverage. I need to keep moving. I need to contact her.

The panic thaws my mind. I move with deliberate, exaggerated motions, coaxing the blood back into my extremities. The cold still stings, but I figure the pain is a better sign than numbness and press on.

I've walked about a half mile when I spot a small shed not far from the river. I note a pile of chopped wood at its side and knock. When there's no response, I let myself in. The shed is small, roughly ten by ten, but it's a goldmine. I spot a coat hanging from a hook on the wall and a series of tools neatly arranged on a worktable. I manage to snap off the handcuffs with a pair of rusty bolt-cutters and slip into the dusty coat before leaving. I toss the cuffs into the river and keep heading north. I'm careful to keep out of the mud, wary of leaving tracks. I glance over my shoulder every few minutes but see nothing.

It takes a while longer for the shivering to stop. The heavy coat chafes against the scars on my chest and I wince against the pain. Bruises and small cuts on my scalp and face abound. Still, so long as the adrenaline is pumping, I can manage. The mental sluggishness passes as my body warms, though I still have no idea where I'm headed. I'm hungry, too, and I scold myself for not making a more careful search of the shed for something to eat.

I keep following the river upstream, well aware that getting lost in the forest would be just as dangerous as the peril I'm fleeing. I estimate I've walked about two hours when I see tire tracks in the mud of the riverbank and turn to follow them inland. They lead through a forested area but there's the clear outline of a trail. The mud eventually gives way to a broad gravel path, and after another mile or so it joins a two-lane stretch of paved asphalt. I choose a direction at random and walk along the shoulder of the road, though I'm careful to keep close to the tree line in case I need to dive for cover.

I duck behind some bushes as the first few cars pass. Most are moving slowly, weighed down by trailers and full loads on their roofs. They almost look like they could be going camping, but the tense expressions of the passengers reveal a different story.

After a while I conclude it's unlikely that Meade and his goons will be riding in any kind of vehicle, and decide there's no need to hide from the cars. When a navy blue Honda sedan stacked high with cardboard boxes wrapped in a plastic tarp and bungee cords passes, I decide to play it cool. I avoid eye contact and try to keep my face out of sight. Though I think it's too soon for any kind of organized manhunt, I can't afford to risk it.

My pulse quickens as the car passes and slows. I can feel the passengers' eyes staring me down but I try to ignore it. I can only imagine what they're thinking as they look me over. I'm wet, muddy, and limping slightly, the muscles in my legs still not completely recovered from the previous night's electrocutions. I hear the squeak of the brakes as the sedan comes to a stop.

That's when I run. I leap over a few shrubs and charge into the woods as the car's doors open behind me. A woman shouts, but I don't stop until I realize what she's saying. She's shouting my name!

I chance a glance over my shoulder. A couple is standing at the edge of the road with matching quizzical expressions. It takes a moment to place the faces. It's the family I met a few weeks back at the hospital before Amy had woken up. The boy and the get well card.

"Is that you, Luke?" the man calls out, squinting. I nod cautiously but keep my distance.

"What are you two doing here?" I shout, trying to catch my breath. They look at me oddly. I am, after all, a runaway prisoner lost in the woods.

"We're headed up north," the woman says as their names finally dawn on me. Ashley and Marc.

"What's going on, Luke? What happened to you?" Marc asks, looking me over. I shake my head slowly, unsure how to answer. A truck passes us on the road and slows, the faces looking over us suspiciously. Ashley and Marc exchange a glance. Finally, Marc motions me over.

"Why don't you get in the car with us, Luke. We can give you a ride to… wherever you're headed."

Ashley nods in agreement and gets in the backseat. Marc pulls a towel from one of the boxes and hands it to me. I wipe most of the mud off and wrap the towel around my waist before getting in the passenger seat. Their son, Matthew, is sitting in the backseat in a booster chair, and I can tell something's not right. He appears to be sleeping, but his face is covered in sweat and his skin is white and splotchy.

"What happened to your son?" I ask.

"We're not sure," Marc says with a sigh. "It could be this cow flu everyone's talking about. The symptoms seem to fit. It came on suddenly. He was fine a couple of days ago, and then yesterday he could barely move. We would've left the house sooner otherwise. Could've beaten the gridlock on the freeway."

"He looks pretty bad. You don't want to see a doctor?"

"We would have, but most of the clinics have shut down, and it's impossible to get near the hospital."

"St. Mary's? Why? What happened?" I ask nervously, thinking of Amy.

"Rioters, I think. People started panicking. There was a big shootout when the police finally…" Marc's voice trails off and he shoots me a glance. "Amy got out of there ok, didn't she?"

"I don't know. I haven't seen her in a while."

"Why? Where have you been, Luke?"

I mull the question over and consider my options before answering. "I was in a car accident."

Marc looks me over and frowns. "Why were you all the way out here? And what happened to the car?"

I shrug, trying to play dumb. "I can't remember. I guess I was thrown from the wreckage somehow. I've been wandering around in the woods."

"Why did you run when we stopped the car?" Ashley asks from the backseat.

"I don't know. I'm not thinking too clearly. Everything's still a blur." True enough.

"Weird. Well, it's a good thing we found you," Marc says with a sigh. "I doubt anyone else would've stopped. People are going completely insane with everything that's been going on."

"Yeah, thanks for stopping. It's quite a coincidence," I grunt.

"Maybe it wasn't a coincidence," Ashley says quietly from the backseat. I turn to look at her and she smiles hopefully.

"So do you have a specific place that you're headed to, or what?" I ask. Marc makes an uncomfortable expression and frowns.

"Yeah, we're headed… to meet some friends of ours."

"How far away are they?"

"Oh, another few hours at least."

"A few hours? Is it past the state line?" Marc nods, but I can sense he doesn't want to go into detail. "Hey, would it be possible for me to borrow one of your phones? I'm really worried about Amy. I want to make sure she's safe."

Marc shakes his head slowly with a serious expression. "I'm so sorry, Luke, but I can't…"

"Dead battery? What about yours, Ashley?" I ask. She looks at me in the rearview mirror strangely.

"It's not the battery, Luke. We left our phones behind."

"What? Did you forget them?"

Marc shakes his head. "No. It's a bit hard to explain. But it was safer, leaving them."

"Safer? But what happens if you have car trouble? Why would you leave something like that behind?"

"We were told to," Ashley says suddenly. I wait for an explanation.

"They can track our phones," Marc says under his breath.

"Who can?"

"The authorities."

I take a deep breath and rub my temples. "Ok, back up. What authorities are you talking about, and who told you that you were being tracked?"

Marc remains silent for a long moment. He's gripping the wheel tightly and biting his lip, clearly unsure of whether he should reveal anything. I sigh and decide to take a chance.

"Look, I'm gonna come clean with you guys," I say softly. The tension from Marc and Ashley is palpable as I pause. "I wasn't in a car accident. I was arrested by federal agents. They tortured me and interrogated me in a prison cell." I hear Ashley gasp from the backseat.

"Why?" Marc asks. "What did they want to know?"

"They wanted to know about you people. The Witnesses."

Marc nods slowly and oddly seems to relax a little. "Did you tell them anything?"

"I didn't *know* anything."

"But why were you in the woods?" Ashley asks.

"I managed to escape. They had me in a truck on an overpass and we got caught in a stampede. Everyone abandoned their cars. The guards tried to move me and I jumped over the barricade and into a river. I wandered for a few hours in the woods until you found me."

"That's incredible," Ashley says, and for some reason a smile creeps onto her face. Marc glances at her in the rearview mirror and nods knowingly.

"Well, Luke," he says. "It looks like you're with us now."

12:29 PM
AMY

It's well past noon when we finally reach the property. We drive a mile or so up a gravel road and come to a large open field of grass. As we wind up the hill, a huge swath of pavement comes into view. A man sitting under a canopy stops as we approach and Walter rolls his window down to wave.

"Hey, Fred," Walter says with a smile.

"Good to see you, Walter," the man says as he peers into the windows and jots something down on a clipboard. "Three of you total?"

"That's right. Chelsea and I, and this is Chelsea's Bible student, Amy Harding. She should be on the list."

Fred squints at his clipboard and nods. "No phones on you, right?"

"Batteries died sometime last night while we were on the highway."

"You still have them?" Fred asks. Walter and I nod. "Ok, you'll have to leave them here. We need to dismantle anything than can be tracked."

"Understood," Walter says. I hesitate for a long moment, feeling as if I'm severing my final connection to my husband.

"Amy, we need to follow the directions. I'm sorry," Walter says somberly. I finally nod, wiping a single tear away from the corner of my eye, and hand my phone over. Fred places the phones into a metal bin.

"Alright, you're good to go. Keep following the road up that way. You can park on the north side of the hangar. We've got attendants there."

"Are all of these people our brothers and sisters?" I whisper as we round the corner behind the hangar. Two young men with walkie-talkies motion for us to park in a narrow lane between two other trucks.

"The attendants all are and I imagine that most in that building are, too. But Bible studies and publishers were invited as well, and we made a special effort to contact all the inactive ones. Even unbelieving mates were welcome."

Walter pulls to the side and retrieves my wheelchair before parking. The brothers jog over to help as soon as they notice my leg.

"We're sorry, brother, we didn't realize you had anyone injured. We've got handicapped spaces near–"

"No, no need. We can wheel her in. Save those spaces for the seriously injured," he grunts, lifting me and setting me gently in the chair. The brothers nod and run back to their posts as another car pulls up. It leans unsteadily on a wobbling spare tire, and the rear of the vehicle is badly scratched and dented. The driver, a tall black man, leaps out as soon as he's parked and bear hugs the two attendants. Tears streak down his face.

"I almost didn't make it. It was so close. Thank Jehovah!" he exclaims, looking up at the sky with a bright smile. He spots Walter trying to get Chelsea out of the car and runs over to assist. The attendants race off to direct more cars as they approach.

"I've got her, brother," Walter says to the man. "But maybe you can help me wheel her inside," he says, motioning in my direction.

"Of course, my brother," the man says, spotting me and jogging over. His face is still shiny from his tears, and he beams at me.

"My name is Akusa Odelawe. And who are you?" he asks in what must be an African accent as he takes the handles of the wheelchair and points me towards the building.

"Amy Harding."

"Sister Harding. It is a pleasure to meet you!"

A brother opens the doors as we reach the building and greets us with a smile. The scene takes my breath away. The floor area is crammed with hundreds of people. PVC pipe frames are draped in fabric sheets and blankets to form a labyrinth of partitions. Cots, air mattresses, and stacked quilts neatly line the wide walkways. I survey the sea of smiling faces, and the realization that these are all my brothers and sisters brings tears to my eyes. I've never seen so many of us together. Shortly after I started attending meetings, many of our activities were moved underground, robbing me of the opportunity of ever attending an assembly. I look back and notice I'm not the only one crying. Brother Odelawe has stopped pushing my chair as he holds two palms to his face and sobs.

"It's so beautiful," I hear him say.

An attendant approaches us and politely asks a few questions. I explain that I'm from Haliford East Congregation, and Brother Odelawe gives the name of a congregation I've never heard of. The attendant welcomes us each with a small paper bag filled with an assortment of toiletries.

"Please use it sparingly, everything is very limited here," the attendant counsels as he moves us on. Many of the friends embrace with tears in their eyes and glowing smiles. Others are praying in small groups with bowed heads. There's an electricity in the air that surpasses even those times long ago when we used to have meetings at the Kingdom Hall.

We eventually run into a few faces I recognize from my congregation. Brother Odelawe wishes me the best and heads off into the crowd to find his congregation's section.

I hear a few gasps and squeals of excitement as the sisters from our congregation gather around me. We exchange hugs and the questions begin. Many have heard about our accident and are eager for details. How serious were the injuries? Am I in pain? How can they help? Walter arrives a few moments later with Chelsea. The sisters quickly prepare a bed for her and Walter sets her down. She's stirring slightly, but the drugs still have her heavily sedated.

He takes a deep breath and begins trembling as the emotions take their toll. "It's so good to see you all," he says softly to the friends around us.

"And it's good to see you, Walter," says a familiar voice from over my shoulder. I turn to see an elderly brother sitting in a wheelchair similar to mine.

"Brother Harris!" I exclaim. "I haven't seen you in ages."

"Same here. I'm glad to know you're safe. I was worried when you all didn't show up last night. The freeways have been a mess since this morning. I fear for any of our friends who are still out there. You should've left sooner," he says to Walter in a mildly scolding tone.

"We would've, but the odds were stacked against us. With their injuries and all the chaos in the city, we were fortunate to get out at all."

"Jehovah was looking after you, I'm sure," Brother Harris says. "You should hear some of the other stories going around. It'll be enough to write our own yearbook."

"So, what's the deal with this place?" I ask, looking high up at the steel girders and walkways.

"This used to be a private airstrip. One of the biggest in the Southeast, in fact. It was owned by a brother and his wife. They passed away about a decade ago and donated the property to the organization. I always thought it would eventually become an assembly hall one day, but now I realize that would've never worked."

"What do you mean?" I ask.

"Assembly halls are great for assemblies but not so great as refugee shelters, unless you can get the chairs out."

My eyes widen as the realization dawns on me. "You mean this was all planned? They knew we were going to use this place as a shelter?"

Brother Harris shrugs with a smile. "Well, I'm sure Jehovah knew, but as for the rest of us... *Who can know the mind of God?*"

We listen intently for a few minutes as Brother Harris relates some encouraging experiences. He shares a scripture from Luke 21:28 to remind us that our deliverance is near, but warns that there are still tests ahead. As he finishes, Walter pulls him aside to speak privately. I try not to eavesdrop, but I hear my husband's name mentioned a few times and wonder.

"Can I ask what that was about?" I ask Walter quietly once Brother Harris has left. Walter is taking Chelsea's pulse and frowning.

"Neither of us is sure if there's anything more we can do for Luke, Amy. All we can do is pray and leave the rest up to Jehovah. It's in his hands now."

I'm nodding sadly. Walter pulls my wheelchair towards him and wraps an arm around me. "I'm so sorry, Amy. We tried. We have to trust in Jehovah. He always knows what's best."

"I know. I know," I say, struggling to believe it.

12:55 PM
LUKE

We meander the wooded roads for miles but after three hours of driving we're still nowhere near our destination. Without their phones, Marc and Ashley are forced to navigate by an ancient Garmin GPS. I doubt the maps are even up to date, but there's little point in bringing it up. I try to sleep, but despite my utter exhaustion my mind refuses to rest. I fret constantly over the fate of my wife and keep wondering if there's any way to contact her.

"Does this thing show any towns coming up?" I ask, pointing at the dash-mounted GPS.

"I think so. But if you need to use a bathroom, I'd suggest doing it here in the woods. You need me to stop?"

"No, it's not that. I was wondering if I could get to a payphone. Maybe try calling the hospital."

"I'm sure Amy's fine, Luke," Marc says.

"How do you know?"

"Well for one thing, she's probably with Walter. He was with Chelsea last I heard from him, and they were in the same hospital ward. And for another, she's got Jehovah on her side."

"I wish I had your faith," I say with a grimace.

"It takes time. But after all we've been through, we are one hundred percent sure Jehovah has been helping us."

"Yeah?"

"Absolutely. We've experienced his helping hand countless times, especially in the recent months. When I lost my job the friends were right there to help. We ended up living with another family. It wasn't easy, but we managed."

"Where are they now?" I ask.

"They were evacuated to a different location. We weren't in the same congregation."

"Congregation. I've heard the term before."

"It's a term for a group of witnesses assigned to meet and do the ministry together. Each congregation is taken care of by a group of older men, called elders."

"Yeah, I figured as much. That's what my interrogators wanted to know. Who all your elders were."

"Walter's one of them," Ashley says.

"Figures," I say. "So how were you all organized? The feds said they were monitoring everything, but they seemed to know very little."

"We were very careful. Our organization had us prepared well in advance. We used encrypted software and internet connections to do everything."

"What about cell phones?"

"We used them, but always encoded our messages. When we had to make phone calls or send texts, like to Bible students, we had a system of code words."

"And was this just locally?"

"No. Every congregation of Witnesses around the world had the same instructions. We were communicating with them up until the moment we had to evacuate."

"But you left your phones at home?"

"We got a message a few days ago saying that the encryption for the app we use was compromised. Something about a hack attempt. The branch told us to be sure to not bring our phones to the safe house."

"Branch?"

"Yeah, it's the term we use for a department that cares for the congregations under its supervision."

"I had no idea you people were so organized. You've got it more together than your government."

"More evidence we've got divine backing. Governments are in turmoil all over the world, and yet we've managed to stay completely united and organized. In fact, we've probably become *more* unified."

I find myself nodding in amazement. "So everyone is being evacuated? Worldwide?"

"That I'm not sure of. I know that many in larger urban areas have been directed to move to other areas. I can't say that it's the same everywhere, though. But it's been the right call."

"Why is that?"

"In all the instances I've heard of so far, once the friends were safely evacuated, something catastrophic happened in the city they'd left. Fires, anarchy, rioting, you name it. There was even one instance in Europe of a nuclear meltdown at a power facility right after the brothers left. If the friends paid attention to the warnings and got out in time, they were safe. Sadly though, some didn't heed the warnings."

"What happened to them?"

"Well, as an example, a brother in one area south of us decided it would be safest for him and his family to build an underground bunker and begin stockpiling supplies. This was long before the evacuation orders came through. Our organization has never recommended this, but apparently he was pretty adamant about it. Even started urging some of the others in his congregation to do the same. Once it was built, he filled it with canned goods and jugs of water and propane tanks and so on. He spent most of the family's savings on the project. Well, eventually some of his neighbors got wind of it. One night a group of masked men with guns stormed his house and forced him and his family out. They eventually made it to the safe house, but it was a nightmare. They barely made it out of the city with their lives."

"But what about people like my wife, who were trapped in hospitals, or hurt? What if they didn't get out?"

Marc draws a long breath before answering. "I can't answer that, but I know that Jehovah never leaves people behind. He'll find a way. In any case, we need to stop soon for gas. We'll see if they have a payphone."

It takes us another forty-five minutes to reach the gas station. I expect the place to be lined with cars trying to fill up, but there's only one other vehicle at the pumps, an old Jeep with mud caked in the wheel wells, a hunting rifle up on the racks. The hood is up, and a large bearded man stands glaring at the engine in frustration. He gives me a cold look as we pull up. At the side of the building I find a payphone and place a call to St. Mary's. An automated message tells me the lines are down.

Frustrated and helpless, I return to the car and wait while Marc fills the tank. Ashley is tending to their son, whose condition has worsened over the last couple hours. She wets a towel and places it gently on his forehead. "He's burning up," she says when she sees me staring. "I hope they have a doctor there."

"Me too," I say, and freeze. Just outside our car, the bearded man from the Jeep is standing just outside our car. In his hands is the hunting rifle, its glistening tip leveled straight at us.

"Get out," he growls.

1:03 PM

AMY

A little after noon an announcement comes over the PA system. The voice offers a brief prayer and asks us to form lines for lunch. Walter and I make our way to the line and chat with others idly as we wait. Despite the sizable crowd, we're served and back at our cots within half an hour. The meal is simple: a bowl of diluted tomato soup, side salad, ham and cheese sandwich. Still, no one's complaining, especially after we see the news.

A few screens installed high up on the walls of the hangar are turned on shortly after lunch, eliciting a wave of gasps from the crowd. Aerial footage from a helicopter is being broadcast as a reporter solemnly delivers his lines. Atlanta is an inferno. Countless structures spew long columns of black smoke or slowly succumb to climbing walls of flames. Heavily damaged police vehicles with broken windows and spray paint scrawls litter the streets. In spite of it all, throngs of people still mill around in the streets, many with guns slung over their shoulders or exiting buildings with large boxes and containers.

"It's a good thing we left when we did," Walter says grimly as he points to one of the screens. The aerial cameras are now trained on a hospital downtown. Fire pours from a row of windows on the upper floors as people dash about frantically on the roof.

"That could've been us," I say softly. Walter nods without turning to look at me. We peel ourselves away from the news reports after a few minutes and chat with the friends. The exchanges are brief and tense; everyone's happy to be here, but we're full of uncertainty for what lies ahead.

Walter and I make our way back to our cots to find Chelsea awake and peering around curiously. She's frail and disoriented, but it's a relief just to see her sitting upright again.

There's a man sitting at her side holding her hand, and I assume it's one of our doctor friends until we get a little closer and he turns. For a Witness, his hair seems unusually long and unkempt, but somehow he looks familiar. Walter gasps and runs up to greet him. He throws his arms around him and the two weep quietly while I try to make sense of it.

"Amy," Walter says, finally turning to me as he drags his sleeve across his eyes. "This is our son, Jesse."

My eyes widen as I make the connection. A perfect meld of his parents, really. Jesse looks oddly at me and offers his hand. He looks down at the floor as his father pats him exuberantly on the back.

"It's so good to see you, son. Did you have any trouble getting here?"

Jesse shakes his head. He glances at me quickly and then turns away. "No, your directions were pretty straightforward, once I could decipher them."

"Good. And what about Isabelle?"

Jesse shrugs and shakes his head. "She didn't want to come."

"That must've been a difficult choice, son," Walter says with a sad look and sighs.

"I'm ok. We'd… hit a rough spot lately. It's good to see you and mom. It's been a long time." Walter nods, and for a moment the two study Chelsea silently. "Her memory loss seems pretty bad," Jesse says quietly. "She seemed to recognize me at first, and then she forgot who I was."

Walter nods. "She comes and goes. The doctors said there was some serious trauma to her frontal lobe. They believe that's what's causing the amnesia. But at least we know it's temporary. All this is."

Jesse turns to his father and nods.

"You got rid of the beard," Walter says, stroking his son's cheek.

"Yeah, well, I figured they might not let me in here if I still had it. I guess Witnesses still don't do the beard thing, huh?"

"Not in this area, usually. I wonder if things will change after, though. We'll have to see. You looked handsome with a beard."

Jesse's face reddens somewhat and he smiles. "Didn't get a chance to cut the hair though, sorry," he says abashedly.

"I wouldn't worry about it. I'm sure we've got a barber and a pair of scissors around here somewhere. But that's not important now. Tell me, how have you been?"

I decide to give the two some privacy and wheel myself quietly away from the partition. I only make it a few yards when I see brother Odelawe bounding up the walkway towards me.

"Hello, Sister Amy! It is good to see you. Have you eaten?"

I can't help smiling. "Yeah. You?"

"Very full. It was so good to have a meal with my brothers! Where are you headed?"

"Just thought I'd get a look around the place. It's a lot bigger than it looks from the outside."

"Oh yes, it is. Where would you like to go? I can help you." And without another word, Odelawe is behind me pushing my wheelchair.

We make a circuit around the outer walkway. Brothers are putting up signs for a help desk, bathrooms, an outdoor shower area, a cleaning and laundry department, a commissary, an exchange area, a lost and found, even a nursing room.

"It's amazing they set this all up so fast," I say under my breath, though Odelawe still hears me.

"Only Jehovah's people. This is a taste of the New World! Very organized, very peaceful."

I'm nodding quietly, but secretly hope he's wrong. It's a little too cramped for my taste, and the smell of sweaty bodies seems to be getting stronger as the day wears on.

"So, is it just you here?" I ask over my shoulder. Odelawe looks down to smile at me.

"Yes, I am the only one here, but I have family in Nigeria who are also Witnesses."

"Oh? That's nice," I say with a touch of envy.

"They learned the truth years ago, shortly after I moved to America to attend university. They would call me often and try to preach to me. At that time, I belonged to a church. I was told by my pastor to disown my family, that they had left the true faith and would burn forever in hell for their sins."

"But you didn't listen," I say, casually wondering where that pastor is now.

"No, but it took me a long time. I flew back to Nigeria often, and would argue with my family every time, trying to convince them that they were being deceived by those *'Watchtower devils'*. But I soon realized that I had no way of proving myself with Bible scripture. Although my parents were much older than me and not as educated, they had no trouble finding the verses to support their faith. I eventually realized that it was *I* who was being deceived." Brother Odelawe lets out a laugh.

"That's great. I'm glad you had a change of heart."

"As am I. And I learned an important lesson: Never give up on anyone! Especially your family."

I nod quietly as Brother Odelawe pulls us back into the spot where Walter and Jesse sit next to Chelsea, who has fallen back asleep.

1:35 PM
LUKE

"I said *get out*," the man repeats, his voice icy. He shakes the muzzle of his rifle at me. It's enough to get my hands in the air and my mind racing to assess the situation.

"What's going on?" I ask calmly.

"Jeep's dead. I need your ride."

"You're hijacking us?" Ashley says in disbelief.

"Yeah, that's exactly what I'm doing. Now all of you, get out."

I'm not stupid enough to argue with him, but I keep the conversation going as I open the door and slide out. I risk a glance at Ashley, pale-faced as she glances at her son.

"Look, maybe we can help you take a look at your car, see if we can get it running. We've got a sick kid here, man," I say gently. The man glances at Matthew momentarily, but the look in his eyes doesn't budge.

"Not my problem. I'm out of time and I need the car. Now get out."

"Time for what? You're not going anywhere. The roads are a mess. You won't get far. Let us help you," I say, avoiding Ashley and Marc's questioning stares.

The man growls, eyes narrowing. "Just get away from the car already!" He brings his rifle to the level of my chest and chambers a round.

"Luke, it's ok, let him have it," Marc says, his voice shaky. "We'll find another way."

"Listen to your friend," the man hisses, wiping a line of sweat from his brow. I glare at Marc and Ashley, who look at me in resignation. Ashley removes Matthew's booster seat and sets it on the ground beside the car. He stirs and whines, looking worse than ever. A rash is creeping up his neck and his face is damp and splotchy. The man seems to ignore all this, hovering over us anxiously with his gun as we struggle with the boxes from the roof of the car.

It takes us at least five minutes to pile everything from the car's roof onto the ground as the man watches coldly. If anyone's watching from the convenience mart, they're keeping awfully quiet. Surely this is all being captured on CCTV somewhere, but with the general state of chaos I suspect we'll never see the footage, or the car.

It makes me shudder, realizing how quickly people can come to this. How fast lawlessness sets in when the authorities can't be relied on. How swiftly people become predators and prey. Maybe it'd be different if I was in uniform. Surely this man would have second thoughts if he saw my Glock 9-millimeter holstered at my hip. But not today. Today I'm just a civilian, easy pickings for this dope and his rifle. It's enough to get my blood boiling.

There's a sound down the road, a vehicle lumbering our way in a cloud of dust. We crane our necks in time to see a dirty minivan climbing up the drive. It turns into the gas station just yards from us. Our hijacker lowers his rifle to appear as innocuous as possible; he even has the audacity to turn and wave. It's an opportunity I don't dare to miss.

I've been eyeing the ten feet of ground between us, and have my footsteps clearly visualized. I can do it in three paces and disarm him, I'm sure of it. I summon all of my strength and wits and leap into action.

Despite the mental focus and adrenaline, I simply don't have it in me. In the last two days I've been tasered, electrocuted, underfed, and nearly frozen to death. My body has had enough. My movements are sluggish and clumsy, as if it's all happening underwater. The man steps back, easily dodging me. He grabs the back of my neck in a thick hand and throws me to the ground. Either he's very strong or I've simply nothing left to resist, or both. I slam face down into the dirt, sucking in a plume of dust.

The sole of a heavy boot lands squarely between my shoulder blades, pinning me down. I hack up the dirt in my lungs and pant heavily as the man puts more of his weight onto my back. The fresh burns on my chest and legs sting with the pressure and I grit my teeth, refusing to give this bully the satisfaction of hearing me scream.

"Everything okay?" a man's voice asks. The driver of the minivan, I think. I hear his approaching footsteps, but keep my burning eyes shut tight.

"Just fine. This fella was gettin' a little outta control. Needs some time to cool off, I'm afraid," chuckles the man with the gun.

"Oh. Uh, ok," the other man says, and I can tell by the shuffling footsteps that he's retreating backwards to the safety of his ride.

"We just about done here?" the man with the gun growls at Marc and Ashley.

"Yeah. It's all yours," Marc mumbles. I hear a set of keys passing hands and the boot leaves my back. I half expect a kick in my side or worse, but instead the man simply walks over to Marc and Ashley's Honda and gets in. If he senses that there's no fight left in me, he's got it right. The engine cranks over once and he's gone.

Marc rolls me over gently as soon as the man leaves.

"You ok?" he asks in a flat voice, frowning.

"Yeah, just fine. Guess I wasn't as strong as I thought."

"No, I guess not." Marc helps me sit up and brush myself off. "To be honest with you, that was a stupid move you just pulled."

"Well, I wasn't going to just sit there and watch him drive off with our only hope of getting out of here."

"He was armed, Luke. He could've been extremely dangerous with that rifle if your little stunt had annoyed him a bit more."

"Gee, sorry for trying," I say with a snort. "It's not really in my nature to get shoved around by some jerk with a gun."

"It wasn't your vehicle to lose, Luke."

He has a point, so I simply shrug. Marc walks back to his wife, who's sitting on one of their boxes with her hands covering her face, her chest rising and falling in spurts. Marc puts his arm around her and says something to console her, but I can't make it out.

I sit up and glance over at the man filling up his minivan, who's watching us carefully and no doubt trying to make heads or tails of all that's just unfolded. He finally walks over a few paces.

"Y'all okay?" he calls out, clearly hesitant to get too close.

"Yeah, it's fine. Just got carjacked," I say with a wave of my arm, trying my best to show I'm not a threat.

"Well, that's terrible. Really sorry 'bout that. Where y'all headed?"

"We were on our way towards the state line," Marc says.

"Huh. Goin' to see family, or what?"

"No, we have some friends there."

"That your boy?" the stranger asks, gesturing curiously towards the booster seat. Marc nods.

"He looks like he should be in bed. Why y'all in such a rush to see friends with him looking like that?"

"We've just... Got a very important appointment. We should've been there by now," Marc says with a glance at his watch.

"Huh. Where'd you say you were headed, again?" the man asks, cocking his head slightly to one side.

"Past the state line, a place near Greenville."

"Huh," the man repeats, rubbing his knuckles against a couple of days' worth of facial stubble. He has a young face, probably not much older than myself, but the grey streaks at the side of his head put on a few years so it's difficult to say for sure. He keeps glancing back and forth between each person in our group, as if he's trying to decide something. I'd be a lot more worried if we actually had something of value. As it is, I'm still sitting on the dusty ground with my elbows on my knees. I suddenly realize that nothing on me is actually mine, and I doubt there are many valuables in the boxes littered around us. In any case, the look the man is giving us isn't a dangerous one. If I had to guess, I'd say he's curious.

"Say, this might seem like a funny question, but do y'all know anyone by the name of Donovan Harris?"

I glance back at Marc, whose expression melts away. His eyes widen and his shoulders go back. "I do."

"You know where he's staying these days?"

"1159 Oak Ridge."

The man rubs his face for a second or two, continuing to measure us up before speaking. When he does, I notice that a crooked grin has worked its way into his features. "Well, isn't that interesting."

Marc is beaming now, and runs over to Ashley, where he sweeps her up in his arms in a spinning bear hug.

"I'm Andrew Gillespie. Small world," says the man, stepping forward and hugging Marc and Ashley. Marc introduces himself and his family and finally points down to me.

"This is Luke. He's a friend of ours. His wife's already there." I get up and brush myself off. Andrew shakes my hand, but there's an odd look in his eye, as if there's something he doesn't understand. It's a feeling I can relate to.

"So what, what just happened?" I ask.

"We'll explain soon enough," he says happily.

"Let's get you all loaded up and get back on the road. There'll be plenty of time for chitchat," Andrew says as he bends over to grab a box and haul it to the van.

1:50 PM
AMY

Walter and I spend an hour after lunch navigating the narrow hangar aisles. I don't know, maybe we're looking for distractions. We see a few familiar faces, but neither of us is in a chatting mood. The latest arrivals to the hangar are injured and have been bandaged and medicated as best as possible under the circumstances. A handful of the friends here have medical training, but supplies are limited.

Wandering in circles like this is enough to drive me mad, even if I'm surrounded by my brothers and sisters. I look into faces wondering if some, like me, are waiting on news of loved ones. Walter suggests we head outside for some fresh air and I eagerly concur. We follow the yellow duct tape arrows along the walkways to locate the nearest exit.

It's warmer today than it has been in weeks but there's an odd smell in the air, like a campfire where someone's carelessly tossed in assorted trash. Lifting our eyes, we discover the culprit. Littering the horizon above the trees are dozens of smoke tendrils weaving high into a grey sky. Some originate from the direction of the highway, but I'm not sure about the others. Houses, maybe? The wail of distant sirens fills the air. A shiver dances on my spine and it isn't from the cold.

"Is this how you imagined it would be?" I ask Walter. A distant helicopter catches our gaze as it arcs over the tree line and disappears, propellers chomping the air noisily. I glance at Walter in time to see him shrug.

"No, I guess… I never really imagined it, to be honest. But Jesus did say it would be a tribulation like nothing that had been seen before, nor would be seen again. I guess anything is fair game."

"I'm glad we got out when we did," I say softly after a long pause, although my relief is tainted with a heavy dose of anxiety. Knowing that Luke is still out there somewhere brings sharp and suffocating pangs to my chest. I hear footsteps behind us and turn to see a young man walking briskly in our direction. His head is hunched below his collar and his hands are deep in his pockets. It's Jesse.

"Hey dad, something happened," he says with a thumb over his shoulder. "You're probably gonna want to see it yourself."

Jesse flashes a brief glance in my direction. *That look again.* It's as if there's something he knows, something that he wants to tell me. I forget it as Walter wheels me back to the hangar. The odor of bodies is even more pungent now after being outside and I hope the brothers are looking for ways to solve the ventilation problem. But for now, something else is occupying everyone's attention.

The flatscreens above are back on and tuned to CNN. My eyes flutter over the scrolling marquee at the bottom of the screen and my heart jumps into my throat.

MASSIVE CALIFORNIA FAULT EARTHQUAKE, MILLIONS POSSIBLY IN PERIL

Despite the sensation of needles pricking my skin, the meaning of the words takes a moment to reach my brain. I'm numbed by the news. It's as if everything is moving through a fog. It's a feeling I've experienced before, years ago, when I watched live as a passenger jet crashed into the South Tower. Before the bell rang for our second period class, it had already fallen. Like they say, it's just one of those things you never forget. I deeply suspect that this is another one of those moments.

The room is deathly silent as everyone stares into the screens, waiting for the inevitable footage to start rolling. The first clip, from a cellphone, is shaky and blurred, but the sounds alone are horrifying. Crashes and a loud rending noise can be heard as the image sways back and forth, as if the whole world is riding on the back of a hacksaw chewing its way through the earth. We hear glass shattering as items pour from shelves and countertops. It's a wonder that the user survived long enough to upload the video, I think, until I realize that it's from a live-streaming app. There's a blood curdling scream and everything goes black. The connection is dead, and the news anchors are left with pale, horrified expressions and no words to fill the air.

The lead anchor mumbles something incomprehensible and bows his head, shuffling papers on his desk. Even his thick layer of makeup can't hide the line of sweat climbing down his brow. Just like 9/11, I think. No one knows how to react.

The co-anchor eventually grabs the reins and rehashes what we've just seen in the cellphone broadcast. She's buying time, of course, but she won't need to for long. Pretty soon there'll be a steady trickle of footage, and then a flood. It'll be all we see, a twenty-four hour news cycle laced in gruesome headlines and harrowing images.

"Hey Walter," I hear someone say in a low voice from behind us. I turn to find a man staring wide-eyed up at the screens with a look as dire as the rest of us.

"Yeah, Ralph?" Walter says without turning.

"You think the friends in California were evacuated?" the man asks, his voice trembling slightly.

"I sure hope so."

As if on cue, a 3D topographical map of California flashes on the screens as part of the newscast, the San Andreas Fault outlined in flashing red. It runs for hundreds of miles through the state like a giant zipper, a dozen cities sitting right atop it.

2:15 PM
LUKE

"So where y'all coming from?" Andrew asks as he winds his Honda Odyssey through a mountain road lined with thick pines.

"Haliford," Marc says. "It was already starting to come apart when we evacuated. We would've left sooner, but we held out, hoping to get Matthew checked out by a doctor before hitting the road. In the end, there just wasn't any time. And you?"

"Marietta, Georgia. It was more or less like you described in our area, too. Lots of fires, sirens. Lots of damage done by the looters. The police did what they could to maintain order, but I can't imagine they'll hold out for long. And what about you, Luke?" Andrew asks with a quick glance back at me in his rearview mirror. I'm in the middle bench by myself. Ashley and Matthew are in the far back. Matthew was fussy after the commotion at the gas station but seems to have settled down some. Ashley hovers over him with a distraught look and a rag she keeps dampening with a water bottle and placing on his head.

"Same as Marc. Haliford," I say.

"Oh, ok. Y'all family, then?" Andrew asks.

"Just friends," Marc says. Andrew nods a couple of times but there's a deep crease in his forehead that tells me he's still piecing it together.

Shortly after getting in the van, Marc and Ashley scrounged through their belongings and tracked down a few cans of beans and corn. We ate it cold with half a loaf of bread and bottles of Gatorade before continuing on our journey. It was then, between mouthfuls of cold preserves, that I learned from their conversation that Andrew is also a Jehovah's Witnesses. They were able to piece everything together through Brother Harris, who used to visit their congregations and is well known in the area. I didn't bother mentioning that I know him too.

What are the chances?

Add to that the miraculous night of restful sleep despite the blaring music. The distracted federal officers on the bridge. Somehow surviving that drop into the water despite the handcuffs, the temperature, and the fact that I was in the custody of armed officers. That I somehow managed to not just escape, but run into two of the only people who might know where Amy is. And now this.

I mull over it in silence for a few minutes before my mind is subdued by a wave of drowsiness. My eyelids go heavy as my gut processes the first decent meal I've had in nearly a day. I have plenty to be thankful for, and whether or not God is a part of that, I guess I'll just have to wait and see. For the time being, I'm happy to be in the company of these people, happy to be far from the clutches of Agent Meade and his goons. I allow myself to relax a little and lay my head against the back of the seat. I hear a snippet of something on the radio, something about California, and that's all I remember. I'm out like a light.

When my eyes flutter open, it's impossible to gauge how much time has passed, but judging from the angle of sunlight it hasn't been long. The asphalt has run out, and we're now crawling along a country gravel road at a snail's pace. Marc speaks softly with Andrew. I close my eyes again, pretending to sleep as I tune into the conversation over the crunch of the wheels along the road.

"*Police officer?*" Andrew mutters in a hushed tone.

"Yeah, I know what you're thinking. I thought the same thing," Marc says.

"And how long's the wife been studying?"

"Over a year. Already a *UP*. She would've gotten baptized at this upcoming assembly, had it not been for the evacuation."

"Huh. And you just ran into him in the woods?"

"Yeah, can you believe it?"

"Sounds pretty incredible. Almost too much so. Y'all consider the possibility that…you know?"

"What, that he's spying on us?" Marc says. I hear his head swivel back and can feel him looking me over.

"Well, yeah," Andrew says.

"I did. But it just doesn't add up. He was running *away from us* when we came across him. He was terrified. Either he's a top-notch actor or he'd actually been through something bad, just like he said."

"So you're thinking something else is at work here."

"That's what it seems like. I keep praying about it."

"Huh," Andrew grunts. "I guess we'll just have to see how it all plays out then. Leave it in Jehovah's hands."

"Yeah. Although, I think I do need to have a talk with him about–" Marc stops suddenly and gasps. The van slows to a crawl and Andrew speaks next.

"Is that what I think it is?"

"Sure looks like it," Marc says. I hear him turn around and reach over the seats to rouse his wife, who's asleep in the back row. "Babe, Ashley, take a look." There's a yawn from the backseat as Ashley pulls herself together and leans into the window, and then gasps.

"Our car!"

3:04 PM
AMY

When the earthquake footage finally gets rolling on the airwaves it's a flood, a disaster in and of itself. The extent of destruction is breathtaking. Roads buckling, cars and trucks swallowed into the earth. A cliffside highway shrugging off into rocky waters below, passengers rolling into the foamy seas in their toy cars. San Francisco is a hilly sea of fire and smoke. It's hard to imagine anyone walking away from any of it.

The Golden Gate Bridge somehow managed to survive, but the footage of it swaying left and right, the *twang* of those giant cables straining and snapping, is seared into my mind like the flash of a camera in my eyes. I realize that even if the news cycle were somehow forced off, it'd all be playing just the same in my head. And the chaos– the destruction, the fire, the piles of debris–isn't even the worst of it. The screams are.

Blood-curdling. I can't think of a better way to describe it. It's the sound of terror and hopelessness. The realization of imminent death. Sounds powerful enough to put ice in veins and haunt dreams. I'm not the only one. The faces of brothers and sisters watching with me are stony with shock. It's too overwhelming to bring on tears, but I imagine the tears will come later on tonight, when we're lying awake in our cots and it all finally sinks in.

Unanswerable questions are whispered over shoulders, families worrying about members and friends last seen in California. Even the kids, who until this moment were unfazed by the reality of life in a refugee camp, have sidled up somberly to their parents, soaking in the news cycle with fixated, gaping stares. But for all its shock and horror, no one is able to tear their attention away.

I guess that's why they decide to pull the plug. There's a small ripple of discontent at the realization that the news stream has been broken intentionally until a brother climbs up a raised platform and holds his arms out for us to be quiet. It's a tense few moments as the room settles down. If these weren't my brothers and sisters, I realize, this could have easily become a mob.

It's all very sensible, of course. The elders have discussed it and decided to give the news a break. There's still a lot of work to be done and everyone's help will be needed. They don't want us sitting in front of the screens immobilized by shock and worry. The crowd dissipates as we wander off to our corners.

Walter wheels me back to their partition and I keep Chelsea company. A couple of older brothers I don't recognize whisk him away a few minutes later and I'm left sitting next to my friend, wondering what's going through her head. It's clear from a glance that she isn't herself. There's something childlike in the way her eyes dart from the curtains that make up the three walls of her room and the bed and me. The gravity of the situation is completely lost on her.

I miss her so much and yearn more than ever for her guidance and reassurance. Instead, she gives me an innocent smile and nods as if there's nothing to worry about. We might as well be on a camping trip. She lies back down on her pillow and is sound asleep within minutes.

"You've known my mom a while, huh?" a voice asks over my shoulder. I turn to see Jesse standing behind me with a head of scraggly wet hair and smelling like a fresh shower.

"Yeah, I guess so," I say. Jesse hands me a wet can of Coke and I'm surprised to find that it's icy cold.

"Brought a cooler of stuff in my pickup," he explains with a shrug. I nod in thanks and we enjoy our sodas together as we watch Chelsea sleep. It's odd, I think, sitting next to Chelsea and Walter's son and knowing nothing about him. He's appeared out of thin air, and I can't help but wonder.

"She was studying with you, wasn't she?" Jesse asks without looking at me. He finishes his can and crushes it on the floor.

"Yeah. We were good friends. We spent lots of time together. She was like a mother to me." I glance over at Jesse and can't decipher his expression.

"By any chance, is your husband a cop?" he asks.

"Yes, he is. How did you know that?" Jesse won't look at me now and it's clear he's hiding something.

"Jesse," I press. "Do you know something about my husband? Please, if there's something–"

"Look, I don't know where he is now, if that's what you're asking," Jesse says, tensing, leaning away from me.

"But you do know something, don't you? What is it?" Jesse's shaking his head and looking down at his dirty sneakers. I wait for what feels like an eternity before he finally speaks.

"I met him."

"You *met* him? How? Where? What are you talking about?"

"He came to my house."

"Your house? How did he know where you live? *I* don't even know where you live."

"How would I know? Maybe he did a search online, maybe the cops have me in their database. Who knows?"

"So, why then? What did he visit you for?"

"He had some… questions."

"Questions? What kind of questions?"

"Questions about my parents. About me. And about the Witnesses."

"When was this?" I pry. Jesse shrugs.

"I guess about a week ago."

"And that was it? You only saw him once?" Jesse nods quietly as my mind reels. It doesn't make any sense. Why would Luke question him? What was he after?

"It wasn't a long discussion. Probably not even ten minutes. I sort of chased him off my property." I stare at Jesse, waiting for more. Perhaps he wants to talk. Whatever he's about to say, he's uneasy.

"It was the craziest thing, your husband showing up like that. Me and Isabelle, my girlfriend–ex-girlfriend now, I guess–had been fighting that morning. It was over something stupid, as usual. There was a time when I thought things would work out between us, way back when we'd first met, but… Whatever. Things change, I guess. I found myself wondering more and more what my life would've been like if I'd stuck with the truth. If I'd turned Isabelle down when she first invited me out bowling with her and her friends way back in high school. If I'd listened to my dad and mom, maybe even got baptized. I felt so… empty. The Witnesses would come around every few months and I always turned them down, or I'd let Isabelle take the door and shoo them away. Then they just… *stopped coming.*

"A few months later the news of the religious restrictions hit, and all I could do was think about the fall of Babylon the Great that we used to study in *The Watchtower* and at bookstudy… I still remembered those images from the *Revelation* book. Sometimes I couldn't sleep at night, and when I did, I always saw that prostitute on the back of that leopard thing, head cocked to the side, holding the cup of blood in her hand with that wild look in her eyes. I remembered how the book talked about government attacking false religion. I even remember handing out those tracts about it when I was a teenager. I hated that campaign. I was terrified of what the householders might think. I guess that was always my problem, though, wasn't it? Fear of what other people thought. Fear of classmates, fear of teachers. And where are all those people now? Why did I care so much about what they thought?

"I'd almost made up my mind to come back. I was worried it might be too late, but what was there to lose? Things were going nowhere with Isabelle. Neither of us was happy. I finally prayed about it one morning. Wasn't easy. But I pushed myself, and no sooner had I said 'amen' when I heard a knock on our front door."

"My husband."

"Yeah. He asked specifically to talk with me. I wasn't worried. I had some misdemeanors long ago, but I'd been on the straight and narrow for the past few years. And it wasn't your typical cop interrogation. He didn't throw his weight around or make it seem like I owed him anything. Actually, he seemed pretty *nervous.*"

Jesse's voice trails off momentarily and he casts me a sidelong glance, as if he expects me to fill in the gaps for him, but I'm not ready to offer anything until I hear the whole story.

"That doesn't sound like him."

Jesse shrugs and makes an expression that irks me. "I dunno. But the questions he was asking…"

"What? What are you trying to say?"

"He was after information, ok? He specifically asked about meetings, like how and when they were held."

"And?" I ask, feeling my discomfort mount.

"What, you don't think that's a little odd? A cop trying to dig up info on the Witnesses? And why come to me? He already knew my parents, didn't he? Why not go to them?"

"Maybe he wanted a different opinion," I say.

"Yeah, or because he thought I'd be willing to sell the Witnesses out. Maybe he thought that I'd be some kind of outcast or something, that I'd tell all."

"Stop it!" I hiss. "Stop talking! You don't know my husband! And why should I trust you, anyway? You just show up out of nowhere because you see the world's coming to an end, and now I'm supposed to believe what *you* say? Where were you all those years while your parents worried themselves sick, huh? Your mom was so hurt that she couldn't even hear your name without crying. And now look at her!"

The words are sharper than I intend, and their effect registers instantly on Jesse's face. The silence is an icy current that he decides not to fight. It carries him swiftly along until he looks down at his feet quietly, long, wet hair covering his face.

"I wasn't trying to hurt you," he says softly. "I just thought you should know."

"Yeah, well thanks a lot," I sneer. Jesse gets up and disappears into the crowd.

3:34 PM
LUKE

"Y'all positive that's your car?" Andrew asks.

"Yeah, that's our license plate," Marc comments. "Looks like it's been in some kind of wreck." There's a ragged horizontal gash that spans the left side of the vehicle, and the two right wheels are off of the road. A long muddy track trails behind the car.

"Must've been another car that did that," says Andrew uneasily, studying the damage before taking a look around us. "Nothin' else it could'a hit around here. No walls, no guardrails. Pretty weird."

"Where's our hijacker?" I ask, sitting up and surveying the area uneasily.

"Doesn't look like he's around. Car's empty."

"The wreck doesn't look that bad. Certainly didn't total it. I wonder why he left it?" Ashley asks.

"Well if it's not wrecked we might as well see if we can get it back on the road, huh?" Andrew says hopefully. The others mull over this for a moment and then begin nodding their heads. But something doesn't feel right to me.

"Keep a sharp eye. He might not be far. And don't forget, he's armed," I caution.

Marc slides the van door open and reaches for the handle of the sedan, which opens without issue. He peeks into the vehicle cautiously, and I see his shoulders drop slightly with relief.

"Looks ok to me," he says with cautious optimism.

"Did he leave the keys by any chance?" asks Ashley, trying to get a look inside.

"Not that I see."

"Weird. Very weird," Andrew mutters. I hop out for a quick inspection of the scene. Andrew's initial estimation of what pushed the car off the road seems accurate. Paint from another vehicle has rubbed off near the sedan's door handles and there are black tire tracks on the road about thirty yards in front of us.

"Any ideas, Luke?" Marc asks as he inspects the inside of his car. He's fishing through the pockets and under the seats, apparently looking for the keys. I circle around the vehicle and discover our first clue: the gas tank cover is open and the cap is dangling.

"Is the tank empty, by any chance?" I ask Marc.

"Yeah, looks like it. It was full when he hijacked us, should have at least half a tank left at this point. Doesn't make any sense."

"Unless it was siphoned," I say.

"Why would he siphon his own tank?" Ashley asks.

"I've got a feeling it wasn't him that did it," I say. "And I think we ought to get out of here."

"Why? What do you think happened?"

"I'm thinking someone ran him off the road, then stole his gas."

"And what about the driver, the guy with the gun, he just disappeared?"

"I'm not sure, but he might still be around, and he might still be dangerous. It's not safe here. We need to get back on the road," I say anxiously.

"And just leave the car?" Ashley says.

"It's no use to us now with an empty tank. Our best bet is to stick together in the van."

I expect a bit more resistance from Marc and Ashley, but they're reasonable people, and they concur after a few moments of contemplation.

"Alright, you're right. Let's hit the road," Marc says, exiting the vehicle with one last reluctant glance inside. I circle to the rear of the car, heading for the van, when something catches my eye, a tiny sparkle of light from among the tall grass in a low ditch to the side of the road. It's something shiny and metallic, and my curiosity drives me closer. I reach out to brush the weeds away and gasp.

It's the hijacker. He's contorted unnaturally and partially covered in leaves and dead grass. I'm sure I would've missed him, had it not been for his glistening rifle stock. His clothes are soiled and torn and bloodied in spots, and his face is swollen and cut nearly beyond recognition. I'm not sure if he's dead or alive till I see his chest rise a fraction of an inch.

"Luke! What are you doing? Did you find something?" Marc yells from the van, its engine idling.

"Give me a second, and stay in the van!" I yell back. I reach down carefully and pluck the gun from the grass, getting it out of the man's reach, just in case. He stirs with the realization of my presence and struggles to open his eyes. One eye is swollen shut. The recognition dawns slowly in his eyes.

"You," he says.

"What happened here?"

"Why do you care?"

"I want to know if my friends and I are in danger."

"Bunch'a punk kids ran me off the road. Too quick for me."

"They were after your fuel?"

"Who knows? They attacked... I fell. Don't remember anything else."

"How long have you been lying here? Can't you get up?"

The man tries to maintain the hardness in his stare, but his fear seeps through all the same. He tries to rise, but his head flops uselessly to the side, his face smearing against the muddy weeds. I clear away some of the leaves and get a closer look at him, and it's not good. His legs are clearly broken and there are deep lacerations on the exposed skin. There appear to be other wounds, too, judging from the bleeding under his shirt. I've seen roadside victims of car accidents in better shape.

"That bad, huh?" he says, catching my expression. Typically I'd fib my way through a situation like this, tell him whatever necessary to keep him calm in time for the paramedics to arrive, but there are no ambulances on their way now, no chances of survival. There's no point in lying. This filthy roadside ditch will be his grave and he knows it.

"I'm sorry," I say.

"I'm sorry too. Sorry for ever being stupid enough to hijack y'all in the first place."

I have no response to this. It occurs to me now that had he not pulled his gun on us at that gas station, it could very well be us lying in this ditch now. I'd like to think that the sight of a sick five-year-old would've kept us from becoming targets, but then again, it didn't stop this guy.

"You were desperate. People do foolish things when they're desperate."

"Yeah, guess that's true. Never stole anything before, you believe it? Not so much as a pack of gum or a bottle of beer."

"I believe you," I say. I feel sorry for him. He's cold and alone without a thing of comfort in the world.

"Guess I'll never have the chance to steal again, neither."

"No, I guess not."

The man's breathing is shallow and uneven, and his face contorts with a sudden wave of pain. His eyes focus on some indiscernible point in the distance and I suspect it won't be long. It's hard to imagine that the last time I saw him he was a viable threat, an imposing figure holding our lives in the balance.

There are no more words shared between the two of us as the last of his life ebbs away. I never learn his name; he never learns mine. And all I can think of is my own mortality, how life can be taken in an instant, and how, somewhere out there, my wife must be worried sick about me.

I glance at the glistening, bloodied rifle in the grass for a moment before jogging up the embankment back to the waiting van.

5:01 PM
AMY

By the time late afternoon rolls around, the tomato soup and ham sandwiches are a long forgotten memory and I can barely wait for dinner. Families begin sending members to their cars in the parking lot to retrieve cans of food, snacks, and bottles of water. Everyone's still doing their best to maintain the mood, but the strain is beginning to show. I try not to think about what conditions will be like in a week or two. I can't imagine the hot showers and the electric generators working forever. What then?

When the call for dinner finally goes out, a line of eager faces forms instantly. But when we make it to the serving tables, our expressions change. Each adult is allotted a couple of slices of white bread and an apple wedge lathered in a slim layer of peanut butter. The kids get half that.

"This is it?" someone asks. One of the serving sisters nods with an apologetic look.

"I can't eat gluten," says someone else. "Is there anything else?"

"I'm sorry," she says. She glances over her shoulder at a brother behind her, signaling for assistance. The brother steps forward and tries to smile through a wide white mustache, but his eyes are frowning and he looks very tired.

"Sorry folks, this is the best we can do. We had a truck loaded with food and water scheduled to arrive this afternoon, but it never showed up. We haven't been able to raise the driver on the CB radio, so we're not sure what's happened. Keep him in your prayers."

This seems to put things into perspective for all of us, and no one else fusses over the slim rations. The brother gives us a slight nod of his head and walks off briskly to care for some other task.

"This is where our Christian qualities will truly be put to the test," Walter says to me when he's wheeled me back to our cots. The paper plate in my lap is already empty.

"Endurance?" I ask, scraping the last bit of peanut butter from the edge of my plate into my mouth.

"Yes, and patience, brotherly love, all of it." Walter parks my wheelchair in the corner of our small alcove and checks on his wife, who's sound asleep. Walter spreads out on one of the cots and peels off his shoes. I suddenly realize that I didn't see him grab a plate in the dinner line.

"Did you already eat?" I ask.

"Dinner? No."

"Why not? You'd better get it while it lasts." Walter simply smiles back at me and closes his eyes.

"I'm ok. I'm sure we'll be taken care of. Truth is, I'm not too hungry. I figured I'd let others have my portion."

"That was generous," I say, looking guiltily at my lap.

"Like I said, I'm sure it'll all be taken care of."

Walter gets comfortable on the cot and soon he's asleep, leaving me to my thoughts. I find that I've got enough strength in my arms to wheel myself around the hangar, and so I decide to do some exploring.

The camp is a lot quieter as everyone settles in for the night. It seems a lot emptier, too, without bodies milling around in the aisles that weave between the partitions. A few new arrivals file in after dinner, stragglers with belongings piled high in their arms and strapped to their backs. They're happy to be here but thoroughly weathered from the journey. Every one of them will have a story, I'm sure.

At the far end of the hangar, next to the serving tables, the brothers have erected a four-foot high stage. As I sit there in my wheelchair, contemplating all that's happened in the past weeks and months, a small cluster of brothers forms, moving in a huddle as they near the platform. Two scribble feverishly in notebooks as the others communicate. Pages are torn from the books and shoved into the hands of one of the brothers, someone I'd seen earlier talking to Walter when we first arrived. He takes the notes and clambers up the steps to the stage. He clears his voice and raps a knuckle twice on the microphone. A mask of perspiration covers his face and he's nearly out of breath. There's the screech and whistle of feedback as the microphone is turned on.

"Brothers and sisters, may I have your attention please," the brother says, organizing the pages in his hands and taking a quick swipe at the sweat on his face. Curious heads poke from behind the sheets of the partitions. Some friends gather expectantly on the empty floor space around me.

"We have a couple of important announcements to make," the brother continues, clearing his voice. "I'm sure many of you are wondering how our brothers and sisters are faring in California since the quake. Well, today we heard from the branch that before the earthquake struck, most of our friends in the major cities had been evacuated. They were given instructions last week ago to travel inland, and if they followed those directions, they would've been far from the epicenter during the worst of it." A collective sigh of relief rises from the crowd, but there's still tension in the air.

"As for the second thing... What I'm about to tell you may come as a shock, and it will perhaps be a challenge for many of you who have just arrived. About fifteen minutes ago, we were contacted directly by a branch representative, who relayed the instructions he received from the branch committee late this afternoon. We're being told to evacuate."

The tension in the crowd erupts in confusion. Questions and fears are whispered quickly over shoulders. *Evacuate? From here? Where could we possibly go?*

A few of the elders standing at the foot of the stage turn to face the crowd and raise their arms, trying to calm the friends, but it's no small task. Some are raising their hands with anxious expressions, hoping for answers to endless inquiries.

"Please, friends, try to remain calm, I know this is difficult to take, and frankly, it's the last thing any of us were expecting. But please keep in mind that up till now, our brothers and sisters have been carefully maneuvered by the branch, and it has saved lives. It's happened with many of us, and as we've heard tonight, it's happened again in California. We must accept these directions as coming directly from Jehovah. It could mean the difference between life and death."

The brother pauses here, and I wait for the clamor in the audience to resume, but the air is still and quiet.

"Now, we know that many of you must have questions, and we will share everything that we know. Unfortunately, there's not much time. We've been told to evacuate this building before sunrise tomorrow. Yes, that means no sleep tonight. We will evacuate as soon as we can. Our goal is to be out of here by midnight if at all possible. As you all know, the highways and roads are a mess right now, so we will make the journey on foot. Of course... this means we'll have to leave our vehicles behind, and many of our possessions.

"We'll be following a nearby hiking trail and heading north. If you are unable to walk, we have a few spare wheelchairs, which should be able to handle the terrain. Because we'll be moving on foot, please only pack your essentials. If you've come with go bags, it'd be a good idea to bring them along. Of course, food and water are top priority. Family heads, please take the lead in making sure your families pack responsibly, and be sure everyone is ready to go as soon as possible.

"It will take us about a day of walking to reach our destination. Rest assured that Jehovah will see to it that each and every one of us makes the journey safely. Just as Jehovah cared for his people in times past, he will be certain to sustain us!"

The crowd is silent when the brother finishes. Perhaps we're all too shocked or overwhelmed, just as he said we'd be. A second brother is called to the stage to offer a prayer, and it's during these moments that the reality of it all sinks in. This is it, the end. We are on the run. The final showdown can't be far off. And yet, all I can think of is Luke. Will I ever see him again?

I cover my tear-streaked face and wipe the wetness away, quickly wheeling myself back to our partition.

5:25 PM
LUKE

Progress is slow. Minutes turn to hours as we crawl along nameless dusty back roads. To make matters worse, the GPS is useless. While Marc remembered to grab their Garmin when we stumbled across their car on the side of the road, he forgot the charging cable. Luckily, someone had enough foresight to pack a compass, so at least we know which direction we're headed. Our exact location, however, is anyone's guess. There's a dispute about whether we've even crossed the state line into South Carolina or if we've possibly made it as far as North Carolina, but there's simply no way to tell. On any other day, armed with my smartphone and a 4G network, this trip would be a cinch, but today the cards seemed stacked against us.

Then again, we've managed to survive this long. I think back to the man in the ditch and I realize just how much I have to be thankful for.

The sun is just beginning to dip behind the horizon when the dirt road we're on abruptly merges with a two-lane stretch of highway. We follow it for about ten miles without seeing a single other vehicle. It's just us, and we still have no idea where we are. Still, the compass tells us that we're headed in approximately the right direction, so we press on.

At six o'clock the gas tank is nearing empty and Andrew's beginning to get nervous. We decide as a group to risk a pit stop in the next town and hope for the best.

We exit the highway to discover that Maynard is less town and more a miles-long smear of asphalt lined with typical small-town hallmarks: a diner, a pharmacy, a hardware store, a bank, a couple of small churches and so on, all doubtless established and run by locals. The main source of revenue here appears to be sport tourism; gaudy posters and billboards promise adventure from places like *Jim's Whitewater Tours* and *Uncle Jeb's Ski Rentals*.

"Anyone spot a gas station?" Andrew asks, head swiveling as our van creeps slowly along the main road. There's no response as we survey the quiet town with its empty sidewalks and streets.

"Where is everyone?" Ashley asks.

"Good question. Sort of looks like everyone packed up and left," Marc says.

I ponder the buildings as they slide by on either side of us. It's odd–many of the windows are caged or boarded in and many of the roll-top security doors have been pulled down over storefronts. It's as if the evacuation was organized, orderly, and thoroughly prepared for. It isn't long before the shops fade away into the residential part of town and the roads begin to branch and wander.

"Did we just miss it, or is there no gas station here?" Andrew says, dumbfounded. He makes a U-turn in an intersection and we retrace our path, carefully surveying the businesses for signs of a place to refuel. I'm again overcome with unease. *What is my gut trying to tell me?*

"There!" Ashley finally exclaims, thrusting a finger over the back of my seat and towards the right-hand side of the road. The gas station only has a couple of pumps and is connected to some sort of deli; it's no wonder we missed it. Andrew pulls in and hops out to inspect the pumps. The rest of us pile out to stretch our legs and I decide to have a look around.

"Darn, no power!" Andrew laments, scratching the back of his head with the brim of his baseball cap. "Ideas, anyone?"

"We'll have to siphon a tank," I say, a plan already forming in my head. I jog to the back of the café and find precisely what I need: a hose wound in neat loops hanging from a hook on a wall. I quickly unscrew it and bring it back to the van as the others observe curiously.

I have Andrew pull the van closer to the front of the shop where several diesel trucks sit, abandoned. I manage to pry open the gas lid on one of them and get the suction going. And that's when it hits me.

The vehicles! That's what's out of place here. Cars, trucks, motorcycles, pickups, all lined up along the shoulders of roads, sitting in parking lots, parked neatly along the curbs. All of it perfectly normal, if it weren't for the lack of drivers. Not a soul in sight, but plenty of cars. How could they have all left without their cars? *Unless they haven't left at all.*

I cautiously explore the other side of the building as our van's tank fills up on siphoned gas, wondering how many pairs of eyes are watching us. I glance down the street with a casual expression, my eyes lingering for a moment on a line of rooftops just above a grocery store. There, nearly concealed by a waist-high brick wall, lurk two dark figures. Both are deathly still, so much so that I question if they're people at all. I resist the urge to hold my gaze and avert my eyes, resolving to keep calm despite the thudding in my chest. My temples throb with adrenaline but I force myself to keep to a steady pace as I walk back to Andrew and the others.

Another casual glance up the street, this time to the other side of the road. More watchers there, too. And these have guns with long, narrowed muzzles aimed right in our direction. I realize that we must've driven right past them (twice!), though we could've never spotted them way up there from inside the van. They could've shot us then, so what are they waiting for? I turn my back to the street and carefully position myself in front of the deli's windows. Hands in my pockets, I pretend to gaze inside while studying the distant rooftops' reflections. I can barely make out the bodies on the building, but they are moving.

"Hey Luke," Andrew calls from a few yards away.

"Yeah?"

"I think we've drained this tank dry."

"How much gas you get out of it?"

"Barely half a tank. Should we try another car?"

"No," I say quickly. "We need to get out of here." The others stare at me blankly. It takes a moment for someone to finally ask why.

"Because we're not alone here," I say simply. "I don't want you all to panic, but we're being watched. Let's pack it up and head out. Now." There are no further questions as the others make wide eyes at me and pile into the van. Andrew revs the engine and we're about to pull out when Ashley suddenly leaps from the van and heads back to the car we just siphoned. She pulls a scrap of paper from her purse and scribbles something down. I can't make out exactly what she's doing, but she stuffs it and something else from her purse under the windshield wiper before jogging back to us.

We're headed back towards the highway, picking up speed as we near the end of the road, when we all notice that something has changed. A row of pickup trucks has been parked along the road, forming an effective barricade between us and our exit. Andrew slows the van and turns to look at us frantically.

"Guys, what do we do?" he asks shakily.

We're about fifty yards from the barricade when Andrew brings the van to a halt. The pickups span the entire road and the gravel paths at the shoulders are too narrow for us to squeeze by. As we watch, a portly figure in a white Stetson rises from behind the center truck. He's wearing a sheriff's uniform and badge, but none of this puts me at ease. Not with the pistol he's got gripped between his two hands leveled right at us.

"I'm gonna say this once, so y'all better listen up real good," shouts the large man. "I want y'all to exit the vehicle slowly with your hands behind your heads. Leave the doors open and walk to the shoulder of the road. I've got armed men watching you from every angle, so don't try anything stupid, y'hear?"

We do as we're told, exiting and sidestepping our way to the sides of the road. Two men in full camouflage and face paint appear out of nowhere and handcuff us before we can react. We're forced to lie prone on the cold macadam as the sheriff ambles over. I can't get a look at him in my position, but he's got on a pair of gator skin boots and reeks of vapor rub and pomade. He lowers himself on a knee with a grunt and hovers over us for a few moments, no doubt basking in his conquest.

"Welcome to Maynard," he says with the smack of satisfaction.

6:31 PM
AMY

The order to evacuate sends our camp into turmoil. People run around anxiously collecting items from their cars, taking inventory, agonizing over what to take and what to leave behind. Some even try to plead with the brothers to allow them to bring more, but the elders won't budge: each person is only allowed what they can carry. *Stick with the essentials.*

An older sister in the partition next to ours is flipping through a large leather-bound book, seemingly oblivious to the chaos swirling around her. It's her wedding album. The tips of her fingers linger on each of the photos, the look of fond reminiscence shining in her eyes. She peels one of the photos from the page and slips it into her coat pocket. Then she closes the album and sets it delicately on her cot and sighs.

"Are you ok?" I ask softly as she catches me staring. She nods.

"I suppose so. I guess it was wishful thinking to imagine I could take all this with me in the first place. That's material things for you–here today, gone tomorrow. And you?"

I shrug. "I'll be ok. Didn't have the chance to go home and pack. I left with the clothes on my back." The sister smiles gently.

"It's probably just as well. Sometimes it's easier when you don't have to choose."

I think she's right about this. Our brief conversation ends as she returns to the task of packing a roller suitcase with canned food and bottled water.

Chelsea has been roused back to consciousness, though the sea of commotion in the hanger confuses and disorients her. Walter returns from his truck with a couple of duffel bags slung over his shoulders. He's followed by a man I haven't seen before. He's gesturing wildly, clearly upset.

"Walter, this is crazy! We just got here, and now they're making us pack up and leave *again*? I mean, *come on!* You have any idea how many hours it took us to get here? The last thing I'm gonna do is start hiking through the woods in the middle of the night!"

"Eddie, you need to get your head on straight," Walter says sternly. "You're only here, along with your family, because you listened to directions in the first place. What do you think will happen if you start deciding to go off on your own?"

"All I'm saying is that you talk to those elders, ask them to give us another day! My family is exhausted, man!" Walter turns to face Eddie and takes a deep breath, and for a moment I almost think he's going to throw a punch.

"Look, we're tired too, Eddie. We'd all love to rest. But we're also obedient."

"It just doesn't make sense to me. Why now? Why leave in the middle of the freakin' night?"

"Deliverance never makes sense from a human standpoint. You think it made sense to the Israelites to put themselves between the Red Sea and the Egyptian army? You think it made sense to the first century Christians to flee to the mountains after the Romans retreated from Jerusalem? Or what about Noah and the ark? Ridiculers will ridicule and doubters will doubt, but those who listen to Jehovah will be saved."

"Yeah, that's all fine, but my point is that–"

"Your point is that you don't agree with the brothers. *Fine!* I get it. To be honest, I don't understand it myself, but I'd be a fool if I were to start questioning things. Not now, not when we're this close to the end."

Eddie is finally quiet. He lowers his head and stares at his shoes for a few quiet moments until Walter walks over and puts an outstretched hand on his shoulder.

"What's really going on, Eddie? Talk to me."

"Rebecca stayed behind," the man says quietly, shrinking with each word. I turn away as he begins to cry, but there's nowhere to hide in a place like this.

"I'm sorry," I barely hear Walter say.

"I remember that last shepherding call you guys did with us. She was starting to get irregular with the meetings, spending more and more time with her unbelieving family… But I had no idea. She wouldn't even get in the car, Walter. She said she didn't want looters to get into our house. I begged her. My two girls had to see that. They had to see their Dad on his knees begging their mother to come with us… But she just refused. The girls and I… We must've cried for the first hour on the road."

"I'm so, so, sorry," Walter repeats. "But you did the right thing."

"Yeah, I know, but that doesn't make it any easier."

"Let's stick together, Eddie. Get yourself and your girls packed up and meet us back here. We'll make the trek as a team, ok?"

"Yeah, ok, Walter. Thanks."

I hear the men hug and pat each other on the back and my eyes are wet by the time Eddie finally leaves. Walter turns to me and sets one of the duffel bags gently on my lap.

"Can you be in charge of this?" he asks. His eyes are red and soggy.

"Sure," I say. "I wish I wasn't in this wheelchair. I feel like I'm really going to slow everyone down."

"Don't worry," Walter says with a wave of his hand. "I'm sure it'll be fine. And anyway, it won't be me that'll be pushing you. I'll have my hands full helping Chelsea."

"Oh? Then what's the plan?" I ask.

"I'm putting my son in charge of you."

And as if on cue, Jesse emerges from the crowd. He's somehow found the time to cut his hair, so now he actually looks like a Witness. He's got a pack slung over his shoulder and acknowledges us with a nod and a smile. I avert my eyes, unable to look at him. Why is he here when Luke is somewhere out there? I clench my jaw and stare into the sagging bag on my lap.

"So, when do we get this show on the road?" Jesse asks eagerly.

7:09 PM
LUKE

The holding cell is a bleak twelve-by-twelve square barred off on one side and surrounded on the other three by cinderblock walls the color of split pea soup. The three men–Andrew, Marc, and myself–sit on narrow benches that jut from the two sidewalls. Ashley sits on the cold floor in one of the corners, cradling Matthew in her arms. He's been sleeping for most of the day but he doesn't appear to be getting any better. The rash covers most of his face now, and it's clear from a mere glance that he's running a dangerously high temperature. His ragged breaths come through in congested spurts and whines.

It was a quick and quiet ride to the station. Our captors simply handcuffed us and hauled us back, no questions asked. Apparently, the Miranda rights have gone out the window with the rest of the Constitution. On the bright side, we were fed. It wasn't much–cold, raw hot dogs and potato chips–but it was welcome all the same.

The large man in the white Stetson strolls in after we've eaten. He's got his thumbs jammed in his belt loops as he hauls his bulging frame up and down the hallway and studies us seriously.

"So, which of y'all care to explain why you were stealin' our gas?" he asks, scowling. There's a pause on our end as glances are exchanged. Finally Marc speaks up.

"It's a long story, sir. Our car was hijacked this morning at a gas station. We ended up carpooling with our friend here, but eventually we ran out of gas. We've been on back roads all day, trying to avoid the highways."

"Where y'all comin' from?" asks the sheriff after a long pause.

"Georgia. We were just passing through."

"Why the Florida plates?"

Now it's Andrew's turn to speak. "It's my car. I just bought it from my sister, who lives in Florida. Didn't have time to change the plates."

"Why'd y'all stop in our town?" the sheriff asks, grunting.

"We were trying to get our bearings, sir. And we needed gas," Marc explains.

"Thought you could just pull up to a small town and steal a bit, huh? Thought we wouldn't notice?"

"We thought this town was deserted," I say. "Do you all know what's been going on everywhere else?"

"What, y'all think we're so backwards out here that we can't figure out how to turn on a television set?" the sheriff sneers.

"He didn't mean it like that," Marc says. "We ran out of options. We were just trying to stay safe and get to our destination in one piece."

"And what do you think I'm doing?" the sheriff growls. "You have any idea how hard it is to keep this many people from goin' insane like the rest of the country? I've been wearing this badge for forty years, son. I'm already three years past retirement. But this town, it's all I got. No one's gonna put these good people in harm's way."

"I can respect that, sir. You have my word that we meant no harm."

"Yeah, that's what the last group said. Bunch of yuppie kids from Atlanta. Said they just needed a place to rest. Ended up looting one of our stores and stealing a bunch'a motorcycles. When my boys tried to stop them, they drew weapons and opened fire. Could'a killed someone if they weren't such lousy shots."

"We didn't steal that gas," Ashley finally says from the corner. The sheriff looks surprised to hear her voice, as if he's forgotten all about her. He glances at the small child in her arms and for a moment I sense his discomfort.

"Who're you?" he demands.

"I'm Ashley, and that's my husband, Marc. Everything they've said so far is the truth. And we weren't stealing that gas."

"You callin' me a liar, miss? I had four men watchin' y'all like hawks from the rooftops. They saw your every move, and they swore they all saw you siphoning gas from one of our cars."

"That's true, we siphoned it."

"Then how d'you figure you weren't stealin' it?"

"I paid for it, sir."

"Paid for it? What are you talkin' about?"

"I left a note with some cash on the windshield."

It takes a moment for the sheriff to process this, and then he dismisses it with a loud scoff. "Right, a note. Sure you did, kid."

"I'm not lying. Why would I? Have one of your men go take a look. I left a twenty and some change. It's all I had."

The sheriff gives Ashley a long stare before reaching for the radio clipped to his belt. He speaks to someone named Benjie and orders him to check the car for cash, all the while eyeing us suspiciously.

The sheriff returns the radio to his belt and gives us one last scowl before plopping into a rusty folding metal chair and reading a newspaper. An eternity passes as we wait.

"Hey Sheriff, we're at the car now," Benjie says.

"Yeah, go on. Find anything?"

"Yeah, there's some cash in an envelope, like you said. What should we do with it?"

One of the sheriff's eyebrows raises an inch as he glances at Ashley, and then down at the child in her arms. "Give it to Fred, of course. It was *his* gas," he says dryly. Benjie acknowledges and the radio is silent.

"Well I'll be," the sheriff says. "So y'all have some semblance of a conscience."

"We're Bible readers," Marc says. It's an odd comment and I stare at him to indicate as much but say nothing. "We do our best to live by Christ's teachings. I'm sure you're doing the same. We saw the churches down the road."

"Those churches' doors been closed for months. People lost their faith long ago, I'm afraid."

"Not all people. We still believe that living by scripture is the best policy."

"Wish everyone was that way. Make my job a lot easier, that's for sure. So, what, your churches in Georgia didn't get closed down? What denomination are y'all? Baptist? Methodist?"

There's a moment of hesitation as glances are exchanged in our cell. It's Marc who finally answers. "Actually, sir, we're Jehovah's Witnesses."

The sheriff pauses at this, scanning each of our faces carefully. "Witnesses. Huh," he says with a tired grunt, removing his white hat and running his fingers through a thin cloud of hair. The others seem to be holding their breath as they wait for the sheriff to react.

"We had a few of your people in our town, before the laws changed."

"You mean the Liberation Act?" I offer.

"Yeah, that's the one," he says, shifting his weight with an uncomfortable look. "Never did understand it myself."

"Neither did our precinct," I say softly, drawing a puzzled look from the large man on the other side of the bars.

"Come 'gain?"

"I'm law enforcement, too. Or *was*, I guess. It's beginning to feel like another lifetime," I admit. The sheriff looks me over dubiously. In my current attire and state of grooming, I know I don't look the part. "It's a long story," I say simply.

"So you're not one of them? A Jehovah Witness, I mean?"

"No sir, but I've been with them long enough to know they're no threat." An odd look washes over the sheriff's face and he lowers his head solemnly.

"Yeah, that was what I said," the Sheriff says sadly. It's quiet for a few moments as the sheriff loses himself in his thoughts. Then he glances over his shoulder down the hall, rises slowly from the chair, and draws a ring of keys from his pocket. The door to our cell swings wide open.

"Are you letting us go, sir?" Andrew asks, clearly bewildered.

"No sense keeping y'all here. You were telling the truth about the money for the gas. Way I see it, no harm's been done. And if things continue to go downhill as I fear they will, we'll need these cells for the real criminals."

"Thank you, sir," Marc says, rising swiftly from the bench and shaking the sheriff's hand.

"Don't mention it. I didn't become sheriff to be a tyrant. I just want to protect my community. Listen, before y'all leave, we've got a nurse here that I'd like to have check your boy out. He don't look too good."

Ashley rises unsteadily with Matthew fidgeting in her arms. She tries to thank the sheriff but is overcome with emotion. Marc and Andrew grasp her shoulders and manage to keep her from toppling over. The sheriff looks them over with a concerned expression before calling someone on his radio.

"Follow me," he says softly as he leads us from the cell, past the corridors, and back out into the cold night.

11:49 PM
AMY

Morale is not high as we exit the hangar into the frigid winter night. There are groans and sighs as we file through the doors, the pall of exhaustion and anxiety having sapped our strength long ago. I brace against a sudden lash of wind and wonder again why we've been told to evacuate now, of all times, in the middle of the night and the dead of winter.

"This is crazy," someone mutters behind us. Still we press on, huddling together in a feeble attempt to keep warm. It's a slow trek to the tree line, where an old wooden sign indicates the start of a densely wooded trail. One of the elders takes the lead, swooping shadows stretching through the trees as the light from his electric lantern bobs and bounces.

Flashlights are flicked on as the pines thicken and the stippled moonlight yields to thick tree cover. With the heavy loads and the unpredictable terrain, falls and stumbles are common. A few young brothers with first aid kits are quick to assess injuries.

I'm thankful for the wheelchair; I can't imagine making the trek on crutches. Still, it's far from a smooth ride. Jesse, of course, hardly seems to notice. I hear him grunt and complain as we trudge further into darkness.

"You doing all right?" asks Walter's voice from somewhere in the night.

"Yeah, I'm good," Jesse replies before I have the chance.

"Good. Slow and steady. No need to wear ourselves out here. It's gonna be a long night."

"How long?"

"Can't say exactly, but I had a look at a map of these trails before the evacuation. They wind through the hills for miles."

"So you know where we're headed?" I ask.

"The general direction, yes. But I'm not sure of our destination."

"I sure hope *someone* is," says Jesse.

"We'll be taken care of, son. Jehovah will see to it."

Walter gives me a gentle pat on the shoulder as a burst of static erupts from his jacket. He zips it open and retrieves a small walkie-talkie.

"Go ahead," he says into the handset.

"Get the friends to shut their lights off and keep still," says a voice. Walter whirls around and gives the signal as our surroundings plunge into blackness. We wait in utter silence, hundreds of frozen bodies shivering in the dark.

"What's happening, Dad?" Jesse whispers, but Walter is silent.

It's a couple of minutes before the sound above us is realized clearly; the thud of propellers high above the trees. The sound approaches slowly and lingers, and the source is soon unmistakable.

A squadron of military helicopters passes just over the treetops above us, red strobes blinking on their black tails and underbellies. Powerful white searchlights rake and sift through the woods around us. The tree cover afforded by the evergreens above is thick, but I know it won't be enough.

"Keep still," Walter says, his voice barely audible above the helicopters' rotors.

"You think they're looking for us?" I ask. Walter ignores this.

An eternity passes before the aircraft have moved beyond us. A collective sigh of relief is heard from the crowd. Though we can be sure of nothing, somehow this feels like deliverance.

We trudge on for another hour before the leading edge of our party comes to a wide, shallow creek. The brothers call for a short break. Canteens and plastic bottles are topped up though the water is far too cold to drink straightaway.

Despite the dark and the cold, the brothers manage to get everyone across the stream in an organized way. As per their instructions, most traverse it barefoot, arms bent and interlocked at the elbows, stepping carefully with their shoes draped over their shoulders.

"Take it slow," I hear someone caution from the shadows. "This water's ice cold. Getting wet could easily give you hypothermia."

I glance at my wristwatch. It's just past three AM. I'm exhausted from just sitting and being pushed in the cold and can't begin to imagine what the others are experiencing. I study the faces as they cross the streambed: White haired sisters with stony expressions, bags slung over their shoulders. Teenagers and parents trudging across the frigid water with smaller siblings latched on their backs. All quietly resolved to the task of survival and obedience.

Walter appears at my side, brushing the mud from Chelsea's feet, then massaging them gently, getting the blood flowing again after the shock of the icy river water.

"Are we going camping, Walter?" she asks, looking up at the trees and the people all around.

"No, dear. This is not camping," Walter says, replacing her shoes and socks.

"How you holding up?" he asks.

"I'm fine. Feeling a little guilty, getting to sit through this all," I say.

"No need for that. This is how it works. We take care of each other."

"Yeah. I'm thankful for that. How would anyone be able to do this on their own?"

"They wouldn't, not without Jehovah. Remember that even if these brothers and sisters aren't at your side, Jehovah always is. His friendship is the most important."

"You say that like we're going to be split up," I ask, catching a shift in his tone. He takes a deep breath and gives me a long look before speaking.

"I don't want to scare you, Amy, but you need to be prepared."

"Prepared?" Another long pause. Walter scans the crowds before looking back at me.

"Things may get harder before they get easier. We just don't know what's around the corner."

"What are you trying to say, Walter?" I ask.

"I'm saying that I cannot guarantee that I will be at your side through all of this. I can't guarantee that any of these friends will. I wish I could, but I can't read the future. You must understand this."

"Walter, stop talking like this," I say, fidgeting.

"Amy, please, listen to me. You need to know that I will do anything to protect your life and the lives of our brothers and sisters. It is the responsibility of a shepherd. But even if something happens to me or anyone else here, be assured that you will be remembered by Jehovah."

I don't. I can't. Just the thought of losing Walter sends my mind into a panic. I'm shaking my head as Walter takes my face in his hands and gently kisses my forehead.

I'm still in shock and confusion as our convoy resumes its trek through the valley of deep shadow.

7:02 AM
LUKE

We're on the road by sunrise the next morning, feeding on tins of Andrew's food as he drives.

"How's Matthew?" I ask, glancing back at the child wrapped in Ashley's arms.

"Better. The fever's finally broken, thanks to that nurse."

"Glad to hear it," I say. "Looks like we picked the right town after all."

"If only we weren't so far behind schedule," Marc laments.

"Explain to me again this 'schedule', would you? Why the rush?"

"A few days ago, the congregations in our area received detailed instructions for our evacuation. They were very clear on the date we had to leave by, and the date and time we had to arrive at the location by. Unfortunately, we missed that deadline."

"So what does that mean? Surely they'll let us in when they see who we are."

"I've been going over the same question in my head. I don't know the answer, Luke. But it worries me, showing up late like this."

"Well, between the road conditions, getting hijacked, and getting ourselves arrested and thrown in jail, I think your friends will have to make some allowances."

"I hope so. For now, we just need to get ourselves there." Marc chucks his empty tin in a plastic garbage bag and unfolds a map on the front dash, tracing our route with the tip of a pencil.

"According to the sheriff, I-26 isn't backed up like the highways we avoided earlier," he says.

"It'll beat back roads, that's for sure," Andrew adds.

"Yeah, my thoughts exactly. Shouldn't take more than an hour if we can keep our speed up."

"And if we can avoid any more setbacks," I add.

"And that."

"So, what else do you know about these evacuations? Where is everyone headed?"

"I wasn't privy to all the details, but I imagine it's different for every area. The place we're headed to is a decommissioned private aircraft hangar. It should be big enough to hold everyone."

"But for how long? What about food? Water? Supplies?"

"Again, I don't have all the answers, but Jehovah's organization has accomplished some impressive things in the past. In many countries hit with natural disasters, the Witnesses were the first to provide aid to their brothers and sisters. Before the government showed up, before the Red Cross, we were there with truckloads of food, water, blankets, you name it. We'd fix houses or even build new ones for our friends. All free of charge, by the way. No one else knows worldwide disaster response like us. I'm not worried."

"I didn't know the Witnesses were into that kind of stuff. Amy never mentioned any of your public works projects."

"We don't call them public works projects," Andrew mentions.

"And why not?"

"We're not about building schools and hospitals. But we do help our brothers and sisters whenever there's a need."

"So you only help those in your congregations? What about outsiders?"

"We don't ignore others. We spent millions of dollars and billions of hours helping people, but not through handouts. Our focus has always been on preaching the good news of God's kingdom, a real, future government that will rid the earth of its problems once and for all. It's the only solution to this mess."

"I remember Walter mentioning something about a war."

"Armageddon."

"Right. Armageddon," I mutter under my breath.

"We don't fear it, Luke. We need it now more than ever. Just think, an end to crime, corruption, war, greed, suffering. It'll bring the kind of world we won't worry about raising our children in."

"It sounds good. I've always been hopeful, but what you all believe, it just seems... impossible."

"I know how you feel, man," Andrew says from behind the wheel. "Took me a long time, too. Sounds like a fairy tale, huh?" I nod at him in the rear view mirror.

"When I first started studying with the Witnesses, I felt the same way you do. At first I thought the Witnesses were a cult. I was very guarded, very suspicious. But after some time getting to know them, I could see they were just normal people. Still, their belief in a future paradise seemed farfetched.

"My Bible teacher's response was for me to just give Jehovah a chance. Told me to start praying, do a little Bible reading each day, think about what I was learning, and use it. It didn't take long to see the changes. The more I thought things over, the more sense it made. My faith has only grown since then."

"I've never really been a man of faith," I say.

"I don't mean *blind faith*. That's dangerous. The faith I'm talking about is based on facts, based on personal experience, and based on study. It doesn't happen overnight. I think one of the big factors for me was having my prayers answered. When that started happening, I could *see* there was something to this. So I began to think, if God's *listening* to my prayers, he must be *real*. And if he's got the power to do that, why wouldn't he have the power to do the other things he's promised? Like I said, the more I thought about it all, the more it just clicked."

"Take the next exit, then hang a right," Marc quietly interrupts. The off ramp from I-26 spills us into a small town. It's so similar to Maynard I almost wonder if we've somehow circled back. The stretch of road, the ski resort signs, the barred-up windows of shops and homes, it's all very familiar. I instinctively glance up at the rooftops, wary of more snipers.

"Follow this road for a couple miles. Take a left at the intersection," Marc says, the tension audible in his voice as he eyes our surroundings.

Andrew follows Marc's directions carefully, sending us through the heart of the small town. Many of the parked cars sport broken windows or graffiti. The shops are caged in with bars or roll tops; the few left undefended have been thoroughly pillaged.

On the next street, charred skeletons of homes stand on black lawns. A mixed pack of soot-covered dogs, some still in their collars, sifts through the wreckage. A couple of them raise their heads curiously as we pass, memories of their domestic lives flashing momentarily in their eyes, but most seem content in their new feral lives. Andrew gases it a little harder.

"What do you think happened here?" Ashley asks quietly from the backseat.

"Same as everywhere else, I'd imagine," I say sadly. "People see the news, get scared, start stocking up supplies. Then you have the troublemakers, the ones who can't wait for a taste of anarchy. The police stand their ground, hold the people off as long as they can, but eventually opt to protect their own and quit the uniform. It doesn't take much, and it doesn't take long."

"It's amazing how quickly society can crumble," Andrew comments under his breath. The van slows to a stop a few moments later as we near a gravel road that turns off from the main street.

"That's it, that's the road," Marc says with cautious enthusiasm. Andrew points the van up the road without a word and we hold our breaths. Minutes pass before the trees part and give way to a large open field. There's a giant grey building at the far end. As we approach I spot at least a hundred vehicles parked quietly on a vast blacktop.

"Seems awfully quiet," Andrew says nervously as he confers with his watch. It's eight thirty.

"Could they still be sleeping?" Marc mutters as our vehicle approaches. Andrew stops the car near a set of doors and we pile out anxiously. Marc flings open the doors to reveal an enormous hangar.

The floor space is littered with abandoned luggage and piles of belongings. Folding cots are stacked high with electronics, clothing, and accessories. Everything but the people.

"Any ideas?" I ask the others as we round the first corner in the main path. A stage made of scaffolding and plywood sits to my right. A microphone stand is perched atop it, and I suspect that whatever was last spoken through it caused the mass exodus.

"Looks like an evacuation. And they must've only taken the essentials," Marc says simply, lifting an expensive looking laptop from a table.

"An evacuation? But wasn't that the whole point of this place in the first place? To give people a place to evacuate *to*?" Andrew says incredulously.

"I think Marc's right. They left in a hurry," I say.

"So what happens next?" Andrew asks.

"I guess we try to figure out where they went," says Mark.

"Couldn't have been far," I say. "Not with all those cars outside. Wherever they went, they travelled on foot."

"On foot? In the dead of winter? We're talking hundreds of people here. Men, women, children, elderly folks…" Andrew says, shaking his head.

"Wouldn't be the first time," Marc says cryptically. I don't bother asking him what he means. He's deep in thought as he surveys the hollow space around us.

"Ok," he finally says to us. "You guys grab a couple of bags and whatever food and water you can carry."

"What's the plan?" I ask.

"A hundred people walking anywhere are bound to leave tracks. We locate the tracks and follow them."

Andrew and I are left without words, but the two of us quickly realize our options are running thin. We nod and disperse.

9:48 AM
AMY

My eyelids flutter open to reveal hundreds of sleeping bodies knotted tightly together beneath a patchwork of blankets and jackets. A few of the friends are stirring awake or picking their way through the masses hoping to scrounge up some food. Walter appears from the underbrush and hands me a thermos of hot coffee. I don't know how, and I don't ask. We enjoy the warmth of our liquid breakfast in the morning tranquility. With the sounds of birdsong and the squirrels bounding along the branches above us, it's almost peaceful enough to forget the gravity of our situation. Almost.

It's another hour before the entire convoy is up and moving. Many are forced to nibble down their breakfast on foot. My stomach aches for something more substantial than powdered coffee and saltine crackers, but concerns about food rations pale in comparison with all the uncertainty that looms ahead.

"You think we're almost there?" Jesse asks Walter.

"I think so. I talked to one of the brothers in the lead early this morning. He seems to think it won't be much longer till we're there."

"And where is *there*?" I ask.

"We'll know soon enough," Walter says.

Somehow, Chelsea's managed to keep up with the rest of us, but her wandering eyes and the occasional wild gesturing of her hands tell me she's still far away. From time to time something just off of the trail catches her attention and she stumbles after it like a child. Walter is immediately behind her, guiding her gently back to the path. His words are quiet and kind, but the pain on his face is unambiguous.

Eddie, the brother with the two small girls, is never far from us. I hear Walter fall back occasionally to check up on him. The two of them speak softly, keeping the conversation neatly out of his daughters' earshot, but I can't imagine the two girls don't know what's going on. Still, they seem content with this distraction through the woods, plucking the periodic pansy and getting me to stick them in their hair. I keep them occupied with conversation, speaking all the louder when I hear their father charge a few paces into the underbrush and vomit loudly. With these rations, I know it isn't something he ate. Anxiety weighs on each of us in different ways.

The trail opens abruptly into a grassy clearing. A towering abandoned sawmill leans tiredly to one side at the center. The tin roof is old and rust bitten, holes gaping in its panels like dirty cavities. Derelict machinery litters the edge of the property. Parents grip the shoulders of their children tightly, dissuading any curious notions of exploration.

"We're not staying in there, I hope," a sister mumbles behind me.

"This is our rendezvous point," a brother says in a large voice from several yards ahead, relaying the message down the line. We gaze around curiously, struggling to make sense of it.

Eventually the crowd disperses, reclining on the grass and relishing the warming daylight as the sun climbs above us in the sky. It takes us some time to thaw out from the night before and it's just what we need. Before long the children are back to their old selves, running around and playing again; the adults are chatting, relaxed.

Then we hear a shrill scream from deep within the forest. The voices fall silent as heads turn to locate the source of the noise. A column of white steam rising from the pine tops is our only clue.

The ancient train chugs determinedly through the trees to meet us, steel wheels swishing along invisible rails hidden by tall grass. Yellow sparks splash to its sides as it screeches to a halt. The engine and the string of cars it tows are relics from a bygone era. The engine's bronze plating and trim are faded and scratched, but it's no less majestic.

The door to the engine car swings open on creaking hinges and a man emerges. He leans over the chain railing on a narrow metal walkway and gives us a friendly wave before dropping down into the grass and disappearing in the crowd.

"Our rendezvous?" I ask Walter.

"So it would seem," he says with an amused smile.

Doors on rails slide open on the sides of the cargo carriages. Friendly faces and outstretched hands welcome us aboard. Young brothers and sisters clamber atop the cars to lash our meager luggage to the rooftops. When everyone is accounted for–three hundred and eighty-nine in total–the engine whistle screams once more and the line of cars groans back to life.

In the cargo carriages there are no seats, no tables, no beds. With the doors barred tight, the only sources of ventilation are long horizontal slats just inches below the ceiling. It's enough to keep the air breathable, but with nearly forty of us in this carriage alone, the smell of sweaty, unbathed bodies is inescapable. The toilet, a shallow metal dish that opens directly onto the tracks below, probably isn't helping the smell, but I try not to dwell on it.

Mike, the brother who'd been in charge of getting us aboard this particular carriage, smiles as he distributes oranges from a large plastic bin. He lets out a low whistle when he spots me in my wheelchair.

"Couldn't have been easy on that trail," he says with the shake of his head as he hands me the fruit.

"It was a long night. Thanks," I reply.

"Be sure to eat the whole thing. Vitamin C might be a hard thing to come by in the days ahead. We gotta take what we can get now. Not a time for waste."

I nod, digging my fingernail into the fruit and enjoying the faint spray of citrus on my fingers. Soon the whole cabin smells of oranges and everyone's mood is slightly improved.

"So, what's the story behind this train?" Walter asks Mike once the bin has been emptied.

"The engine was owned by a brother. It was his business, I understand. He'd buy old steam engines, refurbish them, and sell them to collectors. The organization contacted him a few months ago and told him to keep his eye out for a few functional engines. He did, and they were purchased by the society and sent to different cities here in the South. The containers were purchased months ago for next to nothing at an auction. They were parked in an old railyard in Florida until a couple of weeks ago, when our congregation was assigned to get them cleaned out for passengers. Not an easy job, let me tell you. These used to be livestock cars. It took forever to get the stink out."

"Well, we really appreciate your hard work. This definitely beats trekking through the woods in the dark," Walter says.

"How long were you out there?" Mike asks.

"Not even a full day, but it felt like a week." Walter motions around to the friends around us, most of whom are sound asleep and snoring loudly, their laps littered with orange rinds. "So, you folks are from Florida?"

"Yup. Been on this train for four days now, picking friends up along the way. You guys were the largest group so far."

"Are there more people getting on at later stops?" I ask.

"I believe so, but I don't know the full schedule. The information is all very compartmentalized, for safety reasons, of course," Mike says with a shrug. Walter nods knowingly.

"It's ok, we understand. Up until this train showed up, I wasn't even sure who was meeting us back in that field."

"Walking by faith," Mike says.

"No kidding. So how were things in Florida before you all left?" Walter asks. Mike is suddenly very quiet, a shadow falling over his face.

"Not pretty. The National Guard was called in a couple of days before we left. A huge crowd of rioters tried to fight back. The soldiers opened fire... It was a massacre. The civilians who survived retreated, got themselves armed, and went back. Eventually the soldiers were overpowered.

"Things only got worse after that. Some locals got a hold of one of the army tanks, went on a joyride through town. Shot up a bunch of buildings, ran over cars. No one could stop them. The police were nowhere to be found at this point, of course. It was total anarchy. Utilities had been shut off, too. No water, gas, electricity. That's when the instructions came for us to leave."

"On this train?" I ask.

"Yeah. By this time we'd finally cleaned it out, gotten the doors repaired, made sure the roofs weren't leaking. It's a good thing we had this as our means of escape, too, because by the time we left there wasn't any other way out. The roads were blocked with abandoned cars and those men in the tank had blown up a few of the bridges to prevent the military from sending in reinforcements. The railway was the only way."

"It sure is incredible, seeing Jehovah's hand in all of this," Walter says with a sigh. Mike nods somberly.

"Makes me wonder what's still ahead, though," he says quietly.

9:50 AM
LUKE

It isn't hard to locate the trail. The hangar was clearly stocked to house hundreds of refugees, and so many people trekking through dampened dirt and grass are sure to leave tracks. After less than an hour of searching, we find the trailhead north of the hangar. It's about half a mile from the building and marked by a wooden sign.

I try to picture a mixed crowd of that size moving through the trees in the dead of winter. There's no point in discussing the motive for their evacuation. We're all in the dark together.

"When do you think they left?" Andrew asks from over my shoulder. I'm at the front of the group, with Marc and Ashley at the rear. Matthew, sound asleep, rides in a stroller his mother salvaged from the hangar.

"Hard to say," I mutter in response. The dirt of the trail is mixed with gravel and rocks, making the tracks harder to distinguish. An occasional discarded item–an empty food tin or water bottle–is all that tells us we're still on the right track.

"By the way, I found this in the hangar," Andrew says, jogging a few steps to my side and matching my pace. He swings his pack around and pulls out a small AM/FM radio. He switches it on and starts scanning for a signal. There's a pause as the scanner desperately searches for a signal, but there's nothing. No morning traffic reports, no news bulletins, no pop music, no call-in radio shows. The airwaves are deserted. A chill runs up my spine.

"Try AM," I say uncomfortably. More static, then another stretch of silence at it scans. Then, finally, something breaks through. It's faint and riddled with static, but the message is clear enough.

"*...Repeat, the National Guard has withdrawn from the following counties: Cherokee, Union, Kershaw, Chesterfield, Williamsburg, and Allendale. If you are a resident in one of these counties, for the safety of you and your family, the South Carolina State Sheriff's Department strongly recommends staying indoors. For added protection, board up windows and keep doors locked at all times...*"

Andrew shakes his head with a low whistle as the cold, mechanical voice rattles off a list of cautionary procedures. To the average Joe it may seem like there's a fighting chance, but as law enforcement I know better. The situation must be hopeless. Chances of being alive a week from now are slim.

My mind goes back to the conversation Walter and I had just weeks ago. The *worst-case scenario*; the man hunkered down in his basement surrounded by canned food and a stocked gun locker. Then I see the hijacker in the ditch, rifle glistening at his side while his life slipped away. Walter was right. It's an uncomfortable admission.

The Witnesses were wise to evacuate.

The deafening whine of a jet engine shreds the forest silence as a grey fighter passes just above us. It vanishes a moment later, heading south. The rumble lingers in the air long after it's gone, and as soon as it fades over the horizon, a new one takes its place, a terrible, ground-trembling blast that can only belong to an explosion.

We exchange tense glances for a moment and pause in our tracks.

"That sounded like a bomb," Ashley says, a dire look in her eyes.

"And it sounded like it came from the direction of the hangar," I say, heightening the tension.

"If we'd been even an hour later, we would've been inside..." Andrew says with a look of shock.

"No point on dwelling on it now, let's keep moving," Marc says, rushing ahead to take the lead. But the sound of a chopper overhead stops him. We dive for cover as the aircraft passes, and as I glance up through the branches I catch a glimpse of three letters that put ice in my veins. *FBI*.

"Luke, c'mon, let's go," Andrew says, tugging at my sleeve. I nod vigorously and rush to catch up. After the explosion and the sighting of the two aircraft, our pace quickens considerably. It's now clear that our only hope lies in reuniting with the other group.

By the time we finally break for a late lunch, we've been walking for almost six hours. We peel our shoes off and massage the blood back into our battered and blistered feet. We finish an entire loaf of white bread and half a jar of peanut butter. Matthew wakes up long enough to join in the meal and falls back asleep immediately after. He looks much better than he did yesterday, but he's still pale and weak.

"So, we appear to have hit a crossroads," Andrew says, wiping breadcrumbs from his jaw with the back of a sleeve. We survey the grassy clearing around us, which branches into two opposite paths on either side through the woods. The good news is that it's clear from the large swath of freshly trampled grass that a sizable crowd of people was recently here. The problem is that their tracks end here. Neither path shows any signs of recent activity.

"Any ideas?" Andrew asks, gesturing first to one of the routes, then the other. The grass on both sides is tall and undisturbed. It doesn't add up. Rising, Marc moves towards an old crumbling building in the center of the clearing.

"Babe," his wife calls after him warily. "You're not going in there, I hope. It can't be safe."

"Just want to get a look around," Marc says over his shoulder. Then, looking down at his feet, he pauses and beckons us over excitedly. We wade through the grass to get a closer look. It's an old rusted set of rails. We stare at them in wonderment for a moment before speaking.

"A train," Andrew says with a smile, catching on. "They don't run on highways, so the traffic can't hold them up."

"Exactly. And all you need is enough coal and a small crew and you can move hundreds of passengers anywhere you like. It's brilliant," Marc says.

"Look here," Andrew says from a few yards up the tracks. "Some of these rail ties have been replaced recently. I'll bet our brothers have been working on this for weeks. Months, even."

"This must've been the plan all along," Marc says, face beaming.

"Seems like a stretch," I say.

"Just like everything else up to this point, but here we are," Andrew says.

"I certainly don't see any other options," Marc says.

"Okay, so we wait here on the off chance that another train shows up?" I ask.

"We could follow the tracks, but there's no indication of which direction they were headed. There's a fifty-fifty chance of getting ourselves even farther away from the rest of the group."

"So we wait," Andrew says, shrugging. "Could use the rest anyhow. We can sleep in shifts, make sure someone's always up to watch the rails." It's a sensible suggestion, and the notion of rest is appealing. We're sore, worn out, and mentally exhausted.

"Ok," Marc says with one last look around. "You guys can sleep. I'll take the first shift."

I plop down into the grass and bundle up in a sleeping bag I found stuffed in an old suitcase back at the hangar. I'm asleep before my head hits the ground.

6:45 PM
AMY

Our carriage slows to a halt just as the sun sets beyond the slatted ventilation windows. We hear the engine ahead of us utter its last sputtering coughs for the day, steel wheels screeching in protest. Once we've stopped the doors slide open, letting the cool evening breeze gush in and wash away the stench of bodies, sweat, and waste.

"Are we getting out, Mommy?" asks a little girl in her mother's arms. The woman frowns and leans forward to gaze out the doorway, the final rays of sunlight glinting through her golden hair.

"I'm not sure, baby."

Minutes pass as we wait for instructions. A man in a pea coat and red baseball cap finally materializes outside the doorway. He looks us over quickly and then jots something down in a notebook. He speaks in quick, rapid sentences.

"Welcome to Wilmington, North Carolina. Y'all will be staying here tonight. It's not the Ritz Carlton, but the brothers and sisters here have done their utmost to make the quarters as bearable as possible. If y'all need anything, ask anyone with one of these yellow lanyards." He holds his up for us to get a look, then stuffs it back into his coat.

"Our kitchen crew will be handing out boxed dinners at seven thirty. Please mark the number of occupants needing a meal on the outside of your quarters with the chalk we've provided. Bathrooms are to the north and south of the property. For safety reasons, once the sun goes down, we don't allow lights. If for some reason you need to get around after dark, you'll find plenty of glowsticks in boxes all around the premises. And friends, please, whatever you do, stay within the fenced perimeter."

The brother pauses just long enough for the last command to linger in our ears. Then, with a curt nod of his head, he disappears. When I'm helped down from the carriage, I see him giving the same speech to the group in the next car.

Our train has come to rest amongst a labyrinth of shipping containers. Old, gnarled cranes tower in the air, their hooks and chains dangling like claws above us. I spot a couple of figures high up on the catwalks, eyeing the horizon carefully with the binoculars glued to their faces.

A sister will silver hair cropped close to her face greets us with a tense smile. She reminds me of the old Chelsea. She wears a yellow lanyard and takes us, without a word, to a row of faded Maersk shipping containers. Their doors are swung open, curious sets of eyes peering at us from within, the expressions just barely visible in the fading light. These are our quarters, I realize.

We come to an aisle of empty containers and the older sister divides us efficiently into smaller groups. She repeats the instructions the other brother gave us, emphasizing once again the no-light-after-dark policy. She hands us a package of assorted glowsticks and a small box of pink chalk.

At the far end of our container room, a hastily welded metal rack houses folded blankets, sleeping bags, and travel-sized toiletries. A collapsible bucket hangs from a bolt near the ceiling along with a shovel and a few other essentials. Some folding chairs and a folding card table occupy another corner. Narrow slits covered in metal mesh near the ceiling are the only windows.

Walter takes a quick headcount and marks the number on the outside of our container as instructed. *Fifteen.* Fifteen people stuffed in a space smaller than our apartment's living room. I think about our apartment now, the bars on the windows, the poor insulation, how cramped it always felt, our nagging dreams for a better life. It's a distant memory now, so petty.

Our world was a facade of stability just waiting to crumble away and reveal the darkness within. I can't say I don't miss it a little, but I'm so glad we didn't have more to lose. The great tribulation has evened the field. We are all homeless and penniless, with nothing to show for whatever material lives we lived prior to this. All that matters is the clothes on our back, a warm spot to curl up for the night, and the hope of a half decent meal.

Our dinner is delivered at seven thirty as promised. Sloppy joe sandwiches, rice, and baby carrots. It's warm and it's incredible. Anything is a delicacy to a neglected appetite.

"So what do you think the deal is with the flashlights?" Jesse asks, licking his fingers. I turn away.

"I'm guessing it's so we won't be easily spotted," says Walter.

"Power's out in the nearby town," says a quiet voice near the door. We turn to look, but the face is in shadow. We hear the crack of a glowstick and moments later a girl's face is illuminated by an unearthly green tinge. I don't recognize her from the train. In fact, I'm sure I've never seen her before.

"I'm Sara. This is my second night here," she says.

"You mean, here in this container?" I ask. Sara nods.

"I'm waiting on some friends from Charlotte. We were split up when we were trying to get to our evacuation point," she says with a faraway look.

"Do you know what happened with the town here?" Walter asks.

"Not everything. This facility is right on the outskirts of the town. Fortunately there's a big wooded area between us and them, though."

"Fortunate?" I ask.

"It's... ugly out there. Trust me, you don't want them finding us." Looking in her eyes, I believe her.

"Well, let's be thankful for having this place, then," Walter says. He suggests a prayer of thanks. Nodding heads can be seen in the fluorescent glow of artificial lights, and so he prays.

8:37 PM
LUKE

I'm stirred to life by a hand on my shoulder. It takes a second to get my bearings. The slender grass sways with a frigid breeze. The wind makes strange, ethereal noises as it passes through the pines. Marc settles into a sleeping bag next to his wife and child as my watch begins.

I flick on my flashlight and rummage through the pack I put together back at the hangar. There are a couple of jars of half eaten peanut butter, a loaf of bread, several sleeves of saltines, and a can of tuna. We agreed earlier today that everything needs to be rationed carefully, so I allow myself two slices of bread with a thin slathering of peanut butter and nothing more. My stomach is rumbling again less than thirty minutes later.

I opt for a distraction instead. I stuff my sleeping bag back into my pack and start exploring the clearing around us. I poke around the outside of the rickety old building but decide against entering after noticing the ragged ceiling and exposed glass and rusty nails. It looks like the whole thing could come down at any second and I'd hate to be inside it, this far from a hospital, if it did.

I next take a short walk up the train tracks. I'm not expecting to find anything of significance, but I need something to keep busy. My stomach protests with hunger pangs and I'm restless.

That's when I hear the train.

It's a low rumble at first, soft and distant, and I can't tell which direction it's coming from. My eyes dart up and down the tracks, looking for the scattered beam of headlights through the trees, but the night remains black and still.

I race back to the clearing to alert the others. They pack their bags quickly as we wait, the rumbling growing nearer. We finally spot an engine's headlamp winking at us through the woods. It's a bare, dull glow, and as it approaches I glimpse the dark plastic tarp that's been rigged against it, likely to keep it from being seen at a distance. This is worrisome, and for a split second I wonder if we should observe from the shadows before approaching, but there's no time. I train the beam of my flashlight on the blackened windows of the engine and can't make out a thing.

"It's not slowing down," Andrew says, dismayed and slightly winded from the excitement of it all.

"Could the conductor be asleep? Maybe there isn't anyone else aboard," Ashley suggests as the engine slides past, followed by a long tail of windowless cars.

"Doubt it," I say. "More than likely they're just ignoring us. With all that's going on I don't blame them." I glance over at Marc, who's shaking his head with a desperate look.

"We need to get aboard this train. Otherwise we'll never catch up with the others."

"How? Most of these cars are closed up, no way to jump on," Andrew says. He throws the beam of his flashlight against the carriages as they whiz by. I gaze farther down the line of cars, and there, towards the rear, is a narrow container carriage with a low metal sideskirt and loose, clinking chain handrails.

"There!" I shout, jogging towards it. It's the third car from the end and our only chance. I run alongside the train, trying to match its speed, and quickly realize it's moving much faster than I thought. Then again, perhaps it's the fatigue or lack of a square meal. Either way, it's a struggle, but I manage to grab onto one of the chain railings and swing my body on board. I wedge my pack securely against the side of the carriage, clench my flashlight between my teeth, and reach out for Andrew's hand. There's fear in his eyes, but he manages to clamber aboard without issue.

It's Marc and Ashley I'm worried about. Marc's got Matthew in his arms, the boy's arms and legs flapping lifelessly with his father's movement. Ashley is a few paces behind and struggles to keep up. Marc's an able runner even with the added bulk of his pack and his son, and he hands the boy off to Andrew and I before leaping onto the sideskirt.

As soon as his footing is secure, Marc turns back to reach for Ashley. We yell at her to throw her backpack aboard first, but she can't hear us. Her face is red and sweaty, her arms and legs pumping as fast as they can, but it isn't enough. She's losing ground. Marc sheds his pack and prepares to jump down to help his wife, but I hold him back.

"I'll get her," I say. "You stay with your boy." There's a moment of indecision in his face. He glances at Matthew, then back at me, and steps back. In a single motion I fling my legs over the railing and brace for the ground. It snags me back viciously like a carpet pulled from under my feet. I tumble in the tall grass, stopping just short of the slicing wheels of the next carriage down the line.

When I'm finally up and running Ashley's even farther behind. Her face is streaked with tears and perspiration.

"I can't! Can't do it!" she screams between ragged breaths.

"Forget the bag!" I yell. Her pace slows even further as she complies, slipping out of the straps and letting the backpack fall and vanish in the grass. The carriage with the others is too far away now. Neither of us will be able to catch up. I scan the remaining cars quickly and spot another low walkway at the end of the last carriage. My legs and chest burn with exertion as I grab Ashley's hand and force her to keep up.

"I can't! Stop it, Luke!" she protests between sobs.

"Shut up and run!" I order. My legs burn as my heart hammers away in my chest, struggling to gain ground on the train. My eyes and throat bulge with the exertion, and for a moment I am sure my heart will give out on me, but I manage to press on, Ashley's sweaty hand gripped tightly in my own.

We finally reach the last car. I yank her arm mercilessly and make sure her hands are secure on the railing. She struggles aboard and collapses on the walkway.

As I reach for the railing, lungs burning, an odd, milky light descends upon me. It is so sudden, so unexpected, that for a moment there is no train, no Ashley, no rails beneath me, no forest surrounding me. There is only the strange, white light. My pace slows, and the carriage slips away, as I turn to gaze up at the sky.

And then I trip. My legs disappear from beneath me. I'm sent sprawling, my body crashing and rolling helplessly against the tracks, bits of sharp gravel biting into the skin of my palms and face. I don't understand it. Not at first. Not until the light from above dims, revealing a familiar shape in the sky.

The helicopter's blades hack at the air, whipping the high weeds into a frenzy. I hear Ashley's voice faintly yell my name, but it's all impossibly far away now, an echo from the bottom of a well. The chopper descends just yards from me, close enough for me to clearly make out the sharpshooter perched on its landing skid.

I run my fingers over the back of my calf and find it covered in slick, warm fluid. The realization hits moments before the pain. Two armed soldiers in full gear dismount from the chopper and rush to my side. One kicks me with the toe of his boot and orders me to lie prone with my arms outstretched. They wrench my hands tightly behind my back and cuff me with thick plastic ties. I'm peeled from the ground and forced towards the aircraft, where they heave me inside and throw a black sack over my head.

I'm lost and disoriented as someone with nimble hands dresses my wound with a tight elastic bandage. I hardly feel the gaping hole in the muscle. Maybe it's the adrenaline; maybe it's a sedative they've drugged me with. In spite of everything, I'm strangely subdued. Calm, even. I can only guess at what awaits me, but I'm deeply grateful for the fact that they've let the others escape. Had it been Ashley shot, or Matthew, or any of the others, I would've never forgiven myself. Whatever happens next, at least the others are safe. I take a deep breath and bow my head, blocking out the thudding rotors above us and the whine of machines from the cockpit.

I pray. I thank God–*Jehovah*–for keeping the others safe. I pray that Amy is with the other group, far from the clutches of these criminals, and that she'll be ok when she hears about all this. I thank Him for the time I had with my wife. I actually smile beneath that suffocating black hood when I think back on those golden years.

Really, there is so much to be thankful for.

8:15 AM
AMY

Last night's sleep was riddled with nightmares. In one, I was being pushed in my wheelchair along a dark, damp corridor far underground. On either side were endless rows of prison bars, and in one of the cells, I saw briefly the sallow, hopeless face of my husband. He looked like one of those starved souls from a concentration camp, eyes deep set, like pinpoints of light in dark tunnels. I tried to call out, but my mouth was stuck shut. I tried to reach out, but we moved too quickly. Luke raised a shriveled hand in my direction and was gone forever.

I wake up shivering. My head is pounding and my stomach growls insistently. Walter's in about the same state, and so he rolls me out to the makeshift mess tent where we scarf down a few slices of toast and two cups of powdered coffee. I try to shake the nightmare from my memory, but it lingers like swamp fog in my mind.

I spot a few familiar faces here, including the brother, Eddie, and his two daughters whom Walter and I accompanied for most of the journey yesterday. I also see brother Odelawe, the Nigerian brother from back at the hanger. Though it's only been days since leaving our homes and our belongings, it feels like months.

Walter wheels me around the premises for some fresh air as the next breakfast crowd moves in. The shipping facility's property is surrounded on all sides by a high chain link fence lined with coils of barbed wire. On one side, a large gate opens to a loading dock and an old railway. I presume it's the same railroad we arrived on last night, but everything looks different in the morning light. I glance up at the crane, where two guards peer over the endless trees through binoculars. At least that hasn't changed.

A small crowd of people in the yellow lanyards sweeps by as we pass, opening the gate wide and fanning out along the loading dock. Within five minutes an old train labors up the tracks, steam erupting with a tired hiss as it comes to rest before us. The doors slide open to reveal a new batch of arrivals. The friends pile out as instructions are relayed to them, just like yesterday.

Dollies and handcarts are unloaded to transport supplies from the train's cargo holds to the shipping facility. Giant water jugs, ice coolers, protein bars, stacks of MREs, and hundreds of cans of food are among the items. It looks like enough to feed an army, all piled up like that, but the reality is that with over a thousand housed here in the containers it'll probably be enough for only a day or two.

The containers gradually empty, and as the last of the passengers files past, I hear Walter's surprised gasp. I turn my head to follow his gaze and instantly spot the familiar faces of Marc and Ashley and their little boy, Matthew. They run, overwhelmed, into Walter's arms and nearly collapse. Matthew's face lights up just a little when he sees me, but he hasn't the strength to leave his father's arms. Marc and Ashley are smiling, but there's a distance in their expressions that unsettles me.

"Amy..." Ashley says shakily, kneeling at my side. I wait for more, but her lips tremble without words and she appears ready to faint. Walter reaches out a hand to steady her.

"Let's get a warm meal in you," he says, propping Ashley against his side as he leads the way back to the mess tent. Marc nods, and our small band follows the rest of the crowd back to camp. We exchange introductions with Andrew, a brother who crossed paths with Marc and Ashley somewhere along the way. He says they only met a couple of days ago, and I sense there's much being left unsaid. Whatever's transpired, they've been through a lot together. That much is clear.

"We need to talk," Marc tells me with a serious look once they've finished their powdered eggs and toast. The breakfast crowd has thinned somewhat, but we're still surrounded by a sea of people.

"Ok," I say.

"It's about Luke." For a second I think I've misheard until I look up to see the grave look on his face.

"My husband? What is it? *What do you know?*"

"He was... He was with us. For awhile."

"*With you?* How? When? Where is he now?"

"We ran into him while we were still in Georgia. We had to take back roads since the highways were so clogged up. And he was just... there, in the woods. We stopped and picked him up."

The words don't register. None of this makes sense. The woods? The last time I saw Luke, federal agents were hauling him off to prison. How could he have ended up in the woods?

"Did he say anything about how he got there?" I ask. Marc, Ashley, and their friend, Andrew, exchange uncomfortable glances before I get an answer.

"He did. At first he said he'd been in a car accident, but later he told us the whole story. Apparently, he'd been in police custody..." Marc pauses here, waiting for my reaction. He's expecting shock, I guess. My lack of expression seems to relieve him.

"Apparently he'd been arrested by the FBI. They'd been... interrogating him." The words are said too gently and I instantly sense how awful it must have been. I feel a churning in my stomach and my pulse quickens.

"But he got away, right?" I say.

"He did. He jumped in a river when the truck he was being transported in stopped on an overpass. It's a wonder he didn't drown. He was handcuffed at the time, the water was freezing cold," Ashley says, speaking rapidly, her eyes sorrowful, apologetic.

The next details come in quick succession. They take turns explaining how Luke rode with them for hours until they came to a gas station, where their car was stolen. Then, by chance, they ran into Andrew and continued on their way. Eventually they reached the evacuation hangar, found our trail, and located the railway, where they boarded a train.

Ashley explains, through tears, how my husband went back to save her when she started falling behind. She describes the bright light, the helicopter, Luke falling.

"They shot him," Ashley says, burying her face in her hands.

"And? No one went back for him?" I say incredulously. The three of them look at me blankly. "After my husband risked his neck to save you, no one thought to go back for him?" I repeat, getting angry. Walter pats my arm with his hand but I shake him off, my ire rising.

"Amy, we *would* have, if that was possible. But those men were armed. They were soldiers, trained to kill."

"And? Didn't you just say that Luke tried to defend you all from the man with the gun who hijacked you?"

"Yes, but that wasn't the right decision. It could've made things a lot worse. We have to trust that Jehovah knows–"

"Don't make this about Jehovah! This has nothing to do with you trusting in Him! *You didn't have the guts to go back!* It's that simple! You were so concerned with saving your own skins that you abandoned him when he needed you the most!"

There's so much more I want to say, the fury building in my chest like stoked coals, but I'm powerless to speak my mind. I feel as if the last bit of hope has drained from my core, and my energy along with it. My chin falls to my chest, tears of anger and frustration cascading down my face and into my soiled lap. Without a word, Walter rises and wheels me away from the table and back to our quarters, away from the others' guilty silence and the staring eyes of faces that will never understand this pain.

8:47 AM
LUKE

When I wake, I find myself in a stuffy grey cell, its metal surfaces covered in a thick, suffocating coat of drab paint, the steel bolts holding it all together reduced to rounded, featureless lumps. On the other side of the bars, segmented pipes snake from the ceiling and floor and run the length of a narrow corridor. I hear them groan and creak as mystery fluids flow their course. The air is tinged with the smell of something like diesel fuel. I glance down the corridor and note the odd tapered corners of the doors, their doorways elevated just inches off the floor, and it hits me. I'm in the bowels of a ship, deep down in what they call the *brig*.

As if in confirmation, a powerful foghorn bellows from above deck. A voice comes over the PA system, but the nearest speakers are several compartments over; the words are too muffled for me to make out. It must be a rallying cry; it's followed by a rousing recording of the national anthem and the rhythmic thud of marching feet somewhere overhead.

Like my last prison cell, this one brims with cold artificial light, making it impossible to tell the time of day. I recall my capture, being forced to board the helicopter, the masked soldiers. I remember lifting off over the trees, the pain setting into my leg, my relief at knowing we weren't pursuing the others on the train. But the rest of it is blank and empty. Did I fall asleep? Or did I simply lose so much blood from the wound that I lost consciousness?

I lift my right pant leg to find a band of pale gauze wrapped tight around my calf. The bandages need changing; a burgundy bloodstain slowly chews its way through the material. I don't bother to test my weight on the leg. The wound is likely stitched shut and too much exertion could rip it back open.

Anyway, moving is pointless. Escape is beyond question. Whatever happens, happens. I've been here before, just days before in the previous cell, but this time feels different. My head's somewhere else. I'm calmer, cooler. I have hope for the others and hope for my wife. Somehow, I know she's safe, and that's all that matters.

The squeal of metal hinges echoes my way as a hatch opens out of sight. The door is shut and locked. Several pairs of feet near my cell as I wait.

I'm unsurprised by the grinning face that materializes on the other side of the bars. The slicked black hair, the smell of aftershave, it's as fresh a memory as the hole in my leg.

"Hello again," Agent Meade sneers, feet spread, shoulders squared, hands locked behind his back. Two naval officers with matching scowls flank him. I opt to ignore them, unwilling to give Meade the pleasure of my misery.

He orders me to stand. The officers at his side glare at me as they step threateningly towards the door of the cell, ready for force. In my current state I'm not sure how much abuse my body would be able to handle, so I will myself to my feet. The pain in my right leg is excruciating but I do my best to hide it.

"You're lucky the sniper missed the bone," Meade says, glancing down at the leg with sick amusement.

"Yeah, real lucky," I say, wincing. Meade smiles at this, then nods to the two men beside him. They turn and leave, the door clanking shut behind them.

"You know, we couldn't have done it without you," Meade says, still grinning as he leans forward against the bars. I'm silent. "What, not curious?" he teases. "Don't tell me you haven't wondered at least a little how we were able to track you down."

"I don't care."

"I'm not sure how much you remember from when we still had you in custody. I'll hand it to you–you held up pretty well under the interrogation. We came close to the limit with the voltage, but you wouldn't budge."

"Because I didn't know anything," I say.

"Yeah, that's what the experts said, too. Fortunately, you weren't a total waste," Meade pauses here, enjoying this immensely. He flashes his wolf smile, grinning hungrily at cornered prey. "You remember George? From Homeland Security? Well, he had the simple but brilliant idea to just *tag* you and then… *let you go.*"

"Tag me?"

"Sub-dermal implant, no larger than a fingernail, inserted into the skin of your scalp. We could track you, see where you'd lead us. We figured that even if you didn't know how to find your wife and the others, they might be able to find *you*. In our wildest dreams, we could've never imagined how big this little ploy would pay off."

"You wanted me to run. On that bridge."

"Actually, no. Our instructions were to take you somewhere else, but with the gridlock we couldn't get there. We had to take a detour, and that's when you bolted. Worked out even better that way, with you thinking you'd escaped. All we had to do was sit back and watch. We had a drone watching you get hijacked at that gas station, had satellite imagery of you and your friends on the highways. Getting captured in Maynard. The fat sheriff. The whole bit.

"Funny thing, it seemed that the longer we let you run free, the more mysteries you helped us solve. You led us to the hangar, for instance. We knew the Witnesses must have had evac points, but weren't able to come up with specifics. We're still not sure how they evaded us for so long. Of course, it's all water under the bridge now."

"So that was your helicopter in the woods," I say.

"A careless mistake. We had men on the ground at the hangar, had to recon with them."

"They bombed it, didn't they? We heard the blast."

Meade nods, smiling proudly. "The Witnesses have evaded us for long enough. But now we're back on top, we're calling the shots. And we have you to thank, at least in part."

"So why am I here, then? Why kidnap me?" I say without flinching, though my insides are writhing like a pit of snakes.

"Kidnap? You make us sound like common criminals."

"Is there a difference?" I sneer, drawing a scoff from Agent Meade, who shakes his head.

"You've drifted, Luke. You don't even know who you're supposed to be serving anymore."

"Do you?"

"My loyalties have always been and always will be to this great country. I'm doing this for the future of America, for the future of my children. This country will rise again, and I'll be there to witness it. And as for why we brought you into custody, well… We need you for one last thing."

"You must be insane if you expect me to cooperate after all this."

"We'll see. In any case, rest up for now. Big day tomorrow." Meade nods once and leaves, whistling as he disappears down the corridor.

10:40 AM
AMY

Walter and I have been sitting in the alley between two containers watching the crowds ebb and flow for some time now, neither of us speaking. I hate that I can't even mourn in privacy here. There are no secrets, no places to hide. My plight might as well be broadcast over the loudspeakers for all to hear. At least that way they'd know to keep their distance. Pity and consolation are the last things I need.

A snap of cold air hits us but I refuse to let it chill me. Not that it'd make the least bit of difference; my whole body is numb anyway. Walter disappears for a moment and returns with a threadbare blanket, draping it over my shoulders and plopping down on the ground next to me.

"I know you think they made the wrong decision," Walter says.

"It's the fact that it was even a decision in the first place, Walter. That's what bothers me. My husband… He never *thought* about whether or not someone needed his help before acting. When Brother Harris was trapped in that burning apartment, Luke didn't *stop* to consider that the roof might cave in, or that the flames might swallow him up. He just acted. He knocked down that door because there was someone inside who needed him. That's the kind of man Luke is. Brave. Selfless."

"Jehovah knows that too, Amy. He won't forget how your husband helped His servants."

"Then why didn't He intervene? Why couldn't the bullet have missed? Or the helicopter run out of gas? Or those evil men not even find the trail in the first place?"

"I don't have the answers to those questions, Amy. We may never know. The most important thing is to maintain our loyalty. We cannot let anything separate us from Jehovah or His organization."

"So what you're saying is that you think Marc and the rest of them made the right decision, then?" I ask, glaring at a spot in the ground. I don't have the heart to condemn Walter, but I feel a need to know where he stands.

"I... I just can't say, Amy."

"Why not?"

"*I wasn't there.* And neither were you. But even if it was the wrong decision, it won't impede Jehovah's will in the long run. We have to trust that things are still under His control despite how bad it looks now."

"Yeah right, easier said than done," I scoff.

"The right things always are," Walter replies, and the words are so gentle and warm that for the first time I feel some of the rage subside. I'm not ready to forgive, though. Maybe I need the anger. Maybe it's an easier emotion to deal with than fright and uncertainty. Maybe all of this is just me trying to cope.

"Y'all stayin' in container twenty-three?" asks a voice from the end of one of the containers. A man glances up from his clipboard, waiting for our response with eyes blinking behind thick circular glasses.

"That's right," replies Walter.

"You'll be moving out in twenty-five minutes. Please get packed and be ready for further instructions." The brother tries to smile, a vain effort to keep the mood light, but his expression is still grim. He vanishes a moment later to inform the others.

"On the road again," Walter says tiredly. Heavy bags tug at his eyes like. His cheekbones rim the edges of his features like parched cliffs. He looks skinnier and frailer than I've ever seen him. Maybe it's the lighting. Then again, maybe it's the narrow road to life that skirts nearest the brink of death.

We stop briefly at our container to retrieve the few belongings that have managed to make it this long. I stare into the bag blankly on my lap, gazing at the items without sentimentality:

A few tins of food.
A flashlight.
Two bottles of water.
A roll of toilet paper.

Supplies to extend my life for another day and nothing more. Here today, gone tomorrow, like every other material possession I've ever owned.

I sigh deeply, helpless to fight the tide of memories as I think back to our apartment, the lumpy mattress in the bedroom, the faded sofa slowly disintegrating in the living room. The smell of coffee and bacon in the morning. Luke and I curling up for old *Spiderman* cartoons on Saturday mornings. The longing is strong, like being pushed by a warm autumn breeze, but it's all from another lifetime. For all I know, our small apartment has been looted by vandals or burned to the ground.

Dust to dust. Just things.

We find our spot among the others from our container and are led across the premises to a large parking lot filled with eighteen-wheelers. One of the attendants keeps us out of the way as a truck passes, its diesel engine huffing and grumbling as it moves along. Suddenly, a sharp, wild noise rings into the air. We instinctively duck and dive for cover. The truck before us rolls to a halt, its hood spewing trails of white smoke.

"Darn carburetor's gone again!" shouts the driver, swinging his door wide open and jumping from the truck's skids. "Just put 'er in a new one last week!"

Several other brothers run over, peering under the hood with worried looks and glancing at their watches and clipboard schedules. Someone turns to mutter something into a walkie-talkie.

"How far you headed?" Walter asks, approaching the driver.

"Less than a mile. It's just up the road." The driver peels his wide brimmed hat from his head and swipes his arm across his brow while grimacing at the truck. "I've got a full load and we're on a tight schedule. I'm back and forth moving people all day. We lose one truck and evacuees will start piling up quick here." It's only at this moment that I realize the cargo he's carrying isn't supplies at all but living, breathing souls.

Walter doesn't respond, instead peeling off his jacket and stepping onto the fender to get a look under the hood.

"I was an on-call mechanic for a shipping company a few years back," he mentions as he flips a penlight from his pocket and pokes the light beam into the crevices of the machinery.

"Yeah? Think you can fix it?" asks the brother holding a walkie-talkie.

"Doubt it, but I might be able to patch it. Won't last long, but it should be enough to take you a few miles."

"Good, let's do it. What do you need?" the brother asks, snagging the pen from behind his ear. Walter thinks for a moment before rattling off a list of tools. The man jots everything down furiously on a piece of paper and begins barking orders into his radio.

We're urged on by our guide, who motions towards a row of U-Hauls in the distance. Our crowd obeys silently and someone steps behind my wheelchair to push me along.

"Wait, stop. I'm staying with him," I say, pointing to Walter. He sees me and jumps down from beneath the hood of the truck, wiping the grease from his hands on the front of his pants. He grabs my shoulders and gives me a hard look.

"I don't want you waiting here, Amy. Go with the others," he says.

"Why? We can go together, when you're finished."

"No. Everyone here is evacuating today. I don't want you hanging around. Jesse and Chelsea are already there, at the harbor. They left on an earlier truck. They'll wait for you there."

"I'd rather go with you, Walter. *Please.*"

"Amy. There's no time. We'll meet up soon, then we'll head north to our final destination."

"North to where? *Why do we keep having to move, Walter!*" The grip on my shoulders tightens as Walter's expression melts. His eyes are red and watery, his lips quivering.

"Please, Amy. *Listen to me.* This is it. We are so close. Just follow the brothers. You will be fine. I'll be right behind you."

There's a loud clamor and clanking behind us as a young brother runs our way with a large plastic toolbox in his arms. Walter approaches him and is swallowed by a crowd of brothers murmuring anxious things in terse voices. My wheelchair begins to move again, and I'm struck by a terrible dread. Slowly but surely, I am losing everyone.

We move swiftly to a dusty U-Haul parked next to the cranes. The friends have already crammed themselves into the dark compartment in back, standing with solemn faces, gripping a trellis of handrails suspended just inches below the ceiling. All of this has been meticulously planned, I realize. The network of evacuations, the transportation. The hangars and facilities and trains and trucks. All of it.

A web of hands reaches out to me, plucking me from my chair and squeezing me onto a narrow wheel well. My chair is folded and carried out of view. I hear it scraping along the roof of the cabin. A small hatch is opened in the ceiling to provide a bit of ventilation, but even in the cold winter temperatures, the air goes immediately warm and stale.

The cramped compartment fills with the smell of gasoline and exhaust as the engine coughs to life and we lurch forward into the next unknown.

11:03 AM
LUKE

The room they've brought me to is stark and still and spacious. Overhead fluorescents form neat lines leading to the other side of the room, where a broad wooden desk sits. It's not something I'd expect to see on a ship. It's an antique, no doubt, with its dark, gleaming surfaces and ornate carvings. The floor, by contrast, is a cheap tilework of frayed carpet squares. Framed photographs of naval officers line the walls, posing before the American flag, shaking hands with politicians, gazing blankly like mannequins into the lens.

"This is Admiral Hawkins," Meade says, gesturing to the man seated behind the large desk.

"Ok," I say without reverence. "What do you people want with me?"

"Have a seat and we'll get to it," the admiral says. I sit in a solitary chair in the middle of the room. "Look like you been through a war," he comments. I consider my options for replies for a moment. Should I relate how I was tased by federal officers in a hospital ward while my wife woke up from a coma? Or what about being attacked by a lunatic at a gas station? Or being shot by my government while trying to save the child of my friend? I *have* been through war and these men know it well. They waged it, they watched it. I remain silent and simply shrug.

"You could say that," I say.

The admiral chuckles. "Hungry?" Hawkins asks.

"Yeah," I say frankly, not about to risk the sarcasm. I'm starved, and how could I not be? I've alternated between being a hostage, fugitive, and captive for the better part of a week. The admiral lifts a phone from his desk and mutters something into it. Not ten minutes pass before the door behind me opens, an irresistible aroma wafting in and washing over me. I nearly faint at the sight of a cheeseburger platter, fries still steaming, a puddle of red ketchup at the corner of the plate.

A small folding table is set in front of me and the handcuffs are removed. The next three minutes are bliss. My captors are silent as they study me with what seems like pitiable expressions from across the room. I consider briefly the possibility that the food is poisoned, but decide it's worth the risk.

Besides, poisoning me now wouldn't make sense. In all likelihood they're building my strength for the horrors ahead, or else this is some kind of bribe. Little bit of carrot, whole lot of stick. I push the thoughts away with a thick steak fry smothered in ketchup and throw it whole down my gullet. Mercifully, I'm left alone as I enjoy my meal in peace, although I eat so fast, and after so long without a square meal, that my sides cramp up with the task of digestion.

I'm about to shove the last handful of fries into my mouth when Meade approaches. He carries an old corded telephone from behind the admiral's desk and sets it on the folding table before me. He returns to the admiral's side and leans against the large desk with his arms crossed, a smug expression smeared on his face.

I'm still chewing my last bite as the phone jumps from the table, its bells clanging with furor. The ringing stops as I cautiously lift the receiver and hold it to the side of my head.

"Hello?" I say, as if speaking into the darkness of a deep, cold well.

There is only the sound of heavy, labored breaths on the other end, like waves driven by storm winds lapping against an unknown and faraway shore, predicting only foul weather.

"Luke," says the gravelly voice of Captain Pryce.

11:10 AM
AMY

It seems we've only just boarded the U-Haul when the vehicle comes to a stop, gravel crunching below the tires. The doors are unlatched and flung open, light searing into our cramped compartment. I'm carefully unloaded with my wheelchair as the others pile out behind. We're led from the gravel lot up a path to the top of a small hill. A wind passes over us, carrying a strange, acrid scent. Our group exchanges looks of worry and revulsion. When we reach the peak of the hill we get our first glance at the town of Wilmington.

The town resembles a fiery landfill. Much of it has burned to the ground, and most of the rest of it is still ablaze. Skeletal remains of vehicles line the scarred streets, charred nearly beyond recognition.

The entire visage is covered in a black pall of smoke–smoke that carries the smell of gasoline, trash, and death. Sporadic bursts and explosions pepper the distant air, but whether this is a toll of the slow burning fire or something more sinister, none of us can be sure.

There are of course bodies, too. From up here, they just look like piles of dirty rags dumped along the curb, but I know better. A few survivors wander about the dead aimlessly; others root through scavenged belongings.

"We need you to keep moving, friends," a brother prods softly from behind us, breaking the trance. The path before us runs down the other side of the hill towards a harbor. Some of the buildings there appear to have been recently dismantled, and from their debris, high makeshift barricades have been constructed to separate this area from the rest of the town.

"Keep heading straight until you get to the brother at the base of the hill," the brother says. "And always keep a distance between you and the barricade." We nod and file silently down the path, eyeing the wall to our left warily.

That's when we first see them, a small group of people hobbling towards us on the other side. Their clothing is torn and stained and most are injured. Their leader, a burly man with a bad limp and facial burns, reaches the fence first.

"Let us in!" he snarls, gripping a section of chain link between his fingers and giving it a fierce rattle. Our group looks around anxiously, unsure of what to do.

"Please step away from the fence," says a brother to the man, quickly rushing to our side and standing between us and the barricade, arms held out at his sides.

"What, you people think you can just save yourselves and leave the rest of us to *die?*" the man yells, spittle lurching from his snapping teeth.

"You had your chance. I'm sorry, but it's too late. Now step back."

"Or what? You gonna throw a Bible at me?" says the man, throwing back his head with a hysterical cackling as he slams his fists against the trembling barricade. The others in his troupe follow his lead, pounding the wall with their fists as they hiss and scream. The barricade wobbles uncertainly under the assault.

"Friends, keep moving, please," the brother says to us in his best attempt at a calm voice. We listen with cautious glances over our shoulders and hasten towards the harbor.

"We can't just leave him by himself," a trembling voice says, looking back at the brother by the fence. "Someone go help him!" Glances are exchanged, and three of the brothers from our crowd jog back. We're no farther than fifty yards from them when the wall finally gives. Bloodied hands shoot through the small space, tearing at the flimsy sheet metal and chain link separating us from them. And then a scream. We stop, in horror, unable to move as we watch the scene unfold.

11:15 AM
LUKE

I stare down at the frayed carpet squares as Pryce continues breathing into my ear. Both of us wait for the other to speak, neither of us knowing what comes next.

"Captain?" I say carefully. "Are you ok? How are–"

"I'm not your captain anymore," Pryce interrupts, the words freezing me with their coldness.

"Sorry? What do you mean?"

"Don't play dumb, Harding. I know everything."

"What are you talking about?" I ask in earnest.

"Your involvement with that cult, the investigation, your arrest. All of it. The feds sent me your file."

"Captain, these men are criminals. Do you even know what they did to me?"

"Of course I do. Agent Meade was the one who first came to me about you being wrapped up in this conspiracy."

"Conspiracy? Captain–"

"Enough! Give it a rest, Harding. *You're finished.* You've been caught. They know you were helping the enemy. It's over."

"Helping the *enemy*? What, are you talking about the Witnesses? You think they're the *enemy*? Do you have any idea how much pain and misery–" Meade stops me with a newspaper tossed in my direction. It lands on the table before me and my eyes sop up the headlines.

RELIGIOUS EXTREMISTS COORDINATE WORLDWIDE ATTACK

New York City, N.Y.–Just three months after congress's groundbreaking legislation to limit the practice of radicalized religion, the United Nations Security Council today reiterated its dedication to the eradication of religious separatism, specifically singling out the Jehovah's Witnesses sect. According to reports from Reuters, the BBC, China Daily, CNN, and numerous other reputable news organizations, the Witnesses have been secretly coordinating worldwide attacks on government buildings and personnel.

The attacks, which have been organized primarily on illegal encrypted messaging services and private networks, reveal a level of sophistication previously seen only in terrorist organizations, such as the now-defunct ISIS. Regarding the ultimate goal of these assaults, intelligence analyst Ryan Carthwright comments…

"You were like a son to me," Pryce says, his voice nearly cracking. "You swore to me that we were on the same side."

"These are all lies, Dale," I say, my voice trembling in fear and anger.

"*Christ! How can you treat me like this!*" Pryce screams. "You'd rather let your country burn to the ground than turn these people in!"

"Captain, listen to me! This country is burning to the ground because the people and their governments are out of control! It has nothing to do with the Witnesses!"

I can feel Pryce seething on the other end. He's angrier and in more pain than I've ever known him before. The phone receiver burns in my hand. More than anything, I want him to know the truth, but there's nothing left to say.

"I don't know how they brainwashed you. You're not the officer I knew months ago. Whatever happens to you next, you brought it on your own head. You're dead to me, Luke. Your secret is out, and I hope I never hear your name again." And with that, Pryce hangs up and the line goes dead.

I'm slumped over in my chair, feeling cold and hollow, the pleasure of a hot meal now a long forgotten memory. Agent Meade and the admiral whisper something inaudibly to one other and shuffle papers on their desk. My table and chair, along with the telephone, are hauled away and I'm summoned to my feet.

The windows darken as grey clouds float above the white-tipped sea outside. Thin droplets of water drum against the glass. A far-off thunderhead glows sporadically with coughs of lightning.

"Not exactly a sweet reunion," Meade finally says with mock sympathy.

"I'm sure it unfolded just as you'd planned," I say weakly, head still staring into the floor.

"Luke, this world is not against you, as you seem to imagine. There is no *conspiracy* here. You simply chose the wrong side. You gambled, you lost. Fact is, this could've all been avoided, if you'd only cooperated. *Will you cooperate now?*"

"What could you possibly want from me?"

"It's simple, really. We just need you to send a message," says the admiral.

"A message? To who?"

"To Amy."

11:23 AM
AMY

A young woman who looks to be about my age is the first to squeeze through the barricade. Her hair is matted and greasy, her face smeared in soot and ash. She tumbles onto our side of the wall and instinctively covers her head, bracing for an attack. Instead, the brothers back away, spreading their arms to keep her contained.

"How have you all survived this long?" the woman hisses with incredulity as she rises to her feet, drawing a sharp sliver of wood from inside her coat and holding it like a dagger in one hand.

Their pack's leader comes through next, cutting his shoulder on the sharp edge of sheet metal as he slides through. He curses loudly and presses his fingers for a moment against the wound.

"Amazing," he scoffs. "Not one of you is armed."

"We don't need weapons," one of our brothers says calmly. The man gives him a malevolent grin before reaching behind his back and drawing a handgun.

It's at this very moment that we seem to be surrounded by the baying and howling of wolves. We see them seconds later, their stained coats flicking through the trees, hair on their backs standing on end. We quickly realize these are no wolves, but ordinary dogs–house pets, no doubt–gone feral.

A dirty German shepherd with a tail of singed hair lunges at the woman with the stick, clenching her arm in its jaws and thrashing its head mercilessly. She falls screaming and writhing on the ground. The man with the gun turns to fire at the dog, but the bullet misses. The sharp explosion of gunpowder sends the animals into a momentary mode of retreat, but they quickly turn to its source, ears back, teeth barred, growling and snapping. The man is buried moments later in a pile of tearing canines.

"*Go! Go! Go!*" yell the brothers. We turn to run, but before we do, I spot two of the larger dogs squeezing back through the hole in the barricade, hungry for more, their muzzles rimmed with red foam. The mob on the opposite side screams as it flees. Some make it; others are caught in the wave of dogs.

We move quickly to the harbor where an enormous ship waits. A dozen gangplanks crammed with passengers jut from the hull like the branches of some large, fallen tree. The friends move in silence, few carrying any sort of luggage. Hundreds more peer towards the harbor from the porthole windows, the multistoried decks, and the bridge. It is, I am quite sure, the most somber departure this ship has ever seen.

When we board, I find that the vast halls below decks have been divvied and partitioned by state, city, and congregation, just like back at the hangar. We squeeze through the crowds until we finally see familiar faces. Jesse's voice is the first I hear.

"Where's my dad?" he asks.

"He's back at the shipping facility," I say, shaking my head.

"Why? How did you get here?" Jesse asks accusingly.

"I came with the others from our container. Your dad stayed because there were some engine problems with one of the trucks. He said he could help."

"He shouldn't have split off on his own like that," Jesse says, biting a fingernail. "Why didn't you talk him out of it?"

"I tried! He wouldn't let me stay. He said he'd be right behind us."

"He'd better be. Storm's coming," he says, jabbing a finger towards the window. I wheel myself a bit closer to the large plate glass, watching the smoldering town below us. From up here, framed in this rectangle of glass, it looks like it could all be happening in some disaster movie. *It can't be real.*

"I'm sure he'll get here soon," I say softly, more to myself than to Jesse.

The sky illuminates for an instant as a brilliant cloud of orange flame erupts from the ground. The sound comes a second later, a deep rumbling from the pit of the earth. People line up at the window beside us, mouthing pointless questions, staring stupidly for answers.

"*What was that?*"

"*Did you see anything?*"

"Was it a bomb?"

"Are we under attack?"

My eyes hone in on the plume of fire, then circle outwards, looking for the source of the explosion. As the smoke clears, I can see in the distance the shipping facility engulfed in flames.

11:41 AM
LUKE

SHE'S ALIVE SHE'S ALIVE SHE'S ALIVE!

My head spins with the news. But how? Was she rescued from the hospital, like Marc had suggested? Did she and Walter escape together to the hangar? What about the highways? How did they manage? The possibility that our paths nearly crossed is both scintillating and maddening. Still, *she got out*, that's the important thing. Though my leg throbs from the bullet wound, I can't help the smile forming on my face.

Distant thunder rolls over us as heavy rainclouds sweep in. They're darker than anything I've seen before, an unearthly, purplish grey, like a murky sea swirling with giant electric jellyfish.

"Luke, the admiral asked you a question," Meade snaps. I turn my attention from the window to see Admiral Hawkins standing a few feet away, hands clasped behind him.

"You want me to send my wife a message. I heard," I say, struggling to conceal my joy. *If only they knew the strength they've given me.*

"That's correct. You'll do it through our radio."

"What's the message?"

"We want their vessel to travel to a set of coordinates we'll provide to you."

"And then?"

"Then, when we rendezvous, we'll extract Amy. The rest will be detained for questioning."

"You expect me to just get them all to turn themselves in? Really?"

"We don't want a confrontation, Luke. We're counting on them being rational. We don't know if their passengers are armed."

"Armed? Are you kidding me? You both are clueless. I spent the last three days with these people, not to mention the last year with my wife. They are about as violent as a litter of kittens. They don't use weapons, not even handguns."

"Good, then we can expect a speedy surrender," the admiral says.

"I doubt that, but good luck anyway."

"Oh? And why is that? Do you *know* something, Luke?" asks Meade.

"Neither of you see it, do you? How do you think they were able to outsmart and outmaneuver you all this time? How is it that they've been able to communicate with each other around the country and organize these massive evacuations? How is it that time and time again, when I was with them, we were able to squeeze out of situations that could've–*should've*–killed us? Something else was working in our favor. And that something is what both of you are pitting yourselves against now. This government and its army is powerful, but not powerful enough."

"What, exactly, are you referring to, Harding?" Meade asks, hovering over me with his hands in his pockets.

"What do you think? I'm talking about something greater than you and I, greater than some stockpile of weapons."

"*God?*" Meade asks, the corners of his lips curling in devilish amusement. "Your captain was right. You've gone and drunk the Kool-Aid."

"Time will tell," I say simply, eyes studying the floor.

"You'll send the message?" the Admiral presses.

"Take me to the radio."

11:47 AM
AMY

The room swirls around me with groans of shock and sick horror.

"He's gone. He's gone. He's gone," Jesse keeps repeating, hunched over on the floor with the wall against his back, his hands clenched into trembling fists at his temples.

"How could this happen…?" I say in a frail whisper.

"You. *You* let it happen," Jesse says without looking up.

"Jesse, please don't blame me for this, I can't–"

"What, like you blamed those others for leaving your husband behind? It's the same thing, isn't it?"

"I lost Walter too, Jesse. I've lost everyone. I'm hurting, too," I say, pleading.

"*You*. It's always about *you*. Do you ever stop to think about anyone else?"

"That's not fair, Jesse. I didn't ask to be–"

"No, it *isn't* fair! After all my parents did for you, after all they sacrificed!" Jesse is yelling now, jabbing an accusing finger in my face.

"After all your parents did for *me*? And what about *you*? *You abandoned them years ago!* Didn't even bother contacting them until the very end when you were out of options. You call *me* selfish! What makes you think you even deserve a spot on this ship?" I hiss.

We glance up, alarmed at the size of the crowd surrounding us, a circle of disturbed and anxious faces wondering whether to intervene. No one speaks. Jesse backs away from me, tumbling through the crowd and disappearing in the mass of bodies.

There's a rumbling bellow as the ship's foghorn lets out a double cry. The stragglers from the last truckload of evacuees clamber aboard as the lights dim by a fraction and our vessel begins to move. I turn to the window as the harbor slips quietly away, almost peacefully, but for the ghostly black cloud mushrooming in the distance where the explosion occurred.

Below us, spindly gangplanks retract and disappear into the sides of the ship. I stare numbly at the docks, where an angry mob rushes from a break in the fence, jeering and screaming at us with wild abandon. Some throw rocks and bottles. A few plunge into the water to give unthinking chase. *Rabid animals in a dark place beyond sanity's reach.*

The humidity spikes as the coast fades behind us beyond the wake. The seas are choppier out here, though we can barely feel the swells in a ship this large. White bundles of foam spill like cotton from the wavetips as the wind howls by. Looming clouds blacken and swirl.

"Brothers and sisters," says a somber, tired voice over the PA system. "Welcome aboard the *Cornelia*. We're glad you've made it here safely." A long pause, a search for words. "We know you've all made tremendous sacrifices, but it will be worth it, in the end. Continue to stand firm… According to our weather data, we'll be skirting around a tropical storm early this afternoon. The seas will be rough. Keep movement around the ship to a minimum to prevent injuries…"

The voice drones on for a few minutes but my mind is elsewhere, somewhere back on shore with Walter and the other unfortunate souls at the facility. Or with Luke, wherever he is.

I inch my wheelchair closer to the glass window and lean my cheek against it, feeling its coolness and the vibration of rain droplets as they pummel the other side. The engines hum a low frequency into my head and it's something like comfort.

I close my eyes and try to think of calmer times. Before the tribulation began, perhaps. Back when Luke and I were still together, when he was inching his way towards a promotion. But even then, all I could envision at night during those long graveyard patrol shifts was the dreaded call from Captain Pryce or one of Luke's buddies at the station. *Hello Mrs. Harding. Are you sitting down? We have some bad news. You see, there was an armed robbery... Would you be able to come down to the morgue...?*

And of course there was Luke's first real brush with death. That kid that he killed at the pharmacy. Just a bottle of Oxycotins. That's what he'd died–and almost killed–for. Then the subsequent nightmares. Luke flailing in bed, his side of the sheets drenched with cold sweat as he relived the horror, waking up, swearing he could still feel the bullet lodged in his shoulder, stumbling around our apartment, rooting through drawers for a pocket knife to inspect the wound... Horrors upon horrors.

Was there ever a time when things were right? When life was peaceful and perfect? As far back as my mind goes, all I can remember is gloom. The light at the end of the tunnel only appeared after I met Chelsea and Walter, and now they're both gone...

"Amy Harding?" asks a voice. I turn to see a man in a wet raincoat, hair damp and plastered to the sides of his face, deep wrinkles creasing his features into a permanent frown.

"Yes?"

"Can you come with me, please?"

"Ok. Is something wrong?"

"We're not sure. But there's someone on the radio, and he's asking to talk with you."

"He? Who?"

"He says he's your husband."

12:07 PM
LUKE

"*Luke, is that you?*" a voice bursts through the crackle of static like a sunray through rainclouds.

"Amy?" I say, not ready to believe, not ready to expend too much hope.

"Oh Luke, where are you! What happened! Are you safe?" she asks, voice shaking on the line. I hesitate as a sheet of paper slides across the table in front of me. Meade's finger taps the words silently, his look stony. *FISHING BOAT. CAROLINA COAST.*

"I... I'm on a fishing boat. Off the Carolina Coast..."

"A fishing boat! But how? Marc said you were shot and captured by soldiers, and–"

"Marc? Marc and Ashley? Are they there with you now? Are they safe?" I ask, straying from the script as Meade and Admiral Hawkins exchange unsteady glances.

"...Yeah, they're all here. We're safe, Luke. How did you find me?" More words pointed out on paper.

"It's a long story, babe, but... I was able to escape. Again."

"But you were shot? How serious is it? Are you ok? Baby, I miss you so much, I..." the words come quickly. She's sobbing now, and it's impossible to hold my tears back. I can visualize Amy cradling the microphone as we talk, her voice warm and full of love despite the static interference from the storm and the coldness of electronic communication.

"I'm ok, babe. I'm ok. I miss you too. What about Walter and Chelsea? Are they with you? Are they all ok?"

"Chelsea's here with me, but... Walter... he's gone. There was an explosion. It was an attack..."

"I'm so sorry, babe," I say, feeling the anger and the hate swell again in my chest. The hate for being so helpless and so far away, for not being able to hold Amy in this crucial moment. Anger at knowing that Walter has been taken. He never deserved this. He's a casualty in a twisted war waged by criminals in uniform with endless resources and no one but God to check their hands.

I glance up at the faces of my captors, both clearly unsurprised by news of the attack. Almost smug, I think. Smug and callous. Meade leans forward and slides the paper closer. Coordinates are written in large blocks letters at the bottom of the page. It's the last part of my message, the most crucial.

They're lying, of course. There will be no capture of suspects for interrogation. They plan to sink the ship, maybe while my wife is still on board. My message to them, these coordinates, is just to get the target where they want it. I'm no expert on naval vessels, but I can guess by the Admiral's total lack of concern for the building fury of the storm outside that this ship is enormous–perhaps a destroyer, maybe even an aircraft carrier. They're armed to the teeth and in no way interested in taking hostages. They'll shoot without question. *And I am their trigger.*

"I need you to listen carefully, Amy. Do you have a pen?" A pause. Noises in the background, the shuffling of faraway things.

"Ok. What is it, Luke? Is everything all right?"

"Just fine, babe. I'm going to give you some coordinates, as in latitude and longitude. Got it?"

"Uh, ok, sure. But what for?"

"Just write it down, ok babe? Make sure you get it right. Latitude: *thirty-six point four eight*. Longitude: *minus seventy-three point five nine*. Can you repeat it back to me?" She does. No mistakes.

"What's this for? What am I supposed to do–"

"Just listen, baby. I love you so much. I always have. There's never been anyone else and there never will be. You understand? I'm sorry for doubting you or your friends. You made the right choice, Amy, and–"

Meade and the Admiral lean another inch in my direction, scowls forming on their faces, their eyes boring into mine. It all comes down to this moment.

"Luke, slow down, what are you saying?"

"Please, just listen. I want you to take those coordinates to the captain of the ship you're on. Can you do that for me?"

"Uh, ok. I guess. And then what?"

"Tell him that whatever happens, get as far away from those coordinates as possible. Do you understand Amy? *DO NOT GO THERE! THIS MEANS YOUR L–*"

The words stick in my throat as a terrific pain explodes from the back of my eye sockets. I crumble to the cold, metallic floor of the radio room, the wires and cables dangling over my head like jungle vines, and everything goes black.

12:10 PM
AMY

"Luke! Are you there? *LUUUUKE!*" I scream into the headset, hearing only the whine of static and feedback on the other end. I try for another five minutes without response. Frustrated, I rip the headset away from me and toss it back onto the table.

"What did he say?" one of the brothers asks. He's the one with the raincoat, the one who fetched me just minutes ago with news of my husband's message. Brother Michaels. There are five or six others in the room now, all huddled around me carefully, arms crossed, leaning inwards, waiting. Brother Harris is one of them. Marc is another. I think for a few moments before answering.

"He said... He said he was on a fishing boat off the coast. He said he was ok. Then he gave me these coordinates, told me to tell the captain to stay far away," I say, holding up the scrap of paper for them to see.

"Not far from here. Not far at all," says one of the men, grey hair swept down over his wide-eyed stare.

"How far?" someone else asks.

"Less than a hundred nautical miles north, I'd say. Three, maybe four hours away."

"Amy, did Luke tell you why we had to avoid this particular spot?" Marc asks.

"No, he didn't have a chance to. Something happened."

"Maybe a bad signal. Could be this storm," Brother Michaels suggests. I give my head a vigorous shake.

"No, I don't think so. He sounded scared."

"Scared?"

"I know my husband. It takes a lot to get him that way, but... He was terrified. Not for himself, but for me. For us. I think someone was there with him, telling him what to say. I don't think he delivered the message he was supposed to. So they cut him off."

"Those men who captured him," Marc says, his voice trailing off. He takes a step back from the circle to look out at the brewing storm. The rain droplets are thick and heavy and rattle against the glass windows.

"This is when you were boarding the train, right Marc?" Brother Harris asks thoughtfully, his eyes hard and serious.

"Yeah. He took a bullet in the leg for us. Without him, my wife would've never made it out of there alive."

"It all adds up, then," Brother Harris says with a grimace. "We have to assume he's still their captive. Maybe they let him on the radio thinking he could get us to head right into some kind of trap."

"No way he's on a fishing boat, that's for sure," says the brother with the hair in his eyes as he glances out the window behind him. "Not in this storm. It'd be suicide."

"Then we avoid those coordinates like he said," brother Michaels says with a questioning look around the circle of men.

"What about my husband, then?" I ask feebly. The brothers cast me pitying glances or avoid my stare completely.

"I'm sorry, Amy, but it's just too dangerous. Luke risked… who *knows* what… to send us this message. We have no reason to doubt him. We'd be foolish not to heed his warning."

"Your husband could have very well just saved the lives of thousands on this ship," Marc says, crouching next to me. "Jehovah won't forget it. Just like I won't forget all that Luke did for us back at that train."

"Jehovah knows how to deliver people, Amy," Brother Harris says, reaching over to grip my arm. "Keep your faith in him. Our deliverance is near."

2:53 PM
LUKE

I awake to find myself in a wide rectangular room lined by downward slanting windows on three sides. A dozen men and women hover over glowing display screens, charts, and glowing arrays of dials and switches. The storm rages on beyond the windows, jagged lightning clawing at an endless expanse of agitated, black sea. We're at least a hundred feet above the waves, and the perspective doesn't quite make sense until I lean forward to gaze down at the acres of steel jutting off like a vast highway below me. Neat rows of military aircraft flank either side of a zebra striped runway that diagonally bisects the ship. On the deck, tiny men in neon raincoats fight the wind, sheets of rain cascading on them from above and then streaming from the sides of the runway. The sheer immensity of the aircraft carrier is breathtaking and difficult to grasp, a veritable floating city. Despite the roaring weather and high seas, our vessel slices through the seas with little trouble.

"Look who's up," Agent Meade says, almost cheerily. He walks over and hands me a Styrofoam cup of hot coffee. I accept with some hesitation, and the handcuffs tethering me to a handrail only allow me to reach so far. "Ever been on an aircraft carrier before?" Meade asks, sipping from a mug as he gazes into the squall.

"No."

"She's a Nimitz-class. Biggest of her kind. Six thousand crew members, runs on nuclear power. She can go twenty years without refueling, and she's got enough firepower to take on an entire fleet singlehandedly. *God bless America.*"

"How many tax dollars did it take to build?" I say, barely able to contain my contempt.

"Millions, billions? Who knows. Who cares? We've got it, and we're the only ones."

I say nothing.

"I'll bet you think you were pretty clever with that stunt you pulled on the radio," Meade says, his tone still amicable, eyes shifting to smile at me. "I suppose you think we didn't expect it?"

I'm silent as I feel the unseen fangs of a deep dark dread clamp down on my throat.

"Hello, Luke? Anyone in there?" Meade says, tapping a finger against my forehead, the smell of stale coffee and aftershave overwhelming me. "Do you really think we would've given you a way to sabotage this operation?" Meade repeats, his smile wide now, teeth glinting.

"What are you talking about?" I mutter.

"You are one dumb cop," Meade sneers, exhaling sharply through his teeth.

"Tell me," I say, teeth clenched tight. It's the first time I catch sight of the two MAs behind me, their rifles at the ready. They step forward to shoot Meade a questioning look. He brushes them off without breaking our stare.

"You're an *idiot* if you think we would've put such a crucial part of this operation in your hands. The one thing we could count on was you turning traitor. You're about as easy to read as that wind sock out there. The coordinates we gave you were right off of the Carolina coast. Their ship would've passed right through it without us sending some message to rendezvous. It's smack in the middle of their course."

"Then why did you make me send the message?"

"So you'd tell them to avoid the spot, of course. We want them farther out to sea. Our guess is they'll swing wide by fifty miles or so, which will be plenty."

"Plenty for what?"

"Plenty to get them over deep waters. They'll be far from shore, with chances of rescue next to zero," Meade says, turning back to the window, that sinister smile growing ever wider on his face. I don't need to ask the next question. I've played yet again into Meade's hands.

"Not that we're really expecting anyone looking our way. It's the middle of a typhoon and the nearest town's been practically obliterated by some redneck anarchists, but still… Orders are orders. And you helped us carry them out. So once again, thanks. Turns out you do better work for your government when you think you're on the other side. If that's not the definition of ineptitude, I don't know what is. Still, cheers," Meade says with a cynical wink and the slight raising of his cup.

The humiliation and agony build to a fever pitch. I feel my fists clench into rocks at my side, hot coffee squeezed from the Styrofoam drizzling over my knuckles and onto the floor. I forget the MAs with their guns, the fact that I'm riding a giant weapon staffed by thousands of military personnel, the fact that they could kill me and dump me into the waves without anyone ever knowing. None of it matters, really. Not after losing this much.

I visualize the violence before my muscles react–my free arm lunging out to grab Meade's coat, dashing him to the ground and kicking him before he can rise to his feet. And then, if I'm still alive, if the guards somehow haven't managed to fire a round, I'll…

"Sir, we've got something on radar. Looks to be about the size of our target," says a young woman, her hair gripped back in a tight bun, eyes dark and alert. She wears baggy aqua colored fatigues, a bright yellow navy insignia embroidered into her lapel. She glances between Meade and the admiral, waiting for one of them to acknowledge.

"Scramble a bird. I want a live feed from the air in ten," grunts the admiral, giving me a brief, emotionless stare before returning to his elevated chair at the corner of the room. The young woman nods and lifts a black receiver from beside a set of monitors and gives the orders.

Not five minutes later, I watch as a fighter jet is catapulted from the deck with a roar, rear engine glowing blue as it pierces the storm and disappears.

"Not long now," Meade says with unabashed glee.

I look around at the youthful faces around me, expressions of determination cast in relief by the upglow of digital readouts and radar screens. They're younger than me, I'd guess, and not so different.

Me just six years ago, a rookie on the force. Me pulling the trigger when it seemed like the right thing to do. Me, blood on my hands. Blood that doesn't wash out, no matter how hot you turn that water, no matter how many bars of soap you scrub through. *Do they know how close they are to spilling that kind of blood? The blood of my wife!* Then again, would it matter? Would any of these kids have the guts to disobey orders, to stand down due to their conscience? Would I?

The anger is gone now, washed away by a sobering reality that I'm no better than the rest of these people. Perhaps this is why our judgment will be the same, why I'm standing on this warship rather than with Amy. I close my eyes, tasting only the bitterness of my fate, and pray to Jehovah.

3:19 PM
AMY

The storm ahead swells and churns and begins to rock our ship. The brothers have been kind enough to allow me to stay with them in the bridge. Perhaps they hope to distract me. This room is a few stories above a deck filled with coils of chains and cables and tarpaulin covered crates. Brother Harris sits at my side, consoling me with scriptures as best he can, suggesting that my husband may still make it out alive. I appreciate his sentiments, but deep down, I know it is too late. Luke has made his choice. He has–for the last time–sacrificed himself.

I watch absently as a team of skilled brothers and sisters rove over the controls, reporting their readings to the brother with the grey hair, our captain.

"How we doing in these swells, Shelly?" he asks, swiveling slightly in his chair, pointing the question to a sister over his right shoulder.

"We're listing about one degree to starboard, but nothing serious, Brother Andros."

"Good. Don, are the stabilizers still functioning normally?"

"Mostly. One of them has been giving us irregular readouts over the past half hour."

"All right. Let's get someone from maintenance to check it out. If the stabilizers go down we'll have a lot of seasick friends on our hands."

"Yes, sir," the brother says, lifting a phone from the controls and relaying the command.

I turn slightly as a hand gently descends on my shoulder. It's Marc. His eyes are red and puffy, his lips quivering slightly.

"Marc? Are you ok?" I ask, worried. He drags a folding chair over and plops down next to me, wiping his eyes with a sleeve before speaking.

"I'm so sorry about Luke, Amy," he says, the grief heavy in his voice. I study him for a moment before answering.

"It's ok, Marc. It was his choice," I say sadly.

"Yeah, I know. Just like the train. I can't stop thinking about it, Amy. Trying to figure out if there was another way."

"It… It isn't your fault, Marc," I finally say. "I shouldn't have blamed you and the others. I know my husband. It's his nature to protect others. He would've wanted it this way. If something had happened to you or Ashley or your son, he would've never forgiven himself."

Marc frowns at the floor and nods somberly. "I keep praying that Jehovah will remember him, Amy. Right now I want that more than anything. He's a good man. I have to admit, when we first found him, in the forest, I had my doubts. But as time passed, it really seemed like Jehovah was guiding things, like he'd led Luke directly to us."

"Luke has always been a good man, Marc. He probably would've come around sooner, had I been less secretive. Chelsea had been on my case for months about it, you know. I was too scared. Worried that Luke would react badly to the news that I was studying. Maybe I have no one to blame but myself for all of this."

"Captain, take a look at these fuel readings," one of the young brothers says from a computer screen to our left. The older brother moves over quickly to peer into the screen.

"Can this be right? We were three-fourths full when we left Wilmington."

"We've been overhauling the engines in this storm, but I think we may also be leaking fuel," says Don.

"How much farther can we get on this tank?"

"It's hard to gauge. Another half day, maybe. And that's if the storm lets up."

"Captain, sorry, but I've got something else here," someone says from the other end of the controls. The voice is sharp and agitated. Everyone in the room freezes.

"Well, go on, what is it?" Captain Andros says, voice soft but concerned.

"Something on radar, coming in fast. I think it's a plane."

"A plane? In this weather?" Andros asks.

"It's moving way too fast to be a boat. Less than a mile now."

Our heads automatically rise, peering through the oily rain and black skies. The room is silent but for the distant rumble of thunder. We barely spot it cross over our deck, and it's gone an instant later, but the unmistakable roar of its jet engine rings in our ears.

"Sam, how far are we from those coordinates we received?" the captain orders, his voice low and quick.

"A good seventy, eighty miles."

"Are you sure?"

"Yeah, unless the GPS is acting up. We've been on this course for hours. I can't imagine it's wrong."

"Ok, ok. Don, get brother Michaels on the phone for me. We need to let them know the news."

"The news?"

"They've found us, son."

3:25 PM
LUKE

"That the best we can do for visuals?" Meade grunts, staring up at a widescreen monitor perched above the admiral's chair. The image on the screen is a hazy, black and white outline of a large cruise liner.

"I'm afraid so," one of the technicians replies apologetically. "The rain's coming down in buckets out there. The pilot's made several passes. We tried infrared, not much better."

"Were you able to positively ID the vessel at least?" the admiral says irritably.

"Yes, sir," the tech says, keying something into the console as a series of still images flashes onto the screen. "You can see here. And here, near her prow. It's the *Cornelia*, alright."

"Good," says the admiral. The young man nods with a faint smile and disappears behind a console. "Meade? What's our move?"

Agent Meade's eyes glow, intoxicated by this delicious and horrible power, like a small boy discovering his father's hidden handgun. He gives me a menacing look and leans towards the admiral.

"Let's see if she's armed. Draw her out. Can we fire some kind of warning shot over her deck?"

The admiral nods before lifting the receiver on his phone and giving the order.

"So this is the plan," I say. "Killing innocent civilians." They've got me locked up to a handrail at the rear right of the pilothouse, where I'm forced to watch this all unfold. I feel much calmer now, and the thoughts of violence towards my captors are gone. Still, I don't expect to just sit by and watch without a word.

"Innocent? Is that how you'd label any other radicalized religious group? Wake up, Harding. *This is a cult.* Our government knows it, our allies know it. For god's sake, even our *enemies* know it. You have any idea how many seats of the United Nations General Assembly moved to ratify the total obliteration of this sect? *One hundred ninety-three.* That's a one hundred percent vote. A landslide. There's not a question in my mind that this brand of extremism is anything but innocent."

"You're wrong," I say, thinking back to the conversation with Marc and Andrew days ago. Their explanation of the tumultuous conclusion of world events, the clear attack on God's people by the World's nations. It was a hard concept to swallow, but here it is. Clear as day.

"So what do you think, then? You think God's somehow protecting these people? Is that it? Then where is *He* now? Because last I heard, most of the Witnesses around the world are either in prison camps or fleeing for their lives like animals on the run. Mark my words, a few years from now, Jehovah's Witnesses will be a thing of the history books and nothing more. Just watch, Harding. Just watch."

"Admiral, sir, our bird's almost back in position," announces a quartermaster.

"My orders stand. Let's show these zealots a thing or two about the US Navy."

"Live video feed on your screen now, sir. Half a mile and counting."

I raise my eyes to the monitors, unable to look away. The picture is grainier than before, but the ship stands out clearly onscreen. The digital crosshairs of the fighter jet weave and bob against the outline of the ghostly ship.

"*Open fire!*"

3:25 PM
AMY

The brothers huddle around the bridge with grim faces as Captain Andros relays the news. Somehow, we've been tracked down. It's only a matter of time before the cavalry shows up.

"What do we do?" one of the elders asks. There is no fear in his voice, only steely determination.

"Tell the group overseers to remain with the friends. Try to keep them calm. Share scriptures. Remind them of David and Goliath, of Hezekiah and Sennacherib, of the three Hebrews and Nebuchadnezzar. Do all you can to keep their minds on spiritual things," Brother Harris instructs.

"What about lifeboats? Are they an option?" someone else asks.

"Only as a last resort. If this ship sinks, they won't do us much good. Not in these waves," Andros says gravely.

"Anything else we can do to protect the brothers and sisters?" Marc asks.

"Keep them away from the windows and sidewalls of the ship. In the event of an attack, those will be the most vulnerable places," the captain says.

"A fighter jet like that, though. One missile aimed at the right place, and–"

"Let's not dwell on that now," Brother Harris says. "Let our focus be on what we can do to bolster the friends. We must keep our determination to stand firm." Solemn nods are made around the circle and one of the brothers offers a prayer:

"Jehovah, the God of Armies, our Rock, our Protector. We thank you for our deliverance thus far. You have been there, every step of the way, guiding and protecting. Your thoughts are higher than our thoughts. You saw the dangers long before human eyes could have. Now, Jehovah, we beg for your strength. Our enemies draw ever closer. If it is your will, oh Jehovah, please frustrate their plans. But if not, know that we will remain faithful, even as this ship sinks down into Sheol. We will never leave you, Jehovah! If we live, we live to You. And if we die, we die to You. Let nothing take away our integrity!"

When we open our eyes, our faces are teary but staunch. The brothers embrace solemnly for what may be the last time before dispersing back into the belly of the ship. The words of the prayer continue to resonate deep within my heart like a cave echo. My fear retreats just enough to allow me clear thought.

"Brothers and sisters, please, what is our status?" Brother Andros says as he eases back into his captain's chair. His voice is soft and gentle, completely belying our peril.

"Fuel less than fifteen percent, Captain. We're definitely leaking."

"Please, call me brother. We are all brothers and sisters here," Andros says, patting the younger man on his shoulder.

"Yes, sir. Brother."

"Ok. Besides fuel, what are we looking at?"

"Stabilizers seem to be holding. We're still listing, but it's not severe," Shelly reports.

"Well that's good," Andros says, smiling. "Anything on radar, Sam?"

"No, nothing. Wait… Yes, something's just shown up. Closing in fast, Brother Andros. I think it's that jet fighter again," Sam says, panic rising in his voice like a cresting wave.

"Ok, keep calm. Let's see what he does."

There is utter silence on the bridge as the pinging radar dot races towards the center of the screen. We turn our heads, peering out the window into the storm. The waves are higher than ever, their tips foamy and agitated. The sky is unnaturally black and moonless, illuminated only by periodic flashes of lightning. Gusts of salt wind howl over us. The smell of the sea is all around us.

In the distance, two yellow strings of light dance in the air. The lights move with incredible speed directly at us. The swells below the ship give way, and we duck downwards, the streaming lights passing just a few stories above our prow. The fighter follows seconds behind the missiles, its jet roaring breathlessly above our deck. And then it's gone.

"That was close," the captain says as we begin to breathe again.

"It felt like inches," someone says.

"It probably was. But that was just a warning shot. They could hit us with something a lot worse if they wanted to."

"Maintain course?"

"Yes. Full throttle ahead."

3:37 PM
LUKE

"A-9, what's your status?" the admiral barks into his radio. The pilot's voice is fed back through the bridge intercom for all to hear. The dozen or so heads around me gaze up intently to listen.

"Warning shots fired, Admiral. Just over their deck. No response."

"Retaliatory fire?"

"No, sir. Seems to be a normal cruise ship. But they do appear to have a lot of items covered up with tarps on deck. Could be weapons."

"Ok. Make another pass at her. Go for her radar tower. Use your Mavericks."

"Roger that sir, standby for visuals." The radio clicks off and smiles around us are exchanged.

"They're probably concealed weapons," Meade mentions to the admiral. "Maybe they're trying to draw out more fighters. I'll bet they're using those quick-mount machine guns."

"It's possible," the admiral says, looking down at a screen. I consider objecting, telling these men once again that the Witnesses are surely unarmed. But what good would it do? And then there's the chance they'd throw me back into the brig, where I'd know nothing of all of this. And as horrible as it is to stand here, not knowing would be even worse.

A sharp ringing splits the air as heads turn to focus on a red telephone mounted on a control panel near the captain's seat. Admiral Hawkins glances at it, stunned for a moment, before quickly lifting the receiver. Meade looks on impatiently, clearly displeased with being out of the loop. But all we can do is wait. The admiral's conversation is hushed and brief. He returns the receiver with a glance at Meade, then myself.

"That was the pentagon," he says.

"And?" asks Meade.

"The president wants to offer a pardon to anyone on that ship willing to renounce their beliefs."

"*What?!*" Meade says, suddenly furious. "He can't do that! The UN's Council specifically ruled that–"

"It only applies to practicing Witnesses. He wants to offer them an olive branch. Apparently other member nations are doing it, too."

"This is *outrageous!* These people have been plotting to overthrow our government, and he wants to just let them walk?"

"He's our commander in chief, Agent Meade. This isn't our call."

Meade grits his teeth at the admiral, and for a moment I think the two might start swinging punches until Meade throws up his arms in frustration and storms off to the other end of the bridge. "Politicians," he growls under his breath.

"A-9, belay those attack orders on the cruise vessel and return to deck. Repeat, return to deck," the admiral calls into a radio. The pilot copies the command a moment later, traces of confusion in his voice.

"Alright, let's re-establish radio communication with our target," the Admiral says to one of the seated female quartermasters. Her fingers dance over the controls.

"I've got them, admiral. Shall I patch you through?"

3:52 PM
AMY

"This is Admiral James Hawkins of the USS Gerald R. Ford. With whom am I speaking?" comes the commanding voice on the opposite end of the radio. We freeze for a moment, unsure of what comes next, until Captain Andros takes the radio transmitter from the console.

"This is Captain Phillip Andros of the *Cornelia*. Our ship is filled with civilians. We are unarmed." A long pause on the other end.

"What is the religious affiliation of those aboard your vessel?" Andros composes himself with a deep breath.

"We are Jehovah's Witnesses, sir." Another agonizing pause.

"We wish to deliver a message to your passengers and crew," says the voice.

"Copy that. What is the message?"

"We will deliver it directly to your passengers. We will rendezvous with your vessel at approximately seventeen hundred hours. We will approach your starboard side and broadcast from our PA system. Do you copy?"

"Yes, we copy. But, well… We could save you a trip if you were to just give us the message now," Captain Andros says. We wait, but there is no response. Andros tries again, but there's only static.

"Do you think it's a trap?" Don asks.

"I've no idea. But we have no choice but to comply. We'll be out of fuel soon, and their ship could overtake us even if that wasn't an issue. All we can do is wait. And pray."

4:01 PM
LUKE

"Attention, officers," the admiral barks, the men and women in the room turning and stiffening like planks at the sound of his voice. "In less than one hour, we will rendezvous with the *Cornelia*. Previously, she was a cruise vessel, but we have reliable intel that tells us her passengers are dangerous. Don't let the civilian exterior fool you.

These people are trained. Keep a sharp eye. At any signs of trouble, we shoot first, understand? Look alert. Back to your stations."

Meade glances back to me, giddy as ever, back to his old self. "Ready for the fireworks?" he asks. I remain silent and turn to gaze out into the storm. The waves climb ever higher, their tips foul tendrils of foam in the lashing wind. The crack and grumble of thunder roll over us.

My pulse quickens as I picture those men and women and children waiting anxiously on the ship. There is no way out. Somewhere, not far from us, is my wife. I can almost feel her drawing closer.

4:51 PM
AMY

We gasp as the ship slides into view. It is a mere outline at first, a jagged, mountainous silhouette in the flashing lightning. The sky is abnormally dark for just four o'clock in the afternoon, but this thought is quickly relegated to the recesses of my mind. The ship grows and grows as it looms nearer, its turrets rotating in precise synchronization. Dozens of jet fighters are poised perfectly on the ship's deck like polished scalpels on a surgeon's tray. Glaring searchlights are switched on, flinging immense beams of powerful light across the waves and over our bow.

Despite the high seas and howling wind, the aircraft carrier moves undeterred. It slices through the water steadily, intrepidly, its bow lamps winking at us between the swells. The tower above the flight deck soars a hundred feet in the air like the dorsal fin of a circling shark. A shark that smells blood.

"It's a floating city," says Don. "Never seen *anything* that big before."

"It's a Ford-class aircraft carrier. Biggest of its kind in the world. But don't let its bulk scare you. It's no match for even a single angel, if that's what it comes to," our captain responds.

The predatory ship lurks nearer, her sheer immensity dwarfing our own vessel. Her searchlights pry through our windows and decks. When a beam lunges through the pilothouse, we shield our eyes against its blinding, searing force. The battleship is now close enough for me to make out the dark shapes of soldiers in fluttering raincoats on the flight deck, manning the weaponry, climbing staircases, standing at attention behind windows.

"*Attention, passengers and crew of the* Cornelia! *Attention!*" comes a sharp, measured voice through the PA system of the carrier. I recognize it immediately. It's their admiral, the one who hailed our captain.

"This is the *U.S.S. Gerald R. Ford.* You are in violation of both domestic and international treaties banning the practice and operation of organized religion. *Stand down.* If you or any of your passengers or crew wish to surrender and renounce your beliefs, we will provide a means of safe transport and immediate evacuation. If you refuse, we are authorized to use force. *Repeat...*"

The message drones on and on, the sound reverberating through the hull of the ship, ricocheting between compartments, working its way into every nook and storage space. As we continue to list and leak fuel, red lights flash on control panels, alarms chirp and buzz like panicked birds. There is simply no way out... *except the one.*

I wonder how many of the friends down below are plagued by similar thoughts, how many of us are ready to accept this ship as our grave. Who of us is willing to spend the final moments drowning in a strange, freezing sea?

"Stand firm," Brother Andros says, his voice low, barely audible. He flicks on the *Cornelia*'s PA system and repeats the words, his voice warm, reassuring.

"Sing to Jehovah," Don says, his face turning towards us with the faintest of smiles, his eyes calm and stoic. The words come a second time, but they sound different. They are accompanied by a melody, a familiar song.

"*Sing to Jehovah,
His great name is highly exalted...*"

Captain Andros turns to the young man, his face glowing with warm admiration. He hands the young brother the radio transmitter so his song can be heard throughout the confines of the ship. The following lines are sung louder as Andros and the others join in. I sing too, as best as I can remember the words:

"*His proud Egyptian foes,
He has cast into the sea.
Praise Jah Almighty,
Besides him there can be no other...*"

Our song echoes down into the bowels of the ship, where our brothers and sisters can surely hear it, where we hope and pray they will be steadfast. And as the chorus swells, we hear them, from the decks deep below, the radios transmitting the staunch singing of thousands of brave souls. Chills crawl up my spine as red hot tears brim in my eyes and stream down my face. I'm singing not just for me, nor just for the friends whom I've come to love so dearly, not just for our dear Walter who was slaughtered today, but for Jehovah God himself, for the angels who must be listening. *And for Luke!*

I watch, warmed by a pure thrill as Andros thumbs the transmission button, sending our explosion of voices back to the admiral and his battleship, back to those enemies of Jehovah. Our voices stronger than any missile, our faith enough to conquer warheads.

> *"See now the nations,*
>   *Opposing the Sovereign Jehovah*
>   *Though mightier than Pharoah,*
>   *They too will suffer shame!*
>   *Doom now awaits them,*
>   *They will not survive Armageddon.*
>   *Soon everyone will know*
>   *That Jehovah is God's name!"*

The walls of the ship tremble with reverberating voices crying out in unison, and in that moment, I know that Jehovah must be close!

5:04 PM
LUKE

The chorus of voices echoes through the pilothouse. My skin tingles at their sound. *Amy's is among them.* And in this moment I am more proud of her than I can bear to express. Tears well in my eyes, more sure than ever that their God, Jehovah, must be listening. I only wish I could know the words to the song, that I could be an extension of their voice, right here, like a knife in the heart of the enemy!

I listen carefully to the melody, trying to get a feel for it's swaying rhythm, the pitching melody so perfectly matched to the rising and falling of the sea around us. Surely this is no mistake, this perfect song of conquest over fear! *I may not know the lyrics, but by God I can hum my heart out, and nothing can stop me!*

By the time the third verse rolls around I've got it, and I'm humming as loud as I can muster, chained to the bulkhead like a blathering fool, but I don't care. The effect is not lost on the quartermasters, nor on Admiral Hawkins or Agent Meade. They're visibly shaken by the sheer power of the resounding voices, stunned as if by the roar of lions. For a moment, I see the flicker of fear in their eyes.

"Turn off that ruckus!" Meade screams, lunging towards the communications officer. She fumbles with the switches, but the volume only increases.

"I–I'm sorry, sir. Something's wrong with the controls, I can't–"

She's cut off by a sudden, chilling silence as the song ends, followed by a strong, low voice bursting through the speakers. It's their captain, Andros.

"Admiral, are you still there?" he asks, no hint of fear in his voice.

"Yes. What's happening?" the admiral responds, flustered and confused.

"You have offered surrender and this is our response: You have come to us with planes and bombs, missiles and torpedoes, an immense warship stocked with unimaginable weaponry. But *we* have come to *you* in the name of Jehovah, the God of Armies, whom you have taunted. If it is to be, our God whom we serve is able to rescue us from your hand. But even if he does not, Admiral, know that we are determined not to let *anything* break our integrity to our God. We will *never* renounce our faith! Over and out!"

Stunned, the Admiral slumps into his chair, a frown etched deep into his face. He's visibly shaken by the entire ordeal and unable to move.

"You heard them," Meade hisses, boiling over with an insane kind of rage. "Burn them!"

5:15 PM
AMY

"Status report!" Captain Andros hollers above the scream of alarms. The cabin is flooded with the strafe of blood red lights, warning lamps spiraling out of control.

"Fuel is completely depleted, sir! Aft chambers taking on water fast! I'm not sure what happened, but we are sinking!"

"She's an old ship, and this is a formidable storm," Andros says dryly. Then, snapping up the radio transmitter, "Get the friends to the higher decks immediately. Tell them to leave everything. Prep the lifeboats."

"We're listing, sir. Four degrees and counting," says Shelly.

"Never mind that," Andros says in a voice devoid of emotion. "This ship is lost. Focus all efforts on evacuating and protecting the friends."

"Yes, sir," she says, immediately switching consoles and chattering commands into a separate transmitter.

"Brother Andros," Don says, pointing out the window at the looming warship. "They're firing."

We turn to watch as a barrage of lighted rockets hiss straight up into the air. Despite the rain, they attain incredible height in just seconds, becoming dull glowing orbs as they disappear into the storm clouds.

Brother Andros turns to hug the young man, then the others, in turn. They ruffle one another's hair and smile, tears again flowing freely. Then they come to me and the others of us waiting in the pilothouse. We share a final embrace as we await death.

5:18 PM
LUKE

"Where are those mortars?" Meade sneers, leaning into the window to glare up at the skies.

"Something's wrong," mumbles one of the officers, checking a readout on an overhead monitor. "The shells exploded prematurely."

"Did any make contact with our target?" the admiral asks, brow furled.

"Uh... Negative, sir. Must be a weapons malfunction."

"A dozen simultaneous malfunctions?" Hawkins asks again, fidgeting in his chair, struggling to look out the window. A bright flash of lightning illuminates the skies outside, the dash of thunder so powerful that the bulkheads shudder like chattering teeth. Admiral Hawkins jumps back from the glass, eyes wide, hand against his chest, laboring over his breaths.

"What is it, Hawkins?" Meade snorts.

"A face. I–I saw a face...on the other side of the glass. The eyes..."

A shadow falls over Agent Meade's face as he leans into the admiral, their eyes just inches apart. "Get it together," he hisses. "Order another attack and end this freak show."

"Yes, yes. Of course. Let's try the Mark forty-sixes. Aim low, boys. Let's crack her hull and get this thing over with!"

Meade's attention snaps towards me. He roughly detaches my restraints from the handrail and grips the back of my collar in a clenched fist. "Walk!" he orders. I comply, nearly stumbling over my own feet as we march across the bridge. The quartermasters' eyes glance up furtively–fearfully, I think–as we pass.

Meade shoves my face into the window, slapping the metal cuffs onto a steel handrail. He shoves my head into the window, my cheekbone catching the cold glass hard and painfully, my eyes forced to witness the impending holocaust.

"*Watch. Them. Burn,*" he hisses in my ear.

On the deck below, I see men in bright green raincoats loading the torpedo turrets. They fumble and slip, the strong wind and the slick deck making normal movement impossible. For a hopeful moment I imagine them toppling overboard, but slowly and surely they manage to load the weapon. The turret groans to life, finding its mark. The men step back. There's a deep thud as smoke erupts form the back of the cannon, then a blur of red as the torpedo dives into the waves.

5:29 PM
AMY

"Sir, the lower compartments are flooding rapidly," Don reports.

Captain Andros into the radio: "Jack, how are the lifeboats coming?"

"We're doing our best, Captain, but in this storm–"

"Good. Keep working on them, get more helpers if you need. Prepare to abandon ship."

"What about all these crates of supplies on deck? They're taking up a lot of space–I'm not sure if we'll be able to get everyone out here."

"Toss it overboard. Get the friends on deck, above the water line. That's the top priority."

"Understood."

The captain switches through various channels, spreading the evacuation orders to each deck and group. When that's done, he sits in his chair and looks at those of us still on the bridge.

"This is where we part ways," he says gently. "I want you all to stick together. I'll find you once all two thousand four hundred and thirty-nine of our friends are accounted for on deck."

There's a long pause before we finally begin nodding. The captain hugs each of us before we file out of the bridge. We ride the lift in silence to the deck, alarms blaring all the while. The doors open to the overwhelming cold and the rain falling in thick sheets. Hundreds of friends have already gathered, gripping each other for stability as the ship lists and rocks.

The crowd presses closer together as our numbers increase. More and more faces bubble up from the bowels of the ship, young children held in the arms of parents, older couples moving slowly, hand in hand. The battleship is still there, having drifted back a few hundred yards from us, but it is silent and still. *Perhaps mounting its final attack*, I think.

Jesse and Chelsea somehow locate me in the crowd. Marc and Ashley are close behind, draping a plastic garbage bag over me and my wheelchair. They reach down to hug me, uttering sweet words that I can't quite make out. Matthew gazes at me from his father's arms with a sleepy, curious stare. I reach up to stroke the tip of his nose and he smiles, and in that moment, everything seems right.

The aircraft carrier is gone, along with the roiling seas and furious skies. The lightning is replaced by a breathtaking sunset, a masterpiece of reds, pinks, and oranges. We are no longer cornered prey waiting as a firing squad takes aim. *We are in paradise.* Beautiful, wooded hills surround us on every side. A family of deer graze near a gurgling stream. A vibrant, blonde Chelsea picks roses and smiles over her shoulder at Walter before placing the flowers delicately in her basket. Matthew runs through the trees, a litter of baby foxes close on his heels. Luke tucks his arm around my waist and pulls me tight as we close our eyes, feeling the retreating rays of sunlight warm us down to our very cores.

And then the explosion comes.

5:39 PM

LUKE

"Direct hit, sir! That last shot finally did it!"

"About time," the admiral says anxiously, thoroughly bewildered by the inexplicable number of misfires. "Where was she hit?"

"According to our sensors, it was dead center, just below the water line. Should capsize her. Won't be long now, sir."

"Good. Good," Hawkins says, wiping a line of sweat from his brow.

"And you really thought God would save them!" Meade says with snarling laughter. "All that singing and wailing, and for what? They'll all be *dead* soon." This brings another bout of laughter as Meade keels over, bracing himself on a console. "You really bel–"

"Sir, Admiral, sir," one of the male quartermasters says anxiously. "We seem to have a problem."

"Go on, spit it out," Hawkins snaps.

"I don't know how to describe it, but… Take a look at these images."

We wait a moment as the feed is routed to the main overhead monitor. The quartermaster walks over and jabs a pencil at the screen. The *Cornelia* is smoking from here and here, but the center appears wholly intact. "Here. This is where that last shell exploded."

"Are you sure?"

"We have footage. From our POV, it detonated right here."

"Where's the damage?"

"I-I don't know, sir. Maybe the shell went off prematurely. Or their hull is reinforced after all."

"Impossible! Even this ship's hull couldn't withstand a Mark forty-six."

"I don't know what else to say, Admiral, except–"

The pilothouse is suddenly plunged into darkness as the electricity cuts out. Every screen and console, every switch and light bulb, instantly goes black. The only light is from outside the windows: a pale, ghostly glow that wavers ethereally between sea and sky. For that dreadful but exciting moment, I am certain that every corridor and cabin of the *Gerald R. Ford* is fearfully silent.

A solitary, jagged scream pierces the stillness in the air. It drifts up to us from the hollow caverns of a deck far below, magnified by the silence of dead electronics. The men and women around me slowly remove their headsets and gape down at the floor, looking to make sense of things, struggling to maintain composure.

"What's going on?" someone finally says, their voice a trembling wire.

"Why aren't the backup generators kicking in?"

"You think it was the storm?"

"Do we have contact with the lower decks?" asks the admiral, followed by fumbling noises from one of the consoles.

"No sir. The power is completely out."

"Jackson. Paige. Take flashlights and go check it out. I want you back here in ten minutes with a full report." The two men confirm the order and jog out through a doorway. We hear their feet clank and clatter down a stairwell as the room remains dark.

The tension in the pilothouse is just beginning to dissipate as another scream echoes up through the deck floors. It's much louder this time, much closer. The admiral curses under his breath, his fear pale and naked. From his side of the room I hear a metal compartment open, followed by the familiar clink of ammunition being loaded.

There are muffled gasps and moans from the officers around me as the two men with flashlights return to the bridge.

"Report! Tell me what's going on!" says the admiral shakily.

"*Empty*. Everyone's gone. Nothing but empty corridors," one of the men says between ragged breaths.

"The ground. It's covered in this... *This black chalky stuff*. It smells. I don't know. I don't know. It's bad, sir. Real bad."

5:50 PM
AMY

The wind and rain lash mercilessly against the deck of the *Cornelia* as more and more people squeeze onto her crowded deck. The entire throng of people–well over a thousand and counting–is gripped by uncertainty. Still, it is determination I see marked on the faces around me, not fear. For the moment, it seems the explosion that sent a geyser of seawater into the air and shook the ship beneath us hasn't cost us any casualties, but we can't be sure. The ship is sinking all the same, the water line climbing higher and higher, the wave tips nearly reaching the prow.

On the raised walkways above us, brothers struggle to lower the lifeboats. I'm not hopeful. The ropes are a chaotic tangle and whip in the wind as the boats swing crazily. I stiffen with horror as the prow of one of the lifeboats nearly smashes into a brother's head; someone shoves him out of the way just in time.

The battleship before us drifts with the waves. It fires a few more projectiles in our direction, but the shots go wild, missing us by a good margin. Then comes a lull. The turrets quit seeking us. The rockets are silent. Suddenly, the whole ship vanishes as the deck lights, portholes, and lamps simultaneously go dark.

"Look!" someone shouts. An arm rises from the crowd, pointing across a turbulent sea. "There! Under the ship!"

Hundreds of bodies turn to look, moving closer to the railing, blocking my line of sight.

"What is it?" I ask, tugging on Marc's sleeve.

"I–I don't know. I can't make it out clearly. But there's a bright light, coming up from the water…"

"Is it some kind of weapon?" someone mutters behind me. More voices, more speculation. And then, like the ring of a bell, crisp and clear, comes the voice of a small child perched high up on her father's shoulders, her oversized raincoat shedding water.

"*Look*, daddy," she says curiously. "Look! There's a *man* coming out of the water!"

5:56 PM
LUKE

An explosion, so loud and close that the entire room instinctively ducks for cover as a plume of bright orange fire erupts just outside the pilothouse's glass windows. Despite the handcuffs, my position affords me a clear view of the flight deck, where I see the smoldering wreck of what used to be one of the parked fighters, the ground around it a wild conflagration of ignited jet fuel.

"*What is happening!*" screams the admiral, leaning into the window, the whites of his eyes glowing brightly in the blaze. But there is no answer. Everyone stares in stunned silence at the deck below, where a scene unfolds that I am sure I will never forget.

There, at the far edge of the flight deck, stands a large man. I think *man*, because this is his approximate shape and form, and yet I know this thought is wrong as soon as it passes through my mind. It is no man. His size dwarfs everything around him; he's at least fifteen, maybe twenty feet tall. His clothes radiate with a cold, blue light, and for a crazy moment I actually think I see streaks of lightning scattering over his arms and face. His eyes are like burning diamonds, emanating a bright white light that hurts my own eyes to look at. And in his hand he wields a long, fiery blade.

A cluster of soldiers emerges from a flight deck elevator. They kneel and take aim at the advancing apparition, but it moves forward undaunted. A barrage of shell fire is unloaded in its direction, but it passes harmlessly through. It lifts its sword once and swings, bringing the sharp, glowing tip down in the direction of the troops. Immediately, the soldiers are consumed in bright, red light. Whatever screams they attempted never made it past their throats. The execution is instantaneous. They explode in a ball of bright chaff, like sparks from a fireworks display. A charred, black cloud of dust hangs in the air for a moment but is quickly smothered by the downpour.

Agent Meade tries the ship's radio, then the walkie-talkie strapped to his side, but everything electronic is dead, as if taken out by an electromagnetic pulse. Below us, the glowing man advances. A second platoon of soldiers forms a line in the rain. They're quick, but I sense their hesitancy. The men in front fire carbines from a prone position, empty shells clinking in streams onto the wet tarmac. Behind them, six soldiers man rocket launchers. Ammunitions cases are opened, the rockets are loaded, and then fired, all with the slick efficiency of military professionals. This ship's best, perhaps. But it is an exercise in futility.

The rockets hiss towards their target with impressive speed, but diverge just before contact as if misdirected by a powerful magnet. They whistle past their mark and launch wildly into the sky. They stall for a moment in midair before collapsing back to the deck, destroying a few million dollars worth of Navy aircraft. The jets burn fast and hard, the low, oily clouds above illuminated by the fire.

The soldiers with the rocket launchers attempt to reload, but the creature reaches them with incredible speed, its sword carving fiery arcs the air. Like the first squad, these soldiers meet their end in a plume of sparks and soot. Here on the bridge, people scream. Meade and Admiral Hawkins bellow frantic orders to no one in particular. Bodies scramble about me, silhouetted by the orange flames from burning aircraft. Trained hands open hatches and bulkheads as weapons and cases of ammunition are removed. More death throes from somewhere below as the glowing figure disappears from the flight deck and enters the ship's command tower.

6:02 PM
AMY

Marc nudges my wheelchair gently through the crowd until I find myself at the deck railing with a clear line of sight over the sea. The aircraft carrier before us has plunged into blazing disarray. Stems of fire blossom from the deck as explosions go off one after the other. The ship seems to be under attack, but no other aircraft or watercraft can be seen. And what about that strange light in the water? No one can locate it now. Struggling to get a clear glimpse through the salt-sprayed air and low hanging clouds without so much as a pair of binoculars is nearly impossible.

To our left, brothers continue to grapple with the dangling lifeboats. There's a loud metallic rending noise as one of the pulleys rips free from an overhead beam. The lifeboat dips as it comes loose, swinging off and bashing against the deck before tumbling into the dashing black waves. I hear frantic indistinct shouting as three brothers struggle to maintain their balance on the slick deck from where the lifeboat has just vanished. A length of rope lies coiled at their feet, and I watch in horror as they lose their balance and topple into the waves. They manage to miss the lifeboat, which has capsized and is being thrashed thoroughly by the high waves. It crashes finally into the hull of the ship and shatters into bits of wood and plastic and orange scraps of tarpaulin.

We wait with our hearts in our throats for the men to resurface. Their heads finally appear, gasping for help as the powerful waves swirl and surge around them. Life preservers are flung down to them, and somehow, amidst the debris and surging seafoam, they manage to grab on, the sea around them rising and descending like hills in an earthquake. The crowd on deck leans forward anxiously as the preserver ropes are hauled in by lines of soaking men.

6:10 PM
LUKE

The dark, cavernous bridge fills with the cold clicks and clinks of hastily loaded ammunition. Heavy cases of gun magazines are dragged to the center of the room, where they're unlatched and placed behind two lines of soldiers facing the doors. One of the doors is just a few feet beside where I've been handcuffed, putting me more or less in the line of fire. For a moment I imagine Meade might just consider turning it into a firing squad while the weapons are out and ready, but he's busy inspecting a carbine strapped to his shoulder. His eyes flicker with fire and lightning, his teeth clenched and glistening.

We wait in silence, the room growing steadily cold and damp with the heaters dead. In the silence of the bridge, the sounds from outside float up towards us, the tossing seas and sporadic thunder, the creaks and groans of the ship.

"You feel that?" a faceless voice whispers.

"What?"

"We're listing. Starboard." There's a moment of shuffling as heads turn to gaze down at the floor. Soon, we all feel it.

"Sir?" someone says, panicked.

"Maintain your positions!" Admiral Hawkins orders. The quartermasters spread their feet as they make an effort to comply, but it's no easy task with the rapidly increasing incline. A few of them finally lose their footing, tumbling into the line of their fellows and sending the bridge back into confusion. Several drop their weapons to brace against the island consoles as the guns and ammo cases scrape by against the floor, crashing into the other end of the bridge and narrowly missing two of the men.

The soldiers are kneeling now to keep their balance, one leg outstretched against the downward slant of the floor. And still the angle climbs. The ground is nearly at forty degrees by the time the command is finally given for everyone to shoulder their weapons and brace themselves. The room complies eagerly, scrambling for the walls and ledges, looping elbows around handrails.

At fifty degrees, one of the men loses his grip. He rolls along the floor, grunting to hold a scream back in his throat. Several hands reach for him, but he's moving too fast. He slams hard into the consoles on the far end of the bridge, screeching in pain. At sixty degrees, the pilothouse has become an elevator shaft, a long, treacherous drop from top to bottom. Three of the soldiers seem to have the right idea, and begin climbing down, using the consoles, hanging monitors, and steel window girders as a kind of ladder. As the ship continues to tilt, compartments topple open, their contents raining down on the men below like miscellaneous hail.

As for me, I'm stuck at the top, the handcuffs still holding me fast to the rails. I prop my legs against a metal doorframe, the gunshot wound in my calf fresh and throbbing. I feel the stitches tear open and grit my teeth against the pain as I brace myself and struggle to hold my position.

Some thirty feet below me, a female quartermaster scaling down the windows slips. There's the pop and snap of plastic as the screen she's holding on to wobbles and comes free, thin plastic wires streaming out behind it. She screams as she falls with the monitor still in her arms, crashing into a control panel below and spilling over onto the windows. And *still* the angle climbs.

Beyond the bank of windows below, the sea looms as if through a glass floor. And yet the waves seem so far away, the width of the flight deck to the left of the tower adding a dozen stories to the fall. Far below me, crumpled against the consoles, lay the bodies of a dozen naval men and women. Many are moaning or nursing injuries; some appear to be unconscious.

Next comes a loud crash, a bulkhead flying open, a heavy metal toolbox spraying its contents from the ceiling. The tools rain down onto the bodies below me. A few hit the glass windows, which instantly sprout spiderweb cracks.

The room is almost completely vertical now as my mind struggles to make sense of it. *What could possibly capsize such an enormous ship?*

6:12 PM
AMY

The men in the water are hauled slowly back up to the deck, their limp, shivering bodies bumping against the hull of the ship like wet fish. I feel sick as I watch.

It's impossible to launch the lifeboats in this storm. The waves are too high, the winds too strong. The brothers move away from the winches, looking over the crowd in sad resignation as our ship continues to sink. The waves begin to crash over the prow, soaking us in sheets of freezing foam. The sky is now nearly pitch black, and I notice for the first time that the rising moon is shrouded in a reddish haze.

There appears, once again, to be no way out.

"Look!" someone shouts, pointing out over the waves and into the distance. A sea of heads rises to peer through the rain. The distant silhouette of the aircraft carrier is just barely visible, but the shape is all wrong. Its soaring deck tower has disappeared, replaced by a jagged, foreign outline.

"Is that the battleship?" someone mutters.

"She's on her side," someone gasps. "She's capsizing!"

6:15 PM
LUKE

The glass in the windows fractures, cracks growing like vines from girder to girder. The consoles beneath the windows and the metal struts encasing them are crammed with the wounded, their arms outstretched, trying to grasp on to something, anything, before the windows give. But there is simply nowhere to go. Tools and scraps of paper continue to rain sporadically down as they shift free from unseen places above.

My arms are now numb, my wrists locked high above my head, the blood vessels pinched off by the handcuffs and the odd angle of my hang. My calf throbs, heavy blood piling up behind the wound. My back and shoulders twist and pop with the weight of my body. The pain is so intense that I feel faint and disoriented.

And that's when the windows go.

The glass explodes outward in a twinkling shimmer. A handful of unconscious bodies, rifles still strapped to their arms, tumble quietly into the downward darkness and disappear into the waves.

"Oh God, oh God," I hear someone saying over and over. A second window goes, and two female officers, hideously aware and conscious, lose their grip and go sprawling down into the abyss. The terrified cluster of remaining personnel try to move away from the windows, but it's hopeless. The ship lurches with a loud crash, perhaps from an explosion on another level, and a few more lose their grip, screaming as the vibration pries them from their handholds and pitches them into blackness.

"Please, help. Help me," begs a feeble voice. I glance down to see the admiral on his back on one of the last remaining windows, a single, thick crack dividing the glass behind him. His arms and legs are spread wide, not daring to test the glass. Above him, on a ledge created by the now horizontal island consoles, is Agent Meade. He glances down at the pitiful man and says nothing. The glass pops and crunches as the crack expands. The admiral lets out a final, horrible scream before the window gives, his body plummeting with the shards in a kind of sick slow motion.

Meade watches him fall, then cranes his head up slowly to glare at me. A flash of lightning ignites his features, his cold dark eyes boring up at me through the shaft.

"*You brought this on us!*" he snarls, his voice powerful, dreadful. "*You* did it! But if you think you're going to walk off of this ship alive, think again!" he screams. He curls over, reaching for something at his ankle, and comes up with a pistol in his hands.

"You're a fool, Meade. You brought this on yourself! You thought… You thought you could fight against God!" I say, barely getting the words out before gasping for air. My body is pulled tight, the muscles stretched to their limit, my shoulders and neck burning with the strain. Meade pauses before pulling the gun to level, his white teeth grinning all the while as he brings the trigger to bear.

"I *am* god!" he hisses.

Just then, the room seems to float around us. Gravity disappears as the chasm beyond windows and the ocean below drop from view. Glass splinters tumble weightlessly in the air; papers and unused ammunition toss and bounce around us. The floor is once again beneath us, the normalcy of the room somewhat restored.

Somehow, the aircraft carrier has righted itself. Meade's shot misses, whizzing just inches from my head and ricocheting off the metal behind me.

I close my eyes. There is no fear left. My mind flits through the images of the last days and weeks and months, and of all the emotions that run through me, I am left with a strong sense of gratitude. Gratitude that Amy will be safe, gratitude that at least I have peace of mind.

The pistol fires again, the deafening shot ringing out, echoing in my head. I open my eyes, ready to behold the wound, ready for death. Instead, I find myself surrounded by the cold crystal glow of an unnatural, blue light. Then I see its source.

There, close enough to reach out and touch, stands the large glowing man from the flight deck. His back is to me, his arms outstretched. Meade fires again, aiming for the man's head. The rounds are absorbed as empty shells hit the ground. Meade curses loudly as he runs out of ammunition. He reaches for one of the rifles on the floor, but the blue figure is too quick. The sword of fire materializes instantly in his hands and he is upon Meade with electric speed.

Agent Meade's features sag for a moment, his grin becoming a howling, grotesque mask of anger and horror. He glows bright red for a second, and then vanishes.

I stand there, behind the figure, stunned and unable to move. Grey dust as fine as spring pollen swirls in the air and settles. The man turns to face me slowly.

"*Luke*," he says, his voice low and strong.

"Yes?" I reply, more curious than fearful.

"What have you to say of this?"

"I... I... Thank you. Thank you for saving them. For saving Amy."

"And you?"

"Me? I don't know. What comes next? Will I be judged? I don't know that I deserve any different from the soldiers on this ship."

At once, the handcuffs snap open and clang to the floor. I collapse to my hands and knees, not daring to meet eyes with the creature. A large, warm hand rests on my shoulder and gently lifts me to my feet. Instantly, the pain in my leg and wrists fades.

"An interesting response."

"I just know that... Whatever happens, I'm willing to accept it. I know Amy will be taken care of. She chose the right side. I'm... *I'm so proud of her,*" I say, my voice catching as tears well in my eyes.

"And *you*–will *you* worship the true God, Jehovah?" he asks, eyes dancing like spinning diamonds in a blue flame.

"Yes. Of course! How could I ever choose anything else after all this?"

"By your faith, you live," the man says, a gentle smile softening his features. I bow my head again, wanting to thank him, wanting to say so many things, but unable to through the powerful sobs and gasps for air. When I finally lift my head, I am alone.

6:30 PM
AMY

The dormant warship settles back into its footprint as the storm begins to abate. The black and purple clouds retreat, drawing back to their distant recesses like frightened vermin. Within an hour the foam-tipped waves have been replaced by a gentle lapping against our hull. The brothers launch the lifeboats without further problems. Shortly after nightfall, before the *Cornelia* is finally pulled below the surface in bubbling swirls of water, all two thousand four hundred and thirty-nine passengers are accounted for aboard the lifeboats.

"What now?" Marc calls from our boat to the captain's. Curious heads bob in the rafts with the rising and falling swells.

"There's only one option I can see," captain Andros calls back, scratching his head as he points towards the quiet aircraft carrier. The suggestion drifts across our tethered convoy of boats, eliciting puzzled responses.

We point our boats in the direction of the *USS Gerald R. Ford*, her turrets limp and quiet, her deck cleared of any visible signs of aircraft.

"Seems awful quiet," Ashley says, resting a concerned hand on her husband's arm. "Could it be a trap?"

"I don't think we have much of a choice," he says, grimacing. But there are no explosions as we approach. No rockets, no bombs, no torpedoes.

It takes us some exploring to find a way aboard, the ship's flight deck towering a good five stories above us. Finally, long after dark, someone locates a trail of rungs leading to an unlocked hatch. A team of brothers led by captain Andros slips in to investigate, armed only with emergency lights and walkie-talkies from the lifeboats. Half an hour later, Marc's walkie-talkie comes alive with a burst of static.

"Come in? Come in? Everything ok in there?" Marc asks.

"Just fine, Marc. You won't believe it. Ship's completely empty," Andros says, a smile in his voice.

"Empty? Did you say *empty*?"

"Well, almost. We did find *one* survivor."

8:36 PM
LUKE

It takes them another two hours to locate the rear platform elevator controls, but once they do, the boarding process speeds significantly. I sit anxiously at a table in one of the hangars, rubbing my shoulders, partly to allay the pain, partly to calm the nerves. Smiling, relieved faces begin to trickle in. Children in their parents' arms, beaming faces of moms and dads, old, wrinkled faces, not fazed a bit by their cold and soaking hair and clothing. Just happy to be alive.

Some of the men in charge discover large folding cafeteria tables and boxes of water and MREs to feed the crowds. The hangar quickly comes alive with animated conversations and gleeful, teary faces.

That's when I finally see her.

Amy. My *wife*. I hold on to the moment in my mind as long as I can, standing from the table and hobbling to her approaching wheelchair. I reach for her and collapse into her lap, holding her tightly and weeping as I never have before. Her warm arms wrap around my quivering shoulders as she leans down to bury her face in my hair. There is so much I could say: *How much I've missed her. How scared I was. How sorry I am. How right she was all along. How Jehovah was there for me from the beginning.*

But the words won't come, not now. Now there are only tears. Warm, happy tears.

EPILOGUE

Of course, our story didn't really end there. In a way, this was just the beginning.

It took the brothers two full days of exploring the *Gerald R. Ford* just to figure out how to operate it and get everyone organized. Perhaps unsurprisingly, the living quarters aboard that aircraft carrier ended up being far more comfortable than anything most of us had lived in for weeks. There was enough food on board to feed an army for months, and the ship's robust nuclear reactor and reinforced hull were welcome upgrades to the leaky, diesel-guzzling *Cornelia*.

Then there were the subsequent four days spent sailing up the Atlantic coast to New York, an exciting time spent reliving our stories of deliverance. We ran into other friends along the way too, many of them aboard damaged vessels similar to our old cruise ship, and each with his or her own incredible tale to tell once they joined us aboard the aircraft carrier.

On the third day of our journey, the brothers organized a special meeting. It was held right on the carrier's runway, our numbers now well above four thousand. We huddled around bonfires made of driftwood and debris carried by the tide and listened as a handful of brothers gave talks and experiences.

Each evening after dinner, wide-eyed children would gather around Luke, asking him to relate, once again, just how the angel had destroyed all those bad soldiers and weapons.

We reunited with our brothers at a port in Manhattan where we docked and deboarded. Much of New York City had been cordoned off by the brothers due to chemical and radiation contamination, but in the safer areas to the north, a sort of refugee camp had been set up for the brothers coming from overseas. This is how life began for us in the New World.

Alas, not all of our stories could fit into a single book, and with the current rationing of paper we had to edit much of it out. Luke and I decided to write in the present tense to capture the thrill and uncertainty of our experiences, from the moment he responded to that Kingdom Hall fire in our hometown of Haliford down to that last, unforgettable day of deliverance in the Atlantic. If our readers find the tense confusing, we apologize. Perhaps we'll do an updated version in a more traditional style once paper becomes widely available again.

In any case, we hope you've enjoyed our story. We know there are many more like it out there, and we hope to hear yours soon. In the meantime, we will continue to keep busy with the New York restoration crews as we eagerly await Walter's resurrection.

-Amy & Luke Harding

THE END

For more information on this project and others like it, please visit: www.criticaltimesnovel.blogspot.com

If you would like to provide feedback regarding the novel, email me at:
allthingsnewnovel@gmail.com

Thank you for reading!

-EK Jonathan